Sounding
the
Territory

Sounding
the
Territory

LAUREL
GOLDMAN

Alfred A. Knopf   New York   1982

THIS IS A BORZOI BOOK
PUBLISHED BY ALFRED A. KNOPF, INC.

Copyright © 1982 by Laurel Goldman
All rights reserved under International and
Pan-American Copyright Conventions. Published
in the United States by Alfred A. Knopf, Inc.,
New York, and simultaneously in Canada by
Random House of Canada Limited, Toronto.
Distributed by Random House, Inc., New York.

Grateful acknowledgment is made to Dandelion
Music Co. and TRO-Essex Music Limited for
permission to reprint a portion from "Get A Job."
Copyright © 1957 Dandelion Music Co. and
Wildcat Music Co. All Rights Reserved. Inter-
national Copyright Secured. Permission to reproduce
World English rights (outside of the U.S.A. and
Canada) granted by TRO-Essex Music Limited, 138
Piccadilly, London W1V 9FH, England. Used by
permission of the copyright owners.

Library of Congress Cataloging in Publication Data
Goldman, Laurel. Sounding the territory.
I. Title.
PS3557.O369S6   1982   813'.54   81–12409
ISBN 0–394–51935–3   AACR2

Manufactured in the United States of America
First Edition

To my mother and father,
who have given me so much

Thanks to all the friends and family
who supported me, literally and figuratively,
during the writing of this book.
Special thanks to my sister,
Terry Vance.

We don't see things as they are,
we see them as we are.

ANAÏS NIN

ONE

I

Last time we were in here together, Jesús Rivera decided I was Jesse James. He told anyone who would listen that I was plotting with Billy the Kid and the CIA to stop him from becoming sheriff of Queens County because he was a Puerto Rican. Jesús is in the state hospital now and I'm back here; and on this ward they still call me Jesse. I wore cowboy boots then and I still do.

This is the fifth time I've been in this place. I don't know what my diagnosis is this time around. When I first started coming here six years ago, the question of my diagnosis fascinated me. It was three years before I stopped copping charts out of the nurses' station. I thought I might find the key to something—some combination of words scrawled by some brilliant resident that would suddenly illuminate the dusty corner of the universe where I sat picking my toenails and nursing a chronic headache.

I would bury my nose in the chart, my heart pounding. "This 24-year-old white male . . ." "This 25-year-old white male . . ." "This 26-yr.-old wm functioning well on the ward, verbal, co-operative . . ." "Problems adjusting to outside stress, family problems . . ." "Some problems with sexual identity . . . scattered job history . . . concerned, middle-class parents . . ." "Character disorder . . ." "Borderline personality . . ." "Schizoid personality . . ." "Psychoneurotic . . ." "Neurotic . . ." "Rule out psychotic . . ." "Rule out schizoid . . ." "Depressive reaction . . ." "Manic-depressive . . ." "Depressive . . ." "Obsessive-compulsive . . ." "Adjustment reaction crisis . . ." "Paranoid schizophrenic . . ." "Rule out schizophrenic." I've been everything in my time, except a simple schiz. That's the end of the line.

The truth is I am not crazy. I hover on the brink, drawing up tiny grey lists in my head, pros and cons, regurgitating this or that failed time. Did I? Why didn't I? Should I? Would I? It keeps me precariously on the straight and narrow. I sway at the edge but do not fall. But I yearn to plunge into the darkness, whatever it is. Babble and scream, hallucinate till I am wrung out and so clean that my bones would be bleached.

In any case, this place has been home to me, and it's getting hard for me to even get in the door. Many of us on this ward have admitted ourselves voluntarily, and some of us stay for months at a time. But things are getting tight. They have a Persona Non Grata list now, which I have so far managed to avoid. For people who "do not seem to have benefited from the therapeutic community program on A-5." That means don't get caught bringing in liquor or dope, and don't come back too often unless you can really fuck up proverbs or are pursued by voices telling you to diddle your grandmother or blow up the Brooklyn Bridge.

Time was when they were suckers for any kind of hard luck story down in the PAO—the admitting office. No more. I generally say I'm suicidally depressed, but these days they want you to have at least some verifiable history of a serious attempt. My days on the ward may be numbered.

In the meantime, I skim the surface of my days and nights, riding crests of waves that never break. I watch the games being played out and never won to my satisfaction. Tomorrow is my touchstone. Patiently I wait. I can wait. I will wait, just a little longer.

Every morning, except Thursday, which is Psychodrama day, I sit in Daily Living Group B from nine to a quarter of ten, following a fifteen-minute break after Community Meeting.

I would prefer to float from Group A to B to C and back to A again, the better to keep my finger on the currents and crosscurrents of ward life and personalities—about which I am something of an expert.

Silas suggested I might propose the idea to staff in Community Meeting, the justification being a study of "the different stresses engendered in patients by the task orientation in certain Daily Living groups versus the therapy orientation in others." Silas is convinced that the way they assign patients to a particular Daily Living group is to pick names out of a hat. My theory is that Suzanne Lynch, chief of the ward, matches up our pathologies with the pathologies of the staff members running the groups.

Silas is in Group B, too. But he rarely comes to Daily Living, although it is required.

We sit in a circle. Gemma S., one of our group leaders, Philip, David, the Princess, me, Michael, Shipwreck, and Mr. Watson, an aide on A-5 ever since he came to this city from the islands forty years ago. Gemma sent Willy out to drag the corridors for the rest of the group—Silas and Ursula. And Sophie R., senior nurse clinician and co-leader of Group B, is downstairs at an administrative meeting.

"Good morning, everybody," sings Mr. Watson. Presently, we all know, he will slump a little in his chair, his woolly head will lurch forward onto his broad chest, and he will doze happily through the hour.

"Let's see how the coffee sales have been going before we do anything else," says Gemma. She is wishing Sophie were here to help her out. Gemma hates coffee sales. She has a hard time coordinating lists and task assignments. She prefers ward and dormitory maintenance, where we all troop around twice a week to see if the beds are made and spend the rest of the time talking.

Gemma is the ward's activity therapist. Silas says the title

doesn't suit her. He's right. Hers is a suppressed energy. It surfaces, I imagine, in violent dreams that leave little left over for
organizing games and crafts and trips.

I would like to fuck Gemma. She always looks surprised
and soft, her brown hair falling into her grey eyes as she pokes
around in her purse to drag out a mashed cigarette or a chewed-
up pen with the cap missing. Can she help me?

Willy pigeontoes heavily into the room, minus Silas and Ursula. "Silas was meditating, and Ursula was in bed, and I didn't
think I should wake her."

Gemma receives this information with a nod. She would have
been amazed if Willy had come back with either Silas or Ursula
in tow.

Lowering himself cautiously into his chair, Willy smiles his
sweet, distressed smile. "Marsha was sitting in the hall, Miss S. I
invited her to come but she didn't say anything."

"Marsha has her own group, Willy. That's where she should
be."

"They don't want her," David says.

"That's because she's inappropriate," Philip discloses.

"That's because she's nuts," Shipwreck snorts.

"Miss R. gave me the list of who does what job for coffee
selling," Michael interjects, "if anybody is interested."

No one appears to be. "We could all go out in the hall together and ask Marsha to come," Willy prompts, leaning forward in his seat. "That way she'd know we really want her."

The Princess nods enthusiastically. "That's a splendid idea,
Willy."

Gemma puts up a restraining hand. "Wait a minute. Mrs.
Morley will keep an eye on Marsha if she doesn't go to her own
group today."

"Hamilton Trevelyan used to come to our group," Willy insists, "and he was in Group C."

Before Gemma can think up a suitable answer to that one,

the Princess is wanting to know who Hamilton is. "I don't believe I've had the pleasure."

"He was discharged before you got here," Philip explains, "but he'll be back. You'll like Hamilton. He was a lawyer."

A light breaks across Shipwreck's battered face. "Maybe he could get me out of here."

Gemma half rises out of her seat. "We must get to the coffee sales."

Her voice attracts me powerfully. It is the faint edge of panic that stirs me so.

"Shipwreck, Veronica and I sold for three hours yesterday afternoon," reports Philip. "We made two-sixty."

Shipwreck twists in his seat. "Listen, man, I feel funny callin' him Veronica. I thought his name was Michael."

Michael clears his throat impressively. "I told you, Veronica is my given name that I gave to myself. Veronica au Lait. It's perfect for the stage, and after my operation I plan to make a career on the stage."

"I didn't know you was sick," Shipwreck says.

"It's not that kind of operation. It's a change operation."

"What's that?" Shipwreck wants to know. "What kind of change?"

"Sex change."

David rocks forward in his chair. "The FBI is following me."

"What is it, David?" Gemma asks. "What's wrong?"

"Nobody wants Marsha," David says, closing his eyes. "She got in with bad company." He opens his eyes. They are the brilliant green of a Mediterranean Sea. He is looking straight at me.

Willy bolts out of his chair. "I have to go. I have to go get Silas."

Mr. Watson opens one eye. "Silas, he is meditating. Meditation is the breath of life." The eye closes. Out like a light. Does he know something I don't know?

"Sit down, Willy," Gemma says. "I think David is trying to tell us he is glad to be with us today."

"I am glad," says David, waggling his large head. "I am grateful to be here."

Willy sits back down, but I notice he does not settle back in his chair. He sits sideways, one cheek on and one cheek off.

"Philip, do you have a pass to go shopping?" Gemma is pressing on, a diversionary tactic she picked up from Sophie.

"Excuse me, Miss S.," says Philip, "but I think we should get back to Veronica's sex change."

"Shhh," says Veronica, admonishing. "It's not necessary to broadcast it to the world."

"Well, what exactly do you mean, sex change?" insists Philip. "This is supposed to be an open forum where we freely discuss our problems. It's not good to keep it all bottled up. Dr. Gruber, my outside doctor, says that's my problem. I don't ventilate enough."

"I have to get a drink of water." Willy rolls off the edge of his seat and lumbers out the door before Gemma can stop him.

"They'll change me into a woman, which is what I really am," Veronica explains. "It's what I am in my soul."

Shipwreck has had it. "I don't like no one shittin' me, man. You can be a fish or a fowl, but you can't have your cake and eat it too."

Gemma catches my eye. Why mine? Is she going to laugh or cry? Perhaps she looks to me to tell her which.

Veronica turns indignantly in his seat. "I don't know what possessed me to think I could confide my most intimate secrets to a boozed-out, dry-docked nigger sailor of your vast ignorance."

"Hold your horses. I didn't mean to hurt your feelings. I've got nothing against queers. Shit, I've sucked some cocks in my day. Of course, that was at sea—out of necessity, you might say."

"What Shipwreck wants to know," says Philip, "is what are they going to *do* to you, specifically."

"Well, they make me a pussy, excuse the expression."

"*What?*" Shipwreck is beside himself. "Oh, my God. Now wait a minute. You either got a pussy or you ain't. You can't go making pussies out of thin air."

"They don't make it out of thin air. They make it out of my dong."

"It's time to end," Gemma says.

"They shove the testicles up inside and redo the dong," Veronica explains patiently.

Gemma stands up, pushing her chair back against the wall. "We really have to end now."

"Very productive session," Philip compliments the group at large. "I got a lot out of this, Miss S. This group might be good for Marsha after all. She could do with a little reality testing."

I am the keeper of the lighthouse. The wide beam of my imagining scans the treacherous seas, searching for distress signals, alert for foundering crafts. Vigilantly I stand guard, ready to rescue all who run aground in the night.

If I put my hand over Marsha's heart, I would feel birds fluttering wildly, struggling to fly free of their cage. I can hear the whir of their wings as she passes me in the halls. I hear the birds in her breast beating their brains out.

I hear her banging on the door of the seclusion room. "Let me out of here. Let me out. Let me out."

I watched her run up to her father earlier this afternoon. She ran at him, butting her head against his chest. He drew his arms around her, leading her to a corner table of the dining room, where they talk in low tones, hands touching like lovers. He lights a cigarette. The pulse in his throat jumps. She watches it jumping under the skin at the base of his throat, where the dark, tangled hair creeps out from under his shirt. His pulse is beating. It is loud, very loud, like a drumbeat. It is accusing her.

From her chair in the nurses' station, Mrs. Morley sees me stop by the seclusion-room door. "Leave her alone, Jesse. She socked her father and then she socked Miss A."

"I know."

"We don't have the staff to watch her on Sunday. As soon as she calms down, I'll let her out."

Marsha has taken to writing me notes. She stuffs them into my hand at the end of Community Meeting, then darts away. They are written on scraps of envelopes, inside covers of matchbooks, on wadded-up toilet paper.

> Jesse James, they are giving me hormones. Save me.
> Marsha.

Why has she singled me out? Did she see me stop by the seclusion room last Sunday?

> Oh, Jesse James, my head is flying loose. I cannot keep it on without your help. Marsha.

But how can I help you? How can I help you if I cannot get inside your head? How can I get inside a head that is flying loose?

> Jesse. Oh, Jesse. My heart is shrinking. It is getting smaller every day. I can feel it knotting up in a tiny ball. Marsha.

Yes, yes, Marsha, I understand. My heart is shrinking too. I love you, Marsha. I will discover myself through you.

Next Community Meeting, I sit next to Marsha, my heart pounding, waiting for her to slip her message into my hand. This time I will not let her run away.

But she is changed. Generally, she sits silent through the meeting, her hospital gown opening to show her long legs, her dark hair streaming around her face like strands of seaweed. Today she is dressed in a brown skirt, white sweater, brown tights and low-heeled shoes. Her thick hair is tamed, pulled back in a tidy ponytail. She raises her hand. I hold my breath. Will she strike someone? Me maybe, because I haven't answered her letters? Is she going to scream curses at me? Will they lock her in seclusion, and will I be the cause?

"I think it would be a good idea to extend weekend visiting hours. I hope to get work-release passes before too long, which would mean I wouldn't be here for weekday visiting. And there are other people in that category."

I sit numb through the rest of the meeting. There will be no note today or tomorrow. No message from Marsha.

That night Silas tells me about his collection of messages from Marsha, and Philip's and Shipwreck's, smiling at me, the sonofabitch, ambiguous as a clam.

The message is there is no message. But I don't believe it. I can wait for the message. I am used to waiting.

2

After the first month of that first semester, I went to class only occasionally. I spent the major portion of my days holed up in a corner booth in the Union cafeteria, drinking cup after cup of coffee, smoking pack after pack of cigarettes, waiting for Debbie.

Dear Johnny,

What do you mean what is college like? All I can tell you is I don't recommend it.

You've got 4 years to come up with a better plan for your life. I'd advise you to start thinking about it.

Love,

Jay

P.S. Tell Mom thanks for the T-shirts and the dried apricots.

I can predict fairly accurately when Debbie will walk in. I have memorized her class schedule. I know that she is presently getting B's or better in all her courses, although she cuts classes with some frequency, that she will probably major in history, that she writes her parents twice a month, that she is going to visit her roommate, Anne, in Cleveland over Thanksgiving break. I know all her close girlfriends by first name and on sight. I know that as of last week she has stopped seeing Buddy, the math major from Chicago, and is now seeing Greg, a journalism major from San Francisco, who writes incendiary articles for the *Daily*, urging students to abolish fraternities and sororities. And I know that, Greg notwithstanding, Deborah has just pledged Tri Delt. The only thing I don't know is why she left me and why I am feeling so lost.

Between the two of us, Debbie and I let everyone know that we have been a "thing" back home in high school. Debbie smiles across the booth at me, leaning against Greg's substantial shoulder, while Greg and I agree on every topic either one of us can think to introduce. Classes are bullshit. Eisenhower sucks. The Kingston Trio is bullshit. Bo Diddley, fantastic. Likewise Jerry Lee Lewis, Buddy Holly, Chuck Berry.

Meanwhile, under the table, while Greg and I are whipping

up a frenzy of amiable agreement, Debbie's leg (inadvertently? advertently?) brushes mine.

> Dear Johnny,
>   There goes my baby with someone new. She sure looks happy. I sure am blue.
>   Bye bye.
>
> Love,
Jay
>
> P.S. What can she see in him? He has no sense of humor. He's good-looking, I suppose, but totally without character. He looks like a million other guys. In fact, he looks like me.

Increasingly, Greg and I bump into each other on campus. Everywhere I turn, Greg is turning there too.

"Drop by," Greg invites me warmly. And I do.

At first we scrupulously avoid mentioning Debbie. But soon it's a regular thing—Greg and me on a weekday night, drinking beer, listening to his records, shooting the shit, and slowly, dancing around each other, we get around to Debbie.

"I think she's really happy with you, Greg."

"Yeah, I think so, but . . ."

"But what?"

"She confuses me."

"What do you mean?"

"She's weird sometimes. I never know what she's thinking. And she drinks too much. But what the hell, I'm weird too, I suppose. Sometimes I think I'm really gone. You ever feel like that?"

Hard to keep Greg on the subject. He rambles after a few beers, while I get clearer, closing in on a straight line. "She's not so weird."

"Who?"

"Debbie." For Christ's sake, can't he keep a thought in his

head? How does he get such good grades if he doesn't go to class and on top of that can't think straight? "Did you know she's gone out a few times with Andy?"

"Andy. Who's Andy?"

"Don't get excited, Greg. I don't think it's anything serious."

"Who the fuck is Andy?"

"My roommate." A pharmacy major from Vincennes, Indiana.

"I never heard of him. Why did she pick your roommate out of fifteen thousand guys?"

Why indeed? "I don't think that had anything to do with anything."

"Is he sleeping with her?"

"I don't know, Greg. I wouldn't ask Andy that."

As soon as I get back to the dorm, I ask Andy if he and Debbie have been to bed.

Andy looks up from his *Principles of Pharmacy.* "No, Jay. No, I never slept with Debbie. What is it with you two? She was always pumping me about who you were going out with."

> Dear Johnny,
>   Don't worry anymore. I'm fine. Fantastic as a matter of fact. I'm sorry if my letters upset you. I'm going to turn over a new leaf, pull myself together. And I'll write Mom today. I promise.
>   Love,
>   Jay

> Dear Mom,
>   Thanks for your letter. I'm fine. How are you? Well, gotta close now. I'll write again soon.
>   Love,
>   Jay

> Dear Johnny,
>   I've been trying. I really have. I've gone to class every day for the last two weeks. I haven't set foot in-

side the Union. I haven't gone by Greg's apartment, and if I see Debbie coming, I go the other way. But it's not working. Something is wrong with me. I am a fish out of water. I flop around, gasping for air, while all the other little fishes swim by me in pairs, pencils sharpened, notebooks ready.

Love,
Jay

Natalie Wood is going nuts wanting Warren Beatty. And she is driving Warren nuts. It's so real to me. Oh, Natalie, can't you see what's happening? Poor Natalie, it's all going to come out wrong for you. It will never be the same. Not for Warren either. First time we made love was at Miller's Pond. No splendor in that grass. Not for her. So was mine a dream? Aggh. Shit. Is Debbie Natalie? Will she go mad at the last in some sunny sanitarium? Or will I?

Tears run down my face. In the darkened theater, Debbie squeezes my hand hard enough to break it. On the other side of her, Greg is stroking her knee.

Dear Sirs:
I have just finished reading your matchbook cover— the one that says, Success and Personal Fulfillment Through Home Study.

Enclosed is my $5. Please rush me my course on training at home to be a private investigator.

Sincerely,
Jay Davidson

Dear Dad,
I thought you would like to know that I've finally settled on a major. I'm going to be a private eye. I realize you might have been happier with a more

orthodox choice, but I think when you have had a chance to mull it over, you'll agree that I'm doing the right thing.

Love,
Jay

Jay. Call me collect at the office. Better make it Wednesday. I'm flying to Dallas to chair a conference today, and I'll be in Washington Tuesday with the chemical people. Dad.

Dear Jay,

Why are you doing this to us? You manage just fine when you want to. You're not a child anymore, Jay. Do you remember when you were 13 how you drove us all crazy wanting to leave the city and then when we moved you hated it? And what about that sleeping sickness business that first summer after we moved? I still have nightmares about that and about your first day at junior high school that fall. I can't go through all this with you over and over for the rest of my life.

Love,
Mom

P.S. I am sending along your old flannel bathrobe and also a very nice letter I thought you might enjoy from Aunt Jenny. I ran into Debbie's mother the other day. She's not quite as pretty as she used to be.

Dear Johnny,

My home-study correspondence course has not arrived yet. In the meantime, I'm reading Dick Tracy and tailing Greg and Debbie.

Love,
Jay

Dear Johnny,

My home-study course got here. It says it's always best to work undercover. You can send away to them for disguises. I thought of growing a mustache and sending away for their blond wig. But in the end I decided to settle for a friendly smile and an ingratiating whine.

Love,

Jay

Dear Jay,

Mom and Dad are driving me crazy asking questions about you. They want to know if you are flunking out and why your letters are so weerd. I don't know what to tell them. Last night they had a big talk about whether you should see a psychiatrist at school. I don't think Dad liked the idea, but he never actually said that. Mom was definitely in favor of it, but this morning I heard her tell Dad that you were playing games.

They're worryed about you, Jay. If you could just tell me what's going on, I could try to make it okay with them. Please write me a reel letter.

Love,

Johnny

Dear Johnny,

They should be worried about you. You can't spell. Where are their priorities?

Yours,

Jay

Dear Sirs:

I am turning in my two-way decoder badge and returning the unused portion of my home-study course. You said if I was not completely satisfied with the results of the course I could expect a full refund of my five bucks. I wanted to find the guilty party. Greg or Debbie. I thought it would be Greg or Debbie. But it's me. I feel it in my bones. I have no proof, no circumstantial evidence even. But I know it's true. I'm guilty. I've always been guilty.

Sincerely,

Jay Davidson

P.S. On second thought, don't bother to return my five dollars.

By February it is cold and I am colder. Steam heat hisses and pops in the radiators, but I can't get warm. I walk around the room with Andy's Indian blanket drawn around me. Still I shiver. It's impossible to venture out. After having been notified that I am on academic probation at the end of the first semester, I promised myself again that I would shape up. Go to the library. Study. Go to class. But my resolve has shriveled with the terrible, drawing cold in my bones.

Andy tries to reason with me: "You've got to pull yourself together. You're going to be out on your ass."

Greg calls me up: "Jay, what is it? What's the matter?" I can barely speak to Greg. Is he so innocent of my deceptions, or is he guilefully attempting to drive me up a wall? No, Greg has no guile, and anyway it wouldn't work. I am too cold and numb to be driven anywhere.

Finally, even Debbie is alarmed. She calls me on the phone: "Jay, don't you see what's happening to you?"

"I see pitfalls and muck, slime and slag."

"If you're going to pull that kind of stuff, I'm going to hang up."

"Oh, Debbie . . ."

"What? What, Jay? What is it?"

"I don't know." That at least seems to me to be the truth.

"I've never lied to you, Jay." That's a lie, of course. We both have lied.

"That's okay, Debbie."

"You're not making sense, Jay. Are you purposely trying to aggravate me?"

"Don't be mad, Debbie."

"I'm not mad, I'm . . . I don't know. I don't know what I am."

"You're the queen of the teens."

"Okay. Fine, Jay. Take care of yourself. Greg sends love."

For the last two weeks, I have limited my movements more drastically. I rarely venture out of bed. I keep a jar of Skippy peanut butter by my bed and a supply of cellophane-wrapped crackers, which Andy kindly brings me from the dining room. My bed is crummy with crackers and smears of Skippy. But I am indifferent to the mess.

Between naps, I read Batman comics and listen to the radio. A low-pressure system is winging in from Canada. Hog prices are climbing. Jesus Christ is coming. Claire Jeffries is screwing around on her husband, Dr. Paul Jeffries, who is due to do delicate heart surgery on Claire's latest lover, Joel. The Coasters are searchin' every whi-ih-ih-ich a way-ayay. It's all the same to me.

It flows through my outer ear. My inner ear is plugged into the tape recorder which is securely locked to the base of my brain. Daily I rewind the tape of my last phone conversation with Debbie. It wouldn't be so bad if I could just let it play back. But I must constantly stop the reel, put on a fresh one and record a different line here, a better response there, a happier ending. Then I have to splice my inserts into the original tape. When I play back my new version, I am no more satisfied than I was with the last one. So I have to go back, erase the spliced material, re-record the original dialogue, which I play back until I am hit by a new inspiration for yet another version. At which point the whole cycle begins again. It is hard work. I am exhausted from my labors. Small wonder Andy cannot budge me from my bed.

"You've got to stop this, Jay. Forget her. I never saw anyone carry on the way you do. You're falling apart."

"You should get yourself another roommate, Andy. You'd feel a lot better."

"I've arranged a date for you. With a friend of Joan's."

"I appreciate it, Andy, but I don't want to go out with her. Or anyone."

"I've already arranged it, Jay. It will put me in a lousy position if you don't go."

"Tell her I just got engaged."

"Okay. Okay, Jay. Fuck it. You know. Just fuck it."

"Don't be mad, Andy. I'll go. I'll go. I promise. Call her right away so I can't change my mind."

Angie, my blind date, turns out to be cute. Small and supple. Brown-haired with straight, little-girl bangs. Perhaps she needs protection. She smiles at me over her dripping pizza. "Zit."

What? What did she say? "How's the pizza?"

"Grabble." She smiles again, a sunny, open smile, winding mozzarella around her finger so it won't fall on the table.

It's very noisy in the Pizza Place. Words get swallowed up, bent out of shape. "So, uh, how do you like sorority life?"

"Sodel bat, sodel git. Trey dir?"

I'm starting to sweat. There is a ball of mozzarella hardening in my throat, and I can't get it down. She appears to notice my difficulty and tries a different tack. Maybe she has hit a sore spot, she is thinking. A sensitive girl it seems.

"Bradel vac suc hys, Jil totel summs lats. Mat zow, Jil lafe ab lib lafe." She gives a wry shrug.

I like her. We might hit it off. I stick my finger in my ear and rattle it around. I've been spending too much time with that radio blaring at me. It's given me some rare but, I am still hopeful, temporary disability. I give her a reassuring smile.

She frowns slightly. "Dingel fase cru siper wats."

A bizarre sorority initiation prank. Her sorority sisters must be planted all over the joint watching to see that she goes through with this. Was Andy in on it? Wait till I get that fucker. Setting me up for this shit. I must keep calm. I take a sip of my beer and feel better. It goes down easily, soothing my outrage. Mustn't get so excited. Two can play at this game. I'll be cool. "Slithy toves." I clink my glass to hers. A toast. A little taken aback, I see. Ah hah. Didn't think I'd catch on, did you, Angie? "Mome raths outgrabe," I say, bringing my fist down on the table for emphasis. This is turning out to be fun. Andy was right. It is doing me good to get out. "Gyre and gimble, gimble and gyre. Diddy do dah day."

People are turning around to stare at our booth, and Angie's mouth is hanging open, revealing beautiful, even white teeth. "Be bop a lula. Bibbity bobbity boo." Must be talking too loud, embarrassing her. Now that the jig is up, she doesn't want everyone in the place to see how it's been turned around.

"Zibble crave," she says indignantly. She seems on the verge of tears. It isn't a gag. I have misunderstood.

"Zibble crave," I implore. Surely she will understand that. She just said it. "Zibble crave," I repeat. Angie's mouth is a thin, hard line. I have completely fucked it up. That much at least is clear. "Crave zibble." My heart is pounding so loudly I can barely hear what I am saying. Angie is standing up. I grab her hand. "Crave zibble." She recoils at my touch, swoops up her suède jacket and runs, stumbling and red-faced, shoving her way through the crowded aisle and out into the street.

What did I do? Jesus, what did I do?

. . .

In my dream my mother is driving. I am sitting between her and Dad in the front seat of a black station wagon.

The windows are rolled up, but I hear an insistent humming, like millions of tiny vibrating insects bumping against each other. It seems now to be coming from the back of my head.

"I think we should go back," my father says. "I should get to a phone."

His voice sounds thin and watery. My mother opens her mouth to say something but closes it again. She looks annoyed—or is she pleased? I can't gauge her expression.

She turns to me. "Why does your father look so sad?"

"Tell her, Jay. Tell her why I'm sad."

"Tell him why I'm sad, Jay," she says. "You tell him."

"Tell her, Jay. Explain it to her."

Must concentrate, piece it together, explain everything. But the humming is distracting me. Louder and louder. It gets louder and louder. I can't make sense of what they are saying. I can't hear right. I can't hear.

Everything in the room is white—bedstead, sheets, sink, walls. Outside the window, white snow is falling. A Health Service doctor, an oriental lady, tiny and alert, is sitting upright in the white plastic armchair, catty-cornered to my bed. I have to strain to see her; my bed is so high and she is so tiny in the big chair, wrapped in a white lab coat too big for her. All I can see are her little black olive eyes.

"You will be happy to know the blood tests show you do not have mononucleosis."

"Uhh."

"We can discharge you this afternoon."

"But, doctor, I need a rest. It's imperative that I get a rest."

"You see, you will have to rest somewhere else. We have right now a heavy epidemic of mononucleosis."

"If you send me out in this condition, I'll just catch mono-nucleosis and have to come right back."

"You have no temperature and your pulse is normal."

"But I am not normal."

"I don't understand."

"It's very simple. I'm not normal. I hear things wrong. I hear things other people don't hear or say. Doctor, listen to me, before I came here I swallowed half a bottle of aspirin." I prop myself up further to get a better look at her reaction. It isn't really a lie—though in fact I stopped at nine. My throat closed up. I went to bed, floating into sleep, and dreamed of staying home from school, my mother, solicitous, carrying fresh-squeezed orange juice and Jell-O and comic books to me, tribute to the ailing king. Had she known all along that I held the thermometer up to the light bulb when she left the room?

The olive eyes widen slightly, and I sink back onto the pillows. I shouldn't have told her. They keep records of these things. For the rest of my life it would be down in black and white—transcripts of attempted suicide sent back and forth through the United States mails to haunt me every time I applied for a job or a bank loan. Do they let people with "attempted suicide" down in black and white on their records renew their driver's license?

"What exactly was the trouble?" Her voice is soft and gentle. Maybe it hadn't been a mistake to confide in her. Maybe she'd let me stay awhile, tell the other doctors I had a little sugar in my urine that she wanted to check out.

On the other hand, if I had swallowed half a bottle of aspirin, I would certainly have thrown up, or they would have found traces of it in my blood or urine. Was she just playing me along, humoring me till I talked myself into a hole? Was she suddenly going to leap out of the chair? *Aiya.* You lied. You never attempted suicide. Yankee imperialist dog. Get out of this hospital.

"Of course," she says, from the depths of the chair, "I am not a psychologist, but perhaps you would like to tell me about it. What is the trouble?"

What is the trouble? I must marshal the facts, tell this lady about Debbie. But I can't get my thoughts together. Are there any facts to marshal? It doesn't seem so. Only thin threads of memories, so finely twisted and knotted that I can't find the beginning or end to unravel them.

"Doctor, I lied to you. I never tried to kill myself. I never took so much as one lousy aspirin. They make me gag. I am a malingerer. Discharge me when you will."

3

The old men roam the corridors of the ward, two old hens, cackling and clucking, chanting in cracked voices the songs of the day. Without me, their songs would fade in the air.

"D'ya hear about Shipwreck?"

"The sailor fellow?"

"Says he's going to elope on his next snack-bar pass."

"I notice he's been restless lately."

"Been like that ever since they discharged Veronica au Lait. Hee hee. Heard him tell Walter if they were letting that crazy fuck loose they should let him out."

"What did Walter say?"

"Nothing to the point. You know Walter. The only topic interests him is when is his mother going to send him money to go back to Vienna to finish up his medical studies."

"It's a matter of principle with Shipwreck, I suppose."

"Seems to be."

"You hear about the Princess?"

"Nice lady. Reminds me of a teacher I had once."

"She stuffs things up her twat."

"How do you know that, I'd like to know?"

"Heard Miss A. telling Dr. Green. She's got a colored pebble from a beach where she met her first lover up there."

"Damn."

"And a swatch of blue silk material. Miss A. said the Princess wants to find more like it to cover some chairs. And a silk tassel off an old dance card."

"How do you like that."

"Not a bad place to keep things when you stop to consider."

"I never said the Princess was dumb."

Franklyn Singleton nods at me in the hallway but never speaks. Tall and straight as a tree, he towers over everyone on the ward. His blue-black skin shimmers like some subterranean ore. I am intrigued by his silence, his great reserve. Perhaps he has the answer.

"I see you're hot on Franklyn's trail, Jesse James," Silas says. "Think Franklyn robbed the Danville train and he's got the gold, eh?"

"I don't know what you're talking about."

"Here's a hot tip. He and the Princess are getting chummy. Follow Victoria Vagina."

The Princess nods good morning, Jesse, as she sails by me, heading toward the dining room, where Franklyn waits for her. She thinks we pass by chance. She doesn't know that I am the ward chronicler.

"Mr. Singleton, I have been assigned to work with you on

table duty. At home we had servants, of course, to attend to such things. But I am quite willing to learn."

"Noblesse oblige, your highness. I have it all ordained according to table. You clear and I'll set. If that's degradable with you."

"Perfectly."

"It's important to do the task perfectly. If you are erroneous, it can destroy you. That's how I turned black."

"But you look very nice black to me. It suits you, I think."

"It was a suitable punishment. I try not to feel sorry for myself."

"I try also to adjust to my lowered position with grace. Grace is important. My late husband and I agreed on that at least."

"I have never entered into the state of holy martyrmony. I am impudent. So I am alone."

"I too am alone now. It all goes by so fast, don't you think? And then you are left alone and old. Of course, you are young yet. May I inquire what is your profession?"

"I have not worked for some time, but my doctor, who is very synthetic to my case, suggests I enter the complacency program here. And I am seriously construing such a plan."

"Ah, yes? Well, I would work too if I thought I could find a fitting position. I have written to Queen Elizabeth. We are related on my mother's side. But I have not heard from her. The post is slow these days."

"Slow but steady wins the race."

"Now that I am old, Mr. Singleton, I agree. But in my youth I didn't hold to that at all. I was of quite a different opinion."

"Princess, I wonder if you would excuse me. I am feeling somewhat oblique."

"Perhaps you should lie down a bit."

"I have enjoyed our symposium. Talking with someone kind helps to twine out the time."

"It does indeed, Mr. Singleton. I hope to see you soon again. Bientôt."

"Do you have any real interest in Franklyn?" Silas asks me at lunch.

"Dr. Weisser asked me the same thing two days ago."

"I don't think you do. Not in Franklyn or the Princess or anyone. You're fascinated, which is quite a different thing."

"Why do you bother to ask me questions, Silas, if you already know all the answers?"

"I don't know all the answers."

"You act as if you do. You act as if you have some secret knowledge of everything, especially me."

"Which is why I fascinate you."

I have the feeling Dr. Weisser is not listening to me. Sometimes toward the end of the session, the look on his face is so neutral, so impassive, that I think he has fallen asleep and is keeping his eyes open with the aid of some ancient yoga trick. Other times he is fidgety: his eyes wander to various points in the room, he shifts his weight pointedly, flicks imaginary pieces of lint off his shirt.

'All right, Dr. Weisser. Come into my parlor. Step into the treatment room.'

'If you can spare a minute, Jesse.'

'What's troubling you, Joel?'

'It's a patient.'

'It's Jay, isn't it?'

'I'm not getting anywhere with him. He seems to think he'll get more out of dogging Silas and Franklyn and the Princess and God knows who all than he will with me.'

'That disturbs you.'

'I must get through to him.'

'Why him especially?'

'He's the greatest challenge of my career. If I can't make it with him, I can't make it.'

'You look angry, Joel.'

'What makes you say that?'

'Your jaw.'

'My jaw is fine.'

'Mmmm.'

'All right, goddammit, I'm angry. They're killing me, Jesse. I don't know what to do about anything anymore.'

'You are tentative. Ambivalent.'

'It's driving me crazy.'

'This morning you couldn't decide whether to have Granola or eggs. Whether to wear your work shirt or your striped shirt. You couldn't decide whether to walk here or take the bus. Now you can't decide whether to have lunch in the cafeteria or in the coffee shop. You don't know whether to do your next rotation in Children or Admitting. And last night you couldn't decide whether to have a beer or a joint or both or neither. Whether to see Fellini downtown or *Citizen Kane* uptown. Whether to keep seeing X or marry Y.'

'What should I do?'

'The pressures are great.'

'Everyone wants something from me.'

'Dr. Lynch.'

'Yes.'

'The army.'

'Yes.'

'Your parents.'

'Yes. Yes.'

'Your women.'

'What am I going to do? Jesus Christ, I'm only twenty-eight. What do they want from me?'

'Shhh, shhh, take it easy. It's going to be okay.'
'Do you really think so?'
'Everything will be all right, Joelie.'
'No one has called me Joelie since I was five.'
'Shhh, Joelie. Jesse's here. Jesse James is here.'

"Are you planning on being here long, Mr. Singleton?" the Princess asks Franklyn as they walk the hall together, with me following at a discreet distance.

Franklyn nods affirmatively.

"This is my first visit, of course," the Princess says. "I told them I wouldn't stay past the season when I first came, but I'm sure they wouldn't object if I stayed on. They were very gracious in the initial interview."

"They sat circling," Franklyn answers her, "throwing questions. Some hit. Some don't. They devaluate you. What you're worth. Good and bad, black and white, you see? I refused to precipitate much. The chief says, We depreciate your conning, and everyone nods and smiles and it's all overt."

"Ah, yes, I see," says the Princess. "Well, perhaps I won't bother to extend my visit after all."

What brought me in this time was the faces. At first, it was just one in a crowd. In a few days' time it was two or three, and by the end of the week every face I saw I knew I had seen before. Every face was a face remembered. I racked my brain, hour after hour, trying vainly to place the time and circumstances where I had encountered each face before. I had to quit my job at the movie on Eighth Street. I became exhausted but I couldn't sleep. I tried watching TV to pass the time and clear my mind of the faces, but they were on the TV too. Every announcer, every actor, every contestant on every quiz show, I knew them all from somewhere. And I couldn't remember where.

My mother called me up from Connecticut to say she was coming to town to do some shopping and would stop by to see me. I told her that I was somewhat strung out and why didn't she wait?

When she knocked on my door the next morning, I peeped out. "Don't I know you from somewhere?"

4

My brother, Johnny, said the week before I came to the hospital for the first time he called me thirty times and got no answer.

> Dear Johnny,
>   Do not bother to try and reach me by phone because I am having my phone disconnected. Jangle my nerves, jar my soul, stop my heart in the dead of night. Reminding me of things I haven't done and people I don't want to talk to.
>
>   Love,
>   Jay

Dear Johnny,
    I ate my lunch in the park yesterday and this pretty girl started talking to me. "Do you eat here often?" she asked me.
    I looked her straight in the eye and I said: "I am 24 years old, a relatively recent college grad, presently employed as a bagger at the A & P. I live on Ninth Avenue in the second-story walkup I have rented from Mr. Kaminsky for the past 3 years."

She grabbed her pastrami and ran. I can't talk to people anymore, Johnny.

Love,
Jay

Dear Johnny,

Furniture oppresses me. I sink into soft, squishy sofa bellies, am smothered by outrageous cushions. My color coordinates. I am salt-and-pepper tweed, russet corduroy, purple silk, but I am never good old pink-and-white Jay, standing out like a sore thumb to be reckoned with. I disappear into the recesses of over-stuffed armchairs. I blend, I fade, I integrate. I am an interior decorator's dream. I might have been planted to enhance the total effect, so nullified am I by chairs and tables and lamps.

Furniture could be the real enemy, forcing us to contort our bodies into unnatural shapes and more un-natural conversations. Do you think everything might be different if there were no furniture? I await your reply. Be chair-i-table to your brother, who is sofa gone.

Love,
Jay

Dear Jay,

I am coming to New York. I have to see you.

Johnny

When Johnny finally came to the apartment, flew to New York from California to see what was going on, he found me cower-ing in the middle of my unmade bed, quoting proverbs and wise old sayings. "A stitch in time saves nine, Johnny. A bird in the hand is worth two in the bush. Better to have loved and lost.

It'll all work out. Time heals all wounds. Listen to your old pal, Jay."

"What are you doing like that in the middle of the bed? I need to talk to you. I flew all the way here to talk to you."

"I've had company."

"Who? What company?"

"Friends. Friends from grammar school, from camp, from the block, from junior high, from high school, from college, friends of friends. Acquaintances. Even strangers. Everybody's been here. They were stacked up in the corners of my room, piled one on top of the other, and they were multiplying by the hour, like cells dividing. The only space left was right here in the middle of this bed. They were babbling at me. Telling me their stories—sad stories, funny stories, blue stories, grey stories. Stories overlapping, stories spawning stories. I couldn't tell where one ended and another began. Maybe they were all the same story. The point is, each one wanted a response, a separate, individual response. You can't say the same thing to each one. Plus, I invited them in. I asked them to tell me how they were. So there they were, piled three deep, using up all the oxygen. I had to sit on the bed to stay clear of them, give myself some perspective. Hour after hour I asked probing questions, made up old sayings, quoted maxims, proverbs, rhymes—an endless stream of words. It's been a strain, Johnny. I was so tired I could barely move, so bored I couldn't see straight—that perhaps is the crux of the matter. And I was getting hoarse. But I couldn't stop talking because I was afraid that if I did they would walk out."

By the time Johnny got me to the admitting office, I was perfectly calm. When the resident asked me to explain the meaning of "a rolling stone gathers no moss," I told him that Mick Jagger might not be gathering any moss but he was getting to be a wealthy man, and if he played his cards right and invested in real estate, he'd have it made.

I had it made too. I was in like Flynn. Safe and sound.

5

Dr. Weisser sat in on our Daily Living group yesterday. After it was over, he stayed behind to have a postsession with Gemma and Sophie. I had a feeling he might have something to say to them about me so I hung around outside the door. Unfortunately, Miss A., Margie, came by. "Are you all right, Jesse?"

"Me? I'm fine."

"Aren't you supposed to be helping set up the coffee?"

"I'm waiting for Philip."

"Philip's waiting for you in the kitchen. I just talked to him."

"Oh, great." I walked off in the direction of the kitchen, but when Margie turned into the nurses' station, I hurried back to the door.

"I hate to rush you, Joel," Sophie was saying, "but I have that meeting with Dr. Lynch about the night staff and I absolutely can't be late. I have some grave reservations about Mr. Theodophilus. Is there anybody else we need to talk about?"

"Jay," Weisser said. "Jay's too comfortable here."

"That's because he's not really here," Gemma said.

I would have stayed rooted to the spot had not the sound of chairs being pushed back propelled me down the hall.

How does Gemma know that?

The Princess has snack-bar passes, and I note that she has taken to bringing Mrs. Stern a cup of tea mid-morning.

"Can they keep me against my will?" Mrs. Stern demands, ignoring the Princess's offering. "There is nothing wrong with me."

"Do please drink your tea. Don't upset yourself."

"Thank you. You are very sweet. Are you Jewish?"

"I had a lover who was a Jewish gentleman—an English lord, an elegant man."

"I have relatives in the House of Lords myself. Lord Stern? You may have heard of him."

"My husband may have spoken of him, but I didn't always listen to him toward the end."

"I kicked my husband out. Good riddance. I managed always fine by myself. I am a dressmaker by profession, and I must get back to work. Otherwise I will lose my apartment on Seventy-eighth Street. Have you seen it? I will have nothing. I will have to sit here in this shmatte of a dress. Do you know what means *shmatte*? I sit like an idiot, an idiot."

"But you are a dressmaker! I am not surprised. You have lovely long fingers, unlined like a young girl's."

"I always had a nice hand. Rings looked well on me."

"My dear Mrs. Stern, do you imagine you could do me the great favor of making me an ensemble? Something simple. I am not young enough to overdo, of course."

"But where would I get material? They don't let me go anywhere. I can't even walk like a free person anymore."

"I might take it upon myself to ask that activity therapy girl, Gemma. I understand she handles things like this."

"Acch. That one with her hair in her face doesn't know what she is doing. She hems her dress with a safety pin. I swear to you. I saw it. She will only have scraps of junk, nothing fine, nothing elegant."

"We must make do, Mrs. Stern, as my husband was so fond of saying."

Gemma and I are in the kitchen making a huge vat of punch for tonight's Mass Activity (the monthly party for all patients from all wards—held in the gym in cold weather, in the yard in warm).

Gemma asked Silas to help out too, but he refused. "I want nothing to do with mass transit, mass media, high and low mass, or Mass Activity. They are all degrading."

I, on the other hand, love Mass Activity. It's like watching a Fellini movie. Hamilton and I used to look forward to it as we did nothing else. But tonight I am mostly interested in the chance it gives me to observe Gemma close at hand.

It's cozy here, alone in the kitchen with Gemma, heads together, pouring out cans of orange and grapefruit juice and bottles of club soda. Gemma is a little frazzled. She has misplaced her requisition slip and without it she can't pick up the cake for tonight from the central kitchen in the basement. On top of that, she has just discovered that the ward record player is missing from the activity therapy office, and she hasn't yet secured another one from one of the other wards.

I can feel the wheels in her mind snagging and slipping. I feel confident and powerful. I will arrange everything. Find the requisition. Get a record player.

The kitchen doors swing open. It is Mrs. Stern.

"What are you doing?" she demands. "Is this a hotel?"

Go away, Mrs. Stern. Go away. "We are making punch for Mass Activity," I tell her. "You will have to excuse us. We don't have much time."

"You are crazy," she tells me, wedging herself between Gemma and me. "Look, miss. You are very sweet, but tell me one thing. Why do they keep me here against my will?"

"Mrs. Stern, please. I'm very busy," Gemma says, stirring up a storm.

Mrs. Stern grabs hold of Gemma's elbow. "What crime have I committed?"

"Look, Mrs. Stern, Miss S. can't talk to you now."

"You are out of this," Mrs. Stern tells me.

"It's okay, Jesse," Gemma says.

It's not okay. "I can leave if you want."

"Good," Mrs. Stern says.

Gemma sighs and leaves off her stirring. "Mrs. Stern, you weren't able to manage alone anymore in your apartment."

"Do you know my apartment? Now I will lose it. Who will pay my rent? Can you tell me that, my dear girl?"

"Your rent has been paid for this month."

"I did not pay it."

"Miss Holland did with money from your account."

"Howling? Who is that? I don't know anyone by that name."

"The social worker," I explain. "You talked to her this morning. I saw you with my own eyes."

Mrs. Stern turns her back on me, tightening her hold on Gemma's elbow. "Social worker? Well, where am I? All alone in this place with colored people and gentiles. My family is all dead. Killed by Hitler. Did you know that? Of course not. What should you know of such tragedies? I hope you never have to suffer as I have. I am going out of my mind. In this shmatte of a robe. Where are my clothes? Are you Jewish?"

"Yes, I am," Gemma says.

"Did I ask you that once before? I sit around here all day. Just sit like an old witch. All my life I have managed by myself. I owe nothing to anyone. I asked nothing for myself. My family is all dead."

"You told Willy you had a sister in Israel," I say.

"What should she do for me? She has a family. How can she help me?"

"And your husband? She had a husband," I inform Gemma, "but she kicked him out."

"He is a spy." Mrs. Stern appeals to Gemma. "He spies on everyone. Do I keep you, my dear girl? You are very busy. I see you always flying around. Don't bother with me."

"You are not keeping me, Mrs. Stern."

"But you are keeping me, hah hah. How can I get out of here?"

"You have to speak to your doctor about that."

"My doctor? I have no doctor here."

"Dr. Weisser. You saw him yesterday."

"Miser. I don't know him. I don't remember such a person. Can you point him out to me?"

"I'll be in my room when you're through," I tell Gemma.

"Jesse, I'll be through in a minute. We've only got an hour to finish everything."

"I have to go to the bathroom. Is that okay?" I stride out of the kitchen, the heels of my cowboy boots clicking smartly as I crash through the swinging doors—saloon doors.

Behind the door, I can hear Mrs. Stern jabbering on: "I have to work again. I am an excellent seamstress. I could make you a lovely outfit if you would just bring me a tape measure."

"Shit," I say to no one, kicking the door, raising clouds of prairie dust.

Silas's mother is here to see him today, all the way from Boston. I saw Mrs. Morley let her onto the ward. I never imagined Silas with a mother like other people. It startled me to see how much she looks like Silas—the same clear, snowy forehead, the slender, surprisingly muscular frame, and that strained agility I thought peculiar to Silas. She has the same absurdly pale hair, but her eyes are an uncomplicated brown. Perhaps Silas gets his smoky grey eyes from his father.

Silas refuses to see his mother. He is sitting cross-legged on top of the sagging Ping-Pong table, swathed in an enormous length of cheesecloth. I am underneath the table, a badminton shuttlecock to my ear, the better to hear with. Gemma is trying to persuade Silas.

"I think you should at least say hello to her, Silas."

"Crates of Mallus, Arrian of Nicomedia, Callimaches of Alexandria . . ."

"She came all the way from Boston."

"Meleager of Gadara, Archias of Antioch . . . I am communing with the spirits of antiquity. They have traveled considerably further than she to be with me."

"You can commune with them later."

"Gemma," he admonishes, "you shouldn't take your work so seriously."

"Did she hurt you?"

"Iamblichus of Syria, Aristarchus of Samothrace, Alexander of Aetolia . . ."

"Okay, Silas. I'm not going to get into a thing with you." Gemma exits downcast.

"Why do you tease her?" I ask him from under the table.

"Why not?"

"Did your mother hurt you?"

Silas descends from the Ping-Pong table, and the cheesecloth flutters over the edge of the table, faintly damping the echo of our voices in the empty room. "X plus Y will never equal Z, Jesse James. You better give it up. They're getting to you with their theorems, but they don't work. Nothing works."

Silas is leaving. I listen to the soft padding of his bare feet on the linoleum floor. There are more questions I want to ask him, but it is cozy here under the Ping-Pong table. I squat, squinting through the fine, foggy mesh of the cheesecloth. It is like looking through sea mist. The legs of the sofa opposite me are broken apart, thin, vaporous lines, dancing loosely in the air, nowhere joined, nowhere solid.

6

Already in high school shapes are beginning to lose their shape for me. The outlines of things are fluid, watery. Nothing is solid. Nothing has substance. Still, I am only dimly aware that things are out of whack.

I take up smoking Lucky Strikes and soon am up to a pack a day. On top of that, I become a Coca-Cola addict. I never go more than four hours at a stretch without a Coke. I read voraciously, indiscriminately, everything that is in the house, and retain nothing. My concentration in school is no better. I commit to memory mathematical formulas, great chunks of American history, French and Latin vocabulary and spew them out again on test papers, which keep me a respectable B average. Stuff it in, spit it out. Nothing registers. I begin to suspect that I might be an idiot. I talk my mother into getting the guidance counselor to give me an IQ test. I couldn't repeat numbers backward beyond the first three digits. I had no idea how many miles it was to Paris, or what continent Libya was on, or how many votes there were in the electoral college. At the same time, I have some idea that I might be a genius. How else was I managing to survive when I had no idea what the fuck was going on around me? I had my B average. I carried on normal conversations, my little brother thought I was impressive, my father talked about my potential and my mother about how good-looking I was getting.

My classmates, on the other hand, ignore me. Perhaps their judgment is sounder, less prejudiced certainly. What friends I could have had I avoid like the plague. I can smell them coming a mile off, with their hair combed the wrong way, wearing the wrong shoes, hangdog, apologetic, pimply. They call me on the

39

phone to invite me to their houses or to the movies. How do they know so surely I am one of them? Was I wearing a stigma I wasn't aware of? On the phone I am kind to them, inventing elaborate, convoluted excuses for why I cannot see them. In school I plan my route from class to class, as carefully as a general plots troop movements, in order to avoid them.

By the middle of my sophomore year, my cigarette consumption shoots up to a pack and a half a day, Cokes are up by four more bottles a day. My energy is flagging badly. I masturbate with increasing frequency, three, four, five times a night. And always afterward, I miss the spilled semen. It is dribbling away and for what? But I am powerless to halt its flow. Initially, I fantasize the cheerleaders at school, one after another, the whole squad, in my bed. Suddenly, I can't get off anymore with the cheerleaders. I try Sandra Dee. But after a few times I can't get off with her. Then Annette Funicello. Sophia Loren. Marilyn Monroe. Same thing. Jesus. I am only sixteen and I am having trouble jerking off. There must be something wrong. I should go to a doctor, but I am afraid to hear the truth. I haven't even fucked anyone yet and I am washed up. Meanwhile I am exhausted. I can't sleep. I wake up red-eyed. Finally, I start hitting it with no thought of sex in mind. I itemize my lunch for the next day, decline Latin verbs, review the questions in the driver's manual. It works like a charm.

7

Martin Dewar has approached me several times to ask if I would consider doing an occasional piece for *News in a Nutshell*, the ward newspaper. "You could do a fine job, Jesse. I've thought about it a lot."

"Thanks, Martin, but I'm too busy to take it on. I couldn't give it the attention it deserves."

"But, Jesse, you don't do anything on the ward."

"I was secretary of Ward Government once."

"You resigned that post. I remember distinctly because I voted for you. You could get passes if you participated more, Jesse."

"I have snack-bar passes."

"I mean passes to go *out*—like a regular person."

"I don't care about passes."

"I feel so pressured sometimes, Jesse. I made a list of pros and cons. Reasons why I should keep being editor on one side and reasons why I shouldn't on the other. The pros list was longer by two reasons. But I might have left something out on the con side."

"You're doing a very good job, Martin. Everyone says so."

"Thank you very much. Dr. Green said that too. This week's lead story is the party."

"Great."

"You weren't there. Here." Martin hands me the latest issue of *News in a Nutshell*. "I'll talk to you again when you've had a chance to mull over my proposition," he says, and hurries off before I can refuse him again.

A-5 HOSTS FABULOUS FETE
by Martin Dewar

On the evening of Sept. 8, 1969, Ward A-5 threw a gala party, inviting B-6 to share in the festivities. Records and a record player were provided by the Activity Therapy Department. Guests and hosts danced to the music, which according to Janine Zybriski, who capably handled the changing of records, included Prez Prado, Johnny Mathis, Flatt and Scruggs, Big Brother & the Holding Company, and Aretha Franklin. Janine said the number of people who participated in the dancing was disappointing. She offered the comment

that if we had had a dance contest with a prize of a
pack of cigarettes as she had originally suggested in
Ward Government, the dancing might have been a
more popular activity. The highlight of the evening
was the delightful refreshments served by the Refreshment Committee, which included chocolate chip cookies, Hawaiian Punch, barbecued potato chips, and a
delectable onion dip. Miss Melinda Aaronson, chairman of the Refreshment Committee, said the shopping for the party was done at Bohack's.

Thank you, Melinda, for a job well done. Thanks
also to Miss A., nurse clinician and head of the Social
Committee, to Miss S., our activity therapist, and to
the Social Committee members, Melinda Aaronson,
Janine Zybriski, and Willy.

Decorations for the party were provided by Janine
Zybriski and Melinda Aaronson. Unfortunately, they
were torn down before the guests arrived by Miss Faye
Howard. Miss Howard, a young newcomer to our
ward, was not available for comment at press time.
Welcome to A-5, Faye.

I fall in step behind the old men. The quiet, rhythmic drone of
their old voices soothes me. It is like raindrops falling way out
on the ocean.

"D'you see all that equipment they lugged in here today?
Color TVs, hi-fis, tape recorders. Hamilton ordered it, before
he was admitted yesterday."

"Trevelyan?"

"Called up Sam Goody's on the phone and charged it to the
Hospital Volunteer Auxiliary Fund. Told them he was the trea-
surer."

"Hamilton makes a good impression. He's got that dignified
way of talking."

"Looks dignified too. Tall and all that and he dresses just so.
I thought he was a lawyer myself."

"He may have been once. He went to school for it. But he's nothing now. Like us. Doesn't do a thing. Just goes up and down, high and low."

"Must be nice to be high."

"He says no. Says he feels worse high than low."

"Well, he must feel bad now then. He's calling Dr. Lynch Suzanne again. I heard him. 'Formality has its place,' he tells her, 'but not among friends.' "

"How'd she take that?"

"She said, 'I must insist, Mr. Trevelyan, that you call me Dr. Lynch like everyone else on the ward.' Then he fixes them bright blue eyes on her, and he says, 'Ah, Suzanne, you are lovely when you become agitated.' "

"Hamilton's got one of them silver tongues. Hear about the time he impersonated a doctor?"

"Everyone's heard that."

"Lectured to the young doctors and everything."

"Makes you wonder."

"Don't it though."

No one, including the doctors, has ever been able to get a reliable history out of Hamilton, except that he has been in and out of hospitals for years and in between times has lived in a variety of welfare hotels, from all of which he has ultimately been ejected for "bizarre behavior."

According to Hamilton, when he is high, that is, he has been alternately a painter, a sculptor, a lawyer, a parachutist, a lumberjack, an inventor, a playwright, and a judge. When he is down, he will say only that he is a failed man, "a failure—a failure as a husband, as a father, and in the study of the law."

His return to the ward is always an event. And now Martin Dewar has seen to it that it is a media event. The lead story of the latest issue of *News in a Nutshell* is an interview with Hamilton in which Hamilton, having learned that the post of vice president of Ward Government has recently been vacated, outlines his forthcoming campaign to be our next v.p. Somewhere in the middle of the article there is a long digression on how pleased Hamilton is to see so many beautiful women on the ward. He managed to cite some particular charm of every woman on the ward, including staff. Sophie, Gemma, Margie, and Dr. Lynch all got glowing notices.

"You haven't changed much, Hamilton," I tell him.

"Is that a criticism, Jesse James?"

"Not at all. I like you exactly the way you are."

"Good. I hope that means I can count on your support."

"Sure. How's the campaign going?"

"I've got Melinda and Janine and Walter and Philip and Marsha sewed up. And I talked to Luis this morning. Did you know he was married when he was nineteen and has five children?"

"Yes, I did. Is he going to vote for you?"

"I don't know. Anyway, I was having trouble with Franklyn Singleton, but I think I can get to him through the Princess. David says he's not a voting member of society yet, so I can't count on him. I'm not sure Ursula understood what I was talking about. She said something about dogs and being on a leash. I couldn't follow it, but I think she was pleased at my mention of her in the article, so there's hope. Willy, you know, has taken a shine to that new girl, Faye, and I think he hoped to persuade her to run. But she told him to fuck off, so somewhat reluctantly he has shifted his support to me. Willy's a good boy, though. I know he'll come through for me. He always has."

"Everyone comes through for you, Hamilton."

Hamilton looks at me gravely. "You are mistaken, Jesse James. Silas is right. You are naïve."

. . .

At one time, I was secretary of Ward Government. I declined at first, automatically, but changed my mind, thinking the post ideally suited to my needs and temperament. I lasted one week. I could not compress my bulky transcriptions of the meeting into a suitable form. Nothing escaped my attention, with the result that my report ran to twenty pages, which I had boiled down from thirty-five after several sleepless nights spent writing and rewriting in the bathroom. Now I content myself with committing to memory the reports of other secretaries:

Ward Government—Minutes

Ward Government was called to order 11:00 a.m. Monday by President Melinda Aaronson. Last week's minutes were read by me, Willy. First order of business was to elect a new vice president since Shipwreck eloped last week. Luis nominated Jesse James. Jesse declined. Hamilton Trevelyan nominated himself and was unanimously elected.

Old business. Mrs. Stern said she was old business. Melinda said that remark was out of order. Mrs. Stern said, "You are out of order." Melinda said, "That's why I'm here." Everybody laughed.

The Skin Committee needs new members and also needs $2 from the treasury to buy aftershave lotion and deodorant. Miss A. suggested we should not buy spray deodorant any more as *Time* magazine says it is bad for you.

Miss A. reported the Social Committee needs $5 for this week's party. Martin Dewar said last week's party was a great success. Philip said it was a flop—nobody danced. They just ate and went away. Miss S. said maybe don't put out the food until the party has been going at least an hour. The Princess said she enjoyed the party and so did Franklyn. Faye jumped out of her seat and said it was the worst party she had ever been to and the whole place was a dump and the Social

Committee was a bunch of dumb shitheads. Miss R. said it seemed that some people liked the party and some didn't. The vote was fifteen to four to give the Social Committee $5.

New business—Daily Living reports. Group A is on serving and said it is going fine. Group B is on coffee selling and said it is going fine. Walter said he hadn't seen anyone selling coffee for two days. Philip said he had been doing all the work on coffee and needed a rest. Janine said Shipwreck did all the work and the reason there was no coffee was that he was gone. Philip said, "I object, Madam President." Melinda said, "Objection overruled." Group C is on Ward and Dormitory Maintenance. Luis said it is going fine. He said the male side was neater than the female side. Walter said Ursula and Marsha haven't made their beds all week. Luis said David deserves special mention for the continued neatness of his bed. Everybody clapped, but David wasn't at the meeting. Miss R. suggested Silas tell David about the special mention, but Silas wasn't at the meeting.

Melinda said all those in favor of ending the meeting, say aye. Everyone said aye. Respectfully submitted. Willy.

My trips to the snack bar are reconnaissance flights. The back wall of the staff meeting room faces the elevator which takes me downstairs. The walls are thin and porous, and a foot from the ceiling there is no wall at all, only a wire grating like chicken wire. I lean against the wall, my ears prickling. I ring for the elevator only after I have gathered enough information to get me through the day.

David is being moved from the dormitory into the five-bed room with Walter and Silas and Philip and me, now that Shipwreck has eloped. It's a reward for his going to Daily Living because other than that he is the same as he was when he first came in. Until last week, he was on steadily increasing doses of Thorazine. Now Dr. Green, his resident, has switched him to Stelazine. It won't make any difference, Suzanne Lynch, chief of the ward, tells Dr. Green. But she lets him do it anyway. He doesn't believe her. He is determined to save David. He watches over him, brooding like a mother hen.

David's presence is unnerving Walter: "I can't sleep with him around. I need my sleep."

"Why?" Silas asks. "You don't do anything all day."

"When my mother sends me the money to go back to Vienna, I'll have to take my final exams. I have to rest up so I'll be prepared."

I can't sleep with David around either. He sits all night on the edge of his bed in his hospital pajamas and his state-issued black shoes that are two sizes too small for him. Bony head bent, he stares at his huge folded hands and rocks silently.

Toward dawn, when he is certain Silas and Philip and Walter and I are asleep, he chants in his strange, pliant singsong: "I believe in God the Father and in his only son, Jesus Christ. I am a good Catholic, but the FBI is after me and the Black Panthers and the JDL. I have offended thee, O Lord, but I want to be good. I want to be in society. I will try harder."

David likes to sit in the sun in the yard. I watch him often. His broad, flat face thrown back on his powerful neck, he stares open-eyed, straight at the sun. Today I follow him and sit next to him, surprised as always by the fact that he is actually shorter than I am. "You shouldn't look at the sun. You will hurt your eyes."

He lowers his eyes. "People taught you things. You know how to live in society."

"I'm not sure how much I know. Would you like a smoke, David?"

"You are a kind person."

"Here. Have a smoke. Please. I have lots more."

He takes the cigarette and sticks it in the pocket of his hospital shirt. "It would be bad if they knew you talked to me."

"Who? Bad if who knew?"

"Nixon and the FBI."

"I'll take my chances."

"If they see you with me, they may hurt you."

"Is that why you stay alone so much? So no one else will be hurt?"

"It hurts very bad to be alone."

"What about your family? Don't you have a family?"

"My family doesn't talk to me anymore. I took up with bad company. I sinned."

"Everyone sins."

"Dr. Green hears my confession. He wants to save me." He pats the breast pocket where he keeps his worn billfold. "This time I am trying very hard. I have my credentials. All in good order."

Faye was the last in a long line to tell me about David's credentials. "He's full of shit," she railed at me. "There's nothing in his wallet. Nothing."

"I believe it will be fine," David says. He blinks at me, shaking his head, and his green eyes shine with the stubborn certitude of an imbecilic, a great faith. He takes my hand, gripping it strongly, pumping it up and down. "Thank you very much. I have to go now. Miss A. is waiting for me."

Silas is doing headstands in a corner of the yard. He looks at me upside down. "Well?"

"I don't want to bother you while you're doing your exercises."

"You don't bother me. My concentration is superb."

"What do you make of David?"

"I don't make anything of him. You do. You make something of everything."

"What's that supposed to mean?"

"You are a mole, digging, burrowing, and what do you come up with? Another turd to add to your collection."

"Fuck you, Silas, you fucking superior fuck. Did you tell Hamilton you thought I was naïve?"

"I think I said you were a mole."

"Fuck you and your stinking riddles. I don't have time to figure out all your mumbo-jumbo."

"But apparently you do, apparently you have all the time in the world, Jesse James, to figure and figure and figure while you ride the range."

The only thing Silas has ever told me about himself is that the first time he flipped out he was in Macy's the day before Christmas and the second time he was in a deserted furniture showroom on Broadway, with one foot in Danish Modern and one foot in Spanish Provincial.

From bits and pieces overheard in the senior staff office, I have put together that Silas fled some prestigious university a month before he was due to graduate with honors. He was only eighteen at the time. His first admission was six months later. That was ten years ago. I'm not sure how many admissions he's had since then; but to hear the old men tell it, it's been a lot. According to them, though, when Silas was eighteen he was in Lebanon or Greece or somewhere on an archeological dig. I couldn't get confirmation of either story from Silas. It wouldn't surprise me if both were true.

I don't know why Silas is here or why he keeps coming back.
Perhaps he is disturbed by something I have never thought of.

Gemma is trying to convince Silas that he should start coming
to Daily Living. They sit on the couch in the dayroom, heads
together, conspiratorial. I am across the room from them, pretending to attend to my solitaire game, which I have laid out on
top of the arts and crafts table in the corner.

"It's to your advantage, Silas. You won't get any passes if
you don't start coming."

"Will you be there?"

Gemma stiffens slightly. "I'm always there. You know that."

"I would rather see you here like this."

Gemma draws her knees together. "You're expected to take
part in the ward routine. It's one way we have of gauging your
readiness for discharge."

"You don't believe that bullshit," says Silas. "Let's talk of
something worth talking about—protons, neutrons, carbona-
tions, fusions. I'll tell you about collapsing stars, Gemma. Stel-
lar lifetimes."

Gemma smiles in spite of herself. She looks so vulnerable. I
would like to pet her like a kitten or squash her like a bug or
hold her in my arms or fuck her till she cries for mercy. I can
never make up my mind. She must have a lover at home. What
sort of life does she go home to? Sometimes she seems very gay,
giddy even. Sometimes sad, abstracted, hair flying, notebooks
dropping. Lately she spends less time with patients. I see her
gliding by—hi, hi. She is avoiding us. Don't think I don't
notice. I slam the seven of spades down on the six, hard enough
to rattle the ancient table.

Now she sits knee to knee with Silas. Her face is flushed. A
sudden rush of warmth shoots up my neck, spreading uncomfortably over my cheeks. Gemma lights another cigarette to
hide behind and looks at Silas through the smoke. The drifting

smoke is making me dizzy. Silas is saying something. Gemma's cigarette drops through her fingers to the floor. What did he say to her? She bends to retrieve her cigarette, but Silas puts his foot over it just as she reaches to pick it up. Gemma sucks her breath in sharply. "Do you want to talk, Silas, or not?"

"I want to make a star with you."

My forehead is wet. My palms are wet. I'm sweating like a pig. The cards stick damply to my fingers, and Gemma's upturned face shimmers woozily in front of me.

"We'll overcome the barriers. Electrical repulsion. We can pierce it. Do you want to? Do you want to come with me? Come with me, Gemma. Come."

Gemma's mouth is open. Her warm, excited breath leaps across the room like a flame. It burns my cheeks. I am burning up.

"We'll fly fast. Fast. Faster faster faster. Rushing at each other. Rushing. O God, it's beautiful. Aaah, here it comes. Here it comes. Now. Heat and light exploding. Rocketing."

Gemma shudders. Goddamn him.

"A star. Feel it, Gemma. A perfect nucleus. A star."

She is lost in it, trying to get back to where she was. I see her flailing, helpless while Silas stares through her, beyond me, to the lonely star he has created. I am suddenly aware of each individual drop of sweat on my forehead as I shiver uncontrollably underneath the star's cold light.

8

Out on the streets of the city, everyone else is shedding their clothes. Men carry their jackets, loosen their ties, ambling in their shirt sleeves, dampened with circles of sweat. The young girls are in sandals and tiny wisps of dresses, barely skimming their asses. In between their breasts I know there is a stream of wet. Everyone is swinging loosely, heads up, while I stalk the streets, head down, hands in my pockets, shoulders hunched against my neck.

The coldness starts in my stomach and fans out from there, penetrates my legs and spreads upward to my chest and arms. My bones are iced clear through. I have trouble moving my eyes naturally because my eyeballs are freezing stiff in their sockets. I can feel my intestines stiffening. My internal juices are drying up. My balls have receded into my tightening scrotum.

As the cold gets more intense, I contract harder and harder against it, till I am hunched over like a cripple. My contortions don't help. Still, I can't straighten up. What began as an instinct for survival has become an involuntary posture.

In order to go outside, I have to wear two sweaters, an army parka, a knitted cap, and leather gloves. Underneath my jeans, I have on long underwear from camp. Very small for me now, it hikes up, cuts into my groin, and squashes my balls, what is left hanging of them. Still, I don't dream of abandoning this underwear. Under my cowboy boots, I wear two pair of long, woolen socks. People stare at me in the streets. Do they think I am doing this for a laugh?

I am getting more and more paranoid in the streets. Fortunately, I don't have to go out much. I lost my bagging post at the A & P when I went to the hospital the first time. When I got out, I made the mistake of telling the lady at the state employment service that I had been incarcerated at a city institution for the mentally deranged.

I still go downtown to get my welfare check. Other than that I go only as far as the Puerto Rican delicatessen around the corner to pick up chicory coffee, bread, and peanut butter.

Mr. Sanchez grins at me. "Hot enough for you?" He loves American slang, relishes its inanity. He thinks I dress like this for his amusement. I only confirm absolutely his belief that the Anglos are crazy. That belief and his amazement at it are what keep him sane in this scummy slum.

Inside my apartment, I can give in to this evil coldness, shiver violently, shaking as if I have a fit, teeth clattering loud and unabashed. Out on the street humiliation makes me fight to keep my jaws clamped tight, strain not to shudder.

I have closed all the windows and sealed the corners with chunky peanut butter to ensure against air seepage. For a time I try to keep to some sort of schedule—do a little reading, watch TV, eat a little—but I can't sustain it. I am so cold that I cannot think straight. I can't concentrate enough to read or watch TV, and my fingers are so stiff that it is only with the most torturous effort that I can unscrew the lid of the peanut butter. So I go to bed in my clothes and pile every blanket I have on top of me.

I stay in bed for three days, huddled under the enormous weight of blankets. But I am as cold as ever. This cold is not coming from outside; it is coming from inside. Still, I rack my brain to think of some way to make the apartment warm. What else can I do? I call my landlord, Mr. Kaminsky.

"Mr. Kaminsky, this is Jay. Jay Davidson in 4D."

"Yes, Jay. How are you?"

"Cold. I'm cold."

"Summer colds can be very bad. Are you taking vitamin C and drinking lots of fruit juice?"

"No, no. I don't have a cold. I am cold."

"What, Jay?"

"I am cold. I'm freezing to death, Mr. Kaminsky. Oh, Christ, I'm freezing to death."

"Jay, what's the matter?"

"Mr. Kaminsky, please give me some heat."

"Heat? Did you say heat?"

"Yes, yes. Heat, heat. Please, Mr. Kaminsky. Please give me some heat."

"But, Jay, it's the middle of July. It's a regular heat wave. People are dropping like flies from heat prostration. Just today Mrs. Kaminsky read me another story about it from the newspaper. A lady in Brooklyn . . . "

"I know all that. But it doesn't change anything."

"Well, I don't know. I never heard anything like it. What can I do?"

"Turn on the furnace. Give me some heat."

"But, Jay, that's impossible. Everyone else in the building is yelling at me because we don't have enough cross-ventilation and no wiring for air conditioning, and you want heat."

"You're a slum landlord. You'd let me die like a dog."

"How can you say such a thing? I live here too. It's not like I live fancy. And I wouldn't let you die like a dog."

"Then help me."

"Did you try turning on the oven? That gives some nice heat."

"I didn't think of it."

"Maybe that's not such a good idea after all. You're not thinking of anything desperate, are you? I mean you wouldn't stick your head in the oven? Jay. Jay, are you there? Now listen to me, Jay. Would you like to go back to the hospital for a little while?"

"No. Oh, shit. No. Goddammit, I don't know. I don't know. I'm too cold to think; my brain cells are petrified."

"All right, Jay. You just stay right where you are."

I hang up the phone and sit huddled next to it, my blankets clutched around me, thinking of electric heaters. Why hadn't I thought of that before? Maybe I could find one in a hock shop somewhere. But it would mean going out. I can't decide whether to risk it or not. There aren't too many electric heaters around in July. On the other hand, maybe I should at least look around the neighborhood. I could call on the phone and make inquiries. Then I wouldn't have to go out. But I remember that I never got my new Yellow Pages or else some kid copped it from in front of my door, and I threw my old one out. Besides I detest making phone inquiries. No, the telephone is out. Definitely out. I would rather go out and tramp all over the goddamn city than call on the phone.

I must have sat for at least an hour trying unsuccessfully to decide what to do when Mr. Kaminsky opened the apartment door with his master key and came in red and shamefaced, followed by one cop, baby-faced, with very clear blue eyes, and one young, bearded doctor in jeans and a khaki shirt with the sleeves rolled up.

9

I wonder as I trail the old men if they were ever anything other than what they are now. Have they walked through their lives, just so, ambling up and down the corridors, telling the news? Is this shapeless shuffling the sum of it?

"D'ya hear about Ramirez?"

"Luis?"

"Not Rivera. Ramirez on B-6."

"I thought they finally kicked him out."

"He came back in last night. Told the admitting doctor his wife and two children were killed in a car crash, and he wanted to kill himself."

"I didn't know he was married."

"He isn't."

"Well, is he back?"

"Doctor told him to produce the bodies and he'd be happy to let him in."

"Hee. Hee. Poor Ramirez. Tough for a junkie to get in these days."

"It's getting tough for anyone to get in. They got that PNG list up in the nurses' station. Mrs. Morley told me about it. It means *persona non grata*."

"What's that mean?"

"Ungrateful person. It means you can't get back in. Too many people want to get in. They have to spread it around a little. Give some new people a chance."

"My name isn't on that list, is it?"

"No, no. Mine either. Don't worry about it."

"I wish you hadn't brought it up."

"If you ever have any trouble, just say you're hearing voices."

"I do hear voices. I told you that a million times."

"You're all right then. That's what I'm trying to tell you."

"First thing you know they'll be wanting a tape recording of the voices."

I am on call, day or night, for the needy and the desperate. It is not necessary to make an appointment with me. I charge no fee, I understand everything, and I do not judge. I am impartial as a stone and as helpless.

I come dazed out of sleep, Walter's fat fingers jabbing at my chest. "What? Walter? What? What's the matter?"

"I have to talk to you. It's urgent."

"What time is it?"

"It's four-fifteen." From behind his thick glasses, Walter squints at his watch.

"Jesus, Walter."

"Shhh. You'll wake them."

I sit up in bed. By the light coming from the corridor, I can see Silas curled up on one side like a baby, face turned to the wall. Philip is spread-eagled, snoring lightly. Across from me, even David is sleeping—flat on his back, arms folded across his chest. So still he might be dead.

Walter is tugging at my pajama sleeve. "Please, Jesse, please, come to the bathroon. We can talk there."

I follow him into the hall. Miss Jenkins is slumped on the bench outside our room, her long feet crossed in front of her, the *Daily News* spread across her rising and falling belly. Slack-jawed, she whistles lightly through her snores. From around the corner, I can hear Mrs. Alton and Mr. Frazer laughing. They are old buddies. They have worked the night shift together with Miss Jenkins on this ward for fifteen years. Mr. Theodophilus, a relative newcomer to the night shift, is around somewhere. I saw him earlier conferring with Hamilton. He is trying to persuade Hamilton to invest in a taco franchise in Queens.

Walter pulls me after him into the bathroom. "It's my ring. My opal ring. It's disappeared."

"The one with the yellow stone?"

"It's semiprecious," he moans. "Semiprecious. Oh, Jesse. Why did this have to happen to me? Now, just now, when I'm so near to everything."

"Hold on, Walter. How can that be? You never take that ring off, do you? I've never seen you without it."

"No. Never. Never." Walter paces in front of the row of sinks. "Someone must have taken it off me while I was sleeping."

"But you would have felt it. You would have waked up."

"But I didn't wake up. I've been getting paraldehyde. Ever since David came into our room, I've been sleeping so badly. I asked Dr. Brenner for a second dose, but he wouldn't give it to me."

"Who would try to get your ring off your finger while you're sleeping?"

"There are some very strange people here, Jesse." Walter lowers himself to the tile floor, unable, it seems, to continue. I can't think of anything to say, so I wait silently for Walter to collect himself.

"I think it's Philip," he says finally, with shaky triumph.

Walter used to look up to Philip. He considered him one of the ward intelligentsia. He respected Philip's flourish, his lively reminiscences of the "outside" Dr. Gruber. Philip's psychiatric jargon thrilled him. And Philip for his part encouraged Walter to talk about his medical school days in Vienna. But ever since Philip smeared shit on himself last year, Walter has dreaded him. He considered it a personal betrayal, incomprehensible and unforgivable.

"Philip wouldn't do that, Walter," I say, joining him on the floor. "Besides he doesn't like rings. Or any jewelry."

"Philip, you may remember, is an ex-convict. A thief. Once a thief . . . "

"Walter. He was desperate. He knocked over one little candy store. He only took fifty dollars. He left a hundred fifty in the register. He only took what he needed."

Walter lets out a long sigh, like a balloon deflating. "Mother will be furious."

"How will she know? Just don't write her about it."

"Oh, she'll know. She knows everything. She'll never send me the money to go to Vienna now. And, on top of everything, I'm constipated. Completely blocked up. I pleaded with Dr. Brenner to let Mrs. Morley give me an enema, but he wouldn't hear of it. I told him the milk of magnesia does nothing for it. Nothing at all." Walter is silent, shaking his head from side to side, wondering at his slew of misfortunes. "Do you think it might be David?"

"Jesus, Walter, please."

"He'd have easy access. He's in our room. And he hardly

ever sleeps. He just sits there rocking back ánd forth. It drives me crazy, Jesse."

"It wasn't David."

"But it could be. It's possible."

"All he has to his name is that tattered billfold he carries around with his credentials."

"He has no credentials."

"It isn't him, Walter."

"Oh, I know, I know." Tears glisten in his pale eyes. "I know it isn't David. I've lost it. I must have taken it off somewhere. How could I?"

"Maybe we'll find it, Walter. We probably will. It'll turn up." But I know it won't. Things don't turn up for Walter. The ring is lost forever. I am certain of that.

"She won't send me the money now. I'll never get to Vienna. And I'm forty-three years old, Jesse. Soon it will be too late."

The cold of the tile floor seeps into my behind.

"Come back to bed, Walter."

"D'ya hear about Walter?"

"Don't tell me his mother broke down and sent him the money to go to Vienna."

"Nope."

"He found his ring."

"Nope."

"He got his enema."

"Nope."

"Well, don't keep me in suspense. I'm not a young man. I may get heart failure."

"He's going to hijack a plane and fly to Vienna."

"Walter? They can't bribe Walter to go 'round the corner to Bohack's. Can't pry him loose to go to the yard. I'd love to see him do it though."

"That's what Dr. Brenner said. His exact words. He said he

would gladly give up his summer vacation to see such a thing."

Superman really is Clark Kent emerging from the phone booth. I knew it all along, else I would not be Jesse James. I cannot tell if the old men believe or disbelieve. But they are light-hearted, which I take to be a good sign.

10

The metamorphosis, if that's what it was, must have been very subtle because I wasn't aware of it at all. One day I was popular. The first day of classes junior year of high school to be exact. Girls bumped into me in the hallways, smiled intimately. Guys greeted me like a long-lost buddy: "Hey, Jay. How's it going? Where you been, man?"

Here. I've been here, you insensitive pricks. Right under your noses. I was naturally suspicious at first. I spent long hours in front of the bathroom mirror, searching for some reasonable manifestation of my new status. It was the same face. Bland, sulky. Not bad-looking.

It was good-looking to tell the truth. I had always been pleased, comforted, to see how good-looking it was. I stole secret glances at it in shop windows. But I knew in my heart that it was not my face. It had nothing to do with me. Other people's faces belonged to them. Mine was a superimposition. Except for the blur around the edges. That I recognized as mine. At any rate, it was definitely the same face it had been three months earlier.

I asked Johnny if he noticed anything different about me. "No. What happened? Did you get laid? Hey, Jay, did you?"

"No, no. For Christ's sake, Johnny."

Perhaps, I thought, it is my destiny beginning to unfold. But it didn't feel like it. The holy seed was dormant as ever, lying fallow. Biding its time.

The days flowed into each other, and I flowed with them, languid as a water lily. Everything is drenched in a heavy, golden fog: basketballs drop into nets for me, term papers get A's for me, my car purrs for me, golden girls come undone for me, the radio sings to me, the telephone rings for me.

But inside me the seed lies shriveled, mocking me. In the middle of the night my stomach churns, burning acid holes in my clean, white sheets.

I am increasingly uneasy in the golden landscape. I taste everything there is to taste; I hold it in my mouth, swish it around, and when no one is looking, I spit it out.

Just when it seems that the creeping boredom will overtake me and paralyze me for good, Debbie appears on the scene, a transfer from some exotic girls' school in the city. She is the true Golden Girl. I have been led astray by counterfeits. Alloys. Here at last the glistening original, come to banish my boredom, to set me on edge, to free me. Honey hair falling thickly down her back, honeyed skin and chameleon eyes that change color depending on her mood. She knows her own perfection, acknowledges it from just the distance that will not disturb her perfect equilibrium.

In two weeks' time, she is captain of the cheerleading squad. I watch her greedily from the stands.

She is totally the split she is executing, fused in the "yea, team" she calls out, yet somehow above and beyond it all. My determination to know her burns like a flame, singeing my nerves till they vibrate. Never have I felt so purposeful, so single-minded, my straying, straggling thoughts reined into a hard core of perfect concentration.

By the end of the third week, she is assistant editor of *The Beacon*, our literary magazine. I am about to make my move. I slap together an essay on F. Scott Fitzgerald, defending him against charges of dilettantism by obscure City College professors dug out of old literary supplements gathering dust under my bed. She may reject it, but at least it will give me a chance to get at her.

I drop the essay on her desk in study hall. "Thought you might want to consider this for *The Beacon*."

She looks up from her book. Her smile unhinges me. It is simultaneously reserved and dazzling, as if she were promising me something but wouldn't say what.

She is saying something to me. What is it? What did she say? She's drawing phallic-looking doodles on the inside cover of her geometry book. "Right?" she says.

"Oh right, right." What am I saying right to? "This whole thing is a mistake."

"What?"

"I'm sorry, I was thinking of something else."

"I said, It is Jay, right?"

"Oh, yeah. Jay. Right. Jay Davidson." What does she mean, it is Jay? We have two classes together—history and English. She knows my name. Is she purposely trying to unnerve me?

"Debbie, it is Debbie, isn't it?"

"Debbie Walker. Hi."

"Hi."

It is a dead end. I have run out of things to say. My mind is a total blank.

"I'll take a look at this now if that's okay with you," she says after an endless, leaden silence.

"Fine. That's fine."

She puts one hand on either side of her head, blocking me out. She giggles.

"What's funny?"

"This is."

"What do you mean?"

"It's funny. Don't you think so?"

"Of course. I was surprised you got it, that's all."

"It's not right for *The Beacon*, though."

"Oh. Okay. Listen, Debbie, I'll tell you what. Fuck *The Beacon* and, what is more important, fuck you." I can't have said this aloud, but obviously I have because Debbie's cheeks flush hot pink and her eyes are changing color. Satisfaction surges through me, watching her narrowing eyes change from grey to green to yellow.

"What?"

"You heard me."

"Are you challenging me or something?"

"I don't know."

"Well, if you are, I accept the challenge."

I have no idea what all this means. But I am excited, so excited I can hardly breathe. I feel that I am finally on the brink of something.

"Here." She shoves my essay at me. "Take this. Call me tonight." I miss connections with the paper and it falls splat to the floor.

I call her that night and the next night and the next and the next. The telephone, my old enemy, is now my lifeline. It is only through that malevolent mouthpiece that we connect. In school we avoid each other by some tantalizing subterranean agreement. Pass each other in the halls without a word.

But there is a secret electricity. We know. We know what no one else can know. I can feel her when she is anywhere near, even if I can't see her. I can smell her and she me.

At home, I drag the telephone into the hall closet to call her. I invent for her fantastic lies of my misspent youth that are

truer than anything I have ever said to anyone. I confide to her
dreams of a future I didn't know I dreamed of.

"Where are you now, Debbie?"

"I'm home, of course. You called me here. Are you losing
your mind, Jay?"

"What room are you in?"

"My bedroom."

"You have a phone in there? I didn't know that."

"What's so interesting about that?"

"I like to place you, to visualize you where you are."

"Where are you?"

"In the closet."

"What? Jay, are you really in the closet?"

"Debbie, tell me what you're wearing."

"You're crazy sometimes."

"What are you wearing?"

"Not very much really. Not much at all."

"Yeah?"

My hand has slid under my jeans, inside my jockey shorts.
"Describe it to me."

"What?"

"What you're wearing."

"It's pale green."

"What is it? Is it a nightgown?"

"It's just a robe, a sort of silky robe."

Would she do it if I asked her? Talk to me and touch herself,
play with herself till she came, till we came together over the
phone. What if the operator happened to listen in? Would she
know what was going on? 'Young man. I know what you're
doing. I know. My supervisor wants to speak to you.' 'This is
the supervisor speaking. Coming over the phone is a federal
offense. I will have to report you to the authorities.'

Oh, Jesus, what am I thinking? Do girls even masturbate?
They must. Certainly they must. I never heard one admit it.
Maybe they don't. "Oh, Debbie, Debbie . . . "

"Jay? Are you there?"

"Unngh, I'm here, Debbie. Debbie, the robe. What's under it?"

"Nothing. I'm naked."

"Oh yeah?"

"Mmmmm."

"Debbie, your legs . . . "

"What about them?"

"Oooh, Debbie . . . "

"They feel soft."

"What does?"

"My legs. D'you ever notice how long my legs are, Jay? I bet they're longer than yours. We should measure them sometime."

"Oh, Christ, sweet sweet Christ. Aagh . . ."

"Jay? Jay? Are you there, Jay? I'm going to hang up if you aren't going to talk to me."

"I'm here."

"You sound far away. Are you talking into the phone?"

"Debbie, listen. Listen to me. We've got to stop this messing around. Talking over the phone. Never seeing each other. It's ridiculous."

She laughs. "Jay, I think I love you."

"You do?"

"I think I do. I think so. Good night."

II

"You ever run into a Jesus?"

"Never did."

"You hear a lot about Napoleons. But I never met one."

"I knew an Athena."

"Athenas are a dime a dozen."

"I fucked an Aphrodite. Of course, that was many years back. She's probably an old hag by now."

"You ever talk to that Ursula girl?"

"No. Can't make out what she's saying, so I pass her by."

"She thinks she's a dog."

"I don't believe that."

"Told me so herself. Barked at me. Woof woof. Plain as day."

"Imagine that."

"I never did think I was anyone but me. I've wished I was. But I never really thought it. Did you?"

"Never. Bona fide crazy all these years and never thought I was anyone but me."

Dr. Lynch is wearing disguises. One day she wears her dark hair pulled back from her head, drawn so tight it slants her eyes and gives a Eurasian cast to her narrow face. Her high-necked, long-sleeved dress falls severely to her ankles.

The next day, her hair flies about her face. She is a gypsy in a dress of flaming colors—bold, with billowing sleeves and a sweeping skirt. Straw sandals on her feet and rows of bangle bracelets clanking on her arms like gypsy bells.

Now her hair falls straight to her shoulders, a bang covers her eyebrows. She wears a tweed suit with an open jacket and a white silk blouse. A watch, suspended on the thin gold chain which dangles from her throat to her waist, hits against her metal chain belt and makes a noise—elegant, assured. Her mood is obscured by her falling hair, covering bangs, half-closed eyes that elude any inquiry.

It is rumored that Dr. Lynch is leaving the ward, the hospital, the country. It is also rumored that she is seeing her ex-husband again, that she may have to have surgery for a disc, that she is redecorating her entire apartment, that she is having an affair with Dr. Pattishall in neurosurgery and is pregnant by him, and that she is taking hormones for hot flashes.

I watch her in the nurses' station, flipping through charts, laughing with the nurses. She calls them darling. She smiles seductively at the residents and they smile back.

'Jesse, Jesse, help me. You see that I'm in pain.'

'Be still, Suzanne. Be still. I see you moving restlessly. Wherever you are, you are already somewhere else and that place will not suffice either.'

'Yes. Yes.'

'You wear disguises.'

'I am so tired of it.'

'You would like to sleep.'

'I crave it. Deep, dreamless sleep. Is today Thursday? I see private patients tonight. UGGH ACCH. Mrs. Miller is depressed and her husband is gone. Well, so am I and so is mine. That's life, Mrs. Miller. Her dreams are so transparent, so like mine. I'd rather listen to the really crazy ones. The crazier they are, the better I can concentrate.'

'It's hard to concentrate.'

'I can't keep my mind on what I'm doing. I have to present in Grand Rounds but my mind wanders. I read charts and I don't know what I'm reading.'

'You're overtired.'

'Of course I am. I've worked hard to get where I am. I put the director of this hospital where he is today, and he can't look at me anymore. He looks over my head and hops from one foot to another.'

'What does he know?'

'Not much. I shaped up two pigsty wards for him before I

came on this one, and now he's afraid of stepping on the toes of some teeny-bopper residents. . . . What time is it?'

'We have time.'

'At ten-thirty I have to supervise Weisser.'

'Ah, little Joel Weisser. He tries, I suppose.'

'It's impossible to teach him anything. He looks at me as if he'd heard it all before.'

'Insolent.'

'Insolent. Exactly. It's very calming to talk to you.'

'Stay. We'll talk some more.'

'I have to go see Weisser.'

'Stay.'

'But we'll be discussing you.'

For other patients, the treatment room is a place to weigh themselves and particularly a place to make free phone calls to the outside world—between the hours of 11 a.m. and 12 (except on Mondays at Ward Government time) and between 3 and 4 p.m. For me, the treatment room is a nerve center of my operation. I consider it my office. I go there several times a day, but I never make any calls. Instead, I stare out the barred window at the river five stories below me. My mind wanders as I watch the river change and change and change. I am attentive nevertheless, listening through the pasteboard partition to the conversations in the senior staff office next door, listening for a key word which will illuminate the changing river.

Silas cannot understand my interest in other people's conversations. "It's all the same," he tells me. "You've heard one conversation, you've heard them all. If you want to be entertained, listen to your saliva flow."

It is not entertainment I am seeking. It is understanding. Understanding, understanding, and more understanding. I will stuff myself with it, sniff it up with every pore, cram it into every orifice. Someday it will pay off. Everything will fall into its proper place, and I will, at last, understand.

"Willy, Mrs. Morley found tuna sandwiches under your mattress."

"I'm saving them, Dr. Green."

"For what?"

"For my brothers."

"They get food in the state hospital, Willy."

"No. Nothing. They don't have nothing. Nobody cares about them."

"Miss Jenkins, several patients have reported seeing you eat the sandwiches Willy puts under his mattress."

"Willy's not eating them, Miss R. He just lets them rot under there."

"Don't you think it might look a little bizarre to patients to see a staff member doing that."

"Excuse me, Sophie, but I been here fifteen years and nobody ever called me bizarre. Fifteen years on the night shift. Imagine. Old as I am, I got to sit up all night, workin' and slavin', taking care of other people's children and she's callin' me bizarre."

None of this interests Silas. Trivia. I do not presume to judge what is trivia and what is not. I lap it all up, file it away. Sometimes I think I cannot find the space to shove in one more piece of information to be processed. But I always do. The trouble is that when I go to look for something I can never find it. Everything is jumbled together. Helter skelter. Nothing is categorized because I can never decide what label to affix to what.

The tiny hairs in my ears quiver as I listen through the partition to Hamilton's soliloquy to Dr. Lynch.

"I don't know why I want her back. She broke me. She's more powerful than God. You all are. After love, she would crawl on top of me and peer down at me from her great height, nose to nose, smiling lasciviously, like some obscene cat who had swallowed a bird of paradise. She knew I was shattered and she'd smile like that, licking her lips, and then chatter at me about some unpaid bill or other. Up she'd bounce, my come dribbling down her long legs, and bring back a salami sandwich and eat it, dropping bread crumbs on my naked limbs. Then, not ten minutes having passed, she'd want it again. Like a greedy child stuffing in penny candy—and that's just how much I satisfied her. When I couldn't, she'd finish off her salami in thundering silence and turn her sullen back on me and be snoring in two minutes, her still slippery buttocks pinning me against the wall."

12

Driving home from school on Monday, the snow was already flying down, covering the streets with fine snow dust. By the time we passed through downtown and were climbing into the small wooded hills beyond it, toward Debbie's house, the snow was swirling around us, whipped by a sudden tossing wind into tiny, flying whirlpools. We are snug in my car, drifting slowly through the thickening whiteness, listening to the radio, which announces warnings to motorists, reports of telephone lines down and electrical wires sagging upstate. Schools upstate closed tomorrow. Delays on all commuter trains. Locally,

Greenfield Elementary School closed tomorrow. Millburn Junior High closed, Sedgewick High closed. We smile at each other, savoring the gift the snow is making just for us.

We sit parked in front of her house in the darkening car watching the snow pile up on the roof, bending it down to us. Everything is soft, transfigured in the dusk. We are transfigured too. We roll the windows down to smell the sudden night. Slicing through the open windows, keen as the stinging cold, comes my fear. The promise is slipping away, ebbing out again into the icy night.

In March I am restless, twitching in my sleep, dreaming of Debbie and me locked in uncomfortable embraces in the front seat of my car, in the back seat, in the linen closet of her house, under the Formica-topped tables in study hall.

In my dreams, I touch her till my fingers ache, kiss her till my tongue is sore, suck her till my mouth is dry as dust. But as soon as I try to enter into her, she vanishes.

The reality is the same—only vaguer, less visceral. I am holding up better, fascinated into lethargy by her passion that flares up so soft and strong, then breaks up into sullenness and cold, implacable, virgin determination.

Driving home that March night after seeing *Some Like It Hot*, I tell her her ass is almost as nice as Marilyn's. She laughs luxuriously. "Almost?"

"You want everything."

"Yes," she says. "I do."

"Do you really?"

"Yes."

I pull up at the side of the road.

"Miller's Pond," she says. "We're right by the pond." She pulls at my hand. "Let's walk."

"Do you think we need a blanket?" I ask. "It's kind of cold."

"Do you have one?"

"I don't actually."

We get out of the car. By the moon's light we can make out the worn footpath leading to the pond. She walks in front, holding my hand, leading me on. At the clearing we stop. By day the pond is stagnant, scummy, with beer bottles floating at its edge. It is so different in the moonlight. A satiny sheen plays over the dark water; a trick of light rippling the still surface like waves.

"I smell spring," she says, breathing deeply of the cold air, drinking it in.

I take off my windbreaker, crouching to spread it over the muddy ground. "You're not cold?"

"Yes, I am. But I love it. I love it that it's cold right now." She rushes her words together as if she were rushing toward something, flying to me.

I pull her onto her knees on the windbreaker. I can smell her peppery smell. I sink my hands into her long, thick hair, and sparks fly around her head.

"Static electricity," she says. "The cold does that sometimes."

"Take off your coat." She slips it off and I hurriedly bunch it up to make a pillow for her.

She puts her arms around me and draws me down on top of her. "Make me warm, Jay." She slides her hands under my sweater, under my shirt. My blood surges up in a hot, pounding rush. "I've been wanting you for such a long time, Debbie."

She is watching me. I kiss her eyes shut, but she opens them again.

"Take your clothes off." My voice sounds harsh to me.

I lift myself from her, watching as she raises herself onto one elbow. She tosses her head sideways and her hair flies swirling back. She holds it captive with one hand, unbuttoning her sweater with the other, then stands, shaking herself out of her loosened sweater.

"I'll do it," I say, jumping up in front of her. "Let me do it."

I move my hands over the front of her silky bra. I can feel her nipples under the slippery cloth. My heart is beating very fast. I reach around behind her and undo the hooks, pulling the bra from her shoulders.

The skin of her breasts is so white in the moonlight, blue white almost against the darkish nipples.

I slide her skirt, pants over her hips. They fall around her feet, and she kicks them away. She is rooted in the spongy earth. Strong legs opening.

"You're naked."

She blushes, flushing warm all over: cheeks, breasts, stomach, flushing. "I've got my shoes and socks on." She laughs. "I feel dumb."

"You're beautiful. Like a tree."

"A tree. I don't understand you sometimes. But it's all right. You don't understand me sometimes."

"I don't understand anything," I say, pulling at my shirt. Zipper. Shit. It's in my way. "Everything is in my way," I moan.

"Watch out," Debbie warns, laughing at me. "You're going to trip over your jeans."

"No, I'm not," I say, finally free of my clothes. "I'm not going to trip, I'm going to get you." I make a grab for her. She screams, laughing, darting out of my reach. I run after her, catching her around the waist. "Now," I say. "This second it's clear. Everything is clear. I see you."

"I see you, Jay. I see you clear as crystal."

I pull her to me. She makes a tiny gasping sound. "Do I feel good to you like this, Debbie? Does it feel good?"

"Yes, yes."

"Oh, God, Debbie."

"Wait," she whispers hoarsely, backing away. She sits down on the ground again, pulling off her shoes and socks, rearranging things, spreading her coat underneath her, taking my windbreaker, bunching that up for the pillow.

"How much longer before we get to move in?"

"What? Oh." She laughs, embarrassed. "I'm just straightening the bed."

I did it backward, windbreaker for her to lie on, coat for her pillow. I should have done it the other way around. "It looks wonderful. You look wonderful."

"Lie down with me," she says, reaching up for my hand.

I fall beside her on my back, looking up at the huge sky. "Do you love me?" I ask her, sucking the icy air deep into my lungs.

"Yes."

I turn over her, touching her face. I can read it with my fingers.

"Do you love me?" she asks.

I put my hands over her breasts, brushing my fingers over her cool nipples. They stiffen and stand up under my hands.

"Do you love me, Jay?" She wraps her legs around me.

"Yes," I say. I feel her swaying under me, opening. I put my hand between her legs, and her juice spills over my hand.

She squeezes the small of her back into the ground so she is lifted against me, pressed smack against me. I feel it all wet and juicy, delicious, rubbing against me. I slide down, running my hands over her belly, kissing the inside of her strong thighs. I spread her with my fingers, bury my face in her. She is moving under me, moving like waves, rolling under me, pulling me down.

"Jay, Jay, Jay." She pulls my head away, lifts me hard to her, kissing me roughly. "I can taste myself. I can taste myself in your mouth." She shivers. "Do it. Do it."

Her shiver goes through me, driving me straight, deep into her. I can't hold back. I am falling, wheeling through the turning sky. Outside myself. For the first time. First time ever. Ever in my life. Let me go. Let me go. Fuck it. Fuck you all. Spinning out with her into space.

I am flung across her, half in a perfect dreamless sleep.

"Is that all?"

I cannot realize what she has said. "What?"

"Is that all?"

I raise myself from her. I can't see her face.

"It was so fast," she says. "I was loving you so much. And it was over. You were gone. Off by yourself somewhere." She pulls away from me, drawing her coat around her, dragging it to the fallen log that lies nearby. She sits on the log, wrapping the coat around her, holding herself. "You left me alone." Her voice is flat. Ground down. She stands, stooping heavily, gathering her clothes as if they were rocks she gathered, stones, heavy stones, weighing her down.

13

"I'm bored. I'm so bored it's choking me."

"Why don't you do something."

"I'm an old man. What is there for me to do?"

"There's crafts in an hour. You could go up there and make an ashtray or a belt or something."

"I made seventy-five ashtrays and forty-five belts over the last fifteen years. What do I need more for?"

"You could go up to the library and get a book."

"Books don't interest me anymore."

"There's always cards."

"How long can a man sit and play cards, I ask you? I'm tired of cards. I'm tired of everything. I'm tired of you."

"Well, I'm tired of you too."

"Sitting around this ward waiting to die."

"You could always elope, fly the coop."

"Where would I go to? Hole up in one of them shitty welfare hotels. Barricade the door so the bastards don't steal the pants off me while I sleep."

"We're probably better off here, when all's said and done."

"If I had somebody to give a fuck, it might be different."

"Don't take it so hard. It's a mood you're in. There's good days and bad."

Is that me? A hundred years from now? Shrunken and wheyfaced, pacing up and down, up and down, waiting. What am I waiting for? Something. Something is going to happen. A miracle. But I am not ready yet. I have to prepare myself. I am taking notes, underlining everything. Who knows what might turn out to be important?

Gemma leaves bits and pieces of herself scattered around the ward, a chewed-up ballpoint pen, bobby pins, a key, a brown woolen glove with holes in two of the fingers, cigarettes that have fallen from the pack. She leaves a trail like Hansel and Gretel for me to follow.

From odd corners of the dayroom, I ferret out wadded-up pieces of paper with her notes to herself:

> Remember to pk up cake for Mass Activity
>
> Margie wnts me to encourage Philip to run fr Chairman of Social Committee—talk to him
>
> Toilet ppr, tmpx, oranges
>
> Last night he said—negative forces come in disguise. Does he think I don't know what he is saying?
>
> Do tax stuff

Silas thinks it is idiotic, this obsession I have with other people's waste. But I feel like an explorer.

"Narcissus looking in a pool," he warns me. "Watch out you don't fall in."

"Why did you fuck her with your crazy moon talk?" I ask him.

He looks at me blankly. I don't know if he doesn't remember or is pretending not to.

I have found a way to get into Gemma's office at night. Willy showed me how to do it with an old charge plate he found in the trash. I slip in when no one is watching. I sit at her desk, which is strewn with song sheets and memorandums, rubber bands, paper clips, uncapped Magic Markers, and endless scraps of paper with her notes to herself.

In the bottom drawer of her desk, stuffed away under an old phone book, I find sheets of yellow paper with her slanting writing on them. Every time I come back there is new writing. I pretend she writes to me.

My secret closeness to Gemma is creating a barrier between Silas and me.

"You won't find any answers that way."

"How do you know?"

"Don't tell me about it. I don't want to hear her secrets. Or yours either."

I am transcribing Gemma's notes into a small black note-book which I asked Gemma herself to purchase for me. I told her I was keeping a journal. I didn't lie. Gemma's journal is my journal. Her dreams are my dreams.

It weighs on me like a stone—unanswered letters, unreturned phone calls, clothes not taken to the cleaner's, bills not paid. Still I don't make a move to do any of it. Where would my mind go if I threw off this burden?

It is a farce my being here. Nodding at patients, drawing them out with my compassion that has no focus and spills over everything and everyone indiscriminately, uncreatively.

I use sex like a blanket to comfort myself.

It is a grey city day, silent and cold. I am walking down the streets where we used to live. Next door to the brownstone where I went to second and third grades is another brownstone, similar to the school. I open the door and enter a courtyard. It is dusk here, the long, slow dusk of a spring evening. Flowers bloom everywhere, a profusion of color, green, yellow, orange. I hear water splashing, a waterfall, a fountain, somewhere nearby.

In the center of the courtyard is an enormous tree with huge, spreading branches and thick roots sunk straight through the courtyard stones, deep into the earth. Underneath the tree, resting in its shade, are a mother and her young daughter. The slanting sun illuminates their faces. They are totally absorbed in their task of shelling butterbeans. Yet they noticed me as soon as I entered the garden. The mother smiles at me, inviting me to join them. I sit beside them under the tree, leaning against its broad back, and she hands me my portion of beans to shell.

He rests his head on my shoulder the way he used to.

Meaningless comfort to patients. Prattling advice off the top of my head.

Why can't I show him I love him? What is the matter with me?

Sometimes I am paranoid. I think people can see through me. They will turn away from me, despising my true face, which is not soft but hard, my vision that is not loving but swift and uncompromising. I have to get tighter and tighter not to show my true face.

Could joy begin when the worst finally happens? But the worst of it is that the worst never happens. It is always just about to happen.

14

Something is going to happen. The apartment is like an armed camp: my mother, stalking silently, biding her time till she can strike; my father, pinned against the sofa, babbling as the drink takes hold.

Johnny is eight years old. He skitters uneasily around my mother, his skinny legs fluttering. She hugs him absently. Disconsolate, he leaves her, tagging after me, treading on my heels.

"Leave me alone," I tell him. "I don't feel like playing ball."

"You never feel like doing anything. You just sit around like a grownup, and you're only twelve."

"I'm reading. Can't you see I'm reading?"

"You're always reading."

"So, what's it to you?"

"You'll go blind."

"Yeah."

"Then tell me a story, Jay."

"I can't tell you a story."

"Why? Why can't you?"

"I don't know any stories."

"Make one up."

"I can't make one up."

"You used to. You used to make them up all the time."

"Well, I don't anymore."

"I hate you."

But it's not true. Johnny loves me without reason. And I love him. He is the only one I know I love. But I am implacable against him. He is a wound I cannot heal. I turn my back on him.

I wish every night that I were somewhere else, but I am here in my room, trapped between my mother and my father, listening through the wall to her raging and his pleading. I wish that he would strike her down. I wish I could coax her to smile. I wish I could banish him.

In my dreams she comes to me, sits on my bed. Her beautiful face is wet with tears. They fall endlessly, splashing on my bed sheets. She pours out her heart to me in words that are as familiar to me as my name yet so strange and garbled that no matter how I strain I can't make them out. I listen mute, unable to respond.

Suddenly I am laid low by the flu. I have a fever and my bones ache. My eyes are burning and covered with a thick, whitish slime.

For three days and nights I float suspended, days and nights sliding into each other with nothing to mark their passing. Then suddenly the fever goes down. In the night, the first that I can separate from day, I feel it draining out of me. By morning it will be gone. I fight to keep it in me, tossing violently in my bed. But it is going, ebbing away, leaving me cool and wasted in the dawn.

15

Willy and Philip and Faye and Melinda and Janine and Luis and Silas and I have come to the yard with Gemma. Gemma organizes a basketball game of sorts, but Silas and I decline.

"You look funny without your cowboy boots," Faye calls out as Silas and I walk away. "I wouldn't let you on my team looking like that."

"He's a good player," I hear Willy tell her.

"Silas is better," Faye says loudly. "Silas is much better."

"C'mon, Jesse James," Silas challenges me, "I'll race you around the yard. The loser has to eat two of Mrs. Harper's Jell-O surprises."

"You're on." I pull off my jacket and toss it onto the bench beside the old wooden picnic table.

"The table will be the starting line and the finish line," Silas says, dropping into a deep knee bend.

"Whenever you're ready," I say, running in place to warm up.

Silas moves into position. "Okay, get down. On your mark, get set. Go."

We take off, running hard around the fenced-in perimeter of the big yard, a distance of about a quarter of a mile. The ground is dry, and I can feel the gravel through my old sneakers.

"Hey," I call out to Silas, who is a good ten yards ahead of me. "Why are you trying so hard? What does the winner get?"

I shouldn't have expended that energy shouting at Silas. I'm already winded. By the time we're halfway home I've got a painful stitch in my side. I put on a tremendous push as we circle the last stretch, but Silas edges me out by a hair.

He falls flat out on top of the wooden table. "Not bad," he says, when he's got his breath back. "You almost caught me."

I flop onto the bench. "Next time," I assure him.

Silas closes his eyes, getting the sun. "How about an icy-cold beer in a big frosty mug?"

"We'll send Gemma off to the tavern."

"I'll leave it to you, Jesse James."

I pick up my jacket and bring out the black notebook into which I have transcribed the notes I copied from Gemma's yellow sheets the night before. It gives me a strange feeling to know that Gemma is less than twenty feet away, urging Willy on to make his basket. I bury my head in my journal.

I am avoiding patients.

"What are you hiding in?" Silas asks me, unmoving, eyes closed, face to the sun.

I saw Daddy yesterday. We are strained with each other. Awkward, like failed lovers.

"Reading the notes I copied from Gemma."

I have always had faith. It wells up in me like a spring. I don't know where it comes from.

Silas snorts and shifts his weight away from me.

"Listen, Silas. Listen to this." I lower my voice, conscious of Gemma's closeness.

I can feel it. A mass of signals, jumbled contradictions, strangling the natural impulse. The mind cannot turn off. It twists and turns, watching itself. Perpetual tension spiraling, with never a release, no climax, only finally exhaustion, disgust, and loathing —masturbation of the soul.

I can tell Silas is listening.

"Well?" I ask him.

He crosses his arms across his chest, holding himself. "Well what?"

"That says nothing to you?"

"What good is that?" He sits up suddenly. "What good is it?"

"Silas, look. I'm sorry."

"You're not sorry. You're never sorry. You're just guilty."

"I don't know what we're talking about."

"That's fine."

"I won't talk about the diary, Silas. I'll put it away."

"It's all right, Jesse," he says sadly. "I'll see you later."

I watch Silas walk away and seat himself on the sidelines of the basketball game, closing his eyes again, turning his face to the sun. I close my journal.

The game is ending. Willy waves at me, signaling it is time to leave. I wave back. "I'll come up in a minute." Gemma nods okay. I have pass privileges now so it's okay for me to stay here by myself.

I watch them troop away. Gemma leading her straggling flock. I wish Silas would turn around, look back at me, wave. But he doesn't. He walks ahead of the rest of the group, turns the corner of the building, disappears.

The sun has shifted. It is almost at my back. I am uncomfortably cool, and it's almost time for supper, but I feel reluctant to go in. I draw my jacket around me, and the journal slides off my lap. The pages flutter anxiously as they fall together. My heart is beating very fast. No one is in the yard now except me. No one can see me.

16

My mother circles the dining room. Around and around the big, silent room she moves, stirring up particles of dust in the beams of late-afternoon sunshine that slant into the room. Nothing is real to her except the shadows on the rug, the dust she stirs, the salt tears warming her cheeks. I can feel her sadness. I feel it. It is all around me. I should do something. What can I do? Around and around in circles she wanders, spinning a web of sadness, fine gauzy mesh that moves and sighs and moans. It comes down, twisting and sighing, covering me. I am invisible to her. I am five and I am invisible.

There they are above me, mother, aunt, grandmother, bumping into each other, touching off smells, murmuring pleasantly over coffee and rolls and cigarettes. Comforting voices like wind or rain or waves, seashell in my ear. Occasionally, one of them stoops to pat my head or scoops me up, smothers me with kisses, scolds me or smiles, but for the most part I am invisible and do not affect their rhythms—intimate, magical rhythms.

Now they are yelling. They puff up. Their faces are purple. Their eyes pop, bulging from their heads. They will explode in pieces. But the noise cuts off at its peak. Just when they must burst, they are deflating. Woosh, woosh, they are losing air; they flop around limp, exhausted. The room fills with silence, heavy, smothering silence, warning me of the explosion still to come.

17

It is Group B's week to do Evening Nourishments. Hamilton and I have forty peanut-butter-and-jelly sandwiches to make. Hamilton is not in Group B, but Ursula is not up to it tonight, and Hamilton always volunteers to make peanut-butter-and-jelly sandwiches.

"It gives me a feeling of having roots," he says, sticking his head into the enormous vat of Welch's grape jelly, sniffing deeply like a cocaine freak snorting. He pulls his head out of the jelly and plunges into the peanut-butter vat, his voice echoing up at me. "It links me with all the children of America —all my brothers and sisters eating peanut-butter-and-jelly sandwiches all across the nation in all the scrabbly corners of gargantuan metropolises, in every barren kitchen in every prairie town. It's our shared humanity, our collective unconscious."

"What about the Lone Ranger? Superman?"

"No, no, Jesse." He comes up for air. "It's not the same. Say *Kemo Sabe* to a ten-year-old, and he will look at you cross-eyed. And Superman killed himself, Jesse. He's dead as a doornail. Only peanut butter and jelly is universally American. Spanning all the generation gaps, obsoleting cross-cultural barriers. As soon as it hits the roof of your mouth, instant déjà vu. We have all been there. All of us."

"Okay, okay, Hamilton. Calm down. I'll vote for you."

"Will you really?"

"Against my better judgment."

"Your judgment is only poor to fair, according to your chart."

When Philip was in prison for robbing a candy store, he smeared shit all over the wall of his cell, thus getting himself out of prison and to the hospital for observation. I asked him once if he did it on purpose to get out. He said he wasn't sure.

Silas avoids Philip like the plague.

"Why?"

"He whines. He plays with shit."

But the fact is that last year when Philip was fingerpainting in shit in the seclusion room, Silas was intrigued. Maybe Silas likes a show and he's already seen Philip's. Is Silas after all like me? Or is he onto something I don't know? There is always that hope. What if I decipher everything, all the codes, all the secrets, all the bleeding hearts, and come up with nothing?

Gemma is more than usually distracted. Yesterday she walked onto the ward with her raincoat on inside out. Willy pointed it out to her. Everyone, Gemma included, thought it was very funny. But I know what's going on. She is thinking of her lover.

'He is always right, Jesse. But he is wrong too. Wrong in some way I can't get to. Some subtle lack in him that so precisely nails my lacks.'

'Go on.'

'He speaks in images. They stun me with their accuracy.'

'You can't answer. You are inarticulate next to him.'

'Last night I cooked him artichokes on that miserable hot plate. It takes an hour for the water to boil. I wait wait wait for the bubbles to stir the surface of the water. There is something obscene about eating artichokes, he says.'

'You are obscene, Gemma, butter dripping down your chin. He thinks you are obscene.'

'This dishrag is nasty, he says. He drops it in the sink.'

'He means you are nasty, like a dishrag. Soiled, limp, used up, smelly.'

'How did you know?'

'Our time is up.'

It's five of five and Philip has smeared shit all over his face and is posted at the door, waiting for someone to notice him. Everyone notices. But dinner has started and everyone is busy eating, and Philip did the same thing last year, so for most of us it's no big deal to watch this time around. If you hadn't seen it, you had probably heard about it.

I dip into my tuna casserole, but keep an eye cocked on Philip. Here comes Margie sailing down the hall on her way home.

"Philip. Good God."

"I'm sorry, Miss A."

"Philip, it's five o'clock."

"You should go home. You deserve some relaxation."

"I think we need to talk about why you did this, Philip. Go clean yourself, and I'll wait right here for you."

"No!" Philip takes two giant steps forward.

Miss A. looks on the verge of tears but no one comes to her aid. I busy myself with my spinach, shifting my seat so I will be upwind of Philip but still able to hear what's going on.

"Dr. Brenner thinks I'm ready to leave the hospital, but I don't feel that I am."

From the safety of the stands, I watch Margie swallowing hard, fighting to keep down her lunch and her hysteria, both of which I can see rising in her throat. "Miss R. tells me you're a leader in Daily Living."

"It's a bad time to look for a job, Miss A., and since I'm an ex-con it's even harder."

In her steady retreat from the advancing Philip, Margie has

backed herself up against the wall. She has nowhere to go. There is a long silence. She's down for the count. No. I was wrong. "Have you gone on any interviews at all, Philip?"

"I was going to go yesterday but I didn't get any sleep at all the night before. The aides were carrying on, and David was chanting all night. He's driving me crazy. Walter says the same thing."

"What about today?" Margie pleads.

"Nothing in the paper, Miss A. I scoured the paper and nothing. Also I'm chairman of the Social Committee now, as you know, and I thought you wanted me to be here for the meeting."

"Don't you have an apartment you could go to?"

"My wife kicked me out." A knockout punch. Propped against the wall, Margie sags under the weight of the futility of helping Philip—of ever helping anyone with anything.

"And I can't take those welfare places. Miss Holland was talking about it, but I can't do it. There's holes in the mattresses, Miss A., and dope fiends stealing you blind and shit on the bathroom floor. It's disgusting."

Philip's hands are trembling. He jams them into his pants pockets, but they are shaking so badly that they threaten to throw him off balance. He withdraws his hands from his pockets, despising them as they jump at his side without his consent.

Margie reaches out, gathering his trembling hands into her own. She looks terrible. "It's all right, Philip. We'll talk some more tomorrow. Clean yourself off now and get some supper. You only make yourself feel worse when you do things like this."

"Will you talk to Dr. Brenner and tell him I'm not ready to go? I can't, Miss A. Do you understand? I can't."

"I understand, Philip."

"I'm very depressed, Miss A. I'm very depressed."

"I'd be depressed too if I looked like Al Jolson," Mrs. Morley intrudes. She has been watching with a baleful eye. "Get that shit off your face, Philip, and stop carrying on."

Philip grins sheepishly through the shit. But over the rim of my coffee cup, I watch Margie watching Philip's hands trembling like leaves in the wind.

18

Sha da da da
Sha da da da da
Sha da da da
Sha da da da da
Sha da da da
Sha da da da da
Sha da da da
Sha da da da da
Yip yip yip yip
Yip yip yip yip
Mum mum mum mum
Mum mum
Get a job

Everyone is yapping at me—yip yip yip yip—get a job.

Johnny writes me a worried letter from Berkeley. Don't I have a job yet? I have been out of college for over six months. I will feel more like a person if I quit living off Mom and Dad. Please write back and tell him what I am feeling. I shove his letter into a drawer with my underwear. But every time I go fishing for my jockey shorts it is there yapping at me.

At dinner, my father tells me he can line up several interviews for me with corporate presidents and vice-presidents who owe him favors. I sit hunched over my mother's good cooking, wishing he would shut up and leave me in peace.

My mother's silence is worse than my father's yapping. Silent yapping. I feel her thoughts bombarding me. She has no respect for me. I am not a man to her.

What do they want from me? What has a job got to do with me? Who ever thought it would come down to this.

"Don't you want to get your own place in the city?" my mother asks me.

"Of course I do, Mom. Jesus, of course I do. You think I like being stuck out here?" But the fact is, I'm not sure. I don't want to be at home. On the other hand, the thought of looking for an apartment—call people on the phone, go to brokers, take strange buses and subways, get lost on Houston Street, streets I don't know, Charles or Perry, Columbus or Amsterdam, way uptown or downtown where I have never been—it's impossible. I am not ready for it. Besides, as soon as I have an apartment there is rent to pay and gas and electricity and phone bills and Christ knows what all. And that means I *have* to get a job. The two go together like peaches and cream. Well, I abstain. I'll stick to my mother's cooking even if it means eating humble pie. I would rather eat shit than go looking for jobs and apartments. It is not even that I would rather. I can't do otherwise. Does no one understand that? I can't do these things that everyone takes for granted I must do. I can't.

In desperation, I try to placate my parents by grabbing the back pages of the *Times* out from under their noses. On Sundays, I spend the entire day on the living-room floor, ploughing through reams of newsprint, circling apartment and job items with a red pen. I circle indiscriminately, wildly (Lower East side 3 rms, kitch, bdrm, $95), filled with a hopeless passion that I will lull my parents (Riverside Drive, coop, 4 bdrms, $600) into forgetfulness.

"Why don't you type up a résumé?" my mother suggests. "Then at least, if you find something in the paper or you hear of something, you'll be ready."

"Good idea, Mom. That's a great idea." But I don't know the first thing about résumés. So I don't do anything.

My mother writes to her sister who has always had good jobs, and asks her if she would send me a format for a résumé. It takes almost two weeks for my mother to get the letter off, and we wait for my Aunt Jenny's reply. In the meantime, there is something of a truce in the house. "I wish Jenny would hurry up and answer," I tell Mom. "I really want to get going on that résumé."

I'm starting to relax a little. Maybe Jenny will never reply. Maybe the mails are fucked up. The résumé format has gotten tossed into a wastebasket in a remote corner of some dingy post office in Peoria by a retarded post office worker who passed the civil service exam by some outrageous fluke or through corruption and bribery in high places.

But the letter comes finally, and in it the format. I retire to my room to work on the résumé.

NAME: Jay Davidson
DATE OF BIRTH: Feb. 3, 1940
ADDRESS: 38 Old Oaks Road, Wilson, Conn.
TELEPHONE: 203-227-2889
MARITAL STATUS: Single
EDUCATION: High school—Sedgewick High, Wilson, Conn.
EXTRACURRICULAR ACTIVITIES: Wrote several articles for school paper and several pieces for literary magazine
ORGANIZATIONS: Varsity basketball, home room council

So far so good.

HIGHER EDUCATION:

Now how can I do this? I can't put down University of Michigan, flunked out end of freshman year. Bridgeport University one year to make up freshman credits, Columbia General Studies summer school, Indiana University, another summer at Columbia to make up more credits, and back to Indiana for two more years.

On the other hand, if I don't put it down and just put Indiana University 1958–63, B.A. English, they will wonder about that extra year. They may check it out and find that I went to Indiana my sophomore year. They might contact Michigan and find that I was thrown out. They might even have it down on my record that I swallowed a bottle of aspirin if that Chinese lady doctor ever reported that. And I'd only swallowed nine. I was bogging down.

I hadn't even any jobs to put down. How would that look? Except three days waiting tables in the women's dorm at Indiana. No one was going to be impressed by that. The only good thing I had was the names my father had given me for personal references: Gerald Sommers, Account Executive, BBD&O; Edward Martin, Business Manager, *Forbes Magazine*; Andrew Stoddard, Vice-President, Chemical Division, Continental Can. Even that was dangerous. I didn't know any of these men. Except that I had met Mr. Martin at a dinner party at the house when I was fifteen.

If they contacted Mr. Sommers at his office, he might be deep into maneuvering for a client. How could he be expected to remember that it was Jack Davidson's son they were asking about, when he was on the verge of closing the biggest deal of his career. "Who? Jay who? Davidson? Never heard of him."

I abandoned the résumé and went back to circling things in the *Times* with my red pen.

. . .

My father's face is sagging with disappointment. My mother circles around me, clearing plates over my head. After dinner, she retires to the kitchen to clean up, and he goes to bed.

We are barely speaking to each other, or rather they are barely speaking to me or I to them. They are, however, speaking to each other. Their mutual disgust, mistrust, worry over me have drawn them together. It gives me solace to know that in the privacy of their bedroom they talk of me. I am a bond between them.

After dinner, I closet myself in the den with a box of Mallomars and watch TV, only occasionally bothering to switch the channel. I see old reruns, *Dobie Gillis, I Married Joan,* the early show, million-dollar movie, the late show, the late late show. I gaze at the TV through a gathering cloud of cigarette smoke. It is incredibly comforting to sit smoking cigarette after cigarette, eating Mallomar after Mallomar, watching the figures on the screen running, jumping, crying, kissing, punching, shooting, sighing. It is all the same to me what they are doing. I judge not. The more absurd their gyrations, the better I like it. The more lacking their motivation, the more pleasure it gives me. The more inane the manipulations of the plot, the more soothing it is to me. I could watch forever. I sink lower and lower in my chair as the knot in my stomach diffuses and my brain gets duller and duller, till finally I know I can fall asleep like a baby.

Dear Jay,
    You could get a job. Anyone can get a job. Why don't you write to me? Are you OK? This place is huge, but I'm learning my way around. It's sunny and warm here.

Love,
Johnny

Dear Jay,

It pisses me off that you won't write. You could write a post card. Mom and Dad don't say much about you except that they are worryed. I have some crummie courses and some good ones. Organic Chem is my favorite but I really have to work at it. I'm auditing some extra chem courses to give myself some background. Write me.

Love,
Johnny

Dear Jay,

I heard of an apartment for you. It belongs to a friend of a friend of mine. He's moving out here in two weeks. Living room, bedroom, kitchen, bathroom, long hall. East Eleventh Street, elivator, 3rd floor. Only $65 and the block is OK acording to this guy. Call Michael Wertz OR 9-2567. Will you at least call him? I bet you won't. I'm trying out for soccer and I'm looking around for a cheap bike. What do you think about my applying for a summer work-study program in England? I was thinking I should get a handle on research just in case the clinical stuff doesn't pan out.

Love,
Johnny

Dear Johnny,

I appreciate your concern about jobs, apartments, etc. but mind your own business.

Love,
Jay

Dear Jay,

You are infurriating. One of these days the shit is going to hit the fan for you. Did you ever call Michael Wertz? Don't stay living at home Jay really, please.

I am playing piano a lot. The girl under me has a piano and she lets me use it.

>Love,
>Johnny

Dear Johnny,

Your spelling still sucks. Glad to hear you have a girl under you. Wish I could say the same. The shit hit the fan for me a long time ago. I am covered with shit if you want to know the truth while you are playing the piano and being a pre-med student. How did that happen, Johnny? Do you understand it?

>Love,
>Jay

Dear Jay,

Yes. I do understand it. If you want to hear about it, I'll write and explain.

>Love,
>Johnny

Dear Johnny,

I am not going to write you anymore. It is wearing me out and I need to conserve my strength.

>Jay

My mother announces that my father has set up an appointment for me Monday morning at 10:30 a.m. with a Mr. Shubeck, vice-president in charge of planning at some ad agency. I have lost the battle. I am not clear what the battle signifies or how I have lost, but the terms of my defeat are clear. Interview Monday morning at 10:30, arranged by my parents without my knowledge or consent and presented to me ironclad, fait accompli. It is humiliating. But there was never any way to win. If there were no ultimatum, no interview, it would have been just as humiliating.

That night, in my dream, my mother sits on the edge of my bed, looming over me like some enormous bird of prey.

"I bet you have fantasies of being tied up," she says coolly.

"No. No. I don't. I really don't."

I wake up with a start, sweating in my bed. I have a headache that clamps the back of my head and bruises my eyeballs, and a hard-on.

The instant the train plunged into the tunnel leading into Grand Central Station I went crazy. I saw flashes of propane blue light going off at timed intervals, orange and red sparks jumping up from the tracks, shooting parallel streaks into the rushing darkness.

The train shudders to a jerking halt, stripping ancient gears. My eyes roll in their sockets. I put one finger in front of my nose to test the state of my vision, which is, I know, not working properly. I see two fingers—incredibly long, tapering fingers—growing out of the one knuckle. Squinting beyond my finger at the horizon, I see that my perspective is out of whack. The train car is elongated. It looks like a half hour's hike to the door, when, in fact, it is more like a three-second hop.

My appointment at Felton Advertising with Mr. Shubeck is for 10:30. I look at my watch, but I hadn't worn a watch. It must be almost 10. I should get to an eye doctor right away. It wasn't possible to walk around in my condition. Misjudging distances, I would fall off curbs, be hit by cabs. Maybe the safest thing to do is just to sit right here and wait till the train pulls out again—heading back to Connecticut. I could call Mr. Shubeck from home or drop him a card—"due to circumstances beyond my control."

I sink back in my seat, closing my eyes. My parents' images blend together in a blurred portrait composed of floating appendages: one impenetrable hazel eye (hers) and one of his—

black as an olive, humorous and melancholy; her pure, clean-sweeping nose and underneath it his softly greying mustache. His ears, large, alerted, and resting heavily on top of them her dark mysterious eyebrows.

I rise from my seat and gingerly make my way to the door. I find that by looking down at the ground rather than straight ahead I can orient myself better. The fact that everything appears stretched out is less obtrusive, and I can proceed more or less as if I saw things normally.

The mental and physical concentration required to keep myself moving in a straight line is so intense that I can feel the energy draining out of me. By the time I finally maneuver myself up the crowded ramp and into the station, I am exhausted. I know I can't make it walking out on the street all the way to Fifty-sixth and Madison, so I hail a cab in front of the station.

Looking out the window of the cab, I see the endless, elongated sidewalks are too narrow to contain the masses of people. They are spilling into the gutter, crashing into each other. I can feel each collision seconds before it happens—whump. But they keep on coming at each other, insulated somehow against the shock because no one seems alarmed or yells or socks his assailants.

My cabbie glides in and out of the tangled lines of merging traffic like an Ice Follies star. I feel secure in here with him at the helm. "You have a lot of guts," I tell him.

"What? Did ya see that? Fuckin' bums. Walked right into me. Some people. Ya know what I mean?"

"Yes, I do. Listen, mister, how do you face this every day? Are you trying to conquer something? Like a bullfighter facing the bull Sunday after Sunday?"

"Not me, kid. I never drive on Sundays. Sundays I rest, like the good Lord said, and if the boss don't like it, he can shove it up his tight ass. Ya know what I mean?"

I get out in front of 610 Madison, and immediately am

swept up by the crowd, hurled into the revolving doors, and deposited in the lobby. It is a cave, a mammoth cave, dwarfing me. Every noise echoes, bounces off the walls, comes back at me. My stomach is hollowed out by the cave's hollowness. My intestines are on the verge of collapse, my sphincter muscle losing its elasticity.

Masses of people swarm purposefully around me, over me, through me. I marvel at them. Where are they going? They seem to know. I, on the other hand, cannot see straight so how can I possibly know where I am going? I feel in my back pants pocket for the paper with Mr. Shubeck's name and address and office number on it. Got it. I bring it close to my face, but I can't read a thing. It's as if I'm looking at it from a distance of several hundred yards.

"Excuse me," I say to a passing man. He looks old to me, worn out and stooped. But, when I strain to see his face, I realize I am mistaken. He's probably not five years older than I am. "Could you tell me what office number is written on this paper? I'm recovering from eye surgery, and I can't make it out."

"Sure, of course," the man answers kindly. "Room 1505. That'd be the fifteenth floor. Elevator's over there."

"Thank you very much."

"Not at all. I hope you have a speedy recovery."

"Thanks a lot. Thanks."

"So long," he says and disappears into the crowd.

I feel drawn to this man. We are probably not so very different, he and I. How is it, then, I wonder as the elevator zooms me to the fifteenth floor, that he strides through this lobby with a briefcase full of important papers knowing where he is going?

I step off the elevator. The noise is deafening. Innumerable telephones go off like staggered alarm clocks, electric typewriters rat-tat-tatting like machine guns in the movies. In the background is the thrum th-rum steady, rhythmic churning of the Xerox as it grinds out copies.

The red-headed receptionist is preoccupied with the run in her panty hose. She doesn't look up at me. Her right leg is stretched out to the side of her, and she is looking over her shoulder at the snag, touching it with one finger, probing. Her leg looks incredibly long to me, long enough to wrap around the entire reception room three or four times. I worry that passersby will trip over it. Will office insurance cover her for a suit against her leg?

Finally she looks up. I tell her my name.

"He's expecting you. Go on in. First door to your right through there."

"So you're Jack's boy." Mr. Shubeck is heading for me. I want to gauge it right, so I don't miss connections. When I think I am the right distance from him I extend my hand, but my calculations are off. I thought he was further back than he is. My hand jabs into his abdomen, right under his breastbone.

"Uhhhmph."

"Oh, my God. Please excuse me, sir. I'm terribly sorry. I'm having a little trouble with my eyes. I had eye surgery recently and my distance perception is still way off."

"Jack didn't mention anything about it. I'm sorry."

"It's nothing, really. He prefers not to talk about it."

Mr. Shubeck has his hand under my elbow, guiding me across the room to his sofa.

"Thank you. Thank you. Sorry about this."

"Not at all. There. This isn't a permanent thing, I take it."

"Oh no. I'll be fine in a few months."

"I'd understood from Jack that you were ready to start work any time."

"Well, he's trying to pretend it never happened, like I said. But it won't be long before I can work. A month, two months, three at the outside."

"I see. Well, we might have some trainee spots opening up in a few months."

"Terrific. That'd really be terrific."

"You think you'd like agency work? Jack says he thinks you'd make a fine copywriter. Of course, we couldn't start you off as that."

"Oh, sure, I understand that. Yeah, I think I'd like that. I did a little radio stuff in school and editing and writing, school paper stuff."

"You were at Berkeley?"

"Indiana. My brother John's at Berkeley."

"Oh yes. I think Jack did mention that. Fine school. Well, how is Jack?"

"Oh, he's fine. Really fine."

"Still hustling, huh?"

"Still hustling, yeah."

"Well, listen, you give him my best and go easy on him about the eye thing. He's just concerned, you know."

"Oh, sure, I understand that."

"We'll put your résumé on file, Jay, and we'll be in touch in a couple of months if anything turns up."

"Fine. Great. Thanks a lot, Mr. Shubeck. I appreciate it."

"Not at all."

As soon as I hit the street, my vision returns to normal. But the next morning, coming back into town for my second interview (my father has made all the necessary arrangements for the rest of my interviews, and my mother has my schedule drawn up and posted in the kitchen for everyone to see), the same thing happens. And the next day and the next and the next. As soon as the train goes into the tunnel, my vision goes haywire.

The lobbies all look the same to me, identical caverns. Good for roller skating or yodeling, but I am not here to enjoy myself. I am here to get a job. Two weeks later and it's the same fucking lobby that I have been in every day for the past ten days. Perhaps it was the condition of my eyes which made it seem so. Same crowds. Maybe they are faking it. None of them have jobs. They mill around till lunch, take a break, come back, mill around till five. Thousands of unemployed, unrecorded schlepps, milling around in countless lobbies across the nation, faking it. I am one of you. I wander blindly down these halls, hoping against hope to avoid the inevitable time when someone will have a job for me.

Ah, it is so difficult, so unbelievably difficult, to attend to what Mr. Shubeck, Mr. Morrison, Mr. Stoller are saying when I am having to contend with all manner of visual distortions, at the same time remaining alert enough to make sure that the gold, green, rust, beige walls of their inner offices do not cave in on me.

Mr. Geiger of Grenville Publishing gives me a test assignment, reviewing one of Grenville's new novels, *Time Out of Mind*, by Richard Clemmons. If I pass the test, I become an editorial assistant. I try to read the book going home on the train.

I try again at home that night, but it's no use. I can't get past the first page. Is *Time Out of Mind* a trap? A clever editor's scheme to separate the wheat from the chaff? On a piece of yellow lined paper I write, "An obvious hoax," and sign my name. But it doesn't look right. I cannot read the book. Nevertheless, I feel driven to write the review so I can cross Mr. Geiger of Grenville Publishing off my list, which will leave me only two names to go.

After rereading the first page and skimming the last, I write my review and mail it to Mr. Geiger.

> Richard Clemmons's *Time Out of Mind* is a quietly explosive novel depicting the terror, the comedy, the pathos, and the joy of the human condition. Seldom does a novelist so transcend his material, illuminating

the dark corners of all our lives. Clemmons's characters
are vividly drawn, vulnerable, driven, tragic. They are
also funny, warm, and consummately believable. The
tale he tells (and he is an expert teller of tales in the
old-fashioned sense of the phrase) is deceptively simple, for one discovers layer upon layer of significance
in this compelling, if occasionally artless, story of man's
deepest urges. A gem of a novel, flawed if you must,
but deeply felt.

Three days later I got a letter from Grenville Publishing to
the effect that there were no openings at present on the editorial
trainee staff, but thanking me for my thoughtful review and
they would keep it on file with my résumé.

At home, my increasingly elaborate lies about my promising
interviews are met with increasingly stony silences. Only two
names to go on my father's list of contacts and then I'm on my
own. A rat in a trap running in ever-smaller circles, tracking a
piece of cheese that I don't want. I don't want your fucking
cheese. Leave me alone.

My father doesn't actually know George Fast of A & D Music
Publishing, but he is on my list because he is a friend of a friend
of my father's.

Entering the elevator, I whisper to the man nearest me,
"This is the same fucking lobby," but he doesn't seem to hear
me. He is busy tapping his foot to the Muzak version of "Heart-
break Hotel." My heart sinks as the strings soar. My elevator
mates continue to stare straight ahead and above at the lighted
numbers as we go flying into the sky.

George Fast's little eyes dart around in his head, never

settling long enough to focus. Nevertheless, he is straightforward and gets right to the point. "You need a job?"

"Yes sir, I do."

"What can you do for us?"

"I can hoist a jack, I can lay a track. I can pick and shovel too, Lord Lord . . ."

"What? What the fuck is this? Is this your idea of a gag?"

"No, Mr. Fast. No, really. I need a job. I'll do anything. I'll take out the papers and the trash or I won't get no spending cash. If I don't scrub that kitchen floor, I ain't gonna rock and roll no more. . . ."

"Look. I don't know what kind of smart ass you are, but I don't have time for it. I hire lyricists. That's it. Top forty. I don't even know how you got in here."

"I can write songs, Mr. Fast. Just give me a break. Just one break and I'll head straight for the top. Listen, Mr. Fast, before you know it, I'll build a stairway to paradise with a new step every day." Before Mr. Fast can make a move, I scramble onto his eight-seater, white, slubbed-linen sofa:

> "Nitty gritty sure is shitty sometime,
> Oh yeah.
> Nitty gritty, shitty on my mind,
> Uh huh.
> Pussy and titty, help to pass the time,
> A wop bop alu bop a wop bam boom."

I have Mr. Fast's full attention. His mouth is hanging open and his little eyes are bulging.

"You don't dig it. No no. Don't be polite. I can see by your expression you don't like it. But this one is gold. Solid gold:

> "Let's fuck.
> Yeah yeah yeah, let's fuck,

Let's fuck, let's fuck,
Let's fuck till the sun comes up."

I can see, as if through a telescope, a long long way away, Mr. Fast lunging for his desk to buzz for help. I jump down from his couch, dash past him into the secretary's outer office and through there to the hall, where I wait breathless and perspiring for the elevator to come and take me away.

19

The Princess tells me what I, of course, already know from the original source. Walter has received a letter from his mother saying she cannot send him back to Vienna to complete his medical studies. Nor can she come to visit him at the present time.

"Poor soul," the Princess says. "I have some influential medical connections in Switzerland who might be of some use. I could cable them."

"Let's wait and see what happens," I tell her.

"He has threatened to kill himself," the Princess says.

"I know."

"Do you think . . . ?"

"No."

"Neither do I. The longer I live, Jesse, the less I am certain of what is sad and what is not."

"You hear about Walter?"

"Walter again. I'm tired of Walter."

"He attempted suicide. It was in the bathroom. Walter told Silas he was going to kill himself and then he took a deep breath, pinched both his nose holes shut, and held his breath till he turned purple and fell on the floor. Silas told the Princess it was Walter's finest hour."

"Did he really say that? I don't know what's going on around here anymore."

"I can't help you there. I'm just an old man reporting what I hear. No editorials. Just the facts, ma'am."

An abortion, a joke, a half-assed freak failure, but Silas says he was privileged to witness Walter's finest hour.

"Soon Walter will take up his post by the door again, waiting for his mother to come and take him to Vienna," Silas says when I question him.

"What's good about that?"

"It's a miracle of faith, Jesse James. Of faith and patience. You, of all people, should understand that."

In the middle of Psychodrama, David interrupts a scene to say that he had nothing to do with Walter's death.

"David," Sophie says, "Walter isn't dead. He's out on the ward."

"I just saw him," Faye says. "He's alive, if that's what you want to call it."

"Maybe David's feeling guilty about something else," Philip volunteers.

"He thinks Walter's dead because Walter's bed's been taken out of David's room and put in the hall by the nurses' station so they can watch he doesn't try anything again," Willy says.

David groans and heads for the door.

Sophie dashes after him. "Margie, take over," she calls over her shoulder to Miss A.

I slip out the door, shadowing Sophie and David down the hall. Sophie is too intent on her mission to notice me behind her. She grabs David by the hand and leads him to the door where Walter sits, inert as a stone, his pale eyes staring into space behind his thick glasses.

Sophie puts her arm around Walter's shoulder, bends down to him, and up again to David. Up and down she bends, trying to draw them together. I can't hear what she is saying. Walter closes his eyes. Sophie's mission has failed. Reluctantly, she follows David back down the hall.

As they come closer, I hear David chanting: "We are mortally sorry we have offended thee, O Lord. Walter is dead. Walter is dead."

"No, no, David," Sophie sighs. "No, no." She sees me now and stops short. "May I ask why you are skulking around out here? You are supposed to be in Psychodrama."

"I thought I might be of some help."

"Go back to Psychodrama," Sophie snaps. Then, sweeping past me with David in tow, she murmurs, "His dream, David? Do you mean his dream is dead?"

"Walter is dead. Forgive us, Lord. We know not what we do."

Sophie beguiles everyone with the drama she creates by the rise and fall of her voice. It ascends in outrage at the cupidity of Mr. Theodophilus.

" 'Cut-rate Grade A panty hose, sized to your thighs, all colors.' Mr. Theodophilus, Mr. Theodophilus. What am I to think?"

"Who gave you that card?"

"Surely that is beside the point."

"To sell you gotta advertise, Miss R. That's a fact of business."

"We are not vendors here, Mr. Theodophilus. We are caretakers."

"I only peddle to staff, Miss R. I wouldn't jeopardize my therapeutic alliance with patients to make a lousy dime."

"I am relieved, Mr. Theodophilus, to hear that. You have no idea. You will abandon this venture immediately."

She throws her voice this way and that, over her head, between her legs. "Dr. Brenner. It's sexy Jerry Brenner. Margie told me you were tracking me."

"Can we talk a minute?"

"Five, ten, fifteen. As long as you like. Did you want to talk about Philip or Walter or Silas or . . ."

"I want to talk about last night."

"Last night?"

"Sophie, please. I want to see you again."

"Of course, any time."

"Tonight?"

"Oh no, Jerry. Not tonight. Any night but tonight. Tonight is impossible."

Her voice thickens, moistens with sentiment, telling Gemma of a former patient. "A wonderful man, Gemma. So much life in him. I am waiting for a man like that."

The voice thins to a fine line, dry as chalk. "I have been studying yesterday's sign-in sheet for hours and hours, Margie, and your code is still a mystery to me. Would you be good enough to decipher these initials? MPBC."

"Menstrual period bad cramps."

"I should have guessed. And here. Here I have the sign-in sheet for this past Friday. FIT. Did you have a fit, Margie? Are you prone to seizures? What precisely does FIT mean?"

"Fell in the tub."

"Ah. Of course."

Later she will amuse Gemma recreating the story of Mr. Theodophilus, of Margie, of Jerry Brenner, with deft elaborations that leave Gemma laughing, holding her side, begging Sophie for mercy.

'Ah, Sophie. I have been expecting you. Step into my office, Scheherazade.'

'Am I Scheherazade?'

'Night after night you weave fabulous tales to keep yourself alive. No incident is too trivial to become the stuff of your myths. You transform the buying of a salami into a tale of high adventure; on your way to the incinerator, you stumble on the last act for your drama of unrequited love; your doorman is a hero brave as any Greek.'

'He *is* Greek.'

'Do not attempt to throw me off my mark, Scheherazade. I am onto you.'

'Can I not beguile you?'

'You have staved off death, you have enchanted the Sultan. He has forgotten that he came originally to find Sophie. I have not forgotten.'

'Oh, Jesse, I am afraid.'

'Do not fear, little Sophie. We all need someone to lean on and if you want to, well, you can lean on me.'

Hamilton was discharged Tuesday, subdued and elegant in a worn but impeccably tailored grey suit, sober as a judge and looking like a lawyer, saying goodbyes all around in his deep, cultivated voice. Now he is back in less than a week, charging in like a lion, in hospital pajamas two sizes too small, led onto the ward by Mr. Watson.

"Thank you, my good man, a thousand thanks. I look forward to chatting with you, but now I must look around, settle in."

Hamilton saunters over to the dining area, where we are

eating supper. "Please please, don't get up," he addresses the group at large.

"Hey, Hamilton. Hey, how are you?" Willy stands up and waves at Hamilton.

"Nice to see you," Hamilton says. "Nice to see you all. I'll join you later."

Mrs. Harper is watching Hamilton bleakly from the kitchen. "It's too late for you to get supper. I can get you some Jell-O and milk. That's all."

Hamilton bows to Mrs. Harper. "A pleasure to see you, madame."

"They don't bother to tell me about admissions coming in right at suppertime. And then they expect me to have enough."

"The meal looks superb. But don't exercise yourself. I have already dined this evening."

Mrs. Harper squints suspiciously at Hamilton and beats a glum retreat into the steaming kitchen, muttering to herself.

The word is that Hamilton might only be on the ward for a few days and then go to the third floor to become part of a lithium project.

He is as high this time around as I have ever seen him and more effusive. He writes long letters to the Princess and Mrs. Stern in a style that is at once elegant and romantic, though they are both twenty or more years his senior.

Everything and everyone delights him. The food is delicious, the dormitory splendid, the groups entertaining. "I have rarely been in such a congenial establishment," he tells me. "I will certainly come back."

Hamilton has been temporarily transferred off the ward—to research on 3. He sends the Princess and Mrs. Stern picture postcards of the Riviera and the Alps: "Miss you. Wish you were here. Fondly, Hamilton."

Hamilton is back on the ward, holding his medication in his mouth and spitting it out when Mrs. Morley isn't looking. His good humor and effusiveness have dried up abruptly. He paces the halls like a caged animal. Periodically, he halts his pacing to write feverishly in the spiral notebook he carries or to make calls on the pay phone. He calls the mayor's office ten, fifteen times a day: "Look, miss, I don't think you realize to whom you are speaking. This is Hamilton Trevelyan. Hamilton Trevelyan —Trevelyan, Smith, and Edwards. John knows me. He knows me from way back. You just tell him I called." He calls collect to his ex-wife in California, but she does not accept his calls. He calls Western Union florists and orders azalea bushes sent to his wife, to the mayor, and to the home of every staff member. "You can charge that to my Master Charge."

Up on the bulletin board goes a handwritten notice in Hamilton's small, elegant handwriting:

> It is time for us to take our destiny into our own hands. The air is rife with cries of civil rights for Blacks, for Puerto Ricans, for women, for Indians, but nowhere is there talk of civil rights for us. Plumbers have unions, stagehands have unions, carpenters have unions to lobby for their rights. But we have no union. We must collectivize, unionize to lobby for our rights like every other special interest group in this country. I have outlined our demands which I will take to Washington as your representative. We will have no more commitments. No drugs. We will have no more shock treatments. We will have no more locked wards. No isolation rooms. No charted history to be read by every ignoramus who wanders through a nursing sta-

tion. We shall march on the capitol. We shall overcome.

Silas is conferring with Hamilton, pacing with him up and down the halls. Hamilton is talking so fast that he stumbles and trips on his words. Silas walks beside him, holding on to Hamilton's long gesturing arm.

Another notice goes up on the board, over Hamilton's signature:

> We will converge on the capitals of the world, storm the senates with a barrage of hallucinations more devastating than any bomb. We will drown the leaders in our illusions, delusions, fantasies and dreams. We will act out for them, as we have throughout eternity, all the madness they keep buttoned up in their vest pockets. But we will no longer do it unacknowledged and unpraised. We will force them to the rim of the pit. We will show them our sacrifice. Without us there is no salvation.

Transfer agents from the state hospital come Monday and Wednesday afternoons. Dressed in whites, they slip onto the ward, antiseptic ghosts—faceless, nameless, even to staff, bloodless as the title they bear. They are only agents of transfer. Nobody wants to know their names or where they live or how many kids they have. We see them obliquely, out of the corners of our eyes. We don't acknowledge their presence, but the rhythm of the ward responds—skips a beat.

The patients who go with them know they are contaminated. Now that they are going, we want them gone. We don't want to catch their disease or be reminded of it. We only want them to go now; go and close the door behind them.

. . .

The transfer agents have come for David. They wait, patient as stones in their starched whites, leaning against the white wall of the corridor.

I watch Sophie go up to them. She doesn't look at them or even speak to them. Gemma hides behind her. Sophie reaches for the transfer slip they hold out to her, scans it quickly, and hands it back to them, as if it were unclean. "Wait," she says. She and Gemma walk down the hall to our room, to David's room, with me following.

Dr. Green, David's resident, isn't here for the finale. I heard him tell Sophie he couldn't stand to see it. "He just looked at me when I told him, Sophie. He didn't say a word."

David is sitting on the edge of his bed, head bowed, when Sophie and Gemma and I walk in. Silas sits beside him. I try to catch Silas's eye, but he won't look at me.

No one has bothered to turn on the lights. A chink of daylight from the small barred window over Philip's bed lies across the linoleum floor. Other than that, the room is almost dark.

"My name is David," David says, not looking up. All I can see is the top of his large, bony, close-shaved head.

Sophie sways over him. "David?" No one will help you, Sophie. Gemma hangs back against the green wall, and I am in the doorway poised for flight. "David?"

David lifts himself heavily from the bed.

"Do you have a suitcase?" Sophie asks, looking away.

"No."

"He has nothing to put in a suitcase," Silas says.

"You must have something," Gemma says wildly.

"State shoes. I don't want them anymore." David bends down to pull off the ugly black shoes. "I don't ever want to come out to society again," he roars. He opens his mouth and he roars at the top of his lungs. "Not ever ever ever again."

The noise is deafening. It slams against my spine and rattles the tiny window behind its iron grate.

The blood drains out of Sophie's face. "You have to have shoes," she says.

"It will be all right, David," Gemma cries, rushing at him. "You have your credentials. You're all right if you have your credentials."

David tears his billfold from the breast pocket of his shirt. He pulls it open, holding it up to Gemma, holding it open to show her there is nothing there. His eyes are blazing with clear, anguished light. Everything is suddenly transparent and unbearable.

"Now I'll go," he says. He stoops down, sliding his billfold into one of the black shoes. He shoves the shoe under the bed. "You tried to help me," David says, opening his arms to the two women.

Gemma and Sophie collapse against him, and he holds them close, patting them awkwardly.

"You tried to help me," he says, looking over the heads of the two women at me.

He steps back from Sophie and Gemma and turns to Silas, who still sits on David's bed. David clasps Silas's hand, then turns to me where I stand in the doorway and shakes my hand. Moving past me out of the room, he walks the long hall in his stocking feet, and goes to stand by the nurses' station, waiting for the transfer agents who are waiting to take him away.

After supper I go into the room to lie down. David's bed is stripped, but the greying tape with his name on it is still affixed to the foot of the bed. Silas sits across from me, hunkering on his bed like a wizened old mountain man.

"Do you feel a bond with Sophie and Gemma?" I ask him.

"Why should I?"

"David. Everything that happened."

"David went to the state hospital. That's all that happened."

"I didn't feel that way. Sophie and Gemma didn't feel that way."

"You disgust me. All of you. How many people go every week, month, to the state hospital, and I don't see any of you crying for them."

"I know that, I know, but . . ."

"It was bathetic. That's all. It was a movie and you cry at movies. That's what you understand."

"That's not how it was, goddammit. Why are you saying that?"

"No one cries for anyone else, Jesse James. We cry for ourselves. Don't you know anything?"

"I know you're fucked up."

Silas smiles at me, a grin from ear to ear, a Huckleberry Finn grin.

"No, listen, Silas, I didn't mean that. Just talk to me. Let's bullshit a while. Tell me about something that happened to you. Anything. It doesn't matter what."

"I have nothing to say. Nada. Nothing. Niente." He jumps off the bed, bows low like an oriental, and is gone.

20

I woke up late the Sunday my father left the new house in the country for the start of the trial separation, and he had already gone. He had nothing to say to me.

I drift in and out of the rooms of the house, avoiding my mother, who is drifting too, in and out of rooms. Johnny follows silently, first one of us and then the other. In and out and around we float, never meeting, never colliding, never speaking. The day is huge, endlessly unraveling. We will stay like this forever, the three of us, suspended in the dragging hours.

I knew something bad would happen in this house. It had taken only six months for my prophecy to be fulfilled.

As soon as I lay down in bed that night, I felt a sharp pain in my stomach. I seize the pain, suddenly energized. I try to identify the pain, describe it to myself so I can give the doctors something to go on in the morning. I debate whether or not to wake my mother but decide against it. I don't want to see her with that dead look smudging her features. Better to wait. I'd see her hovering over me soon enough, simple, uncomplicated worry about her firstborn bringing her face back into relief, as they wheeled me dazed and drugged into the o.r. for surgery.

The pain is shifting character, defying hard analysis. It had started out sharp and stabbing, localized. But it is diffusing, deepening. I hear a sob from down the hall. She is crying. The juices in my stomach begin to flow and gurgle. Growl and moan. Louder and louder come the noises from deep inside my stomach, blocking out equally the sound of her crying and the noise of the crickets outside my window.

I am awakened in the morning by my noises, sounding from the vast emptiness of my stomach. It's hunger, I think, laughing to myself. I'm hungry. I dash into the kitchen, where my mother sits hunched over the table, slicing oranges in a fury. Zap. She cuts the orange clean through with her blade. Zap, another orange irrevocably severed.

"I'm starving," I tell her. "Ravenous."

She looks up at me. "What's that noise? Is that you?"

"My stomach is empty. I have never been so hungry. Never."

"All right. Sit down. Call Johnny. I'll make you breakfast."

"I can't wait for breakfast. I have to eat now."

"You can wait five minutes. I'm not a machine. You can see I'm getting it."

"You don't understand. My stomach is empty. Totally

empty." I open the refrigerator and pull out bread, peanut butter, jelly. I slap together two enormous sandwiches, which I wolf down, not stopping to chew.

"What's the matter with you?" she says. "Do you think I'm making breakfast to amuse myself?"

"I'll eat breakfast," I assure her, grabbing a banana and shoving it whole down my throat. "I'll eat two breakfasts."

"Oh, my God," she yells at me. "Are you trying to drive me crazy?"

"I'm just hungry. Can't a person be hungry?"

Nothing helped. No matter how much I ate, I couldn't still the noises or even muffle them. If anything, they seem to grow louder, drowning out the sound of her yelling and Johnny's nagging. I eat constantly, all day long, at no more than ten-minute intervals. Frequently, and in secret, I throw up. But I keep eating. My mother, beside herself, threatens to padlock the refrigerator and take me to a psychiatrist.

It had been arranged that Johnny and I would go into the city to meet my father for lunch. She kissed us goodbye at the station, hugging us both to her, tears gathering in the corners of her dark eyes. "Jay, are you all right? Are you all right, sweetie? I love you."

"What did you say? I can't hear you." My stomach is furious, growling at me, demanding to be filled.

"I love you."

"I love you too, Mom."

"Are you okay? Are you going to be all right?"

"I'm fine. I'm just hungry, that's all."

The tears flood over onto her cheeks. She grabs Johnny and holds him tight enough to crush him.

On the train I read *Portrait of the Artist as a Young Man,* trying to forget the noises and the hole inside me.

"Jay, Jay, Jay." Johnny pokes me and pulls the book down.

"What?"

"I'm scared."

"What? I can't hear you."

"I'm *scared.*"

"There's nothing to be scared of. You're nine years old. You're practically an adult." I pick up my book again.

"I hate you."

"What? You'll have to speak up."

"*I hate you.*"

We meet him in front of a small French restaurant in the east fifties. He looks tired, his black eyes sunk back in his large head, their rims red and irritated. He makes a move forward as if to hug us both against his broad chest, but stops, hanging back, uneasy as a young boy at a dance.

"How're my boys?"

"What?"

"Jay can't hear you too well," Johnny explains.

"Why not?" Daddy asks, ushering us into the plush, dim interior.

"His stomach is making loud noises."

Daddy looks at me over the top of Johnny's head. "I don't hear anything."

"Oh, you can hear it if you listen," I say. "Hear it?"

"No."

"I can hear it," Johnny says. "Sometimes. He eats to make the noises go away. But he can't fill up his stomach."

"Well, then," Daddy says expansively, "we came to the right place."

"Sometimes he can hear okay and sometimes you have to really yell at him. Sometimes he can read your lips."

"Well, what do you know about that," Daddy says, signaling the maître d', whose face lights up with recognition.

"Ah, Monsieur Davidson, these must be your sons. For your sons, the best table in the house." Gliding softly, he maneuvers us to our table and presents us with our menus, scribbled in French on small slate boards, then disappears like smoke into the darkness.

Instantly, magically, he is replaced by our waiter, small, rosy-faced, beaming. "Would you care for drinks, monsieur?"

"Double martini for me. You guys want something?"

"Eh?"

"Speak a little louder," Johnny advises Daddy.

"Do you want something to drink?" Daddy repeats, looking up at the waiter, smiling apologetically, including him in some family joke.

"I'll have a Coke," I say. "And could you bring me some rolls? Right away, please."

"Johnny?"

"Ginger ale."

"Fine. We'll order later."

The waiter beams, bows his head ever so slightly, and is gone, only to reappear in the briefest instant with our drinks and my rolls, which I cram methodically down my throat, one after the other.

"Well," Daddy says, pulling at his drink, "how're my boys?"

"Fine," Johnny says.

"That's good."

"How about you, Jay? What's all this crap about these noises in your stomach?"

"Can we order? I'm hungry. I'm extremely hungry."

"Certainly. It's your day. Whatever you say."

"That rhymes," Johnny says.

Daddy laughs. His face is getting red. "It rhymes. Right. That's right, Johnny." He signals the waiter, "Another double for me and we'll be ready to order."

"I'm ready now," I say, finishing off the last roll. But the waiter has disappeared again.

"I don't think you should have any more to drink, Daddy," Johnny says.

Daddy laughs. He is sweating. "Now listen, boys, what would you like to do today?"

"Are you and Mommy going to be together again?" Johnny asks.

"Uh, Johnny. It's hard. You see. I can't. Listen, boys. I love her. I love her very much. . . ."

The waiter is back again. Daddy draws up straight, forms his words carefully, "Thank you, Gerard. That's fine."

"You wish to order now?"

"Fine. Yes." His face is red and hot-looking, the pores opening before my eyes, enlarging. "Just give us a minute to decide."

"Certainly, sir."

"You said we were going to order. I'm starving. I'm really starving."

"Fine, fine, Johnny. Jay, I mean Jay." He opens his mouth, and I watch him throw his drink down the long tunnel of his throat.

The noises in my stomach are getting louder and louder. I am wavering between nausea and pain.

"Don't drink anymore," I hear Johnny say.

"I'm okay, Johnny. I'm just fine. Perfectly fine."

"I don't want you to drink anymore." Johnny is reaching for Daddy's drink. I watch fascinated as the glass topples and the remaining liquid trickles onto the white tablecloth. I watch my father reach out and slap Johnny across the cheek. The slap reverberates, slicing through my noises like the knife through my mother's oranges. It leaves a red mark like a stain on Johnny's cheek.

Inside me, some vast network of machinery has gone haywire. Gears stripping, clanking and screeching, grinding insanely. I jump up. "I'm *hungry*," I shout. "I *need* some food. What kind of restaurant is this?"

The color is draining out of Johnny's face. He is white, white as a sheet, except for the red stain, which burns like a brand on his pale cheek. He sways in his seat and gags. He is going to throw up. We have to get out of here. I grab his hand, pulling him out of his seat.

Somehow we stumble out of there, the three of us, staggering like evil-smelling street dogs, holding each other, lurching past shocked diners, forks arrested in mid-bite over their steaming soufflés.

21

The Leisure Group, of which I am a member, is supposed to go to the Metropolitan Museum to see the Egyptian room, but it is pouring outside, a grey, driving, sleety rain. Gemma and Margie are attempting to herd us together to decide what to do in view of the weather.

We sit in a corner of the female dayroom on brand-new baby-blue benches with chrome legs. The comfortable, falling-apart armchairs have been shoved to the other side of the room (six weeks ago) for re-covering by the Ward Improvement Committee, which has not met since the project was announced.

"Is everyone here, Luis?" Margie asks. Luis is chairman of the Leisure Group.

"Except for six members, we are all here."

"Luis," Philip says curtly, "except for six only leaves three of us. You, me, and Jesse."

"I can count," Luis says.

"Would you like me to go see where everyone is?" Philip offers.

"I am chairman and I'll do my own job. Excuse me, please, if you don' mind."

In a flash Luis is back with the Princess, Martin Dewar, Franklyn Singleton, Willy, and Morris, who arrived on the ward four days ago.

Morris, ten years a postal clerk and three previous admissions that I personally know of—a Jewish joke, a balding schlepp, a schlemiel, a fat mamma's boy, a turd. Morris is destined never to be popular—not at work, not at Hadassah dances, not at post office Christmas parties, not on a psychiatric ward. Nowhere.

God never did shit for Morris. And don't think Morris is about to forgive him or any of his creatures for that. Since age ten (according to his chart), Morris's farts have been gaining him renown. Morris does not and never did go in for ordinary, undirected flatulence. His farts are antiballistic missiles, mapped out on the drawing board, precisely timed and aimed at a specific target. Evil, miasmic farts, annihilating everything in their path. Rising, steaming, from the depths of Morris's angry bowels, they are Morris's revenge.

The Mad Bomber is what we call him, and he loves that title—has posted it over his bed. Silas suggested that we could be out of Vietnam in nothing flat if the military would abandon traditional bombing and just use Morris. Of course, Silas conceded, the military imagination is deficient so the plan would never work. They can't see past the ends of their noses. So how can we expect them, he asks, to see all the way to Morris's asshole?

Morris has never gotten over Silas's compliment. If he has regard for anyone here, it is Silas.

"Where is Melinda?" Margie asks.

"In bed," Luis reports. "She doesn't want to go."

"And Silas?"

Luis grins his slow, unexpected grin. "He says he's not going anywhere with Morris, and he's amazed we would ask him."

Morris draws his lips back in what is his smile.

"Uh, well, how does that make you feel, Morris?" Gemma asks.

"Fine," Morris says, and he zaps Gemma so bad that she almost topples off the baby-blue bench.

"A little rain never hurt anyone," Willy reasons, ignoring the explosion.

"Right, Willy," says Margie. "We don't always have to stop everything or change plans because of rain."

"That's perfectly true, Willy," Gemma recovers, "but we could go to the greenhouse as an alternate plan. That's just around the corner. It's always a good idea to have an alternate plan. It makes us flexible."

"Don't you want to go to the museum, Miss S.?" Morris asks, innocent and wormy.

"Okay, Morris. Morris has picked up on the fact that I personally would rather go around the corner to the greenhouse than go all the way to Eighty-second and Fifth in the pouring rain."

"I've been to the greenhouse ten times," I say, "and the Egyptian exhibit eight, so it wouldn't kill me just to stay in out of the rain altogether."

Faye comes into the room with that tight strut of hers, one side of her mouth twitching at regular intervals as if someone were shocking her with an electrical device. "What's all this?"

"We may go to the museum or to the greenhouse," Willy says. "Do you want to come?"

"I'll go to the greenhouse," Faye says and sits down next to Luis.

"I'm sorry, Faye," Margie says. "We'd like you to come with us, but we can only take Leisure Group members on this trip."

"We don't mean to reject you, Faye," Philip starts.

"What is this? Some sorority or some crap? Sigma Delta Crazy."

"I'm going to get some water," Willy says and takes off, weaving his slow, ponderous bear-walk out of the dayroom.

"At any rate," Morris insists, "you aren't allowed off the ward, Faye. Isn't that right, Miss A.?"

"Look, fuck-face, what makes you think I want to go anywhere with you?"

I can see it coming. Morris is twisting in his seat, preparing to launch an attack on Faye. Faye sees it too.

"You sluggy fuck. You fart at me, and I'll murder you."

"Okay. Okay. Everyone just keep it down." Gemma's and Margie's admonitions are lost in the melee.

Faye leans forward in her seat. "The greenhouse flowers will drop dead if you go near them."

Fzzzz fzzzzz—gasses stirring, seeping, swirling around the base of the missile; whoosh, whoosh, *zaaaapppp*. Morris lets loose, a triumphant smile pasting his lips back over his capped teeth, a birthday present from Momma.

"Suddenly I'm feeling very down in the damps," Franklyn says, reeling from the Morris blast and fallout. He bows to the Princess and sidesteps out of the dayroom.

Satisfied as a Buddha, Morris settles comfortably back in his chair. But he has underestimated Faye. She is sparking like a hot wire. *Wheee*. Here she comes. Jumps out of her seat, dashes flashing behind the circle of chairs, skidding to a full stop behind Morris, plants her hands flat against his back, and slams him a shove that sends him flying, flopping in a heap, dumped like a sack of wet laundry on the floor.

"As chairman of the Leisure Group," says Luis, "I make a motion that we don' go out today."

Faye smiles over our heads at Morris. I've never seen her smile like that—a full, open, sunny smile. Then, before Gemma or Margie can say boo, she pivots clicking on her heels, dancing a little jigging two-step out of the dayroom and down the hall.

"I second the motion," Philip says.

"I third it," Margie says, dropping to the floor beside Morris, who is squirming on the floor like a turtle trying to right itself.

"Well," Martin Dewar says, "I would've liked to go somewhere. I wanted to write it up for *News in a Nutshell*. We were supposed to go."

Margie is panting. She had hold of Morris under his dampening armpits, struggling to haul him up.

"Write this up, Martin," I suggest. "Anatomy of a Leisure Group Meeting."

"I see what you mean, Jesse. Sort of human interest."

Margie is making progress. Morris is off the floor, hoisted on her knee.

"I hope, dear girls, you are not depressed at not going on the trip," the Princess says to Gemma and Margie.

Margie grunts, staggering backward with her soggy load. Morris has gone limp.

"To tell you the truth," Gemma says gaily, swooping up her purse and papers, "I prefer not going out today."

The Princess smiles serenely, rising from her chair. The Princess and Gemma start out of the room, with me, Philip, and Luis following.

"Okay, Morris, you win." Margie eases her arms from under Morris, letting his dead weight slide back down to the floor. "Wait for me."

"Aren't you coming, Martin?" the Princess calls.

Martin is hanging back, looking down at Morris, considering

if he should try to get an interview. But he rejects the notion, pockets his notebook, and follows us down the hall.

"What about Morris?" I ask Silas. We are standing in line in the lobby snack bar, waiting to get Cokes. It is Methadone Clinic day. The junkies are jazzing around us, making connections, stocking up on candy bars. Hopping, strutting, nodding, scratching, clacking together like geese.

"Morris? Please, Jesse."

"What do you think of him?"

"I don't think of him."

"But how can we figure it all out if we don't think about Morris?"

"I am not trying to figure it all out."

"Where does Morris fit in, Silas? Who loves Morris? Who could? Does God?"

"You're so full of shit, Jesse. If you took a shit every hour on the hour from now till Christmas, you couldn't get rid of all that shit. Morris is a sideshow fart freak, a diversion you're hooking on to so you can slop around in questions and compassion."

"You may think you can get around it, Silas, but sooner or later you and I will have to deal with Morris."

"Later, Jesse. A whole lot later. We'll be old and grey before we get back to Morris."

Luis, it turns out, is distantly related to Jesús Rivera who first christened me Jesse James.

"I have a lot of crazy relatives, but only me and Jesús and my wife's sister, Rosanna, have been in hospitals for it. She's four years older than Maria, but she copied her in everything. Rosanna never had nothing of her own, not even her sickness. She had this friend, and this friend she wouldn't fuck anyone because she said Christ was fucking her. Pretty soon, Rosanna was saying the same shit. Finally some social worker who came around for welfare said Rosanna needed to go to the hospital for treatment. Her best friend in the hospital heard voices talking to her in the radio, so pretty soon Rosanna heard voices in the radio. Whoever she likes, she gets their sickness. It always belongs to someone else."

22

Dear Dad,
    I don't know who I am. I seem to be whoever I am with. Did you ever have that feeling?

Love,

Jay

P.S. Could you spare a couple of bucks as I am running kind of low. I don't get paid till next week, and Mr. Kaminsky wants his rent money.

Dear Ann Landers,
    All my life I have had the feeling that I could see through people, that their inner selves, their true motives, were revealed to me, and so I stopped listening to the words they said, because I was listening to what they were behind the words.

    But now it's getting bad. It was metaphorical before. Now I actually do see. Like Superman. My x-ray vision bores through skin and bones and flesh into the guts of people sitting opposite me on buses and subways.

    Naturally it's getting me down to see weariness and defeat taking up the spaces where stomachs and lungs and intestines should be. I can't stand to see it anymore.

My question, Miss Landers, is—What if I were happy, would I still see into people? And what would I see? Am I seeing what is? Or am I seeing myself?

I thought you might have a clue, as you seem to have a lot of answers on hand. I respect anyone who has an answer to anything. Right or wrong.

Respectfully,
Jay Davidson
(alias Jesse James)

Dear Johnny,

I may have to quit my ushering job at the movie on Eighth Street. It's a shame because Mr. Faber is very pleased with my work and I love seeing all those wonderful old movies.

I have fallen in love with Ingrid Bergman, which would be perfectly normal except that I'm haunted by the fact that I've seen her before and not in the movies. And all the people I seat and Mr. Faber too—their faces are as familiar as Ingrid's and as haunting.

Love,
Jay

23

Marsha is back from work early, escorted by two cops. A bad sign. Her hair is matted and her dark eyes are vacant as marbles.

Silas and I watch Sophie fly over to them. She shoos the cops back out the door as if they were summer flies and leads Marsha down the hall.

"Marsha is losing," Silas says, staring after her with an intensity that makes my flesh crawl.

At lunch, Marsha sits by the door, stiff as a board, barelegged in her flowered hospital wrapper, watching the rest of us eat.

Mr. Watson tries to get her to join us. "The good Lord meant us to eat of his bounty." He sits down beside her. "I could give you a pear I brought from home, very juicy and fragrant."

Marsha stares through the old man. Mr. Watson shakes his head. Soon it drops to his chest and he is off, his ward keys dangling around his neck, clanging against each other with each deep, snoring breath.

Sophie comes to sit with Marsha, then Mrs. Morley, then Gemma, then Dr. Green. One by one they grow fidgety and leave. Next to Marsha's immobility, the slightest twitch looks like the mad gyrations of a whirling dervish. People bounce off her mind like gnats off a screen, pling, pling, pling.

She hasn't moved from that chair all afternoon. I decide that, after dinner, I will sit with her. But Silas is ahead of me. He leans against the wall, not looking at her.

"I don't want to hear your tale of woe," he tells her.

"I had a dream last night," she says. "There were holes. Deep holes full of black slime and . . . "

"You should have heeded the warning," Silas says.

"When I woke up, Mrs. Alton and Mrs. Morley were in the room, and Mrs. Alton tapped the side of my bed with her keys. They were signaling: leave or be locked up. I didn't say anything to anyone. I just got dressed and left.

"The elevator man knew. He knew about my dream. 'Third floor, second floor, basement, what'll it be?' he said. There was no one else in the elevator. They got off because they knew I was getting on. No one wants to get their hands dirty. They don't want to participate in the guilt. But they all let it happen. They don't try to stop it. He wanted to take me to the basement and leave me in the slime. But I tricked him. I seduced him with my eyes. The elevator stopped in the lobby, and I walked right by him before he knew what had happened.

"I walked to the corner and the light was green. The green light was my strength to go ahead.

"When I got to the office, the girl who sits next to me asked me to go down to the lobby for coffee with her. She wanted to drag me away so they could plot in secret. But I refused. Then Mr. Schiff walked in and gave a signal with his eyes. All the girls stopped talking and started to type. It was a code. I pretended to be going over my shorthand notes, but I was listening to the code. I knew if I didn't figure it out, the message would control me. But I couldn't make it out. I couldn't understand the message. So they overpowered me and brought me back here."

"Serves you right," Silas says, patting her on the knee. He excuses himself and leaves Marsha sitting there, staring after him, a tiny pinpoint of light flaring up for a split second in her eyes before they go blank again.

Franklyn bows stiffly to Mrs. Stern. "Her Highness, the Princess, and myself request the pressure of your company at a tea party."

"Is that a joke? Hah hah. Who are you?"

"I am an imitation."

"You at least I see have a pair of real shoes. While I am here like a ragamuffin in bedroom slippers. Look. Not even one real shoe to my name. Slippers only. Ersatz. You know what means *ersatz?*"

"I don't know. Please excuse me. I have to go."

"Oh. My God. I don't want to keep you. Don't bother,

please. Why should you bother? We aren't even related."

"Sunday. Four o'clock," Franklyn says, backing down the hall.

I already know of the party. Martin Dewar approached me this morning: "Franklyn and the Princess are co-hosting a tea party Sunday. It's going to be the biggest story of the year."

"That's great, Martin."

"I'm very upset, Jesse. I can't cover it."

"Why not?"

"I'm going to be out of town on another assignment."

"You're what?"

"I was just kidding, Jesse. I have a pass for Sunday. It's my aunt's birthday. I didn't know about the tea party in time. If I'd only known in advance, but this just came at me out of nowhere. Usually Sunday is so quiet here, and now, all of a sudden, it's going to be this gala affair. I can't ask my aunt to change her birthday."

"I don't see how you could."

"I made her a macramé belt in O.T. But I can't remember if she has anything that will go with orange. I should have done it in something neutral."

"She'll like orange fine."

"I hope you're right. I wish Dr. Green was here today. If I could just discuss this with him. I feel a responsibility to cover this event for *News in a Nutshell*. But when you consider everything, family ties and all that, I have at least an equal or, actually, even a greater responsibility to go to my aunt's birthday party."

"If it were me, Martin, I'd go to your aunt's."

"I hate to miss the tea party."

"Martin, would you like me to take notes for you on the party so you can write it up when you get back?"

"I already thought of asking you, to tell the whole truth. But, if you have to take notes, it's not the same as just going to the party as a guest."

"That's okay."

"Are you sure?"

"Really, Martin, it's fine."

"You sound a little annoyed."

"I'm not annoyed."

"I'll give you a credit, of course. An informed source. How does that sound?"

"Terrific, Martin. I'd appreciate it."

Sophie cornered me this morning after Psychodrama. "Jay, can I speak to you for a minute?"

"Did you have an appointment?"

"I didn't know I needed one."

"I might be persuaded to make an exception for you, Miss R. Unless, of course, you're trying to finagle an invitation to the tea party out of me. In which case, you've got the wrong man. It's Franklyn you want."

"Jay, it's about Silas."

"What about him?"

"He hasn't been to an activity in two weeks."

"That's nothing new."

"I mean not one single activity, Jay."

"He values his privacy."

"I want to know if you've noticed any change in him in the past week or so."

"Like what?"

"Anything. Does he seem upset to you?"

"No."

"Is he behaving differently in any way that you can tell?"

"No. I couldn't really say that."

"Nothing at all then? You haven't noticed anything?"

"I don't know. I'm not sure."

"That sounds like you're picking up something."

"The other day, the day the cops brought Marsha back, he watched the two of you walk down the hall, and he said, 'Marsha is losing.' "

"That's all?"

"It was the way he said it. It scared me, Sophie."

"You think he was talking about himself, don't you?"

"Look, you have to understand that Silas doesn't talk to me. Not really."

"More to you than anyone."

"I have to get going. I promised Gemma I'd help her bring down some clay from upstairs."

"Okay. I appreciate your talking to me. By the way, Dr. Weisser thinks you may be ready to leave soon, and I agree."

"Nothing has changed."

Nothing has changed, I think to myself as the old men walk by. I follow them closely. Nothing at all.

"I got a problem to discuss with you. I haven't heard my voices for two months."

"Well, what do you know about that. Did you tell the doctor?"

"I told him."

"What'd he say?"

"That's good. That's fine. You're getting better. You don't need them anymore."

"I guess that's right. Congratulations."

"Is that all you can say? I thought you at least would understand. I want them back. I miss them."

"Maybe it's age. Mine might go too."

"I have you to talk to now, but you won't be around forever."

"Maybe if I asked them real nice, my voices would talk to you, too. Hee hee."

"You can joke now. You see what it's like when it happens to you."

Tea Party Notes for Martin

Table looks good. Folded-up sheet for tablecloth. Centerpiece—crepe-paper flowers, pink and purple. I think Willy made it in O.T. Teacups from the kitchen. Ginger snaps, Oreos and Fig Newtons on birthday-paper plates left over from staff party for Mrs. Morley's birthday.

PHILIP (smiles expansively): That centerpiece is very effective. Just the right touch, Princess.

PRINCESS: Willy made it. I think it's charming.

WILLY (blushes): Franklyn set the table.

WALTER: I wish my mother were here to see this.

WILLY: I wish my brothers could see it.

MELINDA: I didn't know you had any brothers.

WILLY: Four. I got four brothers. They're all in the state hospital.

WALTER: Let's not talk about depressing things.

FRANKLYN: The state represses for our own good.

PRINCESS: Shall we start the cookies around? Franklyn, would you do the honors? (Franklyn passes cookies and Princess starts pouring tea and passing it around.)

WILLY: I'll save some cookies for Faye. I looked all over to find her.

PRINCESS: I had really expected Luis to come. And Hamilton.

ME: Luis is out on pass, and Hamilton asked me to send his regrets. He's working on an important speech.

PRINCESS: My late husband stopped speaking to me altogether toward the end. Tant pis. Tant mieux.

PHILIP: See, you had an advantage. I never had the opportunity to learn a foreign tongue. If I had had a decent education, I wouldn't be where I am today. Of course, my outside doctor, Dr. Gruber, would call that a rationalization. Maybe that's true. Jesse told me Ursula's got a Ph.D. Isn't that what you told me? And look at her. Terrible. Poor thing.

ME: She was a lecturer in political science in Frankfurt.

WALTER: Perhaps she could put in a good word for me in Vienna.

FRANKLYN: Policy is the best science.

WILLY: Where is Silas?

ME: He's a little under the weather.

FRANKLYN: His barometer is too fine.

ME: He asked me to tell everyone how sorry he was he couldn't make it. (He didn't really. I'm not sure he even heard what I was saying: "Come on, Silas, it'll be fun to watch." "Watch this," he said. He ripped a piece of Philip's *Playboy* calendar off the wall, scribbled something on each enormous bunny breast and handed it to me. One breast said, "Know means can." On the other he had written, "Believe means love.")

WILLY (spots Faye strutting around the outer edge of the tea-party circle): There's Faye. Hey, Faye. Faye. Come to the tea party.

FAYE: What is this? The Boston Tea Party? Who's going to be dumped?

PHILIP (pulling on Faye's arm): Sit down for Christ's sake, Faye, and don't make a scene for once.

FAYE: Don't tell me what to do, prickhead. (Smiles, though, and sits down mildly between Willy and Philip)

WILLY: I was going to save you some cookies if you didn't come. Melinda, would you pass the ginger snaps around to Faye?

MELINDA (daintily): Certainly.

FAYE (mimics Melinda, pursing lips): Certainly.

MELINDA: What's eating you?

JANINE (loud stage whisper): Everybody on the ward.

WILLY (flushing crimson): That's a lie.

FAYE: I heard that, you titless bitch.

WILLY: You tell Faye you're sorry, Janine. That wasn't nice at all.

FRANKLYN (gets up suddenly, bows to Princess): I am on the brink of a recession. Excuse me.

PRINCESS: Oh, Mr. Singleton, I'm terribly sorry. This is upsetting you.

FRANKLYN (shakes Princess's hand; bows to table at large): Thank you for your hostility. (He backs off down the hall.)

MELINDA: See what she did. Faye's spoiling the party. You owe us an apology.

FAYE: I don't owe anything to anybody. You think you're a big deal because you're president of Ward Government. You and Janine think you're hot shit. Big deal. You go off the ward for rehab counseling. Big huge deal. Who wants it?

MELINDA: You're jealous.

FAYE: I don't need counseling. I run my own life.

JANINE: She's mad because Dr. Weisser told her she can't get off the ward till she starts participating more in the ward community.

WALTER: I'm getting a headache.

WILLY: She participates. She says stuff in Ward Government.

PHILIP: I'll have to agree with that. I mean it seems to me . . .

FAYE: I don't need any goddamn lawyer.

WALTER: Hamilton used to be a lawyer. Perhaps I should go get him.

FAYE (jumps up): Shut up. Everyone thinks they can tell me what to do. You don't pay my rent. So leave me alone. (Flings her ginger snaps across table at Melinda and Janine)

General disorder. Walter runs down the hall, shouting for Mrs. Morley. Mrs. Harper opens kitchen door, peeps out, and shuts door again. Princess carefully removes Willy's centerpiece from table. Willy, near tears, tries to reach for Faye's hand, but she pulls away violently.

FAYE: Get away from me. I'll take care of myself. I want to get out of here. You can't keep me, you shit-heads. I demand to get out. Let me out. *Let me out.*

24

Suddenly the city is too small for me. I am thirteen, and everywhere I turn I am confined by buildings, walls, fences, signs,

doormen, teachers. Everything is in my way, including Johnny.
I cannot stand the tiny room we share. Always he is running
behind me, smiling his open, anxious smile, chattering, asking
questions. What does he want from me? Whatever it is, I don't
have it.

I have explored all the underground passageways of the
neighborhood, memorized all the lead-ins to all the radio
shows, dug to China, kicked the can, traded all my trading
cards, sent off all my box tops, swapped all my comics, exhausted my friendships. I want out. *Out*. Before disaster comes,
and it is coming. I feel it running after me, breathing down my
neck.

I had craved the country the way a junkie craves junk, and
now, speeding along the highway out of the city, heading for
our new home in the country, my desire drops from me like a
scab.

I sit in the back of the car, leaning out the open window. The
towers of the city are flushed with pink, glowing warmly in the
late-afternoon summer sun. The bridges gleam in high, clean,
curving arches over the sparkling river. Everything I want is in
this city somewhere, locked away in this magical, brooding
labyrinth. I have just never known it till now. Now when it is
too late.

"I want to go home."

"I can't hear you up here with the windows open, Jay," my
father says.

"He said he wants to go home," Johnny says.

My mother takes her hand from Johnny's forearm and turns
around in her seat to look back at me. "I thought you couldn't
stand the city one more minute. That's all I've heard from you
for six months."

"Are we going home?" Johnny asks.

"Will you boys please shut up?" my father says, swerving ahead of the car in front of him. "Dumb sonofabitch."

"I didn't do anything," Johnny says.

"Jack!"

"That bastard was creeping along."

"Oh, please."

I turn around in my seat, away from them. The city is growing smaller and smaller, diminishing behind me. Leaving me. I know you, city. I know your towers, caverns, bridges, rivers. I want to go back, back into the dark, pulsing streets, narrow alleys, sheltering buildings, high and warm and close around me.

I pretend we are just out for a Sunday drive. At dusk we will turn around and go home. We will go home. I slide down on the seat. Soothed by my fantasy, I doze on and off.

I lurch awake, startled out of sleep by some presentiment of disaster, as we swing onto Cedar Lane. Raw-looking houses, one after another, set back from the road. Each one like the other. On each plot a few saplings, naked and absurd.

"They preserved some beautiful old trees further up the road," my father says.

Wave after wave of nausea rises up in me as we drive slowly down the quiet, winding road. It is a totally unremarkable suburban street. But to me it is contaminated, marked by a secret, suppurating evil. Clean, new blank houses, slowly rotting, decaying from the inside out. I alone know the evil festering inside. It seeps into the soft summer air, poisoning the purple dusk, and no one knows or cares but me.

We pull up in front of our house. It is a low frame ranch house, indistinguishable from its neighbors on either side except for its brick-red color and the fact that it is sited differently on its quarter-acre lot.

"I hate this house. Something bad will happen here."

"You're a vicious little shit." She bites off the end of each word, spits them out one by one into her purse.

Johnny is squirming. "I want to get out of the car."

My father puts his arm around the back of the seat behind Johnny, touching my mother's arm. "It's okay, Leah."

"It's not okay." She shrugs his hand off.

"I want to go look," Johnny says.

"Well, what do you think of it?" my father asks my mother.

"It's a little late to be asking me that, isn't it?"

They get out of the car, and Johnny scrambles out behind them, his thin legs dancing, impatient.

"Jay, Jay." Johnny is calling me. His voice bounces lightly, gusting through the window to me. "Look. I found a tree. A climbing tree. Jay, look."

I turn to look out the back window. Johnny is halfway up a massive oak tree. Its gnarled roots sprawl thickly into the ground; its branches are covered with masses of dark green leaves.

"Come play, Jay. Come play in our tree."

I watch Johnny as he makes his way to the top of the tree. I can see him in the topmost branches. I can feel the sharp, tingling stab in his legs, feel the blood rushing in his veins. My heart is pounding. But I don't answer his call. Very deliberately, I turn around. I sit huddled in the back seat of the car watching myself with glum satisfaction as the joy seeps away.

The next morning I am struck down by a mysterious sleeping sickness.

"Jay. Jay. Wake up." Johnny's voice plagues me like the stab of an accusing memory. "Jay, wake up. It's almost twelve. Mommy's been calling you and calling you."

All the heaviness of my soul seems to have settled in my eyelids. To raise them over my eyeballs would require the strength of creation. I can feel Johnny's warm breath on my face as he leans over me, carefully slides my right eyelid up over my eye. Eyeball to eyeball, we gaze at each other.

"Aren't you ever going to get up?"

"Go away."

But he continues to peer fixedly into my open eye, like a mad prophet. Finally, having divined whatever it was he intended to divine, he pushes my eyelid back over my eye, and calls out to my mother in the next room, "He's not getting up yet. He's really tired."

"Well, the hell with him then," she calls back. "Let him sleep. Come get your lunch, Johnny."

"I'll see you," Johnny says.

"Mmmph." I slide down to the bottom of the bed, curling in on myself like a mole in winter, drawing the cover tight around me, covering all of me, even my head, dragging myself down into sleep.

Through the rest of that interminable summer, I couldn't stay awake for more than an hour at a time. I nodded off in the bathtub, at supper, in front of TV, on the toilet.

"I think we should take him to a specialist," my father says.

My mother looks up from her book. "I took him to the doctor three weeks ago. You don't listen to anything I say."

"What did he say?"

"I told you. He said he was rundown, overtired."

"How can he be overtired when all he does is sleep?" Johnny asks.

"Well, I think we should see a specialist," my father says.

"Do what you want."

After that, he never refers to my sleeping sickness again, except to ask me once if I am taking some kind of dope.

As the days get shorter, my naps get longer. My arms and legs are filled with sand and my eyelids lined with lead. It takes what infinitesimal energy I have to drag myself from my bed to the table and back to my crumpled bed, which I now hate with a sheer, physical loathing that makes me flinch at the sight of it.

The only time I can't sleep is when my mother takes her nap in the afternoon. The house is still. Johnny is out playing somewhere with other kids in the neighborhood, and my father is working in the city. We are alone in the silent house. The shades are down. There is no sound except the steady drone of the air conditioning, like the humming of an airplane engine.

Alone in the house, closeted in our separate chambers, we share some guilty, worn-out secret, some wary knowledge of each other that keeps me on guard and awake, stretched out on my bed, pale and rigid as a martyr, waiting for her to get up so I can sleep again.

"What's the matter with you?" my mother demands.

"What do you mean?"

"What do you mean, 'What do I mean'? You're sleeping all day and all night. That's what I mean."

"It's the climate. I can't take this climate. It's too hot."

"What's he talking about?" she shrieks at the ceiling. "It's cooler here than in the city, and we've got this horrible air conditioning."

I make no reply. I am starting to nod out. I can feel myself sliding forward on my chair.

"Do you want to go back? Is that what you want?"

I only half hear her somewhere way off in the distance. I am absorbed by the sweet weariness running through my veins, suffusing me, overcoming me, pushing me to the edge of my chair.

"*Jay, Jay. Goddammit.* I'll never speak to you again if you fall off that chair."

"Ahhhh," I sigh as I slide ecstatically onto the soft beige carpet, swooning in a heap at her feet.

. . .

The summer is wearing down. In between naps, I stand by the window, a sentinel hawk, marking the fading of each separate leaf, waiting for the falling leaves with greedy, doomed anticipation.

Inexplicably and almost overnight, my sleeping sickness disappears. The slumbering dread rises up full at last, making my heart beat fast and my eyes shine. My cheeks have a feverish glow, which my parents interpret as rosy.

25

Gemma has stopped writing her notes to herself. I have ransacked her office four times in the past week and found nothing.

"What does it mean, Silas?" I ask him as we stand over the bathroom sinks washing up before bed. "It has to mean something. You don't think she found out I've been reading her stuff, do you?"

"She's fading away," Silas says. He smiles at himself in the mirror, marking an X over his image with his soapy finger.

The day after Janine is discharged, Melinda turns in her resignation as president of Ward Government:

> I am resigning my position as president of Ward Government because I am depressed as you can see from my writing which is sad and slanting down.
> Respectfully,
> Melinda Aaronson

Following Melinda's resignation, Hamilton makes his acceptance speech as new president:

"Ladies and gentlemen, I come before you today to accept the position of president of Ward Government, which fate has thrust upon me in Melinda's time of trouble. I come not to bury Melinda but to praise her. We are all grateful for her vigorous leadership. She is a credit to her sex, to her dear mother, to this ward.

"There are those among you who fear my radical views. Let me say to you, I will endeavor to drive down the middle of the road during my term of office. To those dissidents among you, let me assure you that my right hand shall not always know what my left hand is doing. My administration shall be a government for all the people, conceived in liberty and dedicated to the proposition that all men are creative, if not equally.

"In conclusion, let me remind you that sometimes we must close a door in order to open it again. Thank you."

As president, Hamilton stumps the ward, entertaining his constituency with almost daily speeches. Everyone turns out to hear Hamilton speak. Even Ursula and Marsha and Mrs. Stern. Everyone except Silas, who doesn't come out for much these days.

Hamilton stands on top of the longest table in the dining room, striding its length as if it were a stage, waving his hands in the air. "Ladies and gentlemen, the theater is not dying, it is dead. Critics drool over dribbling idiots, marquees blaze the lying phrases—incandescent, brilliant, shocking, magical—and we like sheep go meek and unprotesting, bleating and baaing to the slaughter of our senses. They offer us fornication as an antidote to their putrid boredom. I had rather watch our own sweet Faye fucking my friends in the bathtub than watch a thousand pale-eyed ingénucs simulating sex."

At this, the audience goes wild, thumping and stomping. Faye blushes prettily and gives Hamilton the finger.

"Dear friends, continue your brave boycott of the theater. Write your own plays, perform them in the streets. Set fire to imagination and burn the boards behind you."

If anyone should happen to miss a Hamilton speech, Martin Dewar has seen to it that we can read it in the special editions he is now producing—mimeographed copies of Hamilton's speeches under the masthead of *News in a Nutshell*. Martin scribbles furiously as Hamilton declaims:

"Ladies and gentlemen, I say to you that keeping up is a disease as insidious as cancer and crazier than schizophrenia. Do not drown yourself in the tidal wave of trivia which goes by the name of current events. Abjure the gossip, disdain the household tips, forsake the reviews, ignore the analysis, forget the names and dates and places. Leave your magazines, your newspapers behind. Turn off your radios, your TVs. Empty your mind as you empty your bowels. Shit and be done with it. I thank you."

The word goes around at supper that Hamilton will be speaking again tonight. When everyone is through eating, Willy enlists Philip and Martin and me to set up the chairs in a semicircle in front of the long table on top of which Hamilton will speak.

I find myself a seat in the last row of the semicircle, next to Ursula, who is tapping her foot and smiling. The mood in the room is eager, gay, anticipatory. Philip and Willy have mounted the table and are doing a cancan to everyone's great amusement.

Hamilton comes up behind me. "Where is Silas? Good evening, Ursula," he says before I can answer him. Ursula smiles shyly at Hamilton, averting her head slightly. "Everyone else is here. Everyone except Silas. Where is he?"

"I don't know where he is, Hamilton."

"He should be here. He understands the importance of what I'm trying to do."

"Hamilton, you know as well as I do that Silas is very bad now."

We are making Ursula nervous. She puts her hands over her ears so she won't hear us.

"They have stamped out his spirit," Hamilton says. "Ursula doesn't want to hear that, of course. No one wants to hear that."

"Who has? Who is they, Hamilton?"

"Sometimes it's me. What do you think of that, Ursula?"

Ursula shakes her head, hands still clasped over her ears.

"Leave her alone. I can't drag Silas to hear you."

"I'm not talking about Silas. I'm talking about you."

"What do you want me to do? I always come to hear you speak."

"If that is your answer then you must bear the guilt of hearing and not speaking, of watching and not seeing."

"I already do."

"What would we do without our guilt, Jesse? Excuse me, I should be starting. Good evening, Ursula." Ursula nods and Hamilton strides to the front of the room and mounts his podium. . . .

Dr. Weisser wants me to get out more. "You're not using your passes. Go out—take a walk, go to a movie. Take Luis with you."

"I don't want to. I want to stay home."

"This isn't your home."

"Sure it is. Mrs. Morley is Mama and you're Papa."

"I don't believe you see me as your father."

"You're right, I don't. You're a distant cousin."

"I've been thinking about being in this place. A hundred years ago we wouldn't have been in here at all."

"That's right. Poor old geezers like us. We'd be in some asylum with no windows and nothing to crap in but a pail. We'd be wrapped in wet sheets and tied to a chair, and we'd be vegetables because they would've cut out part of our brains."

"No, no, no. I'm telling you we'd be at home with our families."

"I haven't got a family."

"We'd live at home, out in the country, just old wadoyoucallits, eccentrics, and nobody'd pay us any mind. We'd have our own rooms, and we'd sit on the porch in the spring and tell stories to the children or shoot the shit with the neighbor ladies, and we'd die in our beds at age ninety-two."

Joel won't give up. "Does your not going out have something to do with leaving Silas?"

"No."

"Why don't you want to go out, Jay?"

"I don't know, Dr. Weisser."

"You do know."

"There's something out there."

"What?"

"I don't know."

"You do know."

26

The bus for Johnny's grammar school stops at the corner of our road. The junior high bus picks me up a quarter of a mile farther down the road.

There are three other people waiting at the bus stop when I get there, two girls and a boy. I don't know them, which isn't surprising since I had slept all summer and didn't know anyone.

Obviously they know each other. They do a little dance of intimacy, bumping into each other, separating, giggling, coming together again, a ritual from which I feel myself forever excluded. Periodically, they shoot a curious glance my way. I pretend not to notice them. Sweating heavily, I rummage in my lunch bag as if there were something of vital importance concealed underneath my peanut-butter-and-jelly sandwiches. I note with alarm that no one else carries lunch bags. I curse my mother silently for this visible proof of my alien status.

I wait an eternity for the bus to come, dangling ridiculously on the perimeter of the tableau created by the three others, holding my poor sack with its spreading jelly stain.

At last the bus swings up and opens its doors. I stumble on behind the others into a jumbled mass of legs and arms and faces that magically absorbs my three companions and leaves me still on the perimeter, sticking out like a sore thumb, although I am crammed into a back corner and no one speaks to me or even looks my way.

I stare out the window as the bus goes up and down the suburban lanes—Bluebell Drive, Lotus Lane, Park Road, Old Farm Road—a geography of nowhere. It all looks the same, nothing anywhere to explain why one stretch is Cedar Lane and another Riverview Road; no cedars, no river, no bluebells, no lotuses.

The landscape, tidy, bland, monotonous in the bright September sun, oppresses me, but it is soothing nevertheless to ride up and down and around the prefabricated streets. I wish the ride would go on forever.

When the bus pulls up in front of the junior high, a huge, sprawling red-brick building extending in all directions, a shock of panic goes through me.

"Last stop," the driver calls out. I look out the window at that massive fortress and know with the certainty of terror that the whole thing is impossible. If it had been another sort of building perhaps—something softer and more hospitable, smaller . . .

All around me there erupts a violent commotion as people pile into the narrow aisles, shoving and yelling, spilling one after another, one on top of the other, out of the bus and onto the asphalted parking lot.

I am not going to be able to move from my seat. Already paralysis is setting in, stiffening my joints, squeezing my spine. I try to extend my foot and it curls straight up in an aching cramp that makes me gasp.

The driver must have heard me, for he takes his finger out of his ear, looks up at his mirror, and turns around in his seat to get a better look at me. "Hey, this is the last stop. I thought everyone was off."

He is a man in his middle fifties, sandy-haired and open-faced. He wears a blue-and-white baseball cap planted sideways on his head. "Didn't you hear me?"

"Yes, sir, I did."

"Okay. So long, kid. Have a good day." He turns back around in his seat, writes something down in a little book he keeps on the front window, and sticks his finger back in his ear.

My paralysis is creeping upward. My knees lock, both at once, with a small, snapping sound, jerking my legs straight out in front of me. Simultaneously, my buttocks lift and lock so that I am suspended half an inch off the seat, held in place by my thighs, which alone, of all my body, have contact with the seat.

I must have looked peculiar because when the driver finally turns around again he blanches, his baseball cap slides off his head, and he swears softly, "What the fuck?"

"I seem to be having trouble."

"Are you trying to be cute or what?" he says, stooping for his cap.

"No, sir. I'm paralyzed."

"What?"

"I'm paralyzed. I can't move."

"Well, Jesus Christ. What is all this? You're not a crippled kid, are you?" he asks, perplexed, placing the cap back sideways on his head.

"No, sir."

"Then what's the problem?"

"I told you. I can't move."

"Well, you moved to get on the bus, right?"

"Right."

"Then you can move to get off the bus."

We are at an impasse. The driver turns back around in his seat and whistles "Come to Me My Melancholy Baby," with a lot of fancy, warbling trills, waiting for me to get off his bus.

But I can't move. The strain of my position is tiring me enormously. Sweat runs down my chest. "You're a good whistler," I say finally through clenched teeth; even my jaw is starting to stiffen.

"Thanks. I'm not bad if I do say so myself."

"My father can whistle pretty well."

"It's getting to be a lost art. None of the kids today can whistle worth shit . . . excuse me."

"That's all right."

Suddenly, remembering, he turns around in his seat and glares down the aisle at me. "I want you to get off my bus or I'm going to call the principal."

"I can't."

"I'm a patient man, otherwise I couldn't have the position I have. It takes a lot of patience to be a school-bus driver. But I don't take no crap off no smartass kids." He leaps out of his seat and bounds down the aisle toward me. But when he puts his big hand on me, he stops short. "Jesus Christ," he says wonderingly, "you're stiff as a board." He sits down on the seat beside me, putting a protective arm around my rigid shoulders while he mulls over the alternative solutions. "I'll go get the school nurse. We'll work something out here." He pats me on the shoulder, assuring me that everything will be okay, leaving me stiff and strangely peaceful, in the back of the bus.

By the time the driver returns, almost half an hour later, with the school nurse and the principal and my mother and a stretcher and two ambulance attendants in tow, I am in a semi-comatose state.

A pleasant, confused babble of talk flows over and around me as I am lifted onto the stretcher, carried off the bus, slid into the back of the ambulance, and whisked off to the emergency room at Rossdale Hospital, with my mother beside me, grinding her teeth, her hand on my forehead.

During the ride, I have semiconscious, full-color visions of myself laid out in my hospital bed, while interns and residents perform complicated neurological tests on me and pretty nurses administer soothing alcohol rubs to my contracted legs.

In fact, I was never seen by any doctor, because by the time we arrive at the hospital, I am fully, horribly, awake. On the instant of awakening, my paralysis dissipates. My legs go flaccid, my knees and buttocks unlock. I crawl off the stretcher.

Penitent as the holiest sinner, I follow my mother into the lobby, where, tight-lipped and expressionless, she calls a cab to take us home.

27

Mrs. Morley is in a rare bad mood. I heard her snapping at Melinda earlier because Melinda was crouching on the floor outside the nurses' station, sucking her thumb. Mrs. Morley knows Melinda hasn't gotten an answer to any of her letters to Janine. But tonight that fact only increases her irritation at Melinda. She'll be glad to get out of here. Well, she's only got another half hour. It's almost seven. She can just take her key and open that big door and lock it behind her and go home. So could I for that matter.

No one to talk to. Franklyn went to bed immediately after supper. Willy and Philip are nodding out in front of the TV. The Princess told me earlier that she preferred to be alone this evening. "I feel very melancholy tonight, Jesse. It will pass, of course, but tonight I am melancholy."

Hamilton is closeted in his room, drafting an article entitled "Hic, Haec, Hoc," which he intends to submit to the American Psychiatric Association journal. I have no idea what it's about. I'm afraid to ask. Silas wouldn't come to dinner. He's reading a book named *Mysteries*. I tried to engage him in conversation about it, but he said it was a personal matter and he didn't want to discuss it.

I reach in my pocket for my cigarettes—nothing. I remember. Morris bummed my last one. Why did I let him do that? I've never seen Morris smoke.

Ah, shit. What a bad fucking night. I shouldn't have napped before supper. I dreamed of Debbie again. "You left me," she said. And I woke up shivering in my own cold sweat, with Debbie's despair clinging to me like the wet sheets.

Dear God, who can I talk to? I wish Gemma were around. Luis. I'll hunt up Luis. He has a view of things that is reasonable and reassuring. Besides, when I run out of cigarettes, Luis rolls for me.

I find Luis alone in the back dayroom. He is sitting on the couch, strumming the ward guitar, which has never been the same since Faye attacked Morris with it two weeks ago. Still, Luis is making music on it. He finishes the song and lays the guitar aside.

"I wish I weren't here tonight, Luis. I wish I were anywhere in the world except here."

Luis reaches into his pocket and pulls out his cigarette papers and tobacco. I like to watch Luis roll. With one twist of his thin wrist, he's wrapped it all up. He lights both our cigarettes, handing mine to me.

"I'd rather be here," he says. "There are rats in my house and fucking roaches and half the time no heat. And plastic fucking furniture that farts at me that I bought on time, rotting away before I got it paid off. My street is metal and glass and shit, beer cans and bottles and dog shit and newspapers. I never thought about it. I was a janitor in a movie on Forty-second Street, I loaded trucks, I was a guard at a project uptown. Maria and me got married. I went along, you know. Plop plop plop. And I turn around and Maria and me have five kids. Five. Oh, Jesus, shit. In that rat-shit hole with linoleum curling up everywhere, tripping me, and cracks in the windows. Maria and me don't talk anymore or laugh. Money and clothes and food and carfare and doctor bills. That's what we talk about. The babies are crying and screaming, and we're falling all over each other. There is no room. No room to breathe.

"For nine years, since Maria and me got married, I been a meter reader, a gas man. Out in Queens. Go by people's houses, read the meter. Bullshit a little with the lady of the house. I got a little once in a while, but I never liked it. It was dry and dusty pussy. But I did it anyway. I thought it would wake me up because I'm only twenty-eight and I feel dead inside. But I keep reading the meters, bringing the money home plop plop plop. And it drops into the holes and the holes are getting bigger every day. Making love to Maria. It's nothing anymore. Falling into another hole.

"My Uncle Jaime was always coming around in his silk suits and rings to ask me to run numbers for him or deal a little shit. 'What're you bustin' your balls for, man, to live in this shithouse?' I always told him, 'No thanks, Jaime.' It pissed him off.

"One day, one Saturday, I go out. I was only going to walk around the block to get a little air, but I ended up walking from Sixth Street all the way to Sixtieth and Fifth. I been there before, you know, of course. I been all over the city. But I never saw it before—hotels and awnings and doormen in front and cars and cabs and stores and clothes in the windows and people walking around, smiling, talking, looking in the windows, coming out of the stores with packages, getting out of cabs, going into the lobbies, doormen running, rushing to open doors for them. And I realize everybody doesn't live like me. You understand, Jesse? Not everyone lives like me. Some do and some don't. And there is no reason for one or the other. And I felt hate rushing up in me, like oh, Jesus, like coming the best it ever is. I felt the most alive I ever felt in my life. I ran all the way home. I kept thinking my heart would explode and that would be the end of it, but it didn't happen. When Maria saw me, she crouched in the corner like a scared rabbit.

" 'Stand up straight,' I yelled at her. And I hit her across the mouth like swatting a fucking fruit fly, and then I shoved her to the floor and I beat the shit out of her, man, till blood was pouring from her head, and the kids were screaming, crawling all over. And a neighbor called Jaime, and he whizzed over in his big black car, with a fat nurse in a uniform to attend to Maria, and he told me he was bringing me here for observation.

"If Jaime hadn't come, I would probably have killed my wife. Another man in the exact same place as me, he could not. Jaime could not. You see? Maybe there was always some bad thing in me and it would have been there no matter what my life had been.

"On the outside I'm still going along. I do what they ask. My doctor says, 'No, Luis, you are not crazy. You can go home soon. You will not hurt anyone.' But inside me the bad thing is waiting. I want to smash things, Jesse. To feel bones snapping under my fingers. I want to kill someone."

Silas is losing weight. Daily, it seems, his face narrows. His features are etched more and more sharply in his narrowing face. Dr. Brenner is concerned about his physical condition and examines him regularly.

"They are looking for the defect, Jesse. But I don't think they will find it. It's hidden."

Once a week, Mrs. Morley weighs him. "They think I'm losing weight. But it's atrophy. Some vital organ is atrophied."

I have been used to shadowing Silas, and now he is shadowing me. I can feel his thin, cool breath on the back of my neck. I can feel his thoughts dropping randomly through the air, hitting bottom. Nothing to stop them. Falling through the bottom into space.

At breakfast, he watches me lift the coffee cup to my lips, swallow, put my cup down. I repeat the same motions, again and then again.

'Yes,' he thinks, 'yes. Everything is simple. Jesse lifts the cup, swallows, puts it down. It is a cup with coffee in it. It is morning. Breakfast. After breakfast is Community Meeting, then Daily Living, then . . . I can't remember. What comes next? What follows? It's all right. Watch Jesse. See how he swallows, puts his cup down, lifts it again. Everything has a rhythm. This rhythm is simple, solid. It has a round, clear shape.'

Silas stirs his cold coffee with one bony finger. He watches the circles he makes. I pick at my toast, tear off the crust, throw it aside. Silas starts. I have torn something. He looks up at me, defending himself against my cheap understanding. "I am perfectly aware," he says, "that there are parts of me missing. One of which is the part which would mourn the missing parts."

I push my chair back a little from the table, light my cigarette. Blue smoke in curling columns comes out of my mouth.

'He is having a smoke,' Silas thinks. 'Where there is smoke there is fire. Inside Jesse there is a fire raging.'

Silas jumps up. "You have to save yourself," he yells at me.

"What do you mean, Silas? What's the matter?"

"The fire."

"What fire, Silas? There's no fire."

"Inside you. The fire inside you." He sits back down again and puts his head in his hands.

"I can't stand this, Silas. I can't stand to see you this way."

"I'm sorry." He says it simply, without irony.

"Where are you, Silas? Tell me where you are."

Mrs. Harper crashes through the kitchen door. "Breakfast is over. Would you please clear your place and get out of my dining room? I don't have time for this hanging around. This isn't a saloon, you know. You can't just hang around here all day."

Silas lifts his head, smiling at me. He is amused and comforted. The morning is lightening, clearing. Yack, yack, yack. Familiar. Substantial. Dependable. Yack, yack, yack. Mrs. Harper yacking. It is a marker, a way to orient oneself in the world. 'Yes,' Silas thinks. 'Here. This is where I am. That is Mrs. Harper yacking at me and Jesse.'

For days on end, Silas will say barely a word to anyone. Standing at the elevator, I hear them in chart rounds: "It has happened before. He'll come out of it in time. Don't press him. Up the medication."

He is refusing to see Dr. Brenner. "I don't want to understand my dreams," he tells me. "I just want to dream them."

Staff sees that he talks to me and they encourage my being with him. Dr. Brenner asks that I be excused from Daily Living one morning a week so I can be with Silas. But I can't stand it. I go to Daily Living every day, religiously. Never has my attendance been so regular. I rejoin the Leisure Group, go faithfully to Psychodrama, go upstairs to crafts, downstairs to the yard, upstairs again for rehab counseling.

"You're very busy," Silas says to me. "Meeting, minding, plotting, planning."

"So?"

"You are too busy to hear the dying fall. But I hear it. I have the power."

"I don't understand what you're saying, Silas."

"Oh."

"Explain it to me. I promise I'll listen."

"I'm sure you would. That is your calling."

"Explain it to me."

"I don't want to talk anymore. All the energy is draining out of me in words. I mustn't talk anymore."

Silas sits on his bed. Calmly he watches me pull up my bed sheet, throw the blanket over it, center the pillow. He nods his approval. I pull off my T-shirt, sail it across the room to the pile of laundry accumulating at the foot of Philip's bed. Silas watches its flight, craning his neck around, smiling delightedly like a child.

He turns back around. I am sitting naked on the edge of my bed. His smile vanishes. He stares at my genitals. I can feel the heat of his gaze.

"What's wrong, Silas?"

"Anyone can harm you," he says. His voice trembles so violently that it sets off alarms into the air between us. "Women are safe," he says. "Inside, secret, hidden. Men are vulnerable."

I cover my burning genitals with the cool sheet. There is no sound in the room except the sound of my breathing. I hold my breath, listen to Silas's breathing, regulate my breathing now to his. In and out. In and out. The sound is easier, lighter. In out. In out.

Silas lies down on his bed. 'In and out,' he thinks. 'In and out. I am lighter. In out.'

I wake in the middle of the night to find Silas beside me. He has pulled a chair up to my bed and sits curled up, a thin blanket pulled around him against the chill.

"Silas!"

"Shhh," he silences me, motioning to Philip and Walter.

"What's the matter?" I whisper.

"What I can do is recognize the true artist," he whispers back at me. "I know instantly. They are very few. But it doesn't matter. For each of them lights up the world. That is all that matters to me."

I pull myself all the way up in my bed. My heart is pounding so loudly I am afraid it will wake Philip and Walter.

"Listen, Jesse, I am slipping further and further away. I can feel it happening. I am only here a very little part of the time now. Most of the time I am living in the kingdom inside my head, which I am not at liberty to tell you about." He laughs. He is sitting so close to me that I can feel his breath on my cheek. "It's not very interesting anyway—elaborate, but nothing you have not come across before in your extensive research."

He draws the blanket more tightly around him. But I can see he is sweating. His fine hair sticks to his forehead, long fine strands of wheat fall damply into his eyes.

"It is a terrible strain to go from one to the other. No one can touch me. Do you see? No one can enter the intricate confusion I have constructed. I am the supreme architect, the master builder. It is safe in my kingdom. If I Am All The Way There." He separates the words as if each one carried the meaning of a full sentence, as if each word had a coded meaning, a portent of its own. He rubs his palms with his thumbs as if they ached. First the right and then the left. "I can't be here too, Jay. Jay, listen. I will crack right down the middle."

"I don't want you to go, Silas."

"I am afraid of my thoughts, Jesse James."

"But it's the same for me."

"It's not the same."

"Don't go, Silas. You don't have to go."

"I want to," he says, a kind of ecstasy devouring his face. "I want to give in."

He stops. He has finished. He smiles at me with the calm authority of resolution. "You're shivering," he says.

Silas motions me to lie down. He stands up and arranges my blankets, pulls them up around me in a ferocious parody of maternal tenderness. He puts the blanket he has worn around him on top of me.

"Shhh," he whispers. "Go to sleep, Jay. Go to sleep."

The next morning Silas has disappeared. In his place is a very young boy. Every line on Silas's face has been erased. There is no wrinkle, no furrow, no mark on the perfect mask by which to chart the progress of a life. It is wiped away. The boy Silas will not talk to me. He looks through me, past me, as if I were invisible. Up and down the corridor he paces. Vacantly, he side-steps anyone in his path.

"Silas, please talk to me. Please."

"Leave him be, Jesse," Mrs. Morley says. "He doesn't know you're there."

"He does. I know he does."

"No, honey, he doesn't. He's gone for a while now."

I want to get out. Away from Silas's ghost.

Joel—Dr. Weisser—has left me. His six-month rotation is up, and he is now on 4 in Children. I see him sometimes on the elevator.

Dr. March, my new resident, is very big on charts and graphs and lists. The walls of his office are plastered with graphs, show-ing how much reading he can get done in X amount of hours if he takes Y amount of notes as opposed to Z amount of notes. He charts every event of his day in tiny upright letters on his calendar. I am down there—4:00 p.m.–4:45 p.m., Jay.

    4:45–5   jog home
    5–5:15   grocery shop. Buy starter for yogurt.
    5:15–5:30   unwind with beer and mail
    5:30–6   supper
    6–6:30   local news
    6:30–7   CBS news
    7–10   reading for Farber's lecture
    10–10:15   call Alicia about Sat. night
    10:15–10:30   send off for ski weekend information

10:30–11   exercises
11   bed

He is surrounded: by souvenirs from the drug companies—
paperweights, pen and pencil sets, notebooks, calendars; by
plants (african violets and several varieties of ferns); by pictures of Freud, Gandhi, Thoreau, Ben Franklin.

He leans across his desk, his dark eyes holding mine. The
intensity of his listening is agonizing. He absorbs himself in my
words till the boundary between us is erased. I have the feeling
sometimes that I am speaking through him or he through me,
like ventriloquists.

I know him at least as well as he knows me, barricaded there
in his office, staving off the demons with his idols—his pictures
and maps and calendars and charts, prescriptions for success.

The day of my discharge he shakes my hand, and I feel he
wants to embrace me and keep me there in his office, safe from
whatever harm the world might do me.

"You're going to be fine," he says. He blinks at me painfully.
"I feel you are. Don't you?"

"I'll be fine, Dr. March. Thank you a lot."

"You've been doing a lot better in the past month. Participating. Getting involved."

"Thanks."

"You mustn't get bogged down," he says. "Be active and live
simply."

"I'll try."

"Try as hard as you can. And avoid complications."

TWO

28

Dear Johnny,

I'm out. I came home to discover that Mr. Kaminsky has rented my apartment to two girls from the Midwest. He says he only sublet it with the understanding that they would have to get out when I came back. He told them I was traveling. I wonder if he thought I was gone for good this time. They have fixed it all up—chairs and a sofa and curtains and everything. I can't decide what to do about it.

Love,
Jay

Dear Johnny,

I couldn't do what you suggested so we are all living together here—Nora and Carrie and me. It's a little cramped but they were in a real bind and the company may be good for me.

Love,
Jay

Dear Johnny,

Nora has a regular job at a publisher's and Carrie is an actress—aspiring. She goes to acting classes and makes rounds. She was in summer stock last year in Rhode Island, and she has studied with a lot of famous people who think she really has "it"—"it" being what I don't have, I think.

Love,
Jay

Carrie is very friendly. She engages me in conversation about movies and books and records and doesn't seem put off by the fact that I don't have much to say, not having seen a movie or read a book in quite a while. She looks at me a lot and smiles as if we share some secret. If we do, I don't know what it is.

This morning Carrie stood up to pour coffee for Nora and me. As she bent over my cup, her robe fell open at the top and her small, round breasts were staring me in the face; her nipples almost brushed my chin. She pretended not to notice, absorbing herself in the coffee pouring as if it were a task requiring absolute attention. I flushed and felt a sharp pain in my lower side. "Unnhh," I said, I thought to myself, but evidently not because Carrie put her hand solicitously on my knee and said, "Are you okay?"

Nora gave me a cool, even look from across the table through a hole in her English muffin, her green eyes glinting at me. What's her message?

Carrie and Nora grew up in the same small town in Iowa, went to the same high school, different colleges, and then came to New York together.

Carrie was born in Iowa. Nora was born in Mississippi somewhere, but her family moved to Iowa when she was ten. Still, something southern clings to Nora. I can't say what exactly. She has no accent to speak of but a certain lulling fullness, a hesitation at the top of a word that drives me crazy with nostalgia for long dappled summer days and girls in swinging cotton dresses and Dr. Peppers and whiny guitars and red dirt roads, though I've never been south of Missouri. Carrie's voice, on the other hand, is neutral. I'd rather listen to Carrie talk because I can listen to what she's saying. When Nora talks to me, which isn't that often, I fall into a reverie.

When the three of us walk down the street together, our rhythms are out of kilter. I am way out in front. Carrie skips to keep up, jostling against me every now and again. Nora dawdles behind.

"Wait," Carrie says, when we get to the corner. "Wait for Nora." She smiles at me, unblinking. The parts of Carrie's face don't fit together. She has the pouty, sexy mouth of a starlet and the jaw of a commandant. There is a strange fixity in the center of her milkmaid eyes. She always seems to be looking dead ahead, like a horse with blinders.

"C'mon, Nora," Carrie calls out.

Nora looks at me sideways as she gains the corner. Her eyes are green as sea water and as unfathomable. She is simple as dirt and as dark and layered and mysterious. Above all, she is wary.

Carrie leans on my left arm, Nora dangles on my right, as we dash across the avenue. Carrie Nora. I like them both around me. A pinch of this one, a dash of that one. The soup is thick and murky, but warm and nourishing.

When the three of us are together, Nora and I rely on Carrie to facilitate conversation between us. When Nora and I are alone, which is seldom, we barely speak. Yet I have the feeling that if we could once begin we would never stop.

Saturday morning, Carrie left the house right after breakfast for an audition downtown. As soon as she walked out the door, Nora and I fell silent.

Nora looked beautiful. Her chestnut hair was piled on top of her head and a few loose strands fell around her face as she bent over her coffee cup. Her skin is dark, but there is nothing olive in it. It has a burnished glow, reddish, like the lights in her hair.

"Carrie told me you have some Indian blood."

"A little," Nora said, smiling at me. "Some great-great-grandmother or other. Carrie likes to tell people that. She thinks it makes me interesting."

"You look a little Indian. Your skin and your cheekbones. You have very high cheekbones."

Nora poured the last little dribble of coffee from the pot into her cup. "No more coffee."

"We could make more."

"No, it's fine. I don't really want any more."

We fell silent again, gazing into our empty coffee cups. "Well," I said finally.

Nora looked up expectantly.

"I hope Carrie has some luck today."

"Oh. Yes. Me too," Nora said. "She's made rounds every day this week and now Saturday too."

"Carrie's persistent."

Nora looked straight at me. The green of her T-shirt intensified the deep green of her eyes. "Yes, she is."

"Do you think she's good? Is she a good actress?"

"She's always competent. It's clear Carrie knows what she's doing on a stage."

"That's all?"

"No. That isn't all. When Carrie's on stage, she works so hard at it that you want to believe her."

"But you don't."

"No. Most of the time I don't."

"Oh. Well, I've never seen her act."

Nora leaned forward across the table. "I saw her do something once," she said, suddenly animated. "An Off Off Broadway showcase thing. I don't remember what the play was. I don't remember anything about it except Carrie. She had a small part, an old woman looking back over her life. Carrie didn't have on makeup or a costume. No one did. But she was that old woman. She lit up the stage."

"I've never seen you excited about anything before."

Nora looked at me strangely. I couldn't tell whether she was offended or pleased. "She carried everyone with her. She was powerful."

"Powerful."

"Are you surprised to hear that?"

"It makes me understand your friendship better. She's your best friend, isn't she?"

"I understand Carrie and she understands me." Nora reached out to the sugar bowl and ran a finger around and around the rim. "Carrie likes you."

"Do you?"

"Yes, I do. But I don't know why. I don't know you. I don't know who you are or where you come from or what you want. You seem to me to be drifting."

"What do you mean?"

"You're not working, and you never even talk about getting a job."

"Lots of people don't know what they want to do with their lives. I don't get the feeling you do, in fact."

"You're right."

"Your job doesn't seem to matter to you. At any rate you don't talk much about it. Not like Carrie does."

"My job has nothing to do with me. But that's not what I'm talking about."

"What are you talking about?"

"When you found Carrie and me in your apartment, you didn't kick us out. I was glad, of course, but I felt it would've been the same no matter who you found here."

Nora stopped abruptly and looked away. She fiddled with the hairpins at the back of her head, and a clump of silky hair fell loose. She scooped it up, securing it again, then took out another pin and went through the same procedure.

My mouth was suddenly very dry.

"It's as if you're always waiting for someone else to make a move."

My heart pounded painfully in my chest. "You're wrong," I said, and I reached across the table and I kissed Nora.

The table was too wide to accommodate our kiss. Straining to connect across the table, we held on to each other's arms, trembling with the effort to keep our awkward balance.

We broke apart, breathless and flushed, still holding on to each other's arms. We must have sat like that for three minutes, staring at each other, neither of us saying a word, when Carrie's key turned in the door.

I let go of Nora's arms, jumping up from the table with such force that the coffee cups rattled on the wooden table.

"Carrie." I called out, as she walked in the door. "You're back so early."

"I know."

"We were just talking about your audition. You look beat. Doesn't she look beat, Nora?"

"I'm all right," Carrie said, taking off her coat.

I took Carrie's coat from her and threw it on the couch. "I'll get you some coffee. Sit down and have some coffee."

"There isn't any more," Nora said.

"I'll make some." I grabbed the coffeepot from the table.

"I don't want any," Carrie said wearily, slumping into the seat I had vacated. "Sit down, Jay. You're making me nervous dancing around like that."

"I'm just anxious to hear about your audition," I said, sliding into the chair between Carrie and Nora.

Carrie folded her hands on the table and gave me a long look.

"How did it go, Carrie?" Nora asked.

"I never got in the door. They closed out the audition after the first twenty-five people."

"But that's not fair," I protested.

"I'm sorry," Nora said.

"Thanks, Nora. Actually, it wasn't a complete disaster. The woman in line ahead of me told me they're casting for a soap commercial Monday. The casting director is a friend of hers, and she thinks I'm just what they're looking for."

"I still think they should've warned people in advance that they were going to do that," I insisted. "I'll tell you what, Carrie. We'll all go out to a movie or something later. That will cheer you up."

"Okay," Carrie said, smiling for the first time since she came in. "That would be fun."

"I'll pass," Nora said, sliding her chair back. "I have some reading to do for work. Excuse me." She walked back to the bedroom.

"Well, you don't mind if we go, do you?" I called after her.

"Don't be ridiculous," Nora called back.

Three days later, Nora announces she wants to leave. "I found a place on Fifty-ninth Street," she tells me.

"But why do you want to go?"

"I'm not into this."

"What?"

"This threesome."

"I wouldn't call it exactly . . . I mean, it's not a threesome."

"That's right. It's a twosome. That's the point."

"I don't see that. There's no twosome."

"I've already talked to Carrie, and she sees my point."

"She does?"

"Yes."

"Maybe I should move out."

"It was your place to begin with. Why should you move?"

"Well, I don't know. I don't want to break up your friendship."

"Carrie and I are very different. We get more different all the time."

"You sound so cold sometimes."

"I'm not cold."

"I know. I know you're not. Don't leave now, Nora."

"Do you mean that?"

"Of course I do. Yes. I mean everything seems okay just like it is."

"Forget it."

"What? Forget what?"

"Never mind. I'll see you. I want to pick up cartons from Mr. Sanchez, and I have to go give my deposit money. I'll be here till the end of the week."

"Oh. Okay. Sure. Stay as long as you like."

When Carrie came home from acting class, we talked.

"I wish Nora wouldn't go," she tells me. "It's been so nice with the three of us together."

"She said you saw her point."

"Well, I do and I don't. It's silly."

"What?"

"She thinks—you know. That you and I are . . . she feels uncomfortable."

"Oh."

"I told her it was all in her head."

"Mmm."

"I feel guilty about it. We've been friends for a long time."

"You're very different."

"You think so?"

"Yeah."

"Do you think Nora's mad at me?"

"I don't know, Carrie. No. She didn't seem exactly mad at you."

"Nobody's forcing her to go. Maybe I should move out."

"You don't have to do that. I mean you're welcome to stay as far as I'm concerned."

"I am?"

"Sure."

Nora is leaving at the end of the week. Her belongings are stacked in grocery cartons in the living room. They give the room an unaccustomed look, foreboding and festive. Anything can happen. Catastrophe hangs in the air, and we are all very up. Everything is heightened, extraordinary to us now. We are giddy, bursting with energy. On top of the cartons go piles of Nora's clothes; her plants are out of the window and sit on the floor beside the cartons. Her multicolored quilt is bunched up on top of her records.

As the days dwindle down to a precious few, we become increasingly hilarious. None of us can sleep. We whisper back and forth in the night, excited, conspiratorial—three musketeers.

We moved Nora into her new apartment this morning.

Nora and I sit like lumps on a mattress on the floor, watching morosely while Carrie rips open cartons, thrusts dishes into cupboards, books and records onto shelves, clothes into the closet.

"You don't have to do that, Carrie," Nora says glumly. "I'll do it later."

"Just sit there and relax. I'll get you in shape," Carrie says, gathering handfuls of newspaper and stuffing them into the emptied cartons. She sings in little fits and starts, under her breath, as she bustles and hustles around the room, raising little clouds of dust. "This is really a great apartment. It's much nicer than our place."

Nora yawns bleakly and slides further down on her spine. Her T-shirt rides up, exposing her belly button. From where I sit, it looks deep as a well. I could stick my finger in it clear to the first joint. Carrie nods her head toward Nora and smiles indulgently at me. But it's an effort for her. Her smile is ragged. I smile back weakly. Well, that's it. No way I can stick my finger in Nora's belly button. Carrie and I are sharing an indulgent, conjugal smile. I'm trapped. But I can't seem to think of anything to do about it.

When Nora guides us to the door, Carrie starts to cry. "I feel so sad all of a sudden. I'll miss you, Nora. Are you going to be all right here?"

"I'll be fine," Nora says coldly.

Carrie crushes Nora in a bear hug. "Please come see us."

To my surprise, Nora hugs Carrie back. "I will," she says. "I will, Carrie."

I press Nora's arm, which is circling Carrie, hoping she will read in my urgent touch all my desire, my sorrow, and my helplessness.

Coming home from Nora's, Carrie and I are suddenly awkward with each other. We keep a discreet distance between us as we walk stiffly down the street away from Nora's. When some children playing stickball in the street jostle Carrie against me, she jumps away as if she had been stung. "Sorry, I didn't mean to bump into you."

"That's quite all right," I say, almost bowing. "Do you think we should take the bus or walk?"

"Whatever you think."

"It's up to you, Carrie. Either way is fine with me."

"We wouldn't have to go back—unless you want to," she says.

"I don't want to. Unless you do."

"No, no, that's fine. What do you think we should do?" She looks up at me, walleyed.

Down the street, ahead of us, I see a movie marquee. *Two for the Road*. Providential. "Let's go to the movies," I say.

"Oh, that's a great idea." She is uplifted and revived. "I've been dying to see this. Haven't you?"

The movie does wonders for us. Laughing and crying together in the darkened theater, we relish the difficulty of loving. If Audrey Hepburn and Albert Finney can stick it out, maybe we can make it too. We'll love each other bittersweetly, grow wry and sly and real together. How I long to grow jaundiced with my own true love. Oh, boy. Thank God for the movies. I slip my arm around Carrie, and she leans against me, warm and sweet.

29

Carrie absorbs me into her life as easily as she absorbs the oxygen in the air. I go with her to acting classes, and she waits in line with me for my unemployment check. On Tuesdays and Thursdays I pick her up from work—she works part time at an actors' answering service and ushers at an experimental theater downtown. We shop for food at Mr. Sanchez's grocery on the corner. We cook together, eat together, play poker together, listen to records together, go to movies together.

We sit up far into the night, smoking joints and drinking herb tea or wine, talking about our pasts. Or rather, she talks. I listen. Though half the time I find I've lost track of what it is exactly she is saying. Still, I ask question after question to keep her talking so she won't ask me about myself. I can't seem to get the hang of talking. In the middle of telling some involved story, I go blank, as if I had sprung full-grown from a closet with no past at all, no memories.

I now know that she is an only child of parents who divorced when she was three and that she grew up in a small farming town, raised sometimes by her mother and sometimes by an aunt and uncle. She got hooked on movies when she was twelve and knew she was going to be an actress. She keeps up a voluminous and largely one-sided correspondence with her mother, her father, the aunt and uncle, two or three high school friends, and three or four college friends. The only time we are not sharing an activity is when she's writing her letters.

She knows that I have a younger brother somewhere and that I have been in a mental hospital. Well, what could I do? I had to give her something and that was all I had.

She had just got through telling me how lost and crazy she felt when her father, after having been gone ten years, appeared one night out of the blue at the house where she and her mother were living. Carrie was thirteen. They sat in the kitchen and Carrie, in a sweat of longing and confusion, watched her mother and father eyeing each other grimly over their beers. Then they disappeared into the bedroom, and a half hour later, her father reappeared, kissed Carrie on the forehead, and said, "Watch out for your mother."

"I didn't know if he meant it as a trust or a warning," she told me.

Then he was gone, and that was the last she has seen of him. When she tried to talk about him to her mother, her mother only said, "He's something of a loser, you might say."

My telling Carrie about the hospital proved to be a turning point in our relationship. Her blue eyes glazed with tenderness, and she pulled me to her and hugged me fiercely and touched my face, the way they do in movie love scenes. I felt very stirred when she did that. I kissed her. She moaned softly and said my name, and that's the way it went. We made love on the floor. After, lying there on the floor with her head on my shoulder, I looked at her. How small and tidy she is—muscular but round and so firm that she reverberates like a drum skin if I tap her. Which I did. I ran my hand over her small, hard, nuggety breasts and when she turned on her side, I fell head over heels in love with her behind, so surprisingly large and high-rising, glinting at me warmly in the yellow lamplight.

"I love you," I said, talking really to her behind.

She turned and smiled her open smile at me. "I know you do," she said, lifting herself onto my chest. "I knew it all along."

"You did?" My heart simultaneously sank and soared. I felt that I should be making an effort to sort things out in my mind, but sleep overcame me right there on the floor, with Carrie's head on my shoulder, her hair in my nostrils, her arms wrapped around me, and one muscular leg thrown over mine, grounding me.

She always sleeps like that, with both arms wrapped around me and one leg thrown over mine. If I stir in the night, she is instantly awake and alert. "Are you all right?"

"I was just turning over," I say. "Go back to sleep."

The rhythm of our days is languorous, although Carrie is a believer in activity like Dr. March. We plan excursions to various points of interest in the city, go for long walks in the park, attend a steady stream of free lectures and concerts.

Mr. Kaminsky watches our comings and goings approvingly. "You're getting out a lot these days. It's good for you. She's a lovely girl, Jay. She has zing."

She has zing. Zing to spare and a spectacularly beautiful behind. But as the months flow by, one into the other, I become increasingly uneasy.

30

Dear Johnny,

The more we throw ourselves into the city, the less it seems to touch us. It swirls and rages around us, and we walk through it in a dream. Nothing impinges on us—good or bad, ugly or beautiful. We sail through the fire and don't get burned. Like those holy men from India. It's getting me down.

Love,
Jay

Dear Johnny,

I dreamed that Carrie and I lived in a hothouse in the middle of the city. The glass walls are so beaded with sweat that we can't see out. There are no windows and no doors. We have no nourishment, no water, no air.

Love,
Jay

Dear Johnny,

We are starting to look alike. Tonight we got out of the shower; we were drying each other off. I caught sight of us in the mirror. Both of us naked and steamy, dripping onto the tile floor. I couldn't tell who was who. Our features were blurred and our sex too—all a fuzz of pubic hair and rosy skin. What do you make of it?

Love,
Jay

· · ·

Boredom stalks me. I drag him with me through the subway turnstile. He hangs on to my peacoat, sweeping along behind me.

'You are so bored you could scream,' he whispers thickly in my ear.

I am so bored I could scream. *Agghhhh.* Fortunately the roar of the oncoming train obliterates the sound of my scream. But Boredom is undaunted. He will keep at me. Sooner or later, he figures, I will scream in the elevator of a department store, at the counter of a coffee shop, in the men's room at the movies. I take to wearing a wool scarf of Carrie's which I can stuff into my mouth when I feel a scream coming on. This tactic raises a faint smile from Boredom. If anything, my feeble maneuver only spurs him on. He schlepps along behind me, stepping on my heels. 'I got time,' I hear him mutter to himself.

Carrie has plastered the walls of our living room (formerly my living room) with pictures of people who, she says, inspire her. Pablo Picasso, Pablo Casals, Jack Kennedy, Martin Luther King, James Dean, Walt Whitman, and three unidentified Indian gurus. They make me nervous. They smile, sigh, yawn, smirk, ogle, sneer. Who knows what's on their minds?

I talked to Carrie about the pictures. "I think they're plotting against us."

"Nothing I care about is valuable to you. You think I'm some dumb hick, don't you?"

"No, I don't."

"Do you love me?"

"Sure. Yes. Sure I do."

"I love you. If you want me to take the pictures down, I will." But the pictures are still there, and I never said anything more about them.

.   .   .

In the bedroom on top of our dresser is a yellowing photograph of Carrie's mother and father taken six months after they got married. They are turned sideways to the camera, slouching in an easy, arm-encircling embrace, grinning up at each other. The first time I saw it I was startled to see that Carrie gets her sexy starlet mouth from her father and her sturdy jaw from her mother.

We are never apart. It makes my blood boil. Still, if I were bolder I would sit on Carrie and bolt the door to keep her from going to work or making rounds. She is gone for hours and hours. Days it seem go by with nothing to do but snoop around the apartment, hunting for clues.

I sit on the toilet and watch her freshly washed underpants swinging lightly on the line strung over the tub. Bikinis, strewn with delicate flowers on some thin, transparent material. Drying, they give off a sentimental lavender smell. Maudlin and effusive.

Hot on her trail, I lift the lid off the hamper and draw out a pair of her unwashed underpants. I sniff at them, an old hound dog closing in on its prey. Ah hah. Just as I thought. The lavender is a cover-up, a subterfuge. The genuine article smells acrid and angry. Vindicated, I throw the soiled pants back into the hamper.

By now the contents of the medicine cabinet above the sink are as familiar to me as the Pepsi jingle, but I feel compelled to sneak a peek anyway. Cucumber cold cream, avocado shampoo, gold bobby pins with a few fine strands of yellow hair clinging to them, a box of baking soda to brush our teeth with (Carrie says it's better than toothpaste and cheaper, of course). Carrie's blue toothbrush and my yellow one. Both soft bristles because Carrie read that hard bristles grind off tooth enamel. She threw out my old, hard green toothbrush and bought me this yellow one.

All's right with the world in this medicine cabinet. It is conspicuously positive, the only fly in the ointment being my rusted razor and a bottle of Valium I keep on hand, just in case.

I close the cabinct with a gloomy bang, unnerved as always by all that clamoring boldness.

I continue my safari into the living room, where I squat in front of the low bookcase, reading the titles of Carrie's books, which I have already read several dozen times. Each time I read them over, I sink into a stuporous depression, but I keep going back. World Atlas, Webster's Seventh Collegiate Dictionary, Roget's Thesaurus, Bartlett's Quotations. Several books on yoga. Three paperbacks on astrology. Collected works of Walt Whitman. A biography of Beethoven. Several plays by Arthur Miller. Two books by Stanislavski and one about him. *New York on $5 a Day*. Peanuts paperbacks, *Eat to Live, Don't Live to Eat, Walden, How to Improve Your Vocabulary in Two Weeks, Beyond the Drug Experience, Sexual Bonding: The Joy of Love.* Inside almost all the books Carrie has underlined significant passages in red pencil.

Eventually she will draw those careful red lines under me, if she has not already. I wish she were here so I could hold her and keep her safe, stop her from drawing those red lines.

31

Dear Johnny,

Maybe I will marry Carrie. She knows the city like the back of her hand. We spend days and days and days roaming the streets, holding hands in fruit markets, along the docks, on Forty-second Street. We go to museums, to Central Park, to Riverside Park, to indoor concerts, outdoor concerts, Central Park Zoo, Bronx Zoo, Botanical Gardens, to the movies, Sam Goody's, bookstores. We eat in coffee shops, in Nathan's, in little French restaurants, little Hungarian restaurants, Jewish restaurants, Chinese restaurants, Lithuanian, Cuban, Mexican, Greek, Puerto Rican restaurants. We window shop on Fifth Avenue, Third Avenue, St. Mark's Place. But I have this sinking feeling. I think I've seen the movie.

Love,
Jay

Dear Johnny,
I went with Carrie to her acting class today to watch her do a scene. Usually I bring a book and sit outside in the anteroom.

She was Maggie in *Cat on a Hot Tin Roof* and she was in a slip and she was all charged and fiery, bitchy, creamy-looking. Her nipples standing out like crazy. All her classmates and the teacher were turned on to her, and I could hardly wait to get her home and fuck her. But she knew. "You want me because everyone else did. You want Maggie." And that made me really want her because sometimes I think she doesn't see anything and then when she does I think I really love her.

Love,
Jay

Carrie's past is under our bed in an old steamer trunk. It rises up at me, clogging my pores, filling my nostrils with must and melancholy.

Cautious as a thief, I lift the lid of the trunk. There it is, her past, neatly filed in manila envelopes and file folders with typed labels. Each of her serious boyfriends has his own envelope with his name inscribed on the front. I open "Pictures 1955–57." Carrie in a formal strapless dress with a corsage pinned to her breast falls out at me, smiles jauntily. And here is Carrie at a picnic in blue jeans, a sweat shirt, and sneakers, holding up a hot dog, squinting at the camera because the sun is in her eyes.

I stuff the pictures back into their envelopes and force myself to look down into the open trunk. It is an artful selection. Only the good is here. Love letters, honors, certificates of merit, invitations to parties, diplomas, love poems inspired by her, glowing summer stock reviews, pictures of her mother and father grinning at the camera before Carrie was born. A massive, incontrovertible accumulation of evidence testifying beyond a shadow of a doubt that Carrie is loved, Carrie is smart, Carrie is honored, Carrie is talented, Carrie is happy, Carrie exists.

Dear Johnny,

Carrie is writing another seven-page letter to her father. He never answers her. Neither does her mother, except for an occasional postcard from Nassau.

Once in a while she hears from her Aunt Betty. The last letter from her aunt said: "Uncle Bob is doing much better, but he tires easily. How are you, dear? I hope fine. It's nice to hear your acting teacher thinks you have talent. Uncle Bob and I think so too. Acting is such a hard life. I'm sure I could never do it. I'm very happy you have a boyfriend. He sounds very nice. What does he do? You didn't mention in your letter. I made a lovely peach cobbler yesterday. You remember how Uncle Bob always loved them. Well, you could dig into them yourself as I recall. I hope you are eating all right in New York. I talked to Mrs. Cassel on the phone yesterday and she asked after you. She thinks you are so pretty. She says Nanaline is moving to Syracuse because Joe got a new job at the college there, and she is expecting in the fall sometime. Well, I must close now and get supper started or there'll be trouble in the ole corral. You should plan to visit us sometime real soon. Uncle Bob would love that. He talks about you a lot. You could bring your boyfriend if you like. Love, Aunt Betty."

I love her right now. She is so absorbed in her writing. Her head is bent over the paper, and her hair catches the light. She is wearing a work shirt of mine. It's way too big for her—it's sliding off one shoulder. Her mouth is open and she's taking short, intent breaths. Little beads of sweat stand on her forehead as she bears down on her pen, writing furiously as if she had only a little time before someone would stop her and say, "That's all. Time to turn in your blue book."

I wish he would write her. She says he will. She says she knows he will. But what if he never does? The difference between Carrie and me is she can pretend forever.

Love,

Jay

32

As the weeks pass, Boredom gets bolder. He now rides me piggyback. I have become, needless to say, a semicripple.

'You're starting to look like an old man,' Boredom remarks, feigning concern.

'Drop dead,' I snap at him.

'I'll ignore that because I know you don't mean it. You need me.'

'I don't need you. You're crazy.'

'You think you're a smart boy because you can draw fine lines, diddle with analogies, muck around with images and symbols.'

'I need a new act, that's all. I've got a million new wrinkles, a zillion variations on a billion themes.'

'Big deal,' Boredom drones in his earnest deadpan. 'It all ends up a whine.'

Dear Johnny,

No, I am not working. I told you. I can collect unemployment for another couple of months. You're worse than Carrie on the subject.

I know they worry about me. I will write. I promise. Do you want a carbon copy so you know I did it?

Love,

Jay

Dear Mom,

Nora dropped by. I told you a little about her on the phone. Remember? It's the first time Carrie or I have seen her since she moved out. It caught me off guard. As you know, the unexpected makes me sick. My tongue swells up, the blood roars in my ears, and I twitch like a rat in a trap. Nora and Carrie didn't seem to notice anything, though.

It was a stirring sight. The two of them in raggedy cutoffs and faded T-shirts, giggly and flushed, hugging each other, twining arms. From my corner lookout, I watched them plop on the sofa, crosslegged and facing each other like Indians, knees touching. It made me feel sulky and horny and well they knew it. They are in cahoots against me. I can feel it with the tip of my penis, which sends me messages of collusion and conspiracy.

Women are crafty, as you well know.

I think I'm in love with Nora, but I am serious about Carrie and am thinking of marriage, as I hinted

over the phone. I would like for you and Dad to meet
Carrie. You won't like her at first but she grows on you.

Love,

Jay

I keep thinking I see Nora. I run after women on the street I
think are her. When I catch up to them, I am always astounded
to see how little they resemble her. I walk away quickly, my
ears ringing with embarrassment, sick at my loss and weak-
kneed with relief.

> Dear Sirs:
> I saw your advertisement in *TV-Screen Secrets*
> (which I don't usually read, but it was left on the seat
> I took in the bus). It seemed like the answer to my
> prayers. Would you please send me my copy of *16,000*
> *Natural Responses for 8,000 Situations*. I need to know
> what to say to Nora if I should happen to run into her
> on the street. Also what I will say to Carrie if I leave
> her for Nora, or if she leaves me for Nora or if I ask her
> to marry me. Or she asks me or I ask Nora or Nora asks
> me. I must be ready. As you pointed out, it is so im-
> portant to be ready with the right response, otherwise
> life passes you by, as I know only too well. Although I
> rehearse all my responses religiously, it never falls out
> that the response I have rehearsed is the one that is
> called for.
> Enclosed is $5 in payment. I will expect the book in
> plain brown wrapper by return mail.
>
> Cordially,
> Jesse James

Last night I did see Nora. I was crossing Seventh Avenue
and there she was, looking beautiful in a cream-colored dress
that made her dark skin glow under the street lights.
"You look wonderful. You're all dressed up."
"I'm coming from work."

"Where are you going?"

"Home."

"Let me come with you."

"You're with Carrie."

"I'm not with her now. Please, Nora. I want to talk to you."

We stopped at the bar across the street from Nora's to get a drink. When we walked into the small, dark, slightly shabby room, the bartender waved at Nora. "Hey, Nora, how you doing?"

"I'm fine, Mickey. How are you?"

"No complaints," Mickey called out cheerfully, as Nora and I slid into a booth. "A Bud for you?"

"Please."

I signaled Mickey to make it two. "He's friendly."

"It's a neighborhood place," Nora explained. "Everyone knows everyone here. There have to be places like this in this insane city, otherwise we'd all kill each other."

"You must've had a bad day."

"My day was all right."

"Are you sorry I ran into you?"

Nora shook her head.

"You just don't like New York."

"I don't belong here," she said passionately.

"Where do you belong?"

"In the country, where I came from."

"You mean Iowa?"

"No. I mean Mississippi."

"Maybe I'll take you back there someday."

Nora just looked at me and, for a minute, I thought she wasn't going to say anything. Then she reached across the table and touched my arm. "I'd love that."

"They don't seem to do a thriving business," I said, looking around the small room. Except for Nora and me, there were only four other customers, one of whom, a middle-aged man in a grey suit, was playing pinball in the corner.

"It's too early," Nora said, leaning back against the padded booth. "It picks up around seven."

"You don't come here by yourself, do you?"

"Sometimes."

"And the rest of the time you come with a date?"

"Is this an interview?"

"I want to know if you're seeing someone."

"I'm seeing some people."

We were interrupted by the appearance of Mickey with our beers. "You're looking good, Nora."

"Thanks, Mickey. This is Jay."

Mickey stuck out a big paw for me to shake. "Nice to meet you. Any friend of Nora's et cetera."

Before I could reply, Mickey was off to greet a new customer. Relieved, I continued my questioning. "Are you seeing anyone in particular?"

"No, Jay. No one in particular."

"Good." I took a long swallow of my beer.

Nora laughed. "You remind me of my father with the third degree."

"Didn't he trust you?"

"I don't know. He never talked to me. He just asked me questions."

"What about your mother?"

"My mother wanted me to get married and settle down."

"Why didn't you?"

"It was never right."

"Do you think it ever will be?"

"Are you planning to call Carrie?"

"I'll call her before we leave. Do you think it ever will be right?"

"What are you going to say to Carrie?"

"You got good at handling the third degree, didn't you? I'll tell her I ran into an old college friend and we're out drinking."

"You're very facile."

"One of my residents in the hospital said the same thing. Dr. Weisser. He said I was dangerously facile."

Nora drained the last of her beer. "I think he was right," she said soberly.

"Do you want another?"

"No, I'm fine. That's the first time I've heard you talk about the hospital. Carrie told me about it, but you never said anything to me. I thought maybe you didn't want me to know."

"It's not that. I just don't talk about it much."

"What did you do there?"

"I specialized in data collection, storage and retrieval."

"You're not bad at handling the third degree yourself," Nora said.

"I want to tell you about it. It's just that I don't know what to say."

"Do you ever see any of the people you knew there?"

"No. There are people I'd like to see again. Gemma and Hamilton and Willy and Luis and the Princess. And Silas. I dream about Silas sometimes."

"Is he still in the hospital?"

"I think so. He got very crazy right before I left. I'd spent more time with Silas than I had with anyone in the hospital and he wouldn't talk to me. He'd look right through me as if he didn't know I was there."

"But he wasn't always crazy?"

"No one is always crazy. Especially not Silas . . . Listen," I said, easing out of the booth, "let me go call Carrie and then we'll get out of here." I didn't give Nora a chance to respond. I went to the back of the room and called Carrie on the pay phone. I told her I had run into an old college friend and we were out drinking and I might spend the night at his place.

"Why can't you come home?"

"Well, I might. But I haven't seen this guy for ten years, Carrie. We've got a lot to talk about. We may be up till four or five, and I won't want to push for home at that hour."

"All right," Carrie said dully.

"I'll try and get home. I may be able to."

I hung up the phone and hurried back to Nora. "C'mon, let's go. I want to buy you some flowers. Do you think we can find a florist still open around here?"

I made love to Nora in her narrow bed and it was all I had wanted it to be. But afterward she seemed restless and distant. I asked her questions about her job and she answered me. But it seemed to me her mind was somewhere else. She yawned and moved uncomfortably as if the weight of my arm across her middle was oppressive to her, so I let her out of my embrace and we lay apart staring at the ceiling. After a few minutes, Nora leaned over to look at the clock on the table by her bed, and I felt she wanted me to go.

"I guess I'll go then," I said, hoping she would say, 'Don't go. I don't want you to go.'

But she didn't say anything. Not a word. She just lay in the bed watching me as I sat up and pulled on my clothes.

Nora and I are perpetually missing each other. She is sailing up one escalator while I am plunging down the other; she is stepping off the bus just as I step on; she comes blinking out of the early show as I fork over my $2.50 for the late show.

We are together seldom, no more than twice a month at best, but she is with me, more with me now than Carrie, who is seldom without me. Nora whispers in my ear, tugs at my shirt, pulls me to her, then slips away.

JAY: I can't get hold of you.

NORA: It's you who disappear.

JAY: You don't trust me.

NORA: You assume I want you to leave.

JAY: You judge me cryptically, in snatches of poems
and restless sighs.

NORA: You pretend not to judge me.

JAY: You don't touch me.

NORA: You pretend to touch me.

JAY: Your boredom accuses me.

NORA: Your melancholy oppresses me.

JAY: You will leave me.

NORA: You have already left me.

33

Carrie has made of our apartment a citadel, a fortress. Provi-
sions are stockpiled, stored up in every closet, overflowing
every cupboard. Toilet paper, rolls enough to last us through
seasons of diarrhea, tubes of toothpaste to last us till our teeth
rot, bars of soap stacked to the ceiling, row upon row of deter-
gent lined up in formation. Shampoo, razor blades, shaving
cream, dental floss, paper towels, Clorox, Woolite, Kleenex,
Tampax, Kotex, aspirin standing watch. Vitamins A, B, C, D,
E, lecithin, iron, kelp, and in the kitchen every conceivable
variety of canned food, which we never eat as Carrie disap-
proves of canned food except for tuna fish. Dishwashing liquid

in massive unbreakable bottles, hammer, pliers, nails. We are self-sufficient. Everything we could need in this world is stored within these four walls. In the event of catastrophe we are secure, supplied to the hilt. Still Carrie cannot rest in peace; new shipments arrive weekly, are jammed into corners, stuffed onto shelves, crammed into drawers. Compelled to her mission, Carrie stands guard, defending perpetually against the spaces of need, the powers of darkness, deprivation, and emptiness.

I am bored to tears. My tears fall soundlessly on the ground, soaking into the pavement. My tears fall all over everything. They splash down on the shoes of passersby, run into the gutters. They moisten Carrie's cheek and dampen Nora's T-shirt. They turn Mr. Sanchez's grapes sodden and make a soggy paste of Mr. Kaminsky's Sunday *Times*. They flood the bathtub, spill over onto the tile floor, and drip into the apartment below.

Carrie has lined up a job for me. Ushering two nights a week at Carnegie Hall. An actor friend of hers is leaving in a week.

"Who is this guy?"

"His name is Keith. What's that got to do with anything?"

"Keith who? I never heard you mention him."

"Keith Clay. He used to date Nora."

"How could she be serious about somebody named Keith Clay?"

"I didn't say she was serious about him."

"Was she?"

"Why are you dragging Nora into this? You need a job. You should be thanking me."

"Thank you."

"You've only got a month to go on unemployment."

"I said thank you."

"I've been avoiding Mrs. Kaminsky because I'm afraid she's
going to ask about the rent."

"We're only a week late."

"Don't you want to work?"

"Certainly I want to work. Do you think I like being cooped
up in this fucking apartment?"

"I'm not cooping you up."

"I'm sorry. You're right. You're right about everything."

"Sometimes I think you hate me."

"No, I don't. I don't hate you, Carrie."

Carrie strains against me. Sinews, tendons, muscles, bones bearing down on me. I can't breathe. She lets go. She is melting,
dissolving, open and spreading, vast as infinity. I drive into her,
forcing her to cry out.

She is shrinking, becoming smaller and smaller. Tiny and
lost, she lies beside me, hiding against my chest. I feel strong
and remote, passionless. I am omnipotent and gentle. But her
transformation alarms me. I can't take care of you. I shove her
craven smallness from me. I can't help you. I can't.

I am in love with the dance I do to make women love me. I am
a marvel, an acrobat such as you have never seen, tumbling,
jumping, bending, swaying. And when I have won, sweaty and
red-faced, I am peevish and fretful. I hear the melancholy ladies
sniveling in the wings. *Boo hoo* they lower the boom. Thick
crepey curtain of guilt, tripping me up in its intricate folds. I
inspect each seam with the finest-tooth comb, I worry the
pleats, gnaw at the tucks. I lash myself with each worn-out
thread.

Aaaah. Aaah. Aaah.

I have exhausted myself in my efforts to make them love me.

Now, in the nick of time, comes my reward. Nothing. I feel nothing.

Dear Johnny,

Lately it doesn't matter how ingeniously I position myself—curled up in the drainpipe, crouched under the bed, swinging from the TV antenna—everywhere I contrive to hide I see myself in countless mirrors.

Today, for example: There I am rolled up in Carrie's sodden Kleenex, which she is tearing into tiny flakes. Lady Macbeth, because she cannot find the picture we had taken of us together in the country.

"Carrie," I say halfheartedly, "we have other pictures of us."

"It's not the same. It's not the same," she wails, as she lunges through the room, overturning chairs, hurling pillows, uprooting plants—hunting for the picture. "This one was perfect. It's the only perfect one. There will never be another."

Falling in tiny wet flakes to the floor, I seek with her encapsulation of the one, the supreme moment, and am bereft as she at its loss. We had the picture to prove it was real, and now it's gone. Give it back, give it back. I need it to ward off the blues, to comfort myself, to show to my friends. See, see, see. You can't deny what's right in front of your eyes, plain as day.

Whenever I see Nora, I am in her eyes: cold beam searching out the fatal flaw, reconfirming endlessly the immense space between the dream and what she finds to shatter it with. I am in her eyelids which shade the fear, hooding the flickering vulnerability.

And then, just last night, Johnny: I was resting in the mailbox on the corner and the little door opens and I see a small grey woman, a stranger, yet I know her well. She holds her letter in her hands, scanning the address three times in a row to make sure she has it right. She moves to throw it in, falters, and stops. She opens the envelope carefully so she can reseal it, takes out the letter. I can read her lips as she mouths the words to herself, "Hit the road, Jack, and don't you come back no more no more no more no more." Trembling, she reads it through again and again. With each reading, it becomes more impossible. Tears are starting in her pale eyes. She crumples the note in her hand. Feverishly, she rummages in her small grey purse and pulls out a pen and paper.

I whisper up at her out of the mailbox, sotto-voce like a thief or an actor: "Dear Jack, I'll do anything for you, dear, anything. Yes, I'll do anything, anything for you." She takes it all down, scribbling furiously, seals it in the envelope and shoves it in. She smiles abjectly into the box and shrinks away into the night.

Her letter hits me in the corner of my eye and leaves a nasty paper cut that, who knows, may scar me for life.

At this very moment, Johnny, I am peering over your shoulder as you read this and with you I am simultaneously sighing, laughing, weeping, snorting, disgusted at the rantings of

Your brother,

Jay

One by one, my friends and acquaintances are dropping like flies. I have only to say hello and their eyes glaze, their spines sag, and they fall to the ground. Mr. Sanchez has only to look at me and his mustache droops, his knees buckle. The sardonic Latin keels over his fruit bin, squashing his tender berries.

34

There is something seriously wrong with my head. It has swollen to five times its normal size.

The rest of me seems to have shrunken. Although this is possibly an optical illusion caused by the disproportionately large size of my head. In any case, I am in bad shape. My balance is shot. I tip backward or forward, pushed by this great buzzing weight of my head. My body, it seems, has grown so small that it can't ground itself; it flies up after my head, pitching now this way, now that. All this, as you can imagine, has caused me to fall on my head several times, which naturally increases the swelling and thus the chances of falling again. It is a vicious circle.

Clearly the best place for me is in bed. Though it's difficult to lay my head in a comfortable position. Sideways is best. Not good, but it will have to do.

It is a warm summer night and the windows are open. Lying in bed, I hear buzzing. Buzzing inside my head *zzzz zzzzzzzzzz zzzzzz*. Hoards of flying insects—flies, no doubt. I leap out of bed, grab the nearest magazine, and go at them, swatting wildly. But I see now they are not flies, not mosquitoes; they are words, or something akin. They swarm over my head, darkening the air, swooping low and furious.

They are not flies but they are germ carriers nevertheless, infectors of diseases worse than malaria or dysentery. They have nothing to do with thinking, clarity, resolution, action. Turning in on themselves, they circle wildly. I swat at one clump and instantly they regroup somewhere else. I can swat at them from here to eternity and they will not be done in.

One stormy, flashing, summer night, while Carrie is out rehearsing Nora in *A Doll's House*, the real Nora flies in the bathroom window. Dropping her jeans, naked except for cowboy boots with dazzling spurs, she speaks not a word but goes straight to her work. She lifts me out of my rocking chair, throws me onto my and Carrie's bed, and makes love to me as I suppose I had always wanted to be made love to. Her green eyes are somber as she bends me, plies me, teases me, tosses me, covers me, hurls me, digging her spurs into my complaisant flesh. I sigh and moan and turn and shy and whinny and whip my head. She reins me in hard, riding me on, heaving and pitching, her crop in her hand.

Lathered in sweat, my eyes are bulging. But I can't get off. I can't get off, hard as I try.

Finally, she dismounts, her green eyes flickering. She stands over me, naked and gleaming. 'I was going to ask you to come away with me, but I see now it's impossible.'

'What do you want of me?'

'I want someone to tell me what to do,' she says, shading her eyes, which are brimming. For an instant, I think she is going to rest her weary head on my shoulder; if she does I will soften, I will melt, I will be transformed. But some fear, some barrier rises in me, crystallizes, stiffens my shoulder till it is angular and hard, inhospitable for a head to lie on.

'But it ain't you, Babe,' she says. She turns her gaze full on me to pronounce the final sentence. 'No, no, no, it ain't you, Babe.'

'It ain't me you're looking for,' I acknowledge, but I'm not certain she heard me because when I look up she is gone.

Carrie and my mother appear in the room. 'What's going on? Who was that masked stranger?'

I turn away from them, my face to the wall. Carrie bends over and pulls a small, smooth, cylindrical object out of my asshole.

'What is it?' my mother asks her.

'A silver bullet.'

When Carrie came home, I was sculpting little figures out of the organic peanut butter and she knew immediately, with that strange intuition that women have, that something was up.

"What's happened?" she said.

"Nora dropped by."

"I see."

"Carrie, listen, I have something to tell you."

"I forgive you."

"What?"

"I forgive you for fucking my best friend. I love you and I forgive you."

"I don't want to be forgiven," I moan, flattening one of my peanut-butter sculptures in my anguish.

"That's tough. I forgive you, I forgive you, I forgive you."

"You can't do it if I don't want you to."

"I can too. You can't stop me. I forgive you, I forgive you, I forgive you. So there."

Boredom sleeps with me now, lies smack on top of me, breathing his foul breath into my face. Naturally, this new turn of events has disrupted my sex life. Carrie's eyes roll back in her head when I kiss her. Nora dozes off just as I penetrate her. All this seems to afford Boredom a certain pleasure. He is thinking of becoming my lover. He croons love songs to me: 'Your skin is yellowing. You smell of ashes. Your pretty head is stuffed with sawdust.' I am bored to death.

35

The dream sea rages. Massive walls of black water rise around me. Huge, curling, icy waves crash against my fragile bones, booming in my ears. I will be drowned. I know I will be drowned. Dragged against the black rocks, dashed to pieces by the waves.

But the sea is more mysterious than I give her credit for. Suddenly she lunges forward, sweeps me up on the back of a green, foaming wave, and tosses me high, flying in the air.

The next thing I know I am washed up on the beach—a startled fish, bloated and white, flopping on the dry white sand. Now what?

Dear Johnny,

I never told you that Mom and Dad came to see me every time I was in the hospital. Of course, I know you knew, but I never told you. I never told anyone. They came quite regularly. Silas refused to see his mother when she came. I never refused. I would sit with them in the dayroom, fielding questions like fly balls, looking over their heads.

"How are you, Jay?"

"Fine. I'm fine. This peach is terrific, Mom. We don't get fresh peaches. We get canned peaches in heavy syrup."

"What can we do? Is there anything we can do?"

"Not a thing really, Dad. We got up a petition asking for fresh fruit but nothing came of it. And now I'm pretty much resigned to canned fruit."

The doctors and nurses knew they came to see me.

It was noted on daily charts and discussed in staff meetings. My various residents during all my stays always wanted to talk about it. So I let them talk.

But just to show you how it really was, Mrs. Alton, the old night aide who'd been there for a hundred years, used to say to Mr. Frazer when I went by, "That poor boy. His mama and daddy never come to see him. It's a crime the way the folks of some of these poor children do them." And I'd always feel very sad when she said that.

Love,

Jay

Dear Johnny,

I built my church on the rock of the past and, lo and behold, the rock is not a rock but some terrible substance perpetually changing shape according to the slant of the sun, the tilt of the moon, the angle of my shadow.

Love,

Jay

36

The transfer agents have come for Silas.

"Silas!" I wake with a start. My head is throbbing and I have a stabbing pain in my chest. The room is light. I sit up to look at the clock on the little table next to the bed. It's two in the afternoon. I remember. I took a nap. Carrie is out somewhere rehearsing something with Keith Clay. I sink back onto the bed, drifting down again into a restless, murky, twilight sleep.

Luis follows the old men down the hall, shaking his head and muttering in Spanish under his breath, as bits of curling plaster from the decrepit ceiling fall around his head. He spots me sitting alone at a table in the dining room in the house we lived in when I was little. He makes a beeline for me. "You didn't have to sign your life away," he tells me, gesturing urgently. "Nobody asked you to do that."

"Yes, they did," I insist. "I'm sure they did. It was the only way I could get my credentials." More and more plaster falls down as we speak. Big chunks drop from the ceiling, grazing the side of my head as they fall.

At this point my father bursts out of the kitchen carrying a birthday cake. "How did you know it was my birthday?" I ask him, astounded by this turn of events.

"I know a lot," my father says.

He sets the cake down on the table. Luis guides my shaking hand as I cut the first piece. Suddenly, Hamilton and my mother pop out of the middle of the cake. A hunk of falling plaster conks my mother on the head but she doesn't seem to notice. She and Hamilton glide into each other's arms and proceed to do a tango on the tabletop. And, all the while he is dipping and bending over my mother, Hamilton is addressing an impassioned speech to me—in Latin for some reason, so I can't understand much of it. But I can tell from his lively expression that he's encouraging me to do something.

I'm starting to feel tremendously uneasy. Great chunks of the ceiling are falling down on us. Apparently I am the only one who understands that we are all going to be buried if we don't get out of here. Hamilton gives me his blessing: "Sexus, plexus, nexus," he intones, smiling like a cherub, and I scream with terror as the ceiling gives way.

The apartment is shrinking. The ceiling has lowered to the point where I must support it with my head. The walls are inching inward, protruding oddly, waylaying me as I plot my way cautiously from one end of the room to the other, taking care not to trip over Carrie as she tiptoes around me.

"We need a bigger place," I shout at her.

"We need money for that," she says sullenly. "We don't have any money."

"Are you accusing me of something?"

"I'm just telling you we don't have any money, Jay."

"I'm working now, thanks to Keith Clay. What more do you want of me?"

"If I get that tomato-juice commercial, maybe we could do it."

"You're a dreamer, Carrie. You just keep making rounds, making rounds, and nothing ever comes of it. It's just like writing your father. You write and write and he never answers you."

She brushes past me, stiffening, stomps over to the refrigerator, yanks it open, and starts to rearrange the bottles and jars, the little bowls covered with Saran Wrap.

"There isn't even room in here anymore," she moans hopelessly, staring into the depths of the refrigerator, overflowing with leftovers. She slams the refrigerator door and her potted begonia bounces off the top of the refrigerator and crashes to the floor.

Carrie bursts into tears. "You ruined my begonia."

I come up behind her, put my arms around her.

"What's the matter with everything?" she sobs.

"It'll be fine, Carrie. We'll just put it in a new pot. Everything will be fine. Really it will." But I know it's not true, for even as I hold her I can feel that the walls have moved in another inch, and the ceiling is weighing now on my shoulders.

Carrie tosses and turns all night, thrashing in the sheets. Every straining of her muscles, every involuntary jerk of her legs

enters into my own body, into my own fitful sleep. She moans
and grinds her teeth, grinding into me.

I sit up in bed and look down at her. The sheet is twisted up
around her waist, and her thighs and stomach are damp with
sweat. Her jaw is clamped shut, and her eyelids are puffed over
her closed eyes. She looks like some small woods animal caught
in a trap.

I don't recognize her. She has gone away from me into her
own nightmare. Angrily, I force my hand between her legs,
prying them open. Open sesame, goddammit. Open and let me
in. She starts and pulls away from me, but she is not yet awake. I
put my hand on her stomach, gently this time. I stroke her firm
belly, and with my other hand I disentangle the sheet and pull it
out from under and around her. Slowly I bring my hand down
to her thighs, softly brush her with my fingers. I can feel her
muscles loosening. Her jaw goes slack and her mouth opens
slightly. She is only half-asleep now. I can tell by her breathing.
I put my hand between her legs again, pressing gently, searching her out with one finger. "There you are." She moans a little,
opening her legs for me. "There you are." Slowly, slowly. She
strains against me, lifted slightly off the bed, her breath coming
short and fast. But I will not be moved. I am orchestrating this
comeback. Slowly, slowly. It is excruciating. I stop and she
makes a sound and again I move my finger the tiniest fraction
of an inch. She tightens up like a fist. I bend over her, pressing
my face down to hers. I watch her, watch her coming back to
me, watch it washing over her till she is spent. She opens her
eyes.

"What were you dreaming?" I demand of her, moving my
hand away at last.

"I dreamed you left me."

I am tired of me. I am weary of myself.

37

On the crosstown bus on my way to work, I run into my land-lord, Mr. Kaminsky, sitting in the back of the bus gazing dreamily out the window, nibbling a candy bar.

"Penny for your thoughts, Mr. Kaminsky."

"What? Oh, Jay. Hah. How do you like that. Weeks I don't see you and we live in the same house, and now of all places I see you on the bus. Sit. Sit." Mr. Kaminsky is a natural-born host, even on the bus. "Can I offer you a piece of a Hershey bar?"

"No, thank you. I just ate."

"Ah, well. So, where are you off to?"

"Work."

"Twenty hours a week now, Mrs. Kaminsky told me. An usher at the concert hall. Wonderful, Jay. Really, that's won-derful."

"Yeah, it's okay."

"All that great music you hear absolutely free for nothing."

"That's true."

"And you could work up to something else—a manager or something like that. In a tuxedo. Carrie would be very proud of you."

"She got me the job. An actor friend of hers was leaving and told her about the opening."

"How is Carrie, if I may inquire?"

"She's fine."

"Mmm. I'll tell Mrs. Kaminsky. She thought Carrie looked a little washed out lately."

"Mrs. Kaminsky has her ear to the ground apparently."

"Women have their sources. Who knows? I don't try to figure it out anymore."

"What don't you try and figure out?"

"Anything, dear boy. My wife, Carrie, you, rent control, the crosstown bus. It's all mysterious. And that's that." He finishes off his chocolate bar, chewing with satisfaction. "To tell you the absolute truth, Mrs. Kaminsky is hoping you and Carrie will get married."

"Uh. Well . . . "

"Shhh. Don't say a word. I told her, what business is it of yours? Mind your own beeswax, as Mr. Sanchez would say. You want to know how she answers. She says she'd be a very 'limited' person if she only minded her own business. She says her interest in other people 'widens her horizons.' Wonderful. How does she think up things like that? And so fast. Rolls right off her tongue." Seeing I have grown silent, Mr. Kaminsky says, "Don't be offended, please, Jay."

"I'm not offended. I'm nervous."

Mr. Kaminsky pats my knee. "Well, you were always a little nervous. Probably you will always be a little nervous. Anyway definitely you should not get married till you are ready, forget what anyone tells you."

"I will."

"Ho ho. Not bad. Oh, that reminds me. I almost forgot to tell you, you had a visitor the other day. I asked him wouldn't he like to wait for you, come in off the stoop, have a cup of tea. But he said no, he couldn't stay."

The skin on the back of my neck tightens. "What was his name?"

"He wouldn't leave a name. He said, I remember it exactly, 'He's not expecting me,' and then he smiled and said, 'No, undoubtedly he is.' "

It was Silas.

"A remarkable-looking person."

"He didn't leave any message?"

"No. Nothing. He was fair-haired, almost flaxen, and fine-featured. Mrs. Kaminsky stuck her head out to see who I was talking to. She thought he was remarkable-looking too and she only got a peek. She said he looked under the weather and over the rainbow at the same time. So, I'm talking your ear off, and here's my stop coming."

He won't come back. "Are you sure he didn't say anything else?"

Mr. Kaminsky looks at me oddly. "No, Jay, I just told you. Have a good evening . . . Good evening, Jay."

"Oh, good evening to you, Mr. Kaminsky."

Nora meets me Wednesdays and Fridays after the concert. Carrie doesn't know about it. It started six weeks ago. I was running to catch my bus after the concert and caught Nora instead. Tonight she grabs my hand and leads me down Fifty-seventh Street, steering a smooth course through waves of concert goers.

"Sometimes I love this city," she says excitedly. "Bright nights like tonight when you can feel all this energy all around you."

"Listen, Nora, I just ran into Mr. Kaminsky on the bus, and he told me Silas came around looking for me. Where are we going, by the way?"

"To the river. To the East River. Silas is the one you were telling me about in the bar? The one who got so crazy?"

"Yes. It's a long walk to the river, Nora."

"It's a nice night."

"What if he doesn't come back?"

"Who?"

"Silas. Who have we been talking about?"

"Didn't he leave an address or a phone number where you could reach him?"

"No. Nothing. No message at all."

"He wouldn't have come by in the first place if he hadn't wanted to see you, Jay. He'll probably come by again."

"I don't know that. I don't know that at all. Nora, I can't walk all the way to the river. I told Carrie I'd be home around one."

Nora drops my hand. "Go home then. You shit."

"Dammit, Nora, I'm upset about Silas."

"It's always something, Jay. You always have some reason."

"I don't want to go home, Nora."

"You don't know what you want."

"I want you."

"Then leave Carrie."

"I can't, Nora. I can't do it. It makes me sick to think about it. I can't stand it."

"You've ruined us, you know. Do you know that?"

"Don't say that. Please. You make it sound so final."

"I'll never trust you."

"Yes, you will. You will."

"I'm going to stop seeing you." She starts to walk again, striding furiously down the street. "I swear I will do it, Jay, if you don't make up your mind."

"I will. I will, Nora. I promise."

Cut. Cut. This scene oppresses me. I can see the unhappy ending a mile away.

While Nora and I continue to jabber at each other under the marquee, on top of which I am now cowering, I will quail and retch. When I am crazed with remorse, I will dump Carrie and move in with Nora, bringing with me an unreasonable facsimile of Carrie and a vial of guilt, sticky and sulfurous. Whenever Nora moves toward me, which will be seldom since she doesn't trust me, I will hoist Carrie on my back and take a deep snort from my vial. These activities will render me impotent. Whenever I move toward Nora, which will be seldom since I long ago decided she cannot love me, she will stumble on the catalog of my deficiencies, which she has piled up with painstaking care on the bedroom floor, falling backward out of my reach into the open closet.

It makes me desperately sad to see how it will end. I must warn them of what lies ahead. I shout down to them. But they don't hear me.

I see them down there. Nora is blunted and Jay is exhausted. They have worn themselves out. They kiss each other under the marquee and nothing happens, which each takes as a bad sign to wonder about.

38

Silas is waiting for me when I get off the bus. "I figured you took this bus."

"Silas!"

"Your landlord told me where you worked and what nights. It was this or the subway."

"I ran into Mr. Kaminsky just tonight on my way to work. He told me someone came by. I knew it was you."

"I've been here almost two hours."

"I was with Nora, this woman. We meet each other Wednesdays and Fridays when I get off work."

The electric wash of the street light throws Silas's face into sharp relief. He is watching me watching him, his grey eyes level.

"I was afraid you wouldn't come back, Silas."

"Well, I'm here."

The last time I saw you there was nothing in your face, Silas. No sign of recognition or fear or age. Nothing.

There are lines in my face now. Deep lines trailing out from the corners of my eyes and mouth.

Yes, I see them. I feel them wrap around my heart.

"Do I look that bad, Jesse James?"

"No, no, it's not that. I was just thinking. Aren't you cold in that thing?"

Silas throws me a long, mocking glance as if to say, Is that what you were thinking?

"You're wearing Luis's sweater," I say lamely.

"Yes."

"Remember when his wife came to give it to him and it was swimming on him, and we all razzed him after she left?"

"I don't remember," Silas says.

"Sure you do, it was the same week David went to the state hospital."

"Was it?"

"You're going to freeze in that thing, Silas. Don't you own a goddamn coat? I can't believe you don't have one lousy coat to your name."

"Why are you babbling, Jay?"

We start down the block. I'll wait for him to say something. But I can't keep my resolve. "How did you get out of the hospital?"

"I eloped on a pass."

"Do you think they'll be looking for you?"

"Not very hard."

I can see now he hasn't gained back all the weight he lost before I left the hospital. "They think I'm losing weight," he told me then. "But it's atrophy. Some vital organ is atrophied."

"You're still too thin," I blurt out.

"You're still too thick," he says benignly, stepping off the curb onto the broad avenue.

I laugh, relieved. Why am I so anxious? He seems okay. He's probably at least as okay as I am.

Silas seems to sense my relief. "Don't you want to know how things are on five?" he asks lightheartedly.

"How are things on five?"

"The same."

The light changes. Silas darts ahead of me, weaving and bobbing across the avenue, in and out and around the rushing lines of trucks and cabs and buses, all coming at different speeds, bearing down on us. He looks like a basketball player, dribbling up center court, bobbing and dodging, confounding everyone with his speed. He could have been an athlete, I think to myself. If things had been different. A runner, a skater, something like that. An irate driver honks me out of my reverie, and I run for the corner. Silas is waiting for me.

We tramp down the block, falling automatically into a matching step. Had a good wife and I left, left. It's a nice night for walking. The wind gusts at our backs. My old nylon jacket billows out behind me. I feel invigorated. The muscles in my legs tingle pleasantly. We are young, after all, Silas and I. There are days and days and days ahead of us. A profusion of days piled high, like the buildings rising around us. The streets are emptying now as we walk west. The city belongs to Silas and me.

"Gemma sent you her regards before she left," Silas says, jumping suddenly into the air, dropping an imaginary basketball into an invisible hoop. He recovers the ball, dribbling down the block.

I stop short. "Before she left?"

Silas executes a fast turn, raising the ball over his head. "According to Hamilton, she left her boyfriend or he left her, and three weeks later she quit work and left the city. Ready?" Silas tosses the ball to me. "Hey, Jay. You gotta keep your eye on the ball."

"What did she say? Did she say anything about me?"

"I forgot how single-minded you are," Silas says, leaning across me to drop the ball into the gutter.

"What did she say?"

"We gave a goodbye party for her. I didn't go. But she came back to the room to find me. She said she wanted to tell me goodbye and would I give you a message if I saw you."

"What was the message?"

"She said she couldn't think of one. She started to cry. She looks terrible when she cries. Her eyelids puff up and her nose swells and her face turns purple. She apologized for shredding Kleenex on the floor. C'mon. Let's walk. I'm getting cold standing here."

I follow him down the street. "Is that all?"

"I can see I made a mistake not taping it for you."

"Tell me."

"So she apologized for shredding Kleenex on the floor. And I said, 'Why should I give a shit? It's not my floor.' And she said, 'Well, goodbye then, Silas.' She shook my hand solemnly. So I said, 'Goodbye, Major. Good luck in your mission. All the lads will be rooting for you.' And she laughed and laughed and laughed. I could hear her all the way back down the hall. That's it. Verbatim. I left nothing out."

"You don't think she's gone for good, do you?"

"People go away. You can't keep everyone."

We turn the corner, walking straight into the wind. The exuberant wind, the wind I loved, has turned cruel. It blows hard at us, whipping off the Hudson River. A drunken couple weaves their way down the block, coming toward us. They are laughing. The woman smiles up at the man as they pass between Silas and me. Why can't I be happy like that? "They look so happy," I say when they have passed.

"They look drunk."

We walk in silence. I can see Silas's watery reflection in the windows of the stores we pass, superimposed over a display of naked mannikins holding a sign—CUT RATE. MUST SELL. LADIES' WINTER FASHIONS; over bottles of booze stacked high, dizzying pyramids of bourbon and scotch in Ray's liquor store.

"How are you, Silas?"

"Cold."

'He doesn't know you're there, Jay,' Mrs. Morley told me two days before my discharge. 'He doesn't know you're there.'

"I couldn't stand it when you didn't know me, Silas."

I've made a mistake. Silas speeds up so abruptly that I have to run to catch up with him. When I get abreast of him, he drops his head, fixing his eyes on the pavement. "Francine sucks."

"What?"

Silas points with his foot to the graffiti chalked on the sidewalk ahead of us.

"Oh. Hah. Yeah."

"Cocks or lollypops? Which do you suppose, Jesse James?"

"I don't know," I say miserably.

Something in my voice checks him. He looks up at me. "How are you, Jay?"

I seize his question ardently. "It will take me hours to tell you everything."

"I don't want to know everything."

"There's Nora and Carrie," I begin.

"And Carrie and Nora."

"How did you know that?"

"You're not hard to figure out, Jesse James."

"It's complicated. It's gotten so incredibly complicated. No matter what I do, I hurt someone. Just tonight with Nora . . ."

"Do you want to go on a trip with me?"

"What?"

"Do you want to?"

"Wait a minute. I don't understand."

"What don't you understand?"

"You're throwing this at me out of the blue."

"You have responsibilities," Silas prompts.

"Well . . . "

"A steady job, a little woman. Two little women."

"C'mon, Silas. You know perfectly well what I mean."

"I know exactly what you mean."

"Where are you going to go?"

"You're not going to come, are you?"

"I don't know, Silas. Where are you going?"

"Are you going to make your decision on the basis of where we are going? Never mind. Don't answer that. I'll be back tomorrow night. I'll wait for you at that same bus stop. If you want to come, meet me there, ready to go. I'll wait from eleven-thirty to midnight. Like a story. That should appeal to you. If you're not there by the stroke of midnight, I'll disappear."

"That doesn't give me much time to decide, arrange stuff."

"It takes you five years to decide if you're going to shit in the morning."

"Okay, okay. Tomorrow night."

"Good night, Jay."

"Don't you want to come up and meet Nora? I mean Carrie."

"I don't want to meet either of them."

"Have you got a place to stay?"

"I'll be here tomorrow night."

"What if I decide not to go? When will I see you?"

"I don't know."

"But I will see you again, even if I don't go?"

Silas waves his head ambiguously, then wheels around heading back in the direction we came from.

I roll around in the bed, hanging on to my sleeping Carrie for dear life, dragging her with me from one corner of the bed to the other. I would like to chew on her gold hair. Ingest her. In her sleep she struggles to get clear of me so she can breathe. Nora, Nora. I am consumed with longing for Nora, remembering our last vacant kiss under the movie marquee on Fifty-seventh Street. Carrie grunts and pushes at my overbearing hip. I pull her back to me, stay her with my arm. Know me, Nora. Can't you know me beyond what I can show you? If she were here right now, I would bear righteously down on her. Must she have proof of everything? I wish Johnny would call me. What time is it in California? Three hours earlier. Eleven p.m. He could tell me what to do about this trip. Should I go or stay? I could call him right now but that would require getting out of bed and letting go of Carrie, neither of which I am prepared to do.

'What are you prepared to do?' Gemma asks me. She is sitting on the maroon armchair catty-cornered to the bed, throwing bits of Kleenex at me.

'Hey, watch it.' I remove my arm from Carrie, and she rolls to the wall. I sit up in bed. 'You left without telling me. It never occurred to me that you would leave.'

Gemma pitches the last of her Kleenex at me and settles back in the chair. Why doesn't she say something?

'I hear your lover dumped you,' I say sharply.

Gemma nods. 'In desperation, exhaustion, and to even up the score. But most of all to fulfill the prophecy I tattooed across his heart the first day we met.'

'Why does that make me so sad?'

'You're thinking of you and Nora, Jay.'

'Yes.' I slide my hand under the covers, warming it on Carrie's toasty rump. The heat seems to be making me drowsy. 'Silas said you're leaving the city. Where are you going, Gemma?'

'Through self-pity, rage, loneliness, through pain.'

'Spain?' I yawn, letting go of Carrie's bottom, sliding down in the bed. 'I'd love to go to Spain.'

'There's more,' Gemma whispers. 'Much more. More than you or I have ever dreamed of. There's terror.'

'Terror?' I push myself up again with some effort. I am really very tired all of a sudden. 'That's it?' I manage to say. 'The bottom line is terror?'

Gemma leans forward in the old chair. 'No, no, no. There's light somewhere. Clear sight and reclamation of the power I gave to others to wield over me. And somewhere there's glove.'

'Glove?' Did she say 'glove'? I sink down again into the bed.

'Love,' Gemma says. 'Love.'

'Oh. I seem to be drifting, Gemma.'

'What are you going to do, Jay?'

'I don't know. I really don't know. I'm confused. And my eyelids are so heavy.' Holding them open is a terrible strain. Maybe I could just let go of the right one. I do and it drops down heavily, like a stone. I stare at Gemma out of my left eye. 'You don't believe I'm suffering, do you?'

'I gotta go, Jay.' Her voice is muffled and very far away, as if I heard it through layers of sand. 'I put a sleeping potion in the Kleenex I threw at you, so you should sleep the night.'

39

I am up before the sun, sniffing at the new day. I smell spring. Coming in at the window. Unmistakably spring. March is going out like a lamb. It is a sign. I must see Nora. Right away. I disentangle myself from Carrie, who sleeps like a baby, curled up, her thumb resting on her lower lip. Almost in her mouth. I pull on my jeans and scribble a note to Carrie, which I leave on the kitchen table: "Gone to do errands—groceries, etc. See you later."

The dawn sky is white, fresh as a soft, washed sheet flapping in the breeze. It's going to be sunny. Sunny and mild. Something good will happen today. I stop at the corner in front of Mr. Sanchez's grocery store. It is after all too early to go barging in on Nora on a Saturday morning. And I would feel better if I legitimized my note to Carrie. Also I am hungry.

As soon as I open the door, the rich, ripening melons and bananas, roast chicory, oranges, sawdust from the storeroom assure me I was right to make this stop. The store is empty at this hour, cool and fragrant. Mr. Sanchez looks up from his Spanish paper. His handsomeness delights me. Everything in his dark, seamed face is generously proportioned—big, soaring nose flaring out from under the ledge of his broad forehead. Huge, humorous black eyes sunk beneath high, wide cheekbones.

"Good morning, Mr. Sanchez."

"You on the lam, kiddo?"

"What?"

"It's not even seven yet. I never saw you so early. I naturally supposed something was up."

"I am up, Mr. Sanchez. Very up. It's a great morning. A beautiful morning."

"Well, well, well. In that case, buenas días."

"Do you mind if I cop a banana?"

Mr. Sanchez shakes his head. "Please do. My bananas are perfect today."

He's right. The banana is perfect. I chew on it thoughtfully, relishing Mr. Sanchez's generosity and the sweetness of his fruit. How lucky I am to have such a wonderful store on my corner. "I need a few things."

Mr. Sanchez grins at me. "Whatever you need, I can give you—forty percent fewer cavities, relief from nagging backache, toilet paper so strong you can build a bridge with it." He leans over the counter, confidential, conspiratorial. "I can brighten your smile, move your bowels. I can make your breath kissing sweet."

I grab a carton of orange juice from the dairy case, open the spout, and start guzzling, plunking fifty cents on the counter.

"O.J.," Mr. Sanchez snorts. "Could I interest you in some freeze-dried coffee?"

"No thanks. I don't like instant coffee."

"You say that now, but you are still young. I give you three years, maybe two."

"I'll need eggs and milk and one of those long rolls. I guess I should stop back on my way home and pick all this up. I'll get some oranges and . . . Hey, you wouldn't happen to have any CrackerJacks, would you?"

"What a lucky so-and-so you are. A lucky son of a gun."

"You have them?"

"As it happens, I got some in only two days ago. They are not easy to come by anymore. Sometimes you can get them and sometimes you can't. If you go to a baseball game, you can almost certainly get them. But just at your little neighborhood bodega, it's no longer an accomplished fact that you can get them." Mr. Sanchez heads toward the back of the store to get me my CrackerJacks.

"I just felt like something crunchy," I yell back at him.

"Please, don't feel you have to explain to me," he says, walking to the front of the store and handing the box to me. He watches me closely as I munch the gummy CrackerJacks.

"It's hard to swallow CrackerJacks when someone is watching you, Mr. Sanchez."

"I won't look."

I dig down in the sticky box searching for the little prize. Ah. Got it.

"What is it?" Mr. Sanchez asks me.

"It's a crystal ball. This is wonderful." I hold up the tiny plastic crystal to show him.

"Just what you need."

"But it is. It's exactly what I need." I am very excited by this turn of events. I knew this was going to be a lucky day. "I have to go. I have things to do. I'll tell your future someday, Mr. Sanchez."

"No thanks."

"If Carrie comes in, would you tell her I was here?"

"Okey dokey." Mr. Sanchez picks up his paper again.

I sail up Ninth Avenue, a little breeze bumping me along from behind. The sun is up now. The city is stirring, stretching, preparing to tumble out of bed and start the day. A few shop-keepers sweep the sidewalk in front of their shops, trucks rumble down the avenue, half-empty buses cruise along, and dozens of empty taxis fly by.

I hail a taxi, in love with their dashing speed and the daring drivers who maneuver them so skillfully.

"Where to?" The cabbie turns around.

"Hey. I know you. I've ridden in your cab before."

"Yeah? No kidding. Well, it happens."

"It's a good omen. I'm sure it is."

"Aggh sonofabitch, I missed the goddamn light. Now I'll be fucked all the way."

"I threw your concentration off. I'm sorry."

"Forget it. Where you goin'?"

"Fifty-ninth and Second. You don't remember me, huh?"

"Nope." He swings left onto Fifty-sixth Street, heading cross-town.

"It was a long time ago. You picked me up in front of Grand Central. I was looking for a job."

"Everybody's got to make a buck."

"How have you been since I saw you?"

"Terrible. I've got very bad bunion problems which is no fucking joke, let me tell you. Everyone thinks it's some big joke."

I feel suddenly cast down. "I don't."

"Yeah. Well, you're in a minority. Dumb shitheads."

"You haven't changed much, but you seem sadder. Or maybe I just didn't notice that before."

The cabbie leans on his horn, cursing the white Cadillac which has stalled in front of him. "Someday they'll put one too many cars in here and the whole fucking city will come to a halt. They'll have to airlift them out. And who is it screwing things up? The private car owners, that's who. Who needs a car in the city? Inconsiderate rich bastards. They'll be sorry when they're wedged in here like sardines, starving to death in their cars. And I'll be damned if I'll lift a finger to help them."

"I thought you were very brave, a hero of sorts."

"You get along the best you can, and in the meantime you don't let anyone fuck with you."

"Is that your final word on the subject?"

"Are you a wise guy or what?"

"No, no. No offense. I didn't mean anything. It's just strange seeing you again."

"Yeah. We gotta quit meeting like this."

The cabbie curves gracefully up to the curb, like a runner sliding in to home plate.

"Keep the change," I say, handing him a bill, grateful to him for the joke and his skill. "You have a sense of humor."

"I gotta lot of sides to me. So long."

He zooms off in a cloud of exhaust. The purity of the day is smudged by his black exhaust and by my uneasy remembrance of things past.

I didn't know Nora when I rode in that driver's cab. Or Carrie. A lot has happened since then. No. Nothing has happened really. Nothing has happened. It's all the same. It repeats itself over and over. It is the same now as it was in college, as it was in high school. The same with Debbie as it is with Carrie, as it is with Nora. And I'm still waiting for something to happen.

Dear Johnny, help, help, help. Where is he when I need him?

I can't stand on this street corner forever. I came to see Nora. To tell her . . . something. I walk halfway up the block to Nora's little red-brick building. It's quiet in the lobby. I sit on an aqua vinyl-cushioned, wrought-iron park bench, hoping to compose myself. On the wall behind me swans cavort in an aqua pool, underneath a pink sky.

I pull my CrackerJack crystal ball out of my pocket and gaze into its tiny milky depths. I see Nora. She sits straight as an arrow, austere and driven, marking in her ledger book with a pointed pen. With her left hand, she presses buttons on her tiny calculator, adding up the credits and the debits. There is a page for everyone she has known; a column each for injustices, failures, fissures, and a balance sheet where credits are subtracted from the total debit.

'How'm I doing?' I ask, kissing her on the back of her neck.

She stiffens, pulling away from me. 'You're in the red.' She looks up at me, grim but satisfied.

'Everyone's in the red,' I observe, leaning over her and leafing through the book. My fingers are trembling.

'What do you know about it?' She grabs the book away from me, pressing it to her heart. 'Who are you to come busting in here, criticizing what you don't understand?'

'I want to understand. Explain it to me.'

'It's too late. You've never tried to understand what I was feeling.'

'But that was before.'

'You are unspeakably naïve and horribly selfish.'

'You're very hard, Nora. You are too hard.'

Her green eyes burn with a cold, clear flame like the fire trapped in emeralds. 'I am implacable but scrupulously fair.'

'I'm going away for a while,' I tell her.

'I knew you'd run.'

'Oh, Nora, please. I didn't come for this. I came to love you. I do love you.'

'I want you to go.'

'I was so happy this morning.'

'Just go away.'

'Kiss me goodbye then. Won't you kiss me goodbye?'

'No.'

'Hold me then. That's all. Just hold me. For comfort.'

'It would be dishonest.'

She turns away from me, and the swans at my back float disinterestedly by. They don't care what visions I have seen in my CrackerJack crystal. Their future is assured. They will be preening on this wall when Nora and I are dead and gone.

The day is spoiled. There is no point in seeing Nora now. What was it I wanted to say to her? I am going on a trip somewhere. I don't know where. With Silas. I'm meeting him under a lamppost at midnight.

Out on the street, the herds are moving along. Git along, little dogies, git along. Shuffling off to the slaughterhouse.

Carrie will be wondering where I am so long. I should call my parents to let them know I'm going away. Fuck it. You should do this. You should do that. Stuff it up your ass, fuckhead. I'm going to a movie. I step out briskly, heading west, skillfully dodging the cows who threaten to trample me, flatten me, and leave me for dead on Fifty-ninth Street.

On Fifty-eighth Street, there is a rerun of an old James Bond. I duck into the cool, dark theater, pumped up high, ready for action.

But I have misjudged my mood. This is too brassy, flat, fast. It bounces off me, its hard amphetamine edges slick and cold against my clammy skin. I need a movie to loosen the sadness. A beautiful movie about true love. *Elvira Madigan*. She would have loved me. I need to cry myself to sleep. Sleep soundly, exhausted and peaceful, through the two-o'clock show and the five and the seven and the nine. I could stay in here forever, dreaming of Elvira.

Bond's wonder car screams down the mountain, while the gleaming guns mounted on the amazing breasts of his accomplice blast holes the size of hams in the sides of the bad guys.

No. Elvira would not love me. She risks all. And I, nothing.

The clock in the lobby says 2:10. Ten hours till midnight. A long fucking time. And anyway have I really made up my mind to go with Silas? Why should I go anywhere? It will give me the illusion of movement, of freedom. But that's all. It's not the real thing. Coke is the real thing. A murderous depression seizes me by the throat and drags me to my knees under the marquee.

I should have asked my taxi driver what he would advise. He's been around awhile. He must have figured something out in all this time. Or my father. I wonder what he knows. I have no idea. No idea what he would say to me.

The trash man kicks me to my feet so he can spear the candy wrappers under me.

If I hailed a cab, I might hit that same guy again. And that would be a sign of something. "Taxi." No, it's not the same guy. This man is thin and silent. Who is he? Ralph Wilson. Woolson. I can't read his hack license. He has a whole life that I know nothing about. He loves, hates, eats, kisses his children, makes love to his wife, drinks his orange juice and coffee, pisses it out, and none of it has anything to do with me. Maybe I ride right by his house in the bus on my way home from work; I look up and see the lighted window, dim figures moving up above me, and I ride right on by. But the figures go on moving and talking. Maybe he noticed the bus rumbling by underneath his window. Or maybe he didn't.

· · ·

When I arrive at the apartment, Carrie is trying on a new spring dress in front of the bedroom mirror.

The director notes my entrance. He is sitting comfortably on top of our dresser, leaning back in a director's chair. 'Okay, Carrie, you know he's come in, and you want us to know it, but not him. Right? Okay, keep looking at yourself in the mirror but there's this very slight adjustment in your expression. Raise the eyebrows, chin tilted up. See what that does to your face. You look haughty and a little hard.'

She does. It changes her face completely. I feel excited, seeing her like that.

The director signals me to say my line.

"New dress?"

"Yes." She turns her back to the mirror and looks over her shoulder at how good her sumptuous ass looks in the new dress.

"You seem very up about something," I say.

The director is pleased. 'Good, Jay. Just the right edge of irritation.'

Carrie looks levelly at me. Right in the eye. "Where were you all day?"

"I had a bunch of errands."

"A bunch of errands?"

The director leans forward in his chair. 'Menace. More menace. You're not building, you two. Build.'

Carrie tries again. "A bunch of errands?"

"Didn't you get my note?"

"Of course I got your note," she snaps. "You left it on the table."

"So what's up, Carrie?"

'Bad line.' The director is annoyed. He taps his foot on the dresser top, disarranging Carrie's little pots and bottles and pins. Who is he to come barging in here, criticizing my lines and messing up our bureau top? I want to quit this. I hate what we're doing. I hate it.

"I'm going out of town." Carrie smiles a haughty smile.

'Move a little, Carrie. Move. Not so stiff. Flirt with him, keep that dark edge, but flirty. Good. Okay, Jay. Go.'

"What did you say?"

"I'm going to visit Aunt Betty and Uncle Bob."

"Oh."

'Don't throw that "Oh" away, Jay. What is this? You were leaving her and now she's leaving you. Try it again.'

"Oh."

'Better. That's better.'

"Where did you think I was going?" Carrie asks.

"I don't know. How would I know?"

"I'm going to ask Nora to go with me." Carrie sashays around me, almost dancing; the skirt of her new dress sways around her legs.

I grab the hem of her skirt as she dips past me.

'Nice, Jay, but don't push it. We don't want to slide into melodrama here.'

"If you tear this dress, I'll kill you," Carrie snarls at me.

"Why are you asking Nora to go with you?"

"Why shouldn't I? Is there some reason I shouldn't ask my best friend to go with me on a little trip?"

"Don't give me that best-friend crap. You hate her."

"It's you I hate."

'Okay, break it up. Back off, both of you. This shouldn't be just angry. There's a subtle downbeat. Don't you hear it?'

I hear it. I hear it. I don't need you to tell me. I'm going down. Dipping, diving, sinking fast. "Nora won't go with you, Carrie. She won't go with you."

"You're planning to leave me, aren't you? You're going away. Were you going to tell me?"

"I'm not going to Nora."

Carrie slumps down on the old maroon armchair and hangs

her head down so her yellow hair touches the floor. "I think I'm going to throw up."

'No. No,' the director shouts.

"Me too. I want to throw up too."

'No, no. All that's gotta come out. Just keep hanging your head, Carrie. Now, Jay, don't say anything. Take your time, look at her. Wait. Wait. Now go over to her. One two three four five. Okay. You're sad, mad, afraid. One two. Now. Put your arms around her. Comfort her. Comfort yourself.'

I can't. I can't go to her. I can't move. "You'll be okay," I tell Carrie.

The director is miffed. He looks the other way, smoothing out a wrinkle in his corduroy jacket.

"I won't be okay. You don't understand anything."

"I'm only going for a while. With Silas. He's okay again."

'Who the hell is Silas?' the director barks at me. 'There isn't any Silas. You can't just throw in a new character whenever you feel like it.'

Carrie lifts her head. "What if I'm not here when you get back?"

"I don't know."

"What if I'm not here and Nora's not here and no one is here? Not even your precious fucking Johnny?"

'Good, Carrie. Good. You got him with that one.'

I stare at the director. You vicious shit. I'll show you. "I really like you in your new dress, Carrie. I like the way it clings to your hips."

The director is puzzled. He riffles through his script. He doesn't remember this part. I just made it up, you creep.

"You're crazy." Carrie drawls it out a little.

"I'm excited. There's a difference."

The director looks pained. 'Look, this sex thing. If you're going to do it, it has to be very subtle. All right? Don't bludgeon me with it. You can't pull it off. Don't try to be Brando, all right? Just be you.'

"Come sit on my lap in your pretty new dress."

'Is that you?' the director sniffs. 'That doesn't sound like you to me.'

"You are crazy." Carrie is all flushed and rosy. It sounds like me to her apparently.

"C'mon, Carrie. Don't you want to?"

"I don't know."

The director is breathing hard. Little beads of sweat stand out on his upper lip. A voyeur. He's nothing but a cheap voyeur.

"Then I'll decide for you," I tell Carrie.

She laughs far back in her throat. "Okay."

"Yeah, you do. You want to."

The director is leaning so far forward in his chair that I'm afraid he's going to fall off the dresser.

"Do I?" Carrie moves toward me. I can feel her hips rolling under the new spring dress, rolling toward me. She is halfway to me, and it's all over before I can even touch her, before I can even unzip my pants.

"I'm sorry, Carrie. I'm sorry."

The director is in a rage, jumping furiously up and down on top of the dresser. His upper lip is quivering. 'You blew it,' he sneers at me. 'You had a million ways to play it and you blew it.'

'What are you talking about, you supercilious bastard? This isn't a play. It's my life.'

The director glares at me, gathering himself together for his parting shot: 'Well, I hope it has a short run, because it's dreadful.'

40

I sleep the rest of the long afternoon. Around six, Carrie comes to lie beside me. She has taken off her new spring dress. It hangs from the arm of the maroon chair. In her cotton underwear she looks like a little girl.

"I don't want you to go away," she says.

"I don't want to go."

"Then don't."

The phone rings. It frightens us both. "Don't answer it," I command Carrie, though she has made no move to do so. I hold my breath in between the tyrannical rings, waiting for Carrie to tell me it could be an emergency. My mother, my father, Johnny, her mother, her father, Nora. What if it's Nora?

"All right, goddammit," I growl at Carrie. "I'll answer the goddamn phone."

"Do you want me to get it?"

"Yes, please."

She pads into the other room. "Who? . . . Just a minute."

She comes into the bedroom. "It's for you."

"Who is it?"

"He says he's Silas. But he has a foreign accent."

"Silas doesn't have a foreign accent."

"Well, I don't know, Jay. He sounds funny to me. Foreign."

"Okay." I stumble into the living room. Maybe the phone will be dead by the time I get there.

"Hello . . . hello." No answer. "Hello. Silas, are you there?"

"Hello, Jay."

"Silas, is that you?"

"Yes, it's me."

"You sound funny."

"I don't like telephones."

"You sound far away."

"I am far away. I'm on Third Street."

"You sound so young."

"I sound young sometimes. Jay . . ."

"What?"

"I'd tell you if I wasn't okay . . . Jay? Are you there?"

"Yes. I'm here."

"Are you going to come?"

"I don't know."

"You're afraid there's a quirk in my quark."

"What? What did you say?"

"A quark is a theoretical subnuclear particle. It comes in four flavors—upness, downness, strangeness, charm. You fear my strangeness, don't you?"

"I fear your upness and your downness and your charm too," I answer glumly.

"You don't want to come, do you, Jay?"

"I do want to."

"Is that a decision?"

Is it? Oh, Christ, I don't know.

"Just tell me yes or no, Jesse James."

"Yes."

"Good. Hamilton is coming with us."

"*What?*"

"Hamilton Trevelyan is coming with us on the trip."

"Are you kidding?"

"He was discharged two weeks ago. He wants to come with us."

"Silas, I don't know about traveling with Hamilton. You didn't say anything about him."

"Forget about meeting me at the bus stop. We're leaving at eight. From the West Side bus terminal. Port Authority. Hamilton says to meet us in front of the down escalator."

"In front of thc down escalator."

"If it's fair weather. If it's foul, behind the up escalator." Silas laughs. "Got that?"

"Got it."

"Okay." Silas clicks off.

I smile grimly into the black-holed face of the receiver. "I'm leavin' town, Black Bart. Riding out on a bus." I hitch up my gun belt and lope back into the bedroom.

Carrie is sitting cross-legged in the middle of the bed. I sit down beside her, pulling her head to my chest.

"Are you in love with Nora?" she asks me. The sound is muffled in my flannel shirt.

"I'm afraid of Nora," I tell her, hiding my face in the soft, buttery hair at the top of her head.

"I don't want to hear that." She pulls away from me. She looks so plain, stripped of all girlishness or sorrow, like pictures I have seen of country women sitting on their porches, looking out over the land. She takes me in levelly, her blue eyes unnaturally large in her pale face. "Nora is more vulnerable than I am. It makes her stern. She'll only take one chance. If she takes more than one chance, she'll remember always that she did. Now you're loving me, aren't you? Because I said something true?"

"Yes."

She leans toward me, pressing her arms tightly around my waist.

"Nora wouldn't make love to you now. But I will. I will, Jay."

"Do you love me, Carrie?"

She drops her head in the hollow of my neck. "Do you love Nora? Tell me, Jay."

I pull her closer to me, squeezing her bare shoulders. "Let's don't talk."

"What's wrong with you?" she wails hopelessly, shoving me away, falling stomach down on the bed. She starts to cry.

"Don't cry, Carrie."
She turns on her side, face to the wall.

Dear Mr. Muller,
    Please forgive my giving such short notice, but my great-grandmother in Oregon tangled with a grizzly bear and she is asking for me. It may be my last chance to see her. I was supposed to work the Mahler concert Wednesday night. I just spoke to Sarah Felson on the phone, and she says she will cover that concert for me and any others on my schedule until you can find a replacement.
                                          Sincerely,
                                          Jay Davidson

P.S. Please mail my last paycheck to my home address, care of Carrie Morgan.

Carrie Morgan, who is lying in our bed in the next room, her face to the wall. I read the postcard over with distaste. Fuck it. It will have to do. I don't have enough cards to write a new one, and there are others I must write.

Dear Mr. Kaminsky,
    I was going to call to say goodbye, but it's easier to write. That makes it sound like I'm going away forever. How could I do that? All my stuff is here. I'm just going on a little bus tour. Carrie is going to stay on in the apartment. Please give my regards to your wonderful wife. Maybe I can find some trinket to send her. She likes that kind of stuff, doesn't she?
    So. Well, so long for now, dear Mr. Kaminsky.
                                          Love,
                                          Jay

Dear Johnny,

I am leaving New York for a while. Leaving Nora and Carrie, the apartment, my job. I am going on the bus with Silas and Hamilton Trevelyan. Silas seems okay right now. I'm not sure about Hamilton. I will write you postcards along the way.

Love,
Jay

Dear Nora,

I don't know what to say to you. I never do. I came to see you, but I never got there. I am going away for a while.

Jay

"You ruined us, you know," Nora had said. "Do you know that?" Yes, I know it.

I force myself to look up at the kitchen clock. It's after seven. I should go soon. I've done everything I need to do. I've packed my Eastern Airlines carry-on bag and written my letters. I tip-toe back to the bedroom. Carrie has cried herself to sleep. She is scrunched up at the head of the bed, her face buried in the disarranged sheets. I should take a backpack, but I don't have one, and I dread waking Carrie to ask if I can take hers. I sit down on the bed, careful not to disturb her. I forgot to write Mom and Dad. Dear Mom and Dad, I will not seek what you have not found; I will not be what you have not been. That's not it. That isn't what I want to say. I have a sudden violent impulse to shake Carrie awake, to shake her till I can hear her teeth rattling in her head. But as soon as I bend over her the impulse dies. I lean back against the wall. I don't know what I want.

The curtains at the window blow out in the breeze. Some kids are playing in the courtyard three stories below, though it's been dark for over an hour. They'll have to go in soon to supper. "Daddy," someone calls out. "Daddy." I sit up, listening intently. *"Da-a-ad-dy."* The curtains flap hard in a sudden gust of wind.

Whee . . . . the wizard whizzed up the avenue, the tails of his coat fanning out in the breeze. Johnny and me trotting behind, dodging shopkeepers' brooms, businessmen's briefcases, old ladies' string shopping bags bulging with grapefruits and melons and potatoes. The wizard weaves in and out and around the early-morning crowd, clearing a path for us—"Stand aside, stand aside for me and my boys."

"Look at that," he would say. "Look at that and at that." What wonderful sights we see flying up the avenue. Eight blocks up the avenue to school each day he charts our perilous course, battling wild, belching buses and thundering taxis, spinning stories for us as we go.

He spreads his magic everywhere, stopping to enchant every little girl or boy who happens along. "Good morning, miss. What beautiful magic socks. Of course, you know you must never wear them after midnight or before one in the morning. Remember what happened to poor Cinderella."

"What?" the little girl asks, hopping with excitement. "What happened?"

"She lost her left shoe and her right belly button and all she got was a prince."

"How do you do, sir. What a handsome lunch box. May I look at it?" He lifts the box, squinting into it thoughtfully. "The Duke of Duchess was killed in battle by this lunch box centuries ago." He hands the box back to the little boy, who takes it in a daze. "Things were never the same after that," the wizard explains. "Goldie's locks came loose, Snow White melted, and Rose never read again."

So it goes, up the avenue. Johnny and I red-faced, bristling with pride and mortification, as children we knew and children we had never seen fell head over heels in love with my father.

When we got to school the wizard vanished, and Johnny went off with the little kids. Then I'd peer into my lunch bag. My mother was in there, guarding the abundant sandwiches she had made for me, securing the lid on the Thermos of fruit juice, tightening the wax paper around the crisp carrot sticks, tucking away the surprise of the day, a marzipan pear or a walnut or, in cold weather, a chocolate cat's tongue, rolled up in glistening foil. She packed wonderful lunches for Johnny and me to take with us into the world, to nourish and protect us, to use as a charm.

The apartment is so still. The only sounds are the hypnotic drone of the refrigerator in the next room and the soft explosion of Carrie's breathing—poof in out, in out poof.

'In out, in out. Breathe, Jay.'

'Is that you, Mom?'

'Shh. In out, in out.'

'I was just thinking about you.'

'Were you?'

'I don't want to go, Mom.'

'You don't have to.'

'Should I stay, then?'

'You can stay if you want to.'

'I'm already packed. I have my jacket and my cigarettes and my crystal ball.'

'You're ready to go.'

'I'm not ready. That's what I'm trying to tell you.'

'You're forgetting to breathe. Breathe deeply. That's better, in out, in out.'

'What should I do?'

'Just breathe. That's all you have to do. Breathe deeply.'

'Why are you putting me in a trance? I'll breathe when I want to breathe. And, if I don't want to breathe, I won't.'

'Then I'll be sorry.'

'Yes, yes. When it's too late.'

'I must be going, Jay.'

'Wait a minute. You just got here. There may be something I forgot to pack. I bet I forgot my rubbers. Or my toothbrush.'

'Goodbye, Jay.'

'If I get caught in the freezing rain without my rubbers, it'll be on your head.'

The air coming in at the window is cold. Wintry cold. Carrie shivers in her sleep. I was wrong. Spring is not here. I pull the spread up around Carrie. I lean over her to check the alarm clock by the bed, hoping she will waken. But she doesn't. It's 7:30. I'm supposed to meet Silas and Hamilton at 8. There's one last postcard on top of the dresser.

> Dear Mom and Dad,
>
> I am going out of town for a little vacation with some friends. I wanted to let you know so you wouldn't worry if you called and I wasn't here.
>
> Love,
> Jay

Johnny used to say goodbye to hotel rooms, places we had been for a weekend or just overnight. Tender goodbyes, as if to a lover or the closest of friends. Goodbyes to bathtubs and ashtrays, beds and vases and curtains. Fixing them forever in his memory. We will never see this room again, Jay. Ever in our whole lives. Don't you want to say goodbye, Jay?

Goodbye, Carrie. Goodbye, goodbye. Goodbye, apartment. Goodbye, bed. Goodbye, window over the back courtyard with the one spindly tree. Goodbye.

THREE

41

It's clear and cold outside. The city lights blaze like diamonds lighting up the glossy night. The early-evening crowd throbs like a motor anticipating midnight, climax. I am part of the night machine, speeding down the junky streets, shooting sparks of live color into the icy air. Reeling with dreams, reeking of sweat and perfume, we surge through the vivid streets, spill into the terminal.

The terminal is more powerful than the night machine. Its even fluorescence extinguishes the sparks, drains the colors, flattens the dreams. No more razzle dazzle. We are docile now. Tamed. Ready to shell out for tickets, stand in line, nap on a bench, thumb through the papers. Ready to wait.

I spot Hamilton coming toward me across the cavernous terminal, his straight nose pointing the way, like a fine hunting dog's. He moves with the nervous authority of a show breed, sleek, well bred, high strung. As he gets closer, I am relieved to see that his bright eyes are steady, his high, broad brow, smooth and unperturbed, his color, warm. He is elegantly dressed. A rich, camel's-hair coat opens over a handsome grey tweed suit. In his hand he carries a dark leather attaché case, clearly expensive.

"I've been watching you," Hamilton says, as he comes up to me. "You look deflated." He embraces me warmly, then backs off to look at me again.

"You look wonderful, Hamilton."

"I do look good. I'm well rested. They are experimenting

with sleep cures on the research ward. It's a fad, I'm sure. Dr. Lynch took a dim view of the whole thing."

"She's still there?"

"Everyone is still there. Or there again. Except Luis."

"Silas said Gemma's gone."

"Oh, she left, of course. Willy sends love and Philip and . . ." He breaks off suddenly. "I hate this chrome-plated pesthole. If I were not feeling so serene, it would depress me. We had better get to the down escalator. It's almost eight. Silas may be there already."

Hamilton points his nose and moves out. He knows the territory well. He has spent time here—cold nights curled up on those baby-blue benches, restless days foraging through the newsstands, looking to cadge a pack of cigarettes or a candy bar. Hamilton swings his attaché case. It gives him additional momentum as he shoulders his way through the crowd. There are gold initials embossed on the case: S. L.

"Who is S. L.?"

"Suzanne Lynch."

"You lifted Dr. Lynch's briefcase?"

"I am only borrowing it. I left all her papers on her desk. I didn't even read them. And I left her a note explaining. Actually, it's a love note of a kind. She is so lean, Jesse. I have never known a woman so consistently lean, so strained, so harsh. I would love to make love to her. My God, imagine. It would be like smoking a Turkish cigarette. There's Silas." Hamilton swings his case up in the air as greeting.

Silas is standing in front of the down escalator waving his arms. "Hey, Hamilton. Jay. Hey."

"He looks like a schoolboy in an English movie," Hamilton says.

Yes. Silas on the first day of term, his thick fair hair combed back off his face, his cheeks scrubbed and rosy, his grey eyes clear and untroubled. Michael Redgrave, the headmaster, smiles at Silas, thinking to himself, 'What a bright, sunny boy.'

"Jesse James. Cowboy boots and all. I was worried last night. You looked so bad I thought you might be sick."

"Me?"

"He looked terrible two minutes ago," Hamilton says. "It is our good influence that has resurrected him."

"He was always suggestible," Silas says.

Over the loudspeaker, a recording announces that the Golden West will leave from Gate 7.

"That's us," Hamilton says, bending down to open Dr. Lynch's briefcase.

"Where are we going?"

"West," Hamilton answers me. "Across the country. Here." He pulls three tickets out of the envelope pouch in the briefcase.

"You've already bought the tickets?"

"He bought them this morning," Silas explains.

"How much are they?"

"These tickets are my gift to you and Silas."

"Where did you get that kind of money?"

"Before my last admission, I sold two rings my mother left me. I don't remember doing it. I kept them in a safety-deposit box at the bank. I never went near that bank. Never. Even when I was down to nothing. When I got to the hospital, I was wearing these clothes, and in the pocket of this coat they found three thousand dollars and a note with my signature, stating that I had withdrawn the rings."

"Where's the rest of the money?"

"In the bank. After my sleep cure, Mrs. Morley escorted me to the bank. We opened me a savings account on Dr. Lynch's orders. Mrs. Morley tried to get me to put a small amount into a checking account, but I refused. I hate checks. They are so removed from their own reality. Money at least is substantial. You can jingle coins in your pocket, pitch pennies in the street, wad up dollar bills and stuff them up your nose."

"Who did you sell the rings to?"

"He doesn't remember," Silas tells me.

"I didn't get true value. I should have made $10,000 at least, which leads me to believe I pawned them. My mother would be devastated if she knew. Fortunately, she is dead. She set great store by things of sentimental value. The rings had been in her family for generations. Had I been handed down to her from my great-grandmother or even my grandmother, she would have wept bitterly at my decline. As it was, she hardly noticed."

The loudspeaker announces that the Golden West is now ready for boarding at Gate 7. Please have your tickets ready.

Hamilton leads the way, circling the escalator, deftly maneuvering a path for us between a little girl on roller skates and three large ladies walking arm in arm.

"Why didn't I think of that?" Hamilton exclaims, loud enough for the little girl and the women to hear. "Roller skates make all the difference in this miserable Formica pit." He swings his briefcase high to punctuate his enthusiasm. "That is adaptation—the mark of a fertile mind."

The little girl leans into the curve, ignoring the angry clucks of the three women walking abreast. We stop to watch her inscribe a flaring loop around the startled trio. Silas looks after her as she speeds away, skating low to the ground, bending forward at the waist. His eyes follow her as she skims across the floor, skirting lockers and telephone booths, newsstands and lunch counters, dumbfounded travelers, obstacles in her cross-country run. "I used to be a very good roller skater," Silas says. "I slept with my skate key on a string around my neck."

"You mean you were just a regular kid?"

"Nothing is either so simple or so complicated as we imagine it to be," Hamilton says, nodding to the three ladies as he cuts in front of them, heading for Gate 7.

We join the small group huddled in front of the door marked Gate 7, which flies open periodically to let in a blast of cold air and one or two men in uniform—drivers, mechanics, dispatchers—we don't know who they are. They stride by us without a glance. We aren't distinguishable one from another —a smallish bundle of coats and caps bobbing up and down, as we shift from one foot to another, swap our bags from right hand to left, left to right, tap our toes, impatient to be let on the bus, to start our journey.

From somewhere behind me, a child sings out, "Let's go. I'm ready to go."

As if on cue, the door swings open, letting in a gust of wind, chill, invigorating. A medium-sized man in a blue uniform steps inside, sticks a rubber door jamb in place, then signals us to pass through the door behind him. He must be our driver.

One by one, we file through to the curb. Buses are lined up like horses in their stalls. They are raring to go, stamping and snorting, pawing the ground. Clouds of exhaust, like prairie dust, settle on my boots.

The driver, immaculate in his freshly pressed uniform, stands to one side of the open bus door.

"All aboard," Hamilton calls out from somewhere in front. "All aboard the Golden West."

The small clump of passengers in front of Silas and me board the bus. I step up to the door, holding my ticket out to the driver.

"What is your final destination, sir?"

"Ah, I'm not sure."

The driver laughs pleasantly, as if I'd made a joke, and takes my ticket from me. "Los Angeles. Watch your step, sir."

California. I'm going to California. What a nice man.

Silas is ahead of me as we board. Hamilton has taken possession of the seat immediately behind the driver's. His coat is folded on the seat beside him. A small embroidered pillow I recognize as one Willy made in O.T. for Faye (she refused it) is plumped up behind his head. His briefcase is open on his lap, revealing folded-up underwear, socks, a razor and blades, a compass, a toothbrush and toothpaste, a bar of soap, a shirt, and a small linen towel. He looks as if he had lived in this bus all his life.

I motion to Hamilton that Silas and I are heading for the back. Hamilton waves us on.

I follow Silas to the rear of the bus. Something is wrong. Silas slides into the window seat. He doesn't have a bag. He didn't bring anything with him. Nothing. Michael Redgrave frowns, 'The boy brought nothing with him. Odd.' The ruddy, good-natured face of the headmaster darkens as I hoist my bag onto the overhead rack.

The last few passengers are filing in, and the bus is still considerably less than a quarter filled. A red-faced, rawboned man in tan slacks and a yellow shirt lopes down the aisle, lowering himself into an aisle seat in the middle of the bus. He lets his seat back as far as it will go.

A very tall black woman steps up onto the bus, holding the hand of a little boy. She stands at the head of the aisle, surveying this new territory. She will not advance yet. Her eyes narrow, her nostrils open. She is alert as a lioness stalking survival. Hamilton says something to the woman. She nods, almost imperceptibly, but doesn't smile. The little boy breaks away from her, sprinting down the aisle. He must be six or seven. Skinny, with long, coltish arms and legs. His hair is cropped very short, springy black fuzz sprouting out of his small head.

"Hi," he says, as he slides into the window seat across from Silas and me.

"Hi."

The little boy doesn't say anything more. His nose is glued to the window.

I look across Silas out the window. An old man is mounting the steps with difficulty, helped by the driver. Behind him is a portly black man in a dark suit, carrying a large suitcase. I turn my attention back to the interior of the bus.

The tall black woman rolls down the aisle like thunder, scattering my calm before her like leaves in the wind. I smile graciously at her as she stops by the seat the boy has taken, but she doesn't notice me any more than the storm notices the leaves displaced in its wake. She is larger even than she looked from a distance—heavy, broad-boned, powerful. I can't guess her age. She could be forty or sixty. "Do you have everything?" I hear her ask the boy as she sits down beside him. Her voice surprises me. It is lighter than I expected it to be.

The little boy mumbles something in reply. Mumble mumble, I hear over the roar of the engine starting up. Wharrum, the huge motor turns over. Wharrum. Rrumm, Rrumm.

All around me the passengers make small shuffling sounds as they settle in. Like birds, I think to myself, settling into the nest. The homely image pleases me. It's cozy in here. Warm. Already the outside world seems far away, Carrie and Nora artifacts of another age. My body aches with sensuous fatigue. It seeps into my arms and legs. Michael Redgrave puffs on his pipe, watching the fire, musing about the boy Silas. The cinders hiss reassuringly in the grate. 'Everything will come right in the morning,' he thinks to himself. 'It always does.' My eyelids prickle. Sleep will overtake me. I don't have to do anything about it. Life is really very simple.

42

The bus rumbles through the night. Its powerful heart beats in my dream, lifts me from sleep. I surface slowly, coming up into its warm, dark, swaying belly. The overhead lights have been turned off. All around me the passengers breathe and sigh and turn in their sleep, giving themselves up to the protection of the driver, relinquishing their daytime vigilance. There is a little glow of light around the driver. I can see him way up front, leaning forward, steering a steady course.

Lights from passing cars and trucks flash and dim, flash and dim in regular rhythm. I can't tell where we are. New Jersey, perhaps. Pennsylvania. The road is straight and flat. Occasionally, there are signs. Holiday Inn, Howard Johnson, Esso. A few bare trees falling away on either side of the swaying bus. I could be anywhere. I close my eyes. I will slide back down into my rocking sleep. I stretch my legs out. They knock against something soft and bulky, bunched up on the floor.

'Watch out, Jay. You're squashing me.'

I look down. It's Gemma, curled up on the floor, wrapped up in a new red coat I have never seen her wear. 'Gemma! I'm sorry, I didn't know you were there.' I pull her up beside me, and she plops into Silas's seat in a flurry of dust and flying cigarettes. Silas. 'Where is Silas?'

Gemma sneezes softly. 'He moved. He's stretched out in the seat in front of you.'

'Have you been down there long?'

'No.' She pats off her new red coat. 'It's filthy down there.'

'I thought you were in Spain.'

'I am.' She laughs forlornly.

'Are the memories so bad?'

'Yes.' Gemma takes a bent cigarette from the pocket of her coat and lights up. Behind the streams of smoke, she looks sad and weary, old, fine little lines creasing the bridge of her nose.

'I baked bread for him,' she says, staring into the blue smoke. 'When no one was looking, I hurled my rage into the dough in place of yeast. I kneaded and folded and rolled it around on the floor. He sits by the window, watching me grease the loaf pans, butter dripping from my fingers. The bread rises raging, sloshing over the sides of the pan, moving across the room. He leaps up on the chair, "You want to murder me." The dough laps up over the wooden legs of his chair. The bitter dough is rising up around us. It is at my waist. I tear at it, pulling with my fingers, "Help me, please. I'm going under." The dough clings to his calves. "I can't help you," he cries bitterly. "I have to save myself." With one tremendous straining effort, he bends his knees and dives out the open window into the river below. I watch him jackknife into the water. He surfaces, sending up mists of drizzling spray, and swims with long, exhausted pulls to the opposite shore.'

'I understand, Gemma. No one understands you like I do.' I put my arm around her, touch her silky hair with my free hand. 'It would be so easy with me.' I slide my hand down her warm neck. She shivers and arches her neck, bumping her head softly forward against my shoulder. I brush my lips against her ear, whispering: 'Gemma. Sweet Gemma. You don't have to tell me anything. Nothing at all. I will listen so intently that I will hear your dreams, know your thoughts, read the stirring of your restless body.' She lifts her hips, moves them against me, and I bring my hand down to her rising hip, slip it inside her new red coat.

She's not there. She's slithering out of her coat, off the seat, sliding away from me. 'Gemma, wait!' I grab for her arms, trying to hoist her back up to me. It's no use. I am tugging at her empty coat sleeves. She has slipped through my fingers. She slides to the floor, pulling the coat behind her. A red ball rolling under my feet. 'Wait!' The red ball rolls away, disappearing under the seat in front of me.

I scramble down to the floor, hunching up to peer under the seat. She's gone. I can't see anything except an empty raisin box and a broken sliver of mirror embedded in half a discolored plastic compact, its hinges broken. Gemma's I bet. Just like her to carry around a sliver of broken mirror in the pocket of her new red coat. She takes it out a few times a day when no one is looking to study what is written there, astonished to see the fine lines settling into that soft child's face. Damn her.

The mirror winks up at me. This tiny piece of cheap glass set in its mottled plastic backing, this useless piece of shit, appears to be signaling me. I pick the mirror up. It is crisscrossed with broken lines and fogged over like a bathroom mirror when a hot tub is running.

I stare into the glass. Where am I? C'mon, goddammit. I know you're there. The glass is clearing. There I am. No. It isn't me. It's Johnny. Johnny years and years ago. Johnny six or seven. He is bent over something—a book. He bends his body to the book on his lap as if he would subdue its hostile jumble of letters with the force of his weight. He bears down on the letters, willing them to yield their secrets to him. He presses his finger into the page, tearing the paper. I can see the knots standing up on either side of his thin neck. Tiny drops of sweat bead up on his forehead, fall onto the page. His jaw juts forward. He opens his mouth trying to sound out the letters.

I cover the mirror with my hand and shove it back under the seat. I don't want to see anymore. I lift myself off the floor into my seat, arranging myself for sleep, stretching out across the two seats, my feet propped up against the window. I close my eyes. Johnny is there. I remember. The letters will not yield. He will sit there for hours. He will sit there for hours with only his terror and his will for company.

Goddammit. I turn in my makeshift bed, shoving one arm under the seat, feeling for the tiny mirror. Got it. I sit up, bringing the mirror to my face. The glass is densely clouded. 'Johnny? Are you there? I can't see you.' I bring the glass closer. Something is there—a figure. 'Johnny?' Yes, it's Johnny. He's fifteen, all angles and shadows, his nose and mouth too big for his narrow face. He's writing in a book, a diary of some kind. I can see over his shoulder. 'I watch my friends' faces. They are happy. They're laughing. I can't talk to them. They are different than they were last year. But they are not afraid. No one else is afraid. I am ugly and strange. My nose is grotesque. It is so big that it makes my eyes look like dots. Mom says I have a wonderful face. I can't stand it when she says things like that. I can't concentrate on what the teacher is saying. I'm afraid I will cry. I'm falling behind in all my classes. I don't understand what's going on, and even if I did, it's too late to catch up. They'll find out I'm stupid. Everything is so grey. The trees are turning grey. The sky is turning grey. The class buildings, the food in the cafeteria. Mary Ann Lipscomb just slipped a note to Tony, and they smiled at each other. I will never be able to be like them.'

The letters wash across the page, falling off the edge into darkness.

I am exhausted. I have barely the strength to shove the mirror back under the seat. I must sleep. In my dream Johnny holds Gemma's mirror up to me, and I turn my face to the wall.

43

A presentiment of light. I open my eyes.

Sky. A vast expanse of pure, pale sky as far as the eye can see. No buildings, bridges, towers, nothing climbing upward to stand against it. The rising sun alone has dominion in this sky. Silas is awake in the seat in front of me. He puts his face to the window, and the frosty glass bursts into flame, consuming Silas's face in its fiery glow. We watch the squared-off fields catch fire in a quick-moving line, first one and then another and another, glowing ruby red in the cold dawn.

We watch in silence for a long time. The sun is not yet full-risen. Only a few early risers stir in their seats. Hamilton still sleeps. I can see him up front, stretched across two seats. His long legs, gracefully crossed at the ankles, stick out into the aisle.

Out my window the fields stretch away in an endless checkerboard. "Hey, Silas, where do you suppose we are?"

"I don't know. We could be anywhere." He seems pleased at the idea. In profile, in this virginal light, his skin seems porous. If I concentrated, I could see straight through to . . . "Except Essentuki."

"Essentuki? I'm not following you, Silas."

"Or Izmir or Alexandria." Silas turns back around in his seat. I can only see the back of his head. "We lived in palaces with large rooms opening onto each other, great high-ceilinged rooms dangling over the sea. At night the rooms overflowed with women in silk dresses, rustling. Do you know that sound, how much it promises? Gentlemen in tuxedos and robes. Laughter and music—strange instruments sighing, teasing. But in the day the rooms were silent. Enormous empty rooms."

Silas breaks off suddenly. He turns around to look at me over the seat. "Do you think I am inventing this? Never mind, Jesse James. We all invent our own history." He stands up abruptly. "I think I will stretch my legs. Excuse me." He moves out into the aisle.

My left knee is trembling and my neck aches. I wish I had a cup of coffee. Dammit. I need a cup of coffee. I can smell the rich, pungent smell of Mr. Sanchez's chicory coffee blend. I close my eyes. In the steam rising from my coffee, I see Silas roller skating through enormous empty rooms in a palace in Izmir. Where is Izmir? Where are we? I must at least find out what state we're in. I am in a bad state. My neck really hurts, and we've barely started on this trip. I need food. When are we going to stop to eat? Too early. Hardly anyone up yet. The driver's been up all night. Such an ordinary-looking man, from the back anyway. Medium build, medium height, brownish hair. I don't remember his face. It was pleasant, I remember that. And he was very courteous. How tired he must be. He's sitting very straight, though. His spine is straight as a plumb line. He drove me through the night. What kind of man drives a bus back and forth across the country? I guess he doesn't do the whole trip by himself. We'll probably have a couple of other drivers before we get to L.A. I don't like that idea. I am used to this man. I trust him.

Across the aisle from me, the little boy peeps around his companion's great bosom, which moves softly up and down. "Guess what state we're in?"

"You'll wake her."

"No, I won't. Guess."

How different she seems in sleep. Unguarded, she is easy, generous, even opulent. Her head lolls comfortably to one side. Her wide hips sprawl luxuriously, crowding the boy on his narrow seat, warming him.

"I don't know," I tell the boy. "I have no idea."

"Please guess."

"Well, give me a hint."

"It starts with a letter in the middle of the alphabet."

"Ohio."

"You win." He seems pleased.

Ohio. Solidly in the middle of the Midwest. I feel easier.

"My name is Midas," the little boy tells me. "And this is my Aunt Josephine. She looks after me."

Aunt Josephine sits up smartly at the mention of her name, wide awake on the instant.

"Good morning," I say, bending eagerly, automatically, to the task of charming her.

Aunt Josephine nods curtly, indifferent to my affable charm, my straightforward manner, my youthful good looks.

"I never knew anyone named Midas," I tell her in a voice exactly calculated to inspire confidence and to express my great interest in her and her nephew.

"What's your name?" Midas asks me.

"Jay." I smile at Aunt Josephine. "Jay Davidson. How do you do?"

Aunt Josephine yawns. Her teeth are very small and very white.

"I heard that man sitting with you call you Jesse James," Midas says.

"That's my other name."

"That's a cowboy. An outlaw cowboy."

"Don't you think I look like a cowboy?"

"No."

"Quit bothering that man, Midas."

"He's not bothering me. Not in the least. I should say not." David Niven. I'm doing David Niven. "Delightful child." I can't stop. "Oh my God," I mumble desperately, fingering my imaginary mustache.

"Did you brush your teeth?" Josephine queries Midas.

"Ho ho," I laugh painfully. "His teeth. Yes, quite. Teeth."

Midas looks at me quizzically.

"Did you?" Aunt Josephine asks again.

"No."

"Well, go do it."

"I haven't eaten breakfast yet. I'll just have to do it again after breakfast."

"Oh. Hah hah. Well, the lad has a point, eh?"

"It won't kill you to brush your teeth twice," Aunt Josephine says, turning her broad back to me.

"All right." Midas crawls past Aunt Josephine. I smile at him weakly, intending to convey sympathy for the absurd arbitrariness of adult rule, friendship, apology for my foolishness. He doesn't smile back. He thinks I'm a shit. A crazy shit.

Aunt Josephine pulls out her knitting, casting stitches onto her long needles with dizzying speed and rapt absorption. She is knitting a wall I cannot scale.

I turn away from her. People are waking up. It's a small group. Smaller even than I realized last night. There are more empty seats than full ones. Well, it's an off time. It isn't Thanksgiving or Christmas. It isn't summer. It's late March—a good time to stay home. I wonder what Carrie is doing right now. Sipping her coffee, pretending to check audition calls in the trade papers, her eyes so blurry with tears that she can't read. Or is she already hardening her heart against me? Crying aloud, banging her fists on the table. That cowardly sonofabitch didn't even wake me. But she heard me go, and she lay sleeping in our bed. She felt me leaning over her and she wouldn't wake up.

The bus is slowing down. I can feel it pulling under me, groaning as it decelerates, lurching heavily onto the access road, turning onto a side road. We pull up into the parking lot of a small, low brick structure. A sign says MINNIE's. It appears to be a gas station, diner, and, I guess, a bus stop. Ahead of me a few rows, the rangy man with the red face and the yellow shirt and tan slacks reaches up for his suitcase. I had not expected people to be getting off along the way. I thought we were all going west together. And here this guy is bailing out in Ohio.

The driver pulls a lever and the doors wheeze open. He puts his head down on the big wheel and lets the weariness run through him as the passengers file past.

Hamilton is the first one off the bus. I watch him out my window as he surveys the scene, shading his eyes with his hand, turning in every direction. He is a handsome man in his fine camel coat. He looks rested and refreshed, the picture of a man at his ease anywhere. He catches my glance and nods, then turns smartly and advances on Minnie's.

"Aren't you going to get some breakfast?" Midas asks me, scrambling into the aisle after his aunt.

He's forgiven me. I feel grateful to him for his goodwill. "Hey, Midas. Yeah, sure I am."

"Breakfast," I say to Aunt Josephine, flattening my voice to as neutral a position as I can manage. She dips her head, a tiny, regal acknowledgment of my idiotic greeting, and precedes Midas up the aisle. I follow them.

I don't see Silas. He must be off the bus already. Ahead of Aunt Josephine are the rangy man toting his bag and the elderly man I noticed the driver helping to board last night. The old man wears a black overcoat, which rides up oddly in the back, displaced by a bulky hump across his shoulders.

Josephine and Midas and I are the last passengers to dismount. Only the driver remains at his post, waiting to make certain all his charges are safely disembarked. He is making notations in a small blue notebook, but he nods and smiles as we pass by.

Outside Minnie's there is an old beat-up Dodge and a small Ford pickup truck. There is a woman inside the pickup. She gives a short, welcoming beep on the horn, and the rangy man lopes off to meet her.

I am about to ask Aunt Josephine if I may join her and Midas for breakfast, when she opens the door of Minnie's and shepherds Midas away. I catch the door with my hand. Perhaps she sensed my thought. I wouldn't put it past her.

It's warm and toasty inside Minnie's, steam rising cheerfully from half a dozen cups of hot coffee. The portly black man in the dark suit looks up from his coffee as I walk in. His face is startlingly handsome, at odds with the thickening body. I wave and he turns to look over his shoulder to see who I am greeting. In the booth behind him, two women sit side by side conferring over the menu. The woman on the end is plump and grey-haired. She looks like pictures of Carrie's Aunt Betty. All I can see of her companion is the top of her head, swathed in a blue scarf.

I slide into a booth with Silas and Hamilton, who are talking to the waitress, a tall, thin woman with red hair tucked behind her ears.

"And you must be Minnie," Hamilton is saying.

"No. I'm Sarah. That's Minnie over there." She motions toward the counter, where Minnie, a large, burly man with curly black hair, is pirouetting with surprising grace, back and forth between the toaster and the refrigerator and the grill.

"Ah. I see. Well, Sarah, you don't mind if I call you Sarah, do you? I am Hamilton and these are my friends, Silas and Jay."

"Pleased to meet you," Sarah says.

"What do you recommend?" Hamilton asks her.

Sarah squints at Hamilton, the better to determine if he is pulling her leg, but she decides he is sincere. "Ah, well, the eggs are fine. We get them fresh every day. And Minnie baked some coffee cake this morning."

"How wonderful to come upon fresh eggs and homemade coffee cake." Hamilton smiles expansively, warming the company with his enthusiasm. "I'll have two eggs scrambled and a piece of the cake."

"I'll have coffee and coffee cake," Silas says.

I order juice and coffee and fried eggs and bacon and coffee cake.

"He's a big eater," Sarah says, and she smiles shyly at me, before she turns away to put in our order.

Where are Josephine and Midas? I crane my neck. They're over in a corner by the window. Midas is constructing something—a bridge, a house, a tower. Two knives, overlapping, lie across two water glasses. On top of the knives, he is stacking up a pyramid of sugar cubes. Josephine does not see me watching. Her eyes are fastened on Midas. It is not pleasure in his inventiveness that rivets her, but fear that something will strike it down.

"I always liked the name Sarah," Hamilton says. "It's a round, womanly name."

"She's skinny," I say, plucking at my napkin, wondering about Josephine.

"Yes, but did you see the color of her hair, Jesse James."

"She has a lovely smile," Silas says. "I like her."

Hamilton and I look at each other. Silas sees the look and shuts down. I can see it happen as clearly as if he had slipped a paper bag over his head.

Hamilton sees it too. "It is to our everlasting discredit that we rely on each other to be the same today as we were yesterday," he says, leaning forward across the table. "If I go up and down, there are few surprises in it anymore. It is a ritual as formal and prescribed as a minuet." He puts out a hand to touch Silas's arm. Silas picks up his water glass, and his arm lifts away out of Hamilton's reach.

Hamilton's large hand lies awkwardly on the table. It is an embarrassment to all of us, this large protuberance, extended foolishly to nothing. I am grateful for Sarah's return with the coffee. And angry with Hamilton.

We will do this scene over. Take two.

'She's kind of skinny.'

'Yes, but did you see the color of her hair, tucked behind those rosy ears? And Silas was right, her smile is lovely. Take her, Jesse James. You would be doing her a favor. Minnie is too busy to notice her anymore. He is scrambling eggs and baking coffee cakes, while she goes hungry for love. Go ahead, my boy. Silas and I are quite content to sit here and sip our coffee and wait for you.'

Minnie's husky voice pushes its way through my reverie. "Look, Fred, I'm telling you. Your relief man won't be here for another six hours. There's been a fuckup. It happens. I'm sorry, Ned."

Fred? Ned? pushes his coffee mug around on the counter. "The relief man is always here, Minnie. Always. I've been on this route for twelve years and he's always been here."

"I know, Ed, but today he's not here."

"I've been driving all night."

Minnie turns to flip some hotcakes on the griddle. ". . . take to keep you going . . ." is all I can make out.

"I don't take pills, Minnie. That's it. I don't."

"Some guys do."

"Then they shouldn't be driving. Company policy expressly forbids it."

"Company policy is supposed to get your relief man here on time."

"This is the first time this has ever happened."

"Maybe you could just explain to your riders and they can sit here till your relief comes."

"I can't do that. I can't hold people up for six hours."

Minnie catches two pieces of toast as they pop up out of the toaster and slides them onto a plate. "Well, I don't know what to tell you."

"It will reflect badly on the company if these people are held up."

"Listen, Fred, call yourself if you don't believe me."

"Excuse me." It's the elderly man in the black overcoat. He has been sitting two stools over from the driver at the counter. "Excuse me for butting in, but could I offer to drive for a while? I'm an excellent driver, as it happens, and I'm sure some of the other passengers would be willing to help out too. We could take turns, and you could take a nap."

Hamilton bolts out of his seat, startling the old man with the suddenness of his appearance at the counter. "That's an excellent suggestion," Hamilton tells him. "I would be delighted to help out," he continues, turning his attention to the driver. "I have a chauffeur's license, as a matter of fact. And I drove a bus in the city."

Fred-Ed-Ned turns agitatedly from the old man to Hamilton to Minnie. He drops his voice, afraid to draw the attention of anyone else. "I appreciate this. Thank you very much. You're both very kind. But I can't accept. It's against regulations." His round face colors a splotchy red. "It's not allowed. Definitely not allowed. I'm sorry. I'm going to go call in. There's some mistake. I'll get it straightened out." He pulls himself together and speaks up. "Ladies and gentlemen. We have five more minutes at this stop. Please get back on the bus when you've finished your meal."

Hamilton returns to the booth and Silas excuses himself, "I'll see you outside." Hamilton and I finish our coffee in silence, pay up, and troop back out into the chilly March morning, straggling into line with the rest of the passengers.

I don't see Silas. "Hamilton. Silas is gone!"

"He's back on the bus," Hamilton snaps irritably. "What's wrong with you?"

I spin back around in the line, tripping over my tail which drags between my legs. Damn Hamilton. The black man I waved at is in front of me. He must have heard my exchange with Hamilton. He thinks I'm nuts. No. His only interest at this moment is in getting back on the bus. He jiggles coins in his pocket impatiently, waiting for the woman in the blue scarf to board. Why do I always imagine that everyone is interested in me? Suddenly, he turns to address me. "I thought we got a new driver here," he says sharply, swiveling back around to mount the steps before I can respond.

I slink back into my old place beside Silas. He doesn't look up.

By the time we are all seated, the driver is back. He stands in the doorway of the bus, checking to make sure that none of his charges is missing, collecting his thoughts. He fingers his rumpled collar, then, straightening his cap on his head, he sits down at the wheel. He sits quietly, as if he were waiting for some signal, before he picks up his microphone. "Ladies and gentlemen, I'll be driving you on to Indianapolis."

We pull off again with Fred at the helm.

44

"The company let Ed down," Silas says and smiles at me.

"You're not mad at me?"

"Because you and Hamilton made a production out of what I said about the waitress?"

"Yeah."

"Not anymore."

"Good."

Silas is silent, gazing out the window at the black trees and the dark barns and the silver silos that leap away as we fly by them. "Do you believe in the possibility of happiness?" he says finally.

"Yes."

He turns to me, scrutinizing my face as if it held the key to some mystery. "You do, don't you? Of course. I already knew that. But you don't know what your yes means. Not yet."

"No. I suppose I don't."

"I'm not talking about a wish, Jay. Or moments either."

"What are you talking about, Silas?"

"Living there." He turns back to the window, propping his elbow on the tiny window ledge, covering his eyes with his hand. I have been dismissed.

"Obviously he doubted my ability." It's Hamilton talking to the old man with the hump on his back. They are sitting in front of Silas and me. "He doubted my ability," Hamilton says again, motioning with his hand to the driver up front.

"No, I'm sure not," the old man says.

"He was clearly agitated at our offer of help. Clearly."

"He was upset by the whole turn of events. But you shouldn't take it so personally."

"I take everything personally. If there is static on the radio, I take it personally. If a leaf falls, I take it personally. If my wife has her period, I take it personally."

"You don't mean to say . . ."

"I mean everything I say and everything in the universe has something to say to me."

I will my attention away from Hamilton and the old man. Silas's elbow has slid off the ledge; he is asleep. Good. I wish Hamilton would sleep too, slide back down from high to neutral. My stomach is in knots. I wish the old man would sleep. I wish the driver would sleep. Everyone. I want everyone to go to sleep. Go to sleep, Aunt Josephine. Her eyes are closing. Go to sleep. Then Midas and I will fly the coop and leave you all to your own devices.

Midas must know I'm thinking of him. He reaches across the aisle and taps my knee. "You know how I know you're not an outlaw desperado? Number one, you're too sleepy. A desperado is always wide awake." Midas moves out of his seat and into the aisle, assuming the stance of a runner—crouched, alert, ready for the starting gun. "And number two," Midas straightens out of his crouch, "a desperado wouldn't take a bus, he'd ride a black stallion."

"A desperado is desperate. I'm desperate. That makes me a desperado."

Midas leans toward me, taking my measure. "I don't think that's right."

"I don't care what you think anymore."

"Why are you being mean to me?" Midas asks, flopping back down in his seat.

"I'm not being mean."

"You didn't talk to me at all since we got back on the bus," Midas complains. "There's not one single kid on the whole bus besides me. And I can see right now everyone's going to take naps the whole trip. They'll sleep all night and take naps all day."

"I see what you mean."

"Could you play with me?"

"Okay."

"Yay. We can make paper airplanes." Midas whips open his school bag and brings out twenty or thirty loose sheets of lined yellow paper.

"I haven't made a paper airplane in years."

"My daddy taught me how to," Midas explains. "Who taught you?"

"Same."

"When I grow up, I'll teach my children and you do too. That way it will be passed on to each new bunch of kids."

I watch Midas carefully, duplicating each fold of his paper with my own sheet. Before long, my fingers have remembered, and I am turning out sleek planes. Some lift straight up and plummet to earth again in an instant. Some glide up, hanging suspended for the briefest instant before nosing slowly down to our aisle runway. Some abort, dead ending against a foot rail on the runway. An occasional flight ends in the lap of an unsuspecting passenger.

Still, the passengers don't seem to mind, nor the driver. Only Aunt Josephine has misgivings. I can tell by the way she arranges and rearranges her bulk in the seat. But for the time being she has no plans to quash our play, and her displeasure gives just the right edge of danger to our game.

Midas's planes are wonderful. He draws elaborate insignia on each, and spells out names on some. I am about to launch my latest missile, when out of the corner of my right eye, I catch sight of a yellow-lined biplane outside the window. I lean across Silas, taking care not to wake him, prying the window open for a better look. Sticking my head out the window, I can just make out the letters M A I L on the side of the plane. MAIL in big red letters. The cockpit of the biplane is open. It's Gemma at the controls, looking very jaunty in her flying gear. I draw my head in, intending to signal Midas, but just then the plane dives in the open window, swooping low, and Gemma leans out, dropping a packet of letters tied round with a string into my lap. Gemma waves at me then throttles back, disappearing through the open window.

The packet of letters lies on my lap like a stone. Dead apparently. Dead letters. I've heard of them. I clamp my hand over them as one would raise the sheet over the face of a corpse. Something is happening. The string has come undone and the letters thrash around in my lap like fish on hooks. I pounce on the scattering letters, trying to gather them together again. I manage to lash the string around all but a dozen or so of the most active, which continue to jump and leap and spin before my eyes, compelling me to read them.

> Dear Jay,
>   I tried to talk to you every time we came to the hospital. But I couldn't. I was so oppressed by that place. It was so bare and ugly. I can't stand for you to end up crazy in an ugly hall.
>   Dad

> Dear Jay,
>   I have no idea what you are feeling. I've never known what you were feeling. Not even when you were a little kid. You always looked so impassive. Maybe you were in pain. Were you in pain? Why didn't you say something, Jay? Dammit goddammit. Say something to me.
>   Dad

Dear Jay,

I've pushed myself harder than that bastard of a father ever pushed me. I did it to make that miserable sonofabitch choke on his prophecy: You, you'll never amount to anything. You're a good-for-nothing. A loafer. A fool.

But I did it for me too, for the thrill it gave me to pit my will against the world. For my pride as a man. I did it for my sweet mother, to thank her for her abiding faith and tenderness. I did it for my wife—it was my understanding of love. I wanted to give her everything, the world, because she was so beautiful. And I did it for you and Johnny, to pass something of who I've been on to you, flesh of my flesh. I am proud of what I have done.

Dad

Dear Jay,

It makes me laugh to think how much fun I've had working my ass off. Don't do it if it isn't fun, Jay. And don't let anyone tell you what's fun and what isn't. I had a wonderful time when my brother Harry and I beat the shit out of my weasel cousin, Albert.

Dad

Dear Jay,

Maybe this summer when you're home from school you'd like to do some walking with me. There are some wonderful birds in the woods in back of the house. I'm studying their calls. I could show you what I've learned.

Dad

Dear Jay,

You thought if you stepped on a crack you would break my back, if you held your breath I would be the one to choke. You thought if you danced your frantic dance long enough and hard enough, you could hold the world together. None of it was ever true. None of it was ever in your power.

Mom

Darling Jay,

What is it you want? If you could only tell me. Do you want to leave camp and come home for the rest of the summer? If that's what you really want, we will arrange it. But someday you must stop running.

Mom

Dear Jay,

Nothing has turned out the way I thought it would. Love especially. I'm sorry. I ask too much of you sometimes and not enough at others. You are only thirteen, but I am only forty. I am only forty and I don't know what to do.

Mom

Dear Jay,

When you get home, your father will be back at the house. I can't explain it to you. I can't explain it to myself.

Mom

Dear Jay,

You sucked my sorrow out of me, untapped the bitter flow, and I forgot who you were. But out of the corner of my heart I saw how strained you were, holding your breath. I used you. But you have used me too. You needed my sorrow and my rage. I had strength to show you, cheerfulness, good sense, but you did not want them.

Mom

Dear Jay,

The day is bright and sunny. A breeze like a sea breeze blows through the open door. I am eating

strawberries and drinking coffee. Everything smells
so good. The sweet strawberries and the sweet spring
air and the deep, rich coffee. I am gratified in this day
and in the food I have to eat and in the book I am
reading and in the tasks I have to do and in the rest I
will take when the tasks are done.

Mom

Dear Jay,
  Take a chance!

Mom

Enough. I can't read any more. My eyes are burning and the
words jump around on the page as if they had a life of their
own.

Where is Midas? Not in his seat. Aunt Josephine is fast
asleep, and Midas might be anywhere. I left him in the middle
of our game. Silas is still asleep beside me. He wanted to talk
and I didn't say anything. Ah, God, I am all alone here. Hamilton and the old man have dozed off too. I wanted them to leave
me alone, and they have taken me at my word. What can I do?
"I could make a bugle out of Midas's yellow paper and blow
everyone out of their seats," I venture out loud. My little sally
falls flat at my feet. Disgusted, I kick it away.

I push myself up, open my airline bag on the overhead rack,
shove the packet of letters in, and zip it closed.

I take out a cigarette and light up, inhaling the smoke deeply
into my lungs. "Shit. Motherfucker."

"What's the matter?" Silas opens one eye.

"I just bought this pack. It's a fresh pack and it tastes like
it's been lying around for a hundred years. You pay fifty
fucking cents and they palm this revolting stale shit off on
you."

"Put it out then."

"No."

Silas laughs and closes his eye.

"Don't go to sleep on me, Silas. Please."

"I'm not asleep."

"What's going to happen to us, Silas?"

"I don't know what's going to happen to you, Jesse James."

"What's going to happen to you?"

"Nothing."

"That's ridiculous. You were just talking about being happy. A lot can happen. We've got our whole lives ahead of us."

"I told you a long time ago that nothing was going to happen to me."

"No, you didn't. You never said that."

"You weren't listening."

"Explain it to me then. No, don't. I don't want to hear it." The last drag of my cigarette tastes maddeningly awful. "Fuck you anyway, Silas," I swear, stamping out the butt. "I listen to you. I listen and listen, but you never tell me anything."

Silas looks at me with new interest. I might be an aberrant cell under a microscope. "The best I could give you is reasons," he explodes. "Reasons are nothing. Every cockroach has reasons."

"Tell me anyway, Silas. Please tell me."

Silas leans back against the seat, his eyes on the ceiling. In the silence I can hear his breath race in and out of his lungs as if he were running hard. "Everything moved through me," he says finally, "vibrated, sang, stung, groaned. Shadows, stories, bugs, clouds, dreams, sighs, blankets, pissing, kisses, whispers. My green jacket mattered. Stones mattered. Being Stephan's best friend. My mother wiped my nose or didn't, smiled or frowned, hung my drawing on the wall or left it facedown on the table in the hall. My father showed me how to drive a nail into a piece of wood. He didn't get home in time to say good night to me.

"My green jacket got lost when we moved. Anina sang songs for me while she dusted the table tops. One day she wasn't there anymore. She kissed Stephan goodbye. He said she stuck her tongue in his mouth and kissed him.

"At night I listen to my parents humming. Hum hum ho hum, hum mmm. I love to listen to the soft humming. 'They are edging me out,' he roars one night, blasting a hole in the humming. He roared like a bull with a spike through his heart. 'Shhh, darling. Shush, shh,' she whispers. They are edging him out. It is a kind of murder. His voice is bleeding, staining the bedsheets. We will have to move again. He will die. He will leave us.

"He brings my mother a red rose. She throws it in his face. The rose breaks, splinters on the Spanish tiles. She leans across the table, kisses him on the mouth. He wipes his lips on the blood-red napkin at his elbow.

"Stephan drowned at the seashore. The grownups were picnicking on the sand—champagne and melon and crusty bread and cheeses. He was only a few feet from the shore.

"Oh, my God," my mother said when she heard the news. "Oh no oh no oh no."

"I dug a deep hole and lay down in it and covered it over with dirt. I threw my green jacket in it. I threw Stephan in it. I threw in my mother and my father. I threw in my roller skates. I threw in everything I could lay my hands on. But no one knew that I had died. I tried to tell my father the night he left. . . ."

Silas passes a hand over his eyes as if he were dispelling a vision. His gesture overwhelms me with sorrow.

He looks up at me. "You have the same rapturous look on your face you had when David went to the state hospital." He falls silent, staring at his hands, which dangle on his thighs. I have an urgent, almost irresistible desire to lift his hands and take them in my own.

"My mother knows," he says finally. "She's known for a long time. But we don't speak of it. We don't speak of anything."

"What if she could tell you something?" I say, my voice

trembling with the effort to contain my deep, sorrowful happiness. "Perhaps there are things you haven't seen."

"It doesn't matter," Silas says.

"I don't believe you."

"That doesn't matter either, Jesse James."

"I don't believe you." I fairly burst out of my seat.

Silas stares up at me. "Something is happening to you."

Prophetic words as it turns out. Someone has hold of my legs. I look down. My mother is in front of me on her hands and knees, pulling on one leg; my father kneels behind me, yanking on the other. They squint at each other through my legs.

'Let go of me,' I bellow. I must have hit on the signal. My mother winks at my father and, at the same instant, they release their grip on my legs, sending me sprawling flat on my face, tripping over Midas's leg which is sticking out in the aisle.

"You should watch where you put your feet, Midas. You could've killed me."

"I'm sorry."

"Move over."

"Your face is all red," Midas observes. "You look like a beet."

"Where is your aunt?"

"Talking with Mr. Trevelyan."

"She is?"

"Yup."

"How did that happen?"

"I don't know."

"Well, did he just come up to her or what?"

"I was up front drawing, and he started talking to me about my pictures. Then Aunt Josephine came to get me back here to take a nap, and he started talking to her. She likes him."

"Did she say that?"

"No."

"Well, how do you know, then?"

"I don't know. I just think so. Can we talk about something else?"

"Sure."

"I'm going to be an artist when I grow up."

"Really."

"Yes. I may change my mind. But probably I won't. What are you?"

"I don't know yet."

"You don't?" Midas turns in his seat to look at me. "You better decide."

"It may not seem it to you, Midas, but I'm a young man. I have plenty of time."

"What if you die before you decide?"

"I won't."

"How do you know? You could fall off a roof or a monster could get you."

"There aren't any monsters."

"Yes, there are."

"No, there are not, Midas. There are no such things as monsters."

"I've seen them."

I am relieved to see out of the corner of my eye that Aunt Josephine is bearing down on us.

I stand up, trying to move out of her way. She squeezes past me without a word and installs herself in the seat.

"You're supposed to be sleeping," she tells Midas without looking at me.

"He doesn't believe in monsters," Midas tells his aunt.

"He's right. I don't. I don't at all. Surely you don't either."

I back out further into the aisle. "Nice to see you again." I am acutely aware of my physical bigness in this cramped space. If I were just a little smaller, I would not be so obtrusive. Perhaps Josephine would like me better if I were not so big. I try to pull my head into my shoulders, but the effort is too much of a strain. The muscles of my neck and shoulders ache furiously. Anyway, she likes Hamilton and he's taller than I am. She's taller than I am.

"Midas tells me you were speaking with Hamilton. He's an old friend of mine, a very dear old friend. We were in the RAF together. He saved my life." Josephine doesn't bat an eyelash.

Midas sits up, very interested in this turn of the conversation. "What is RAF?"

"I want you to get some sleep now," Aunt Josephine tells him. "Hush and close your eyes."

"Well, please excuse me. I see Midas is set for his nap, and I should check in with Hamilton, see how the old boy is faring. His leg wound acts up on long trips. Couldn't get the shrapnel out. Top-flight surgeons too, but they couldn't do it. Three men died trying—went in and never came out again."

Where is Hamilton? Where is he? I wheel down the aisle, my head booming. There he is, sitting tall and erect, preternaturally alert, his small, well-shaped ears quivering ever so slightly. He turns before I am abreast of him. "Ah, it is you. I thought so. Sit down, sit down. You look bad."

"I don't see what you find appealing about that woman."

"Josephine?"

"She doesn't like me."

"That's why you look so bad. But I fear it is worse than that. She doesn't notice you. You don't come into her scheme of things at all."

"And you do?"

"She is, among other things, a religious woman. I speak to her of my quest for God."

"Did you mention your quest for pussy?"

"For the artist it is all the same," he says with some heat.

"Are you an artist?"

Hamilton closes his eyes. With his eyes shut and his face

lifted skyward, tilted forward on his neck as if he were reaching for something, he looks drunk, wanton, lascivious, as if he would slurp up the very air. Yet something makes him look stern, unbearably stern. It is the large blue vein pulsing in his forehead.

"I aspire to be an artist, Jesse James. In everything I have done, that is what I have aimed for. It matters not that I was hallucinating when I took my law boards. That my decisions on the bench were based not on precedent or a prudent weighing of the juris. They were creatures solely of my mood and fancy. Of my particular passion. And no less sound for that. It matters not a whit that my sculpture was piss-poor. I spoke in my clay, dreamed in it, fucked in it, ate out of it. People pass judgment on art. That is ridiculous. Art is not a matter of opinion. It is a matter of seeing. It is a matter of God."

He leans forward, swaying in his seat, as if in time to music. "I am an asshole," he chants. "An agitator, an alien, an alchemist, an aphrodisiast, an ace. An abject, addled alcoholic. I am an aberrant aboriginal. An abysmal accessory. I am abnormal. Acquiescent. Accursed. I am abundant. I am an archangel. I am amazing."

"Hamilton. Stop. I am afraid of your passion." I am as startled by my outburst as Hamilton, who has the disoriented look of someone wakened in the middle of a dream.

"What did you say?"

"I am afraid of your passion."

Hamilton is wide awake now. "It is not *my* passion you are afraid of."

"Where are we, Hamilton? This bus ride is interminable. Riding around somewhere in the middle of the country. I don't even know where we are. Surely we must get someplace soon."

"Of course we will. We should be stopping soon. It must be close to lunchtime."

The thought of lunch, food, triggers the queasiness I now

know has been lying in wait for me all day. Uggh. The bus sways smoothly round a curving bend in the road, tipping me over into nausea. I can feel the color drain out of my face. "Excuse me, Hamilton, I am going to be sick."

I rise unsteadily, walking very slowly, deliberately, to the rear of the bus. I am going to throw up. Oh no, please no. I hate to throw up. I hate it. Clammy and perspiring, I fall on my knees into the tiny bathroom cubicle, fling up the toilet seat, and stick my face in the bowl.

Good God! Deep in the recesses of the toilet bowl, I see Debbie. Debbie's face reflected in the gently lapping water. The shock of seeing Debbie quells my nausea instantly.

'Debbie? Is it you?'

'It's me all right.' She smiles up at me. Her thick, honey-colored hair trails out in the water on either side of her face. All the old deep longing floods into me. I feel faint with longing. I stick my head deeper into the bowl. 'Oh, Debbie. It's been so long, so long.' My words bounce off the rim of the bowl and echo back at me—so long so long so long.

The echo is unnerving. I pull my head back.

'So how are you, Jay?'

'I'm fine. How are you?'

'I'm fine. How are your parents?'

'They're fine too.'

'And how's Johnny?'

'Oh, he's fine. He's finishing med school at Berkeley.'

'That's good.'

'Debbie. I can't stand this.' Desperately, I plunge my head back into the bowl.

'How do I look to you, Jay?'

'Beautiful. You look beautiful to me. Like always.' Like always, comes the echo. Always always.

'I have a few grey hairs now. And some stretch marks on my belly. I've got two kids.'

'Goddammit, Debbie. I don't want to hear about that.' I pull my head back.

'You never did want to hear about anything real. When I think of all the crap you used to pull on me, Jay Davidson.' She jerks her head the way she used to when she was angry, and the water jumps around her, splashing up at me.

I stick my head into the bowl, furious. 'You deliberately splashed me.'

'You're full of shit,' she says. 'You always were full of shit.'

'Me? What about you? I never knew if I was coming or going with you. You had me on a fucking string.'

'You wanted it that way. You could never stand for anything to be simple.'

I am trembling with rage. 'Then what the hell did you come back for?' I yell down at her.

She sighs a trembling sigh that shivers over her face, agitating the water and touching me with fear. 'I came to tell you that I still dream of you. And you still dream of me.'

'Yes. Yes.'

'I took a big chance coming here,' she says.

The hairs on the back of my neck stand up. 'What do you mean?'

'We may not dream of each other after today.'

'Don't say that, Debbie.'

'Sometimes I really did see you, Jay, and sometimes you saw me.'

'Stay with me, Debbie.' I tip my head closer to her face. My forehead is almost touching hers.

'It's too late for that, Jay. Watch out, you'll fall in.'

'It's never too late.'

'Sure it is.'

I pull my head back, overcome with sadness. 'Did you come to pay me back, Debbie?'

'I wouldn't have come unless you'd asked me to.'

'Did I ask you?'

'I heard you calling me.'

'Will you come again if I call?'

'I'll always come if you call me. But I don't think you will.'

'Oh, Debbie, I want to kiss you again.' I lean forward as far as I can, putting one hand up on the back of the toilet to steady myself as I dip down. My lips are almost touching hers. 'Oh, Debbie, Debbie.'

Suddenly, a monstrous roaring fills my head. Water gushes out at me, flooding from every side. Everything is spinning. 'Debbie. Debbie.' She is disappearing. Her face is swirling around, whirling in ever-smaller circles, breaking apart before my eyes. There is a final massive gurgling and she rushes away from me. She is gone, sucked down the drain. Silence. I hold my breath, my heart pounding, waiting for the water to rise up again. The water comes up clear and still. No Debbie. I remove my head from the toilet, falling back against the wall.

Someone is knocking on the door. "Jay." It sounds like Hamilton. "Jay? Are you all right? We are stopping for lunch."

I step out into a new world. The bus is buzzing with anticipation, humming pleasantly as it girds its powerful loins for its swing off the highway.

"You're looking better," Hamilton tells me. "Come sit with me." He motions to the vacant seats opposite the bathroom. "We're almost there."

"Where?" I ask, settling into the seat beside him.

"Midas tells me we are somewhere in Indiana. It's a lovely name. If you ever have a daughter, you might name her Indiana."

I laugh. Yes, I do feel better. Much better. All around me the passengers stir in their seats. We feel the new rhythm of the bus deep in our bones, make it our own. Humming and buzzing, we shake off the monotony of the morning's ride. Toss aside magazines, knead cramped muscles, comb tangled hair, reach for sweaters and coats.

"Where is Silas?" I ask Hamilton.

"He's up front somewhere with the old man. Indiana looks beautiful this afternoon, doesn't it?"

I crane my head around Hamilton to look out the window. The bus is looping awkwardly around a clover leaf. "I went to school in Indiana, but I can't tell it from wherever we stopped last. Ohio. It could be the same place."

"To you perhaps. Or on a bad day to me. But think of the man coming home to Indiana. He would know at once. He would know with his eyes closed that he was home."

The highway is behind us. The bus races up a one-lane paved road, open fields lining either side. In front of us, I can hear Midas informing Aunt Josephine, "Nobody gets off here. Except to eat. Mr. Bane told me."

"Who is Mr. Bane?" Josephine wants to know.

"Him," Midas says, standing up and pointing to the portly black man who is squinting into his wallet. "He says we just eat and get a new driver here."

"That might be. Zip up your jacket, Midas."

People are standing in the aisles, queuing up, eager to get off the bus. Hamilton and I step up to the end of the line behind a balding man in a brown coat. The driver speaks into his little microphone. "We'll be at Frank's Café for thirty minutes. Your new driver will take you on from here."

I watch him over the heads of the other passengers. His cap sits solidly on his head. He sounds confident and composed. Still, it seems to me I can hear the exhaustion in his voice, amplified by the microphone.

"Next stop is Indianapolis, approximate driving time four hours. You should arrive there right on schedule, as we've made up the time we unfortunately lost on our last stop due to the unexpected mixup about the relief driver. As a matter of fact," he reports, not troubling to conceal his pride, "we are seven minutes ahead of schedule."

"Yay for our driver," Midas calls out.

Everyone laughs and claps. The man in the brown coat turns around to smile at me and Hamilton.

The driver flushes with pleasure, acknowledging the tribute of his charges. "I've enjoyed riding with you and hope I will have an opportunity to serve you again. Have a pleasant trip."

Everyone claps again.

The bus glides to a smooth stop. Our driver has discharged his last duty with all the style at his command. I am last in line, and I watch as each of our small band of disembarking passengers stops to say a word of thanks or a goodbye to our driver before they leave the bus.

"First-rate job," Hamilton congratulates the driver warmly before he steps down. He has forgiven the driver for this morning's slight.

I step up to say my goodbye. Something is wrong. The driver's shoulders stiffen suddenly, and his head snaps backward as if someone had caught him unawares with a jolting uppercut. His cap falls from his head.

"What's wrong?" I ask him. "What is it? Are you all right?"

For answer, the driver hurls himself out of his chair and rushes past me down the steps.

45

I step down into the sparkling March air. No one is moving. The projectionist has stopped the film and the actors are frozen in place. We stand transfixed, staring at the small whitewashed concrete block structure which looms up at us in the bright air. The door has been blown away. A gaping hole like a wound is there where a door once was.

Two small windows on either side of the door are shattered. Tiny slivers of splintered glass catch the sunlight, shining in the dirt. The two gas pumps in front of the building stand bright, indifferent, their oval red-and-blue signs spinning in the breeze over our heads.

The driver is standing beside me. I can hear his heart hammering against the wall of his chest.

"What is it?" I whisper. "What has happened here?"

He jerks his head around, startled by the sound of a human voice. He thinks there's no one left alive. In his frantic eyes I see the building sag and sway in the wind, sloping inward like a house of cards collapsing.

"Frank?"

"I'm Jay. I'm your passenger."

He looks into my face, uncomprehending, then lunges suddenly toward the door.

"I'll go with you."

He crashes through the gutted doorway. My stomach slides out from under me in a sickening, jittery dive. I can't go in there. I can't. I'll stay with the others. I turn back. Silas stands apart from the others. He has picked up a wooden board. He's looking at it with something like amusement on his face, or disdain. Aunt Betty and her friend in the blue scarf flank the man in the brown coat. Behind them, Hamilton and the old man and Mr. Bane and Josephine huddle together. Josephine has both her arms around Midas, anchoring him to her side. The buttons on her coat catch the sun, glinting like armor. Midas sees me staring. His eyes hold mine. What is it, Midas? What are you trying to tell me?

There is a crumbling noise behind me. I wheel around to see a shattered chunk of cinder block fall from its place above the door, smashing into powdery bits at my feet. I run through the door.

It is dark inside the small room, except where two flat

patches of sunlight fall in at the smashed windows. As my eyes adjust to the dimness, I can make out a Formica counter running the length of the room. Six stools in front. Behind the counter, light blue dishes are stacked in tidy rows on stainless-steel shelves lining the wall. Mounted above the shelves is a cardboard sign, white with black letters: FRANK & JOE'S—WE NEVER CLOSE.

I see with a start that the driver is behind the counter. He's staring at the coffee urn. "There's coffee in it," he says. He lays both hands flat against the urn. "It's still warm."

My knees give way. I fall onto a stool and it spins me around one dizzying full turn. "I could sure use a cup of hot *kahve*— that's coffee in Turkish. It's *qahwah* in Arabic. Silas told me that. Silas is a pretentious bastard when all is said and done."

The driver looks up at me.

"I'm sorry," I tell him. "I'm terribly sorry."

I turn slowly on my stool, letting my eyes travel the length of the room. "It's all perfectly ordinary," I say. "Everything is intact." No rivers of blood, no dead bodies, no sign of struggle or flight. Nothing broken or out of place. Nothing speaks of disaster or disuse, except for some few fugitive clumps of dust in the corners. Frank and Joe might just have stepped out for a moment. But the windows and doors are blasted out and Frank and Joe aren't here. And I feel the presence of something malevolent settling in over the room with the dust.

"Hello," I call out. "Hello, is anyone here?"

"What's the point of that?" the driver snaps at me. "There's no one here."

He comes around from behind the counter, trailing dust. He sits on the stool next to mine.

"I never got your name exactly. Mine is Jay."

"I was here last week," he says. "I started from Cleveland on my return run, L.A. to New York. So this was my first stop. They didn't expect me now, of course. I'm supposed to be sleeping now. But I got that all straight when I phoned the company this morning." He drums on the counter top. "I was here last week. Joe and I got on Frank about his hair. Just like always. Everything was exactly like it always is."

Silas and Midas step into the room. I am so relieved to see them that I feel giddy. "There's no one here," I call out, leaping the length of the room to greet them.

Midas looks at me quizzically, sniffing the dismal air, running his fingers along the wall. He knows better.

"Everything looks so . . . ordinary," Silas says.

"We haven't called anyone yet," I explain to Silas.

Silas walks over to the driver, who is still sitting on the stool. "Do you want us to phone your company first? Or the police?"

"Just do whatever you think," the driver says, gazing at the counter top. His voice is flat as the plains.

"Does the phone work?" Silas asks me.

"I don't know."

Midas walks behind the counter and picks up the pay phone that hangs on the wall. "No."

"Everything is written down on my yellow sheet, and the master copy is filed with the main office," the driver tells Silas.

"I don't want to stay in here anymore," Midas says, coming out from behind the counter.

"There's nothing we can do anyway," Silas says. "Hamilton is getting people back on the bus. Let's go."

I take the driver's arm, and we file out of the deserted building into the bright sun. The sudden glare hurts my eyes.

There's Hamilton. He stands by the bus door, herding the stunned, silent passengers onto the bus. He looks flushed and purposeful. Aunt Josephine stands beside him watching for Midas. She catches sight of us and turns to Hamilton, saying something I can't hear. Hamilton smiles at her, touching her elbow.

Midas breaks from us, running into his aunt's arms. She lifts him easily in her powerful arms, cradling him like a baby, and carries him onto the bus.

"There's no one there," I tell Hamilton as we come up on him. "We tried to call someone, but the phone is dead."

"The phone is dead," the driver repeats.

Hamilton looks at him with interest. "I see," he says, wedging himself between me and the driver. "Yes, I understand, sir. Then you would agree there is nothing we can do here. We must restore order and go on."

The driver nods.

"Let's get going," Silas says.

The driver mounts the steps, followed by Hamilton.

"I don't like how Hamilton looks," I tell Silas as I follow him up the steps.

"He looks better than the driver."

"Silas, what was the board you were looking at?"

"A sign. It was lying in the dirt."

"What did it say?"

"Frank's Famous Food & Fries—Gas to Go, See Joe."

Silas and I head for our old seat in the back while Hamilton steers the driver into his seat as you would a blind man. Hamilton picks up the microphone, admonishing the passengers to keep calm. His warning appears unnecessary. No one looks agitated except Hamilton. The passengers slump in their seats, flaccid as rag dolls.

Silas slides in by the window. "Luis bashed his cat's brains out on the sidewalk."

"Jesus Christ, Silas, what are you saying?"

"In a dream. He dreamed it the night before he was discharged."

"I'm afraid. Oh God, Silas, I'm afraid."

"You have never given the evil spirits their due, Jesse James."

I look up to see Hamilton place a solicitous hand on the driver's shoulder. "I think our driver has a few words to say." Gently, Hamilton brings the microphone to the driver's lips.

"*Anngh,*" comes out over the speaker. "*Anngh.*" The tortured sound runs like an electrical current, crackling through the bus.

I leap out of my seat. From across the aisle, Aunt Josephine reaches over Midas, pulling me down to my seat again.

"Ladies and gentlemen," Hamilton announces. "There's been a change of plans. We must welcome change. Rigidity is the mark of a frightened mind. Our noble driver has done yeoman service, and the man is understandably exhausted. He and I have just arranged that I will drive us on to Indianapolis, a short trip of only four hours. Let me assure you that I am not without qualifications. I drove a bus for six months in New York City in 1948, and I have a chauffeur's license."

Hamilton lifts the driver out of his seat. He is propping him up in the front seat on the door side across from the driver's seat, when Mr. Bane jumps out of his seat.

"You're crazy. We can't go on to Indianapolis. We have to find the police in this town and notify them about this . . . this . . . whatever has happened here. We have to contact the bus company. This is a matter for the authorities."

The driver slumps sideways in his new seat, as Hamilton releases his hold on him to turn on his challenger. "Do you imagine they will know what to do better than we? Do you imagine the authorities are any less poor benighted slobs than you or I? We have crowned them out of fear and laziness. We grovel at their fat feet and they throw us crumbs which we gobble up—slogans, statistics, headlines. All of them indigestible."

Aunt Josephine is leaning forward in her seat.

Mr. Bane is stunned. "This is incredible," he gasps. "We must notify someone."

The old man stands up. His hump twitches, quivering, as if it had suddenly a life of its own. "I vote we go on with Mr. Trevelyan as our driver."

Mr. Bane stares at the old man. "We can't do that." He twists his head, searching our faces for some answering echo. "We'll find the nearest gas station and phone from there."

The old man's voice rises. "All those in favor."

"Yes," Josephine sings out. Her voice surges up, breaking over our bowed heads. "Yes."

Midas looks at his aunt's perspiring face, balancing something in his mind. "Aye," he says quietly.

"Aye." Several voices.

"Opposed?" the old man calls out excitedly.

Nothing. Mr. Bane is silent. The ayes have it.

Midas looks at me curiously. "You didn't vote."

"He's a fence sitter," Aunt Josephine says bitterly.

Hamilton bows to the old man. "Thank you. Thank you all for your vote of confidence."

In front of me the bald head of the man in the brown overcoat reddens visibly.

"I'm hungry," Midas complains to Josephine. "When are we going to eat?"

Josephine pulls several packages of crackers out of her bag. "I saved these for you from breakfast. Eat these now. We'll be in Indianapolis soon."

"I hope so," Midas says grumpily, taking the crackers from Josephine.

Hamilton sits down in the driver's seat, turns over the mighty engine, and the bus pulls away from Frank's place.

"Did we just crown Hamilton?" I ask Silas.

Silas laughs. "I guess so."

"I don't know," I hear Aunt Betty whisper to her companion in the blue scarf. "I thought Mr. Bane had some good points."

"I did too."

"We shouldn't have said aye," Aunt Betty worries, twisting her wedding ring.

"I didn't say aye," her friend says.

"Silas, did Hamilton really drive a bus?"

"Probably. Look." The desolate concrete block structure is framed in our window. I can feel the wind dancing through its smashed windows and gutted door. Burned-out eyes staring at nothing. Black mouth, gaping.

46

The bus drones on through the cold afternoon, restoring ordinariness with the reassuring monotony of its heavy, pulling rhythm. I am tired. I am dog tired. Bone weary.

"Sleep," Silas murmurs so softly I think perhaps I have imagined it.

"Silas?"

There is no answer. I can hear his even breathing.

All around me, my fellow travelers are dropping off like flies, mouths hanging open, heads thrown back, hungry for sleep to overtake them. Take me, sleep. Throw me down, subdue me. I close my eyes. Red-and-blue gasoline signs twirl in front of my eyes. It's no use. I can't sleep. I wish I had a TV here.

Ozzie and Harriet, where are you now when I need you so badly? I long to be one of Fred MacMurray's three sons, to be part of a family affair. Robert Young would know what to say to me. Brian Keith would screw his comfortable face into that level grin. 'Take it easy, kiddo, it'll work out.' And I'd believe him. Mr. French may fuss and scold benignly. So much the better. It only proves that neither he nor Uncle Bill can be thrown off base by anything at Frank and Joe's. Father knows best.

'Well, I didn't. I'm sorry.'

'Dad. Where are you?'

'Here. Here. I'm right under your nose.'

'You wouldn't happen to have a sleeping pill with you, would you? . . . Dad?'

He's gone.

What can I do? I wish I had something to read. Those books Mr. Sanchez sent me last time in the hospital. Something by Dostoyevsky and *The Rosy Crucifixion*. I only read snatches. I couldn't read more. I couldn't get through a line without going off into violent, exaggerated daydreams. Still, I understood something. Silas asked me to give the books to him and I did. He devoured them as if they were food. There are only scraps left, but I would gladly settle for that.

The letters Gemma brought me. Not exactly what I had in mind. But it's something to do. I stand up on my seat, reaching for the overhead rack, half hoping that I will rouse Silas by my movements. He doesn't stir. I grab the packet. Four letters fall out into my hands. I see at once they are from Nora.

> Dear Jay,
>
> You brought me wine, perfume, violets. I drank the wine, wore the perfume, put the flowers in a vase. I was afraid to come right out and say, "Give me something real." I knew your gifts weren't freely given. They had strings attached. Miles of string to tie me to you, to trip me, to set the stage for your escape. The wine was bitter dregs, the perfume sour, the violets were dead. I spit on your presents.
>
> Nora

A dark, raging explosion goes off in my brain, ripping through the inside of my nose, splitting my eyes. I crumple the letter in my hand.

The light seems to be fading. Something repulsive and gloomy waits in the dank air, chilling me like a foreboding. I won't read any more. But the letters are insistent. I hear them whispering to me in the gloom. If I do not read them, they will read themselves to me.

Dear Jay,

When I wanted to surrender to your power, you whined and, whimpering, begged me with sad eyes to cradle you in my mothering arms. When I wanted to stand above you, master you with the full force of my love, you threw me to the floor and ground your heel in my forehead.

Nora

Dear Jay,

I know I am illusive (as a fox), changeable (as quicksilver). The pretty words in parenthesis are yours not mine. I say one thing today and another tomorrow. What sets me on fire one day leaves me cold the next. You can't get hold of me. Can't get through to me. You could have said, stop. *Stop.* I wanted you to say it. But you never did, you miserable faltering failed cocksucker heartbreaking bastard sonofabitch.

Nora

There is one more letter. I pick it up but I cannot see to read it. Everything has grown dark. I look up. Thick, knotted vines cling to the inside walls of the bus, covering the windows, twisting upward to the ceiling, where they loop around each other to form a matted tangle of roofing. The aisle is overgrown with weeds and brambles. They have pushed their way up through the floor, fastened onto the sides of the seats.

Something stirs in front of me.

'What is it? Who is there?'

I strain to see through the sulfurous glare that filters through the vine-covered windows. The angel glides toward me over the heads of the passengers in front of me. Her long, loose robe trails out behind her.

'Who are you?'

She glides closer, her face lewdly soft in the yellow light. *I know her.*

'It's you. I know who you are.'

'Of course you know me.' Her silky voice thickens around me, suffocating and dense.

'I can't breathe.'

She smiles indulgently, then holds up her finger to show me her ring. Where the stone should be is a nail. 'I've been waiting to use this on you. It's the crown nail. You gave it to me.'

She lunges at me with the nail. She is going to kill me. I grab her hand, twisting it, straining desperately to turn the nail around. I've done it. Her face is so close to mine I can smell her poisonous breath, feel it scald my cheek. I sink the nailhead into her stomach. It slides in as easily as if I were spooning into Jell-O. 'That wasn't the real one,' she hisses. She holds up her finger. 'Here's the real one.' She's coming at me again. . . .

I scream.

'Shhh shhh shh.'

'Is it you, Gemma? Is it you?'

'Don't open your eyes yet. Just listen to me.'

'She wouldn't die.'

'When all else fails, they beat their halos into swords and plunge them into your guts so they can see you bleed before they go. Every time one leaves, the cold hand of the beast reaches through the open space and touches you with fear. When you are empty, the beast will be there. All around you. In you. Everywhere.

'I have lived my life attended by bright angels, glorious creatures who flew me high above the bitter earth on wings of hope. Don't choose, they counseled me tenderly. Don't make a choice, for that will ground you to that finite ball beneath you, and you should fly. Everything is open to you. You are a vessel of infinite possibilities. Climb up on our backs and no sorrow will truly touch you. No wound prove fatal. It doesn't matter if you suffer now. That's part of the grand design. Only wait, wait. The miracle will happen, the inspiration will come. Everything will be revealed and you will soar. Listen to me, Jay. They lied to us. Don't indulge your foolishness forever, Jay. There isn't time.'

Something touches my shoulder. I open my eyes. The late-afternoon sun slanting in at the window hurts my eyes. I squint against the glare.

Midas is standing beside me, watching me gravely. "You were talking in your sleep."

"What?"

"You were talking in your sleep. I was going to remember what you said to tell it to you, but I couldn't understand."

"Where is Silas? He was here, asleep."

"I saw him talking to the old man before. Do you feel all right?"

"Yes. No. I feel so sad, Midas. I feel so terribly sad."

"I feel like that sometimes."

"What do you do about it?"

"I don't know. I'm just sad." Midas reaches down and takes my hand. "I'll stay with you till you feel better."

Something is lost, something is lost, washing away, rushing out to sea. I can taste the salt. "I'm crying."

"That's okay."

"I don't know how to go on. How do you go on?"

"I don't know what that means."

"I don't know where I'm going."

Midas frowns, perplexed. "Well, first off, you're going to Indianapolis."

I laugh awkwardly, taking my hand away from his. "Yeah, I suppose you're right about that." Midas watches me steadily with clear, dark eyes. "Where are you and your aunt going after Indianapolis?" I say finally, to ease my discomfort.

"Chicago."

I sit up in my seat. "You never said anything about Chicago."

"You didn't ask me where I was going."

"I just assumed you were going to California."

"We don't know anybody in California. Anyway, I don't think this bus is going to get to California."

"Don't you?"

"Uh uh. I don't. Aunt Josephine is thinking of getting off in Indianapolis and taking the train. Do you feel a little cheered up?"

"Yes, I do." But the truth is that the thought of Midas leaving is unexpectedly painful.

"Would you like me to tell you a scary story?" Midas offers.

"That'd be great."

Midas crawls over my legs and installs himself in Silas's seat. "One day in Bombay far away at the old king's stadium, there lived a king with big horns, and he could shoot metal out of them. One day the mean king ordered all his guards to go and find everybody in the world and bring them back. They said, 'But, King, we can't.' And the king said, 'I will shoot lightning into you with my horns.' And the guards were stoned metal—all except for one because he had a wife and three kids. He said to the king, 'But, King.' " Midas takes a deep breath, the first he has taken since starting the story, before plunging in again. "Then the king got mad and almost shot metal into him. But he ducked. And when he ducked he just saw a duck swimming by and a lot of swans. Suddenly, he got shot in the ear and he couldn't hear. He couldn't even hear Bombeer. And he said, 'How queer.' Then his wife came swimming in a boat and the boat sunk. But he swimmed underwater and . . . Look!" Midas breaks off excitedly, pointing to the half-open window. Heavy, yellow-edged clouds hang low in the darkening sky. "A storm is coming."

As he speaks, the bright spring wind which has blown through this day like a warning, dies abruptly. The stillness leans against the bus, pressing like a stone. An unholy yellow light fills the sky. Midas and I watch together as a glowering cloud rides hard across the yellow sky, plunging the bus into darkness.

"Woo!" Midas exclaims. "I'm going to go up front and look out the big windows." He crawls back over me and disappears up the aisle.

I move into his seat, closing the window. Bright white light flashes in front of my face. What is it? Is the angel come back to stab me again? I touch my cheeks. They are feverish. The angel's breath still burns my skin. It's the lights. Hamilton must have switched on the interior lights.

The bus roars on through the darkness. I put my face to the window. Hailstones as big as a man's fist rain down out of the black sky.

A ball of ice hurtles out of the sky, flattens splat against my window. There's a message on it in big black letters, I CAME NOT TO SEND PEACE, BUT A SWORD. Another hailstone comes crashing at me, smashes flat as a pancake across the window. RAGE, DON'T WHINE, I read.

They are coming faster now, one after another, smashing furiously against the window: BEWARE THE ASSASSINS. DON'T TAKE IT SERIOUS, LIFE'S TOO MYSTERIOUS. EVERYTHING THAT LIVES MUST DIE. DANCE. WHAT ARE YOU WAITING FOR?

Not for any more hailstones at any rate. I stumble out of my seat and into the unexpected coolness of streaming water that rushes gushing down the aisle, making little waves at my feet, lapping over my sweat socks. Perhaps the hailstones have melted, causing massive flooding, which now, in the mysterious way of nature, has created a new river where once was only an arid aisle.

Cruising down the river come two figures on a rubber raft— a man and a woman. It's Gemma with some man. Hard to see from this distance but he seems to look something like me—smaller, fairer, leaner, but there is a resemblance. Johnny. It's Johnny. Johnny's come to save me. I plunge into the water, swimming upstream to greet the bobbing raft, pulling cleanly through the white water with long, sure strokes. At last I have hold of the tip of the raft. I hoist myself up, spouting water like a whale. The little raft tips dangerously as I scramble aboard, but Gemma and Johnny seem not to notice the tilting of the raft or my arrival, so engrossed are they in conversation.

They are naked (funny I didn't notice that before), lying side by side, thighs touching, their brown-gold bodies glinting wetly, slippery in the sun. My stomach tilts and sways with the leaning raft.

'Hey,' I call out. 'I'm here.'

Johnny sits up, leaning on one elbow, shading his eyes with his free hand, looking out over the water. He must have heard my greeting, but he still doesn't see me.

I step gingerly across the raft, standing finally spread-eagled directly over Johnny and Gemma, dripping water onto their naked bodies. 'Johnny, it's me. It's Jay.'

Gemma brushes the droplets from her shining belly.

Johnny presses Gemma's thigh urgently. 'Do you know what I mean?' She rolls over on her side so she can see his face. 'Yes, I do.'

I kneel beside Gemma, leaning across her shiny middle to talk to Johnny. 'I've been waiting for you, Johnny.'

He doesn't see me. He looks right through me to Gemma. I bury my face in Gemma's flesh, my nose in her deep, cool belly button. I can feel her even breathing—in out, in out. It's very soothing. I'll just lie here for a while. Sooner or later, Johnny is bound to notice me.

'I had a friend,' Johnny says. 'He named it like you would a beast—a deadly adversary. He despaired of conquering it because it changed and changed and changed till he thought he would go mad. If he managed to lie still when the cockroach dragged its skinny legs across his face, he would see the wolf watching him from the shadows. He saw the red eyes glowing, and knew the wolf only waited for him to cry out before it would leap at his throat.'

Gemma's breath is speeding up; her stomach jumps up and down, popping against my cheeks.

'Sometimes it was only the drip of a faucet,' Johnny says. 'Or a smudge on a white wall. Or the sound of his own heart thumping.'

Gemma shivers. I can feel the shuddering waves all through her. I lift my head, reaching up to cover her trembling breasts with my hands. Her nipples are cold. 'Don't, Gemma,' I whisper. 'Please don't be afraid. Let's stop this whole thing.'

She opens her grey eyes wide, looking straight at me. 'It's your fantasy,' she says, shaking herself free of me.

I move away, going to sit on a corner of the raft, my back to Gemma and Johnny. I pull off my socks and let my feet trail in the cool water.

'Tell me how you met the beast,' I hear Gemma whisper. 'I want to know about you.' Even with my back to them I know she is pressing herself against Johnny.

He is putting an arm around Gemma, drawing her closer. 'One day I ran out of things to do. I couldn't bear it. I couldn't stand the silence.'

'Why didn't you come to me?' I cry, jumping up with such a violent start that the raft tips perilously into the white water, shooting streams of spray into my face.

Johnny has one leg thrown over Gemma. He is rolling slowly over her. I can see her face. She looks simultaneously addled and attentive. 'I came to see Jay in New York,' Johnny tells her, coming to rest on top of her. I watch him run his thumb along the side of her arching neck and softly down into the hollow of her throat. 'But he was dancing off the walls.'

He's crying as he enters her. His tears fall on her shoulder. She is crying too. I bury my head in my hands and the tears fall like rain.

The rain drums down on me. It makes a noise like a heart-beat. There are voices in the rain. I will be still at last. I will listen.

My mother's voice is in the rain and my father's too, falling lightly.

'Yes,' he says to her. 'Yes,' she answers. 'Yes.'

I can sleep now. Yes yes yes. Sleep and let the rain fall on me. Let the rain fall while I sleep. . . .

47

"Excuse me. Excuse me." It's the old man with the hump on his back.

"Are you feeling all right? You've been standing here sway-ing with your eyes closed. Are you sick?"

"No. No. I'm fine, thanks. I'm really fine."

I look around in the dim light. Here I am, standing in the aisle, at the front of the bus. The old man sits to my right, three rows behind the sleeping driver. The two rows in between are empty. Across from the driver, Hamilton leans into the wheel as if his life depended on it.

The old man beckons me. "Would you care to join me?" He makes way for me, moving to the window seat, as I slide in beside him. "Everyone seems to be sleeping. I can't sleep much anymore. Only catnaps. That always puzzled me when I was young—how old people don't sleep at night. It still puzzles me. I wake up at four in the morning."

"What time is it now? Do you know?"

"My watch has stopped. I would imagine it's around seven. A bad night." He looks out at the black, starless night. A sleety, freezing rain slaps against the window. "It's not hailing anymore. That was something, that hail. To tell you the truth, I like bad weather. It stirs me inside. It reminds me of how I felt when I was young. Churning, tumultuous." He savors the words. "Of course, I didn't like that then. I thought of it as an affliction." He smiles ruefully in the dim light. "This bothers me more in bad weather, of course." He reaches behind his shoulder, touching his hump. "Would you like to know what's in here?"

I edge away from the old man, alarmed at his indecent invitation.

"I wasn't born like this." The old man twists in his seat to give me a better view of the knotted bulge on his shoulders. "It came on very slowly, weighing me down further and further, so gradually I didn't see it happening. Old wishes are in here, wishes and hopes for a life other than the one I was given to live." He turns back around in his seat. "I wouldn't let them go and they turned to stone on my back."

My cheeks sting as if the old man had slapped me across the face. You're wrong, you old fool. It's regret in there, old putrid anger and regret for not making your dreams come true.

To my surprise the old man laughs out loud. "You don't understand. My regret is that I didn't make my life come true."

I jump back, startled, my head bouncing painfully against the back of the seat. "I didn't say anything."

"I read your mind. It's all right. Don't apologize. I talk too much. It comes of not having enough people to talk to anymore. I talked the ears off your seatmate," he says, opening his eyes.

"Silas? You've been talking to Silas?"

"You sound surprised."

"No. Not exactly. Midas told me you talked together. But I hadn't noticed."

"He listens with great intelligence and kindness. He seems to know what it's like to be old. Not just to sympathize but to know. He knows it's no different—that's what he knows."

The old man leans back against the seat, trying to find a comfortable position for his hump. He presses his head forward and down like a turtle, settling into himself, into his thoughts. "I overturned my glass at supper the other night," he says softly to himself. "The waitress was irritated. She wiped up the mess without a word to me, her back stiff with reproach. I was furious and ashamed. I wanted to cry. But that's nothing. It will happen to her too. That's why she was angry. I know all that. But still I lay for hours tossing in my bed, planning how I might have tripped her. . . ."

I am drifting away from the old man as he drifts away from me. Three rows in front of me, the driver's neck is bent, broken like the stem of a flower. His head looks naked, defenseless without his cap. Not five feet away, Hamilton, his successor and heir to the throne, gears down, laughing to himself, the pure laugh of the conqueror.

" . . . she understands that it will come . . . she understands, yes . . . more than I did . . . " the old man mumbles.

Mumble mumble mumble. The old man's mumbling washes over me in the darkness. I no longer trouble to distinguish the words. They are part of the rumbling of the bus. Rumble rumble mumble rumble . . .

The driver's neck snaps erect. He shoots straight up in his seat as if he had been goosed by lightning.

I lean forward in my seat expecting to see him rocketing through the roof of the bus. The muscles in my thighs race from danger the way dogs' do in their dreams.

"Why?" The driver's howl explodes, blasting the stillness.

"It has taken me my whole life to understand that time is only a device," the old man confides to the darkness. "And now, hah hah, I am out of time."

I stare at the old man. He hasn't heard it. Nor has Hamilton, who bends to his wheel as if there were nothing else in the universe.

I drop to my knees, thrown down by the same instinct that drops the soldier to his face and slides him on his belly to meet the enemy. I crawl along the aisle on my hands and knees, coming to rest at the feet of the driver.

He doesn't see me. He stares straight ahead, his eyes stretched wide, as if someone had pried them open and held them peeled back against his skull.

I crouch beside him, curled up like an animal, ready to spring or to flee.

He opens his mouth. The cords in his neck jump into prominence, bulging as if they will burst the prison of his skin. His jaw locks with a tiny crunching sound.

Scream, damn you. Open your mouth and scream.

"If they said move to New Jersey, I moved," he whispers hoarsely. "If they said you can't take your kids to the game Saturday, I didn't take them. Leave your wife in her bed, I left her. If they told me don't join the union, I didn't join. If they said join the union, I joined. If they told me to piss into the wind, I pissed straight into the wind." He stops abruptly as if someone had clamped a hand across his mouth. He grabs his knees, rocking in his seat. "I loved the company," he moans. "Oh God oooo oh . . . " He leans forward suddenly, cocking his head, listening for something.

I hold my breath, afraid that he can hear my blood pounding.

"What has happened? Tell me what happened." He waits, listening. "There's no one there," he sneers bitterly. "They lied to me."

He leaps out of his seat with such force that I topple backward on my heels. I scramble up, diving for his legs, but I am too late.

"They've made a fool of me," he sobs, throwing himself across the astonished Hamilton.

"Good Christ! What in the name of God are you doing?" Hamilton swears at the apparition flung across him.

"Hold on to the wheel," I shout at Hamilton. "He's got the wheel. Go for the brake, the emergency brake."

"Make up your mind, damn you," Hamilton curses, reaching for the brake with one hand, bearing down on the wheel with the other. "Get him off of me."

I grab the swinging wheel. The driver slams a fist down on my hand, wrenching the wheel all the way right. The bus lurches across the deserted country road like a wounded buffalo, careering onto the shoulder, plunging through the rain across a field.

Before Hamilton can brake our flying charge, the driver grabs onto the lever that opens the door and flings himself from the bus. Someone screams, an electrifying, earsplitting shriek.

We are heading straight for a billboard. The Marlboro Man smiles confidently in the glare of the headlights. The poster colors bleed and blur, swimming before me in a lovely, rainy haze, as we plough through his massive chest, screeching to a shuddering stop, wedged upright in his guts.

All hell has broken loose. Bodies catapulted out of sleep slide from their seats, shrieking as they spill into the aisle.

Somehow I am still on my feet. Sweaters, magazines, suitcases rain down from the overhead racks. I cover my head and fall to the floor, rolling out of range of a flying canvas case, just in time. A trenchcoat falls softly over my head.

The thick poplin muffles the terrible confusion of sounds breaking over my head. My head is spinning. I can't see a thing. Wait a minute. Someone is here, lying beside me. Someone is with me in my tent. I feel the soft breath on my cheek. 'Gemma!'

'Hello, Jay.'

I peer at her in the darkness of my poplin tent. She is smiling. No, she is accusing me. Tears spring to my eyes. I'm worn down. I can't make any more efforts. She makes a tiny gesture with her mouth. Is she mocking me? No. She is fed-up, disgusted. I grab her wrist. 'Damn you. I'm worn out. Can't you see that?'

The shadows thrown by the folds of the trenchcoat fall across her face. I cannot read her expression. Perhaps she is sad.

'What happened to the driver?' I demand, tightening my grip on her wrist. 'Is he dead?' I press my fingers into her blue-veined flesh.

'I don't know,' she answers me.

'What's going to happen?'

'I don't know, Jay.'

'Is that all you have to say to me?'

She's come to say goodbye. She's going to leave me. The sudden knowledge crashes over me like a giant wave.

'Goodbye, Jay.'

Gemma's voice comes to me from very far away, as if I lay truly at the bottom of the ocean and heard her through all those vast fathoms of black water.

Someone tugs at my hand, yanking me to the surface. The elaborate reconstructions of the past break like sea bubbles turning to foam on the rolling waves. I lie gasping for air, my eyes smarting with salty tears, thrown up on the desolate shore.

"I knew you weren't dead." Midas pulls the trenchcoat off me and sticks his small black face close to mine. He smiles at me.

"Midas." I blink in the light.

"No one's killed," he reports. "Aunt Josephine has a big bruise on her leg and the old man is a little hurt and Mr. Trevelyan bumped his forehead. No one else is hurt even."

"What about the driver?"

Midas sucks his breath in sharply, pressing his hands over his chest as if his lungs ached. "Why did he jump out?"

Hamilton swoops down on us, saving me from the necessity

of a reply. "Ah, Midas, you have recovered him. Are you all right, Jay? You look pale."

"He's okay," Midas says.

It is Hamilton who looks pale. He is white as a sheet, except for two scarlet splotches burning on his cheeks.

"Yeah. I'm okay. What about you?"

"Fine. I'm absolutely fine. Except for this small evidence of the wars." He touches the knot on his forehead. "Everyone is fine. Everything is under control." He helps me to my feet. "I've settled the passengers down. I explained that the driver went crazy. Silas is out looking for the driver now. I couldn't find the driver's flashlight, but Midas had the foresight to bring his own flashlight on the trip." He pats Midas's bony shoulder approvingly. "Midas, please go sit with your aunt. She is not easy about you yet." Midas obeys, and Hamilton steers me to a vacant seat.

"I think it's unlikely that the driver is dead," he says. "I told the passengers that. I was already starting to brake when he jumped. No one is seriously hurt, as I say. The old man has a few bruises. And Mr. Bane appears to be in shock. I mean to say, he looks astonished."

"I see."

"Josephine has a bruise on her calf, but she is a brave woman, a remarkable woman. I am considering asking her to marry me. Don't look so alarmed. Why not? I had dreamed, I will confess, of a reunion with my ex-wife, who is somewhere in Los Angeles in a dingy pink bungalow. But I am abandoning that dream. Fuck her, I say. Fuck her, Jesse James. She doesn't know who I am. But Josephine . . . You think this is a strange time to be thinking of such things. I am not neglecting the present realities, if that's what's bothering you."

To prove his point, Hamilton leaps across the aisle, grabbing the microphone, which miraculously still works. "Ladies and gentlemen, now that things have settled down and we are assured that none of us is seriously hurt, I should like to report to you on our circumstances. We are not, in fact, so badly off. The bus has broken down, of course, but I don't think it's a major breakdown. By my calculations, we are less than forty-five minutes from Indianapolis and not far from the highway. Perhaps those of you who have food—crackers, fruit, candy, whatever —might share with those who have none. In the morning, in the light, we will send out a scout to bring help, and when the bus is repaired, we will proceed to . . . "

Mr. Bane bolts out of his seat as if he had been shot from a cannon. "I'm not proceeding anywhere with you," he bellows. "How do we know it wasn't you who wrecked the bus?"

"I know, Mr. Bane. I saw it. It was the driver."

Mr. Bane glares at me as if I had done him some grave injury. "Why should I believe you?" he thunders at me. "Who are you?" He stops, struggling for his breath. He is almost panting. "I'm supposed to be on my vacation. I get two lousy weeks a year. Two lousy weeks."

Aunt Josephine stands up. "Mr. Trevelyan was talking. Do you mind?"

Mr. Bane twists around to face Josephine. Fury has made him bold. "Do I mind? Do I mind?" It has also rendered him inarticulate.

"We've got to stick together," Josephine says. Something flickers in her dark eyes. Irony? Vengeance? Faith?

"Don't give me that shit. That's shit. You're sticking with him. You're siding with this crazy white man against me."

"Sit down," Josephine commands, "or I'll throw you out the window."

Hamilton turns to me. "My God, look at her. She's monumental. Like a force of nature. She has restored me to myself."

Long experience with overwhelming odds pushes Mr. Bane back down in his seat. "Crazy bitch," he mutters hopelessly, then falls silent, his head sunk on his chest.

Aunt Josephine sits down.

Hamilton bows deeply to her, a bow at once humble and elaborate. Coming up from his bow, he swoops up the microphone, brandishing it over his head like a sword. "Ladies and gentlemen, we will go on. We will go on to Indianapolis. And from there—" he brings the microphone to his lips in a wide, swinging, intoxicated arc—"from there we will go on together —west to California. To Hollywood. Each of us in his heart of hearts wants to be a movie star. It is the apex of our ancient longing, the only balm that can finally heal our miserable, draining wounds."

Mr. Bane does not stir at this outrage. He is chained to his seat, imprisoned by despair as old as the hills.

"Annabel watches the silver screen and the longing builds in her breast. She aches to see herself projected eight hundred times her normal size. Dear God, please rub Vaseline on my lens. Shoot me through cheesecloth. Everything I am inside up there on the magic screen for all the world to see. All my beauty, mystery, passion set free at last. I will fill the screen."

The words spill out of Hamilton. I watch them tumble out on the floor, clogging the aisle.

"It is the same everywhere. Plucky English lads sloshing through the grey drizzle, peeing into puddles; horny little hill-billies lying on their bellies in the red dirt, sucking on their Georgia peaches—all dreaming of the time when they will be revealed. And they sing their hearts out, poor little cocksuckers, tunes whistling through the holes in their heads. They shake, rattle, rock and roll till their eyes fall out of their sockets. And when they've reached the top, the apotheosis, the pinnacle, the peak—it isn't it. It's not enough. They want to burn up the silver screen like Annabel. That's what it's all about."

I look around in a sweat, expecting mutiny.

Aunt Betty and her companion, now scarfless, are thrown back against their seats. They look as if they had been hurled there. The scarf lady seems not to know that she is clutching at the sleeve of the man in the brown overcoat across the aisle from her. For that matter, he seems as unaware of it as she. He has the foolish, glazed look of someone pretending to enjoy the witticisms of the after-dinner speaker through an impenetrable fog of whiskey and creamed chicken.

"Bring out your snapshot of Marilyn in pigtails swilling a Pepsi," Hamilton exhorts us. "We sucked hashish and confidences into our lungs with James Dean a week before he died. Oh to gobble a pastrami sandwich with Liz. Console Warren when he crashes, make Simone laugh, lift Marcello's ennui, let Candice down easy. Advise Ingmar: Liv is perfect for the part. On the other hand, so is Bibi. Kiss them both for me. . . . No, do not smile. Our yearnings are not frivolous. They are the antithesis of frivolity."

I can't stand it. I can't sit still anymore. I jump up, heading for the door. Hamilton sways in the aisle in an ecstasy of zeal.

"Hamilton." I touch his shoulder. His sleeve is drenched with sweat. "Hamilton, I'm going to help Silas look for the driver."

He looks up at me as if he didn't know who I was or where I had come from.

"Please sit down and get some rest. Please, Hamilton. I'll be right back."

His bright blue eyes glide away, tiny fish gliding through the cloudy water.

"Hamilton, you're frightening your passengers. Hamilton?"

He tilts his head sideways, then forward. His eyes float back up to the surface—glossy, brilliant, startlingly blue.

"You're frightening . . ."

"I heard you. You're going to help Silas look for the driver." He turns away from me, pouring his heart out into the microphone. "No, no, it is not frivolous. It is our holy passion to get inside the inside of the inside," he cries to the astounded passengers, as I crawl awkwardly on my hands and knees out the door, emerging from the Marlboro Man's splintered entrails into the cold, wet night.

48

The sleet has stopped. A thin, steady rain thuds down on the soaked earth. I look up into the huge sky. It is empty. No moon. No stars. It is pitch black out here, except for the squares of wavering light thrown on the ground by the interior lights of the bus.

"Silas? Silas, where are you?"

No answer. I walk all around the lighted bus. The Marlboro Man watches me through flinty, narrowed eyes. He doesn't take his eyes off me as I circle the bus. His slightly bared white teeth catch the light, blazing in his weatherbeaten face. Even mortally wounded, he is sure of himself.

"Silas! Silas?"

A dog howls somewhere in the distance. I listen with frozen concentration. "Fred," I call out desperately. "Ed. Tell me where you are. Ed. Driver." The dog howls again.

I'm shivering like a dog myself—a poor, abandoned dog, soaked through. I forgot to grab my jacket. The mean, thin rain slaps at me. The stinging needles hurt my skin through my shirt.

Where is the driver? Where is Silas? Why doesn't he answer me?

I walk away from the bus, away from the light, calling for Silas. The rain lashes down with new fury; torrential sheets of water pour down from the sky. I can't see two feet in front of me. I can't see anything except a wall of water. "Silas. Answer me. Where are you?"

My foot bumps against something soft. A body. Spread-eagled, face down in the mud, embracing the wet ground as if it were a lover. I drop to my knees, my heart beating wildly. The head turns sideways, lifting. "Silas!" I jump back, almost falling over his legs. "What are you doing, Silas? What are you doing lying in the mud? I thought you were the driver."

"No. It's only me."

"Why didn't you answer me? I've been calling and calling. What are you doing? For Christ's sake, what are you doing?"

"I'm lying down in the ground."

I grab his shoulders and roll him over. "You can't do this now, Silas. You can't. Where's the fucking flashlight? Where is it?" Silas points. I grab the light and turn it on him. He winces, turning away from the light.

"Where is the driver, Silas?"

"I can't find him."

"He's got to be here. Get up, Silas, we're going to find him."

"I've walked every inch of this field in every direction five times, Jay. He's not here."

"He is here. He's got to be here."

"He wanted the night to swallow him up," Silas says, laying his face back down in the mud.

I yank Silas upright. "It's you. You want the night to swallow you up."

"Yes," he says, stiffening in my arms. His bones feel so fragile, like a woman's. I could almost imagine I held a woman.

"Don't hold me," he says. "Don't."

I drop my arms. "We'll find the driver in the morning. It's impossible to see in this rain even with the light. You've probably been going in circles."

"God is terrible," Silas says.

"Please, Silas, please. I'm begging you to stop it. Listen to me. Hamilton is exhausted. He's running down."

Silas stares at me. "You think God is your buddy, don't you? You think he's up there watching over you like a mother hen. You think he cares when you can't shit. You think he's listening every time you moan in your sleep. You think he's going to reorder the universe so you won't have to die." He stops suddenly as if someone had pulled a plug. We sit in silence.

The rain splashes down on us, incessant, impartial. What does it care for our yammering or the fact that we sit shivering in the mud?

Silas picks up the flashlight and turns it on me. "You look terrible," he says, shutting it off again. "We should go back."

Silas's hair is plastered to his forehead; his face is streaked with mud. I pull my shirt up, intending to brush the wet dirt from his face. Silas hits me away like a panicked animal.

He stands up, slapping the mud from his arms and legs. "We'll say I tripped in the dark."

We walk back to the bus. How ridiculous it looks, like some ungainly prehistoric monster stuck absurdly in the middle of its prey. The Marlboro Man is still smiling.

We crawl back into the bus. The aisle has been cleared of the falling debris from the overhead racks. The lights are down. It appears that everyone is asleep. Silas's shoes squish forlornly as he pads down the aisle, falling into the seat beside the old man.

I head down the darkened aisle, looking for Hamilton. He is sitting beside Aunt Josephine. She is fast asleep. Hamilton sits upright, spine straight, hands folded in his lap. He is staring at Josephine so intently that he doesn't see me stop beside him.

I touch his shoulder. "Hamilton?"

"Shhhh. My Josephine sleeps. Oh, what I would give to love her, to sink into that deep rain forest, anchored between those dark thighs."

"Hamilton, we couldn't find the driver."

"How her sweet skin gleams. My God, I swear I would polish her every day with the finest creams till I could see my face in her belly."

It's no use. I fall into the seat opposite Hamilton. My old seat. Midas is curled up by the window, asleep, his head cradled in his arms, leaning against the window.

Everything is falling apart. There is no one left to help me. What can I do? Gemma must have left me some clue, some message. The letters. *They're gone.* Where are my letters? They will tell me something.

Quietly, trying not to disturb Midas, I step up on the seat to search the overhead rack. Nothing. My airline bag is intact, my jacket, but no letters. I open the bag and riffle quickly through it. Not there. I sit back down. What about the mirror? Gemma's broken mirror. *It's gone.* Yes, but I will look just to make sure. I scramble under the seat where the mirror was. All I can see is one of Midas's paper airplanes.

I am alone on this godforsaken bus. What am I going to do? It's dusty down here. Why am I scrunched up in this ridiculous position on the filthy floor of this bus? It's stupid. I should get up. There is Midas's paper plane, dust settled on its yellow wings. I extend a hand to snare the plane, but it's just out of my reach. I put out my hand again, wiggling my fingers in a vain attempt to grab hold of the plane. Damn. There has to be some way to get at it. I need a stick or a pencil or something. I know. I pull a cigarette from the sodden pack in my shirt pocket. It's damp but intact. It should do for my purposes.

Poking at the plane with the cigarette, I manage to lure it to me. It's still in almost perfect shape. Only the nose is bent a little. On one of the wings of the plane Midas has drawn a circle, and inside the somewhat irregular circle, listing to the left, is what can only be an eye. The eye gazes at me knowingly. But something about the odd angle of its placement gives it a rakish, even impudent, stare. I return its gaze calmly. "I can look you straight in the eye," I whisper, delighted at the discovery. If he were not asleep, I would open the window and let Midas's plane soar.

I know what I need to know of the past.

I lift myself from the floor, leaning back on my haunches. The muscles in my back and legs are cramped. I fall back gratefully into the comfort of my seat.

Get out of your wet clothes. Yeah, yeah, all right. I stand up on the seat again, pulling a clean shirt and socks out of my bag. It feels good to shed the sodden clothes, pull on the dry shirt and socks. I am warm and dry. I settle into my seat. Silas will still be in his wet clothes, soaked through, covered with mud. Shit. On top of everything else, he'll probably get sick. I look down the aisle to see him. Silas's head tilts stiffly toward the aisle. I can feel the tension in his neck. Oh, Silas, what will happen to you?

"Poor Silas." My thought is echoing. "He chooses to die over and over." It's Hamilton. Across the aisle from me. Hamilton speaking softly to his sleeping Josephine. "Now tell me truly, what do you think of Silas?" he asks her, peering down into her face. "I don't know myself what I think of him. But I do think of him. That counts for something, I suppose. He is more than what I have understood of him. And Jay? Dear Jay. I wish him well, Josephine, from the bottom of my heart. I see him trembling in the wings, and I want to shout, 'Go on. Go out there. Do it. It doesn't matter if you fall on your face. It doesn't matter if you make a fool of yourself. Sing till your lungs burst. Dance till your heart breaks.' But I never said anything. Oh, Josephine, my love, I never said anything.

"Don't look at me like that. I love you. It is true I have said it before. But each time I mean it. Each time it is newborn.

"I know. It isn't that. You cannot depend on me. You see how I spin up, catching the light, blazing with a thousand passions. I cannot bear to climb so high. I know that I will fall. I feel myself winding down. I feel the sadness coming in. I feel it now.

"At the top of the upward curve, there is nothing to do but fall. I dread it. I would do anything to save myself from that descent. And yet I crave it. I long for it to come. Do you suppose I fall hurtling through the sky like a meteor, crashing through the center of the earth, smashed to smithereens? Not at all. I fall with the smallest inconsequential thud. I stop, you see.

I do not plunge into the abyss. I do not go to the bottom of my sorrow. I stop at boredom, meanness. Timidly I peek down and through the cracks in my poor addled brain, I catch a glimpse of terror, and I shut my eyes and will myself, against my will, to rise again into the fire.

"They think I am better on medication. In a way it's true. They are not entirely fools. No one in my experience is entirely a fool. Don't you think that's true? Mr. Bane was right to object to me. Why should he follow me, when I am demonstrably crazy? The poor man only wanted a peaceful vacation. He wants too little, it makes me contemptuous. You were magnificent, Josephine. You put down the insurrection, and you gave me the great gift of your confidence. I will always love you for that. Neither my wife nor my mother had any faith in me. I'll tell you the truth, I cannot think of a single woman who has had faith in me.

"I will do what you say about the medication. It's true it holds me in place. I do not pace, my skin is cool, I speak calmly. But inside I am rioting; my blood races, my heart is on fire. They shoot velvet straight into my veins and still I spin up and up and up. You could stop me, Josephine. Breathe your calmness into me. You think I delude myself, don't you? Yes, I see it in your face. How did you get to be so wise, Josephine? Won't you tell me? You know when to be silent. My ex-wife never knew when to shut up. That's not fair, of course. She thought she was marrying an upstanding lawyer, a charming man with excellent manners and a tireless cock. No. She only wanted me to love her. And I was spinning away. Never mind. I cannot live in a pink bungalow.

"Will you come with me, Josephine? You smile so sadly. You won't, will you? You know too much to follow me. I suppose I would have been disappointed in you if you'd said yes. How perverse I am. So my wife said, and she was right in that at least. Thank you, my dear lady. Thank you for listening to me. I don't want to be alone tonight, Josephine. Let me sleep beside you and I'll be all right."

If only that were so, Hamilton. If only I believed you would be all right. Midas stirs beside me. "I dreamed I was flying on the back of a gigantic fish."

"Was it nice?"

"I was scared. But not too much."

"Go on back to sleep, Midas. It's very late."

Midas settles back into place, cradling his head in his arms again, leaning against the window. I shouldn't have told him to go back to sleep. I'd like someone to talk to.

Midas snaps up in his seat, as if he'd read my mind. "I remember."

"What?"

"The driver."

"We didn't find him, Midas."

"Why didn't you?"

"It was pouring rain, and it was very hard to see even with your flashlight. Silas searched all over and couldn't find him. And I did too. We'll look again in the morning. He's probably okay."

"But he's gone."

"I didn't say he was gone. I just said we couldn't find him."

"But what if he's dead?"

"Damn it, Midas, what is this? A fucking interview? You're supposed to be asleep."

"Why did he jump out?"

"I don't know, Midas. How do I know?"

"You don't know anything. My aunt knows much more than you."

"Well, fuck you, you little shithead. If that's how you feel, just leave me alone."

Midas slides down in his seat. "I don't want him to be dead."

"I don't really think you're a shithead, Midas. I like you very much."

"I know."

"Midas, I don't know what's going to happen."

I don't know what's going to happen. I can't stand not knowing. I jump up on the seat, pulling down my bag.

"What are you doing?"

I unzip my bag, rummaging through the contents—sneakers, cigarettes, jeans, underwear. "I'm looking for something. Here it is." I pull out the tiny crystal ball and hand it to Midas.

"What is it?"

"It's a crystal ball. I got it in a box of CrackerJacks."

"What does it do?"

"You can see the future in it."

Midas brings the tiny ball up to his face and peers into the plastic bubble. "I don't see anything."

"Give it to me." I'm shaking as I take the crystal from him. I stare into its face. Show me something. Please, please. I have to know something.

Nothing. There's nothing there. I can't see anything. Rage swells up in me. I can feel it pushing against the surface of my skin. "Goddammit. Sonofabitch motherfucker."

"What do you see?" Midas asks me.

"Nothing."

"Maybe you should send it back and get another one."

I lean forward in my seat, holding the tiny piece of plastic in my hand. I could crush it between my fingers. Stomp on it, grind it into the floor. Smash it to bits.

Midas is watching me intently. I lean back against my seat. The back of my shirt is drenched. I can smell my own sweat. It smells like stale seawater, brackish and bitter.

"Do you want it?" I say, holding the crystal out to him.

"Sure," he says eagerly. He takes it from my shaking hand and the rage drains out of me, like dirty bathwater running out of a tub.

"What will you do with it?" I ask him.

"Pretend."

"I see."

"Can I lay down on your lap?"

"Of course you can. Are you sleepy?"

"Just a little bit. Not so much." Midas settles down on my lap, resting his head on my thighs, his skinny legs tucked under him, the crystal ball in his hand. "Could you tell me a story?"

"I'm not too good at stories."

"It doesn't have to be so good." His voice is muffled, thick with coming sleep.

"Once upon a time, there was a little boy. And his name was Midas. One day, Midas was swimming in the ocean, riding the waves. Sudddenly he saw this gigantic fish spouting. . . ."

Midas is asleep, breathing deeply. In his sleep, he presses his face against my stomach and wraps one skinny arm around my waist. With each breath he takes, I can feel the soft weight of his body moving lightly against me. I slip my arms around Midas to hold him more securely. A deep sense of physical comfort, of immense ease, runs through me like a steady, flowing river.

The river flows steadily on. On and on and on it flows into the bottomless sea. . . . Anything might happen to Midas. He could be killed by any car in the street. He could grow up to fight a war, be blown to bits by a bomb.

Don't you know you could fall off your bike and split your skull? Disease could waste you, stupidity thwart you, indifference grind you down. You could slip in the tub. You sleep so soundly in my arms. You give your trust so easily. Oh, Midas, I wish you well from the bottom of my heart.

My eyes are heavy with sleep and the weight of tears behind my lids. I can sleep now.

I dream of my grandfather. I'm a little boy playing with my grandfather. My mother's father or my father's. He's both, it seems. But he looks like Mr. Kaminsky. My grandfather smiles as he tosses me up in the air. Up he throws me. Up. Up. I hang swaying at the top of a curve of joy and terror, suspended in mid-air. I scream, laughing with fear and delight, as I spin down into his waiting arms.

The sky is growing light. Outside my window the thick bars of darkness dissolve as the sky turns slowly to cream. The sun tips into view. Its fiery edge throws streaks of rose across the white sky. The black, furrowed earth gleams wetly, sleek as a seal. Feathery shoots of new grass, drenched by the night's rain, lie flat against the black earth.

No one stirs. No sound. Only the soft breathing of the sleeping. Over the top of the seat, I see the old man, the back of his head thrown forward, thrust out of its hard turtle shell. And next to him, Silas. The collar of his shirt is caked with mud. But his flaxen hair holds the sun's first glow as if he were himself a source of light.

Midas's eyes move behind their lids. Sprawled on his back, face up in my arms, he is abandoned to his dream.

Soon the others will wake. The driver may be dead.

I look across at Hamilton. His head has slid down onto Josephine's broad shoulder. But he rests uneasily there as if he expected to be thrown off at any moment. He looks unspeakably tired, as if he had been running all night in his sleep.

The sun climbs in the sky. A fan of light spills on Midas. He opens his eyes.

A NOTE ON THE TYPE

This book was set on the Linotype in Electra, a
typeface designed by W. A. Dwiggins. The Electra
face is a simple and readable type suitable for
printing books by present-day processes. It is not
based on any historical model, and hence does not
echo any particular time or fashion.

Composed by Maryland Linotype, Inc.,
Baltimore, Maryland
Printed and bound by R. R. Donnelly & Sons,
Harrisonburg, Virginia

Designed by Judith Henry